BEAT COP

Vincent Casale

Cover design by Trisha Lewis

Photo Credit: taken in the early 1980s unknown photographer

Edits & Layout & Publishing via Van Velzer Press
ISBN: 978-1-954253-04-9

Printed in the United States of America

VanVelzerPress.com

FOR MY FRIENDS,

AFFECTIONATELY KNOWN AS LOSERS.

CPOP 1986

momentarily he would surrender to this fantasy and fire a bullet into his own head. In his mind's eye the long branches from the curbside trees shadowed the roof of the Cape Cod style house, where tall Leyland Cypress trees lined the fence in the rear yard and puddles from the sprinklers formed pools along their trunks allowing small chirping birds to cool. The grass was evenly cut and finely edged. A plane flew high above the pretty surroundings creating a distant roar in the clear sky. The only apparent imperfection of this suburban dream landscape was that damned **For Sale** sign posted on the front lawn. He was envisioning it all with his eyes closed.

He would sit in a striped beach chair, splintered and no longer taut, a precious memento his mother left when his parents moved to Florida. "Honey, when are you going to get rid of that relic?" Kathleen would have teased.

"But it's my—"

"Yes, I know, it's your mommy's chair, but it is old honey."

He would have smiled. Her reality always made him smile.

This was to be our home, Frank thought. *This is where I imagined it would be good for me. Now the dream is lost forever.* He leaned forward and put his face into his hands. His wife's signature was on the papers and now his was required sooner rather than later.

Frank looked up, thinking of a time when she could have been in the doorway, unbeknownst to him. "Are you smoking again, Frank?"

"Only a couple of drags," he would have replied.

Funny, in recollection her voice seemed softer, her fair features exaggerated and ethereal.

Frank walked to the bedroom then slid himself into a small white bench in front of her vanity. All her clutter was gone and only the paper and pen he placed there earlier was on the table. With his breathing labored he gripped the pen, glanced at his reflection, and began to write his letter *for* Kathleen...

To the unfortunate bastard who gets to read this first, pass it along.

Please! Do not! I repeat -Do Not- blame Kathleen Colleri for my death. It's not a woman who drives a man to take his own life. She can breach his sanity, and can add fuel to a fire, but that fire is burning long before the woman no longer desires the man. For a man to commit an act so cowardly the answer must rest deep inside himself where something so hidden would not surface until…well, until it is too late.

Please, reader, do not misconstrue this telling as only a confirmation of my suicide or as a testament to a few dribbles of unhappiness that have clouded my life. My purpose here is to clear the name of a woman that I have shamelessly besmirched.

I have blamed Kathleen for moving on with her life when the reality is, that is what people do. I'm sure she dug deep into her hurt and attempted to pull out some relevance. How bold of me to assume I was infallible about the broken end of what became an inconsequential relationship.

I do! I do take responsibility for my failed marriage. I did stomp it further into the ground with my rantings hoping anyone would feel sympathy for me. Truth be told, details of our shortcomings were out in plain sight for those who knew us intimately. One friend told me, 'You did what you wanted. You were always out with the guys, flirting with other women. You repeatedly lied to her, saying you had an arrest so you could go out, or to avoid her family. Basically, you fucked her around corners.'

I'm shaking a little now. I feel hot and I am suddenly thirsty. If I were to speak, the sound would be a slow dry stutter. My gun is in my hand and I am still at this very moment wondering if I am really going to do it. Am I going to hurt those who do love me no matter what? My family. Oh, my God! Is it too late to purge myself of this pain? Soon I will lift the revolver to my temple where I will push and grit. Or I will just stick it in my mouth.

Although all I will need is one bullet to do the trick, I leave my weapon fully loaded. No Russian roulette crap for me.

I guess pulling the trigger will be simple and quick, and I hope painless. There will be no mistakes, no embarrassing turbans wrapped around my head. Unfortunately, I don't have a world of time to contemplate. I didn't have to wait for mail order poison. I carry it with me every day, and no one was smart enough to take it away.

I feel I'm starting to ramble, sounding more like a lunatic, so I'll end with a sudden thought of compassion. There's this sweet girl I met not long ago. Ann Caputo is a kind and decent person who did not deserve the twisted nightmare she was handed. We are compatible in grief and I just hope she can dig deep inside herself and pull out her pain, and maybe somehow be able to look at a better day.

After countless prayers and months of self-pity I believe I have had my day. Insecurity is a bitch.

EARLIER THAT

YEAR . . .

CHAPTER 1

ngelo and Teresa Caputo were proud of their daughter. Proud that Ann was idealistic. And as far as they knew, proud that their daughter practiced many of their own beliefs concerning life's values. The Caputo family lived in a stereotypical Italian-American Brooklyn neighborhood. A stronghold where its residences protected their own from the radical way of thinking that began in the 1960s. A place where mothers raised their children and fathers busted their ass working two jobs to afford a decent life for their family.

When Ann entered the New York City Police Department as a new cadet, she surprised many of her family and friends, because she had always exhibited the demeanor and character of a devoted teacher. Moving forward she believed she could accomplish some good, that she could comfort or help the unfortunate citizen victimized by crime. And it was a noble job. A good-paying job with important benefits. Ann's protective father, a union iron worker who certainly didn't want his daughter to follow in his footsteps, thought, if not a fine housewife like Teresa, then maybe a teacher, a lawyer. If not, why all the college?

Angelo was against the idea of his daughter swinging a nightstick, however slightly comforted by reasoning 'She packs a rod.' She was a good shot, too; scoring consistently in the high nineties on all training sessions at the firearms and tactics range, where many of her points were in the desired chest area of the bad guy caricature on the down range target. Pointing his thick forefinger out and his thumb up, her father would tell her, "Ann, shoot first, question later...and don't tell your mother what I said, please."

Ann would always smile and assure her father, "I won't. Pop, don't worry." They would embrace and laugh affectionately about the little secret they kept from her mother.

By the time Ann reached her second year on the job with the department, she had built up enough confidence in herself to handle the responsibility of living on her own. So, against her parents concerned wishes, then eventually their approval after Ann puppy-dogged them with forlorn eyes, she moved into her own apartment. Now she was an independent young policewoman.

Ann enjoyed the advantages of being single. She rented a quaint yet airy studio apartment in the northern section of College Point, Queens.

An enclave that was once an old fishing village, though the only recent signs of any fishing was the smell at low tide and two broken-down tackle shops. Her landlords were a young couple newly married and welcoming of a tenant who was reliable in the rent they needed to supplement their own mortgage. There was a private entrance off to the side of the house and the block was a quiet one, conveniently close to where she worked.

Most cops who had a 'hook' (a connection) chose the best precincts for convenience. Knowing his daughter's desire to work in a Queens precinct, her father was insistent, using the excuse that a friend from the Knights of Columbus was dying to help his daughter and would not take no for an answer. Many young cops bragged about their assignments in tough ghetto precincts but when it came right down to it, not many rookie cops would deny themselves a 'hook' precinct.

Ann fit in with her squad immediately. She wasn't afraid of work, and more important, she didn't use flirtations to her advantage for choice assignments. Therefore, she was well-liked and respected by her male co-workers. An uneventful stint at the Police Academy now seemed light years away as Ann fell into a life of new friends and a precinct she enjoyed patrolling.

It was a different sort of independence, something she certainly had not felt as a secretary. Ann relished the idea of being what one New York magazine dubbed 'The New Breed of Cop.' The name stuck because of the immense hiring over the past few years, starting in 1980, where recruits came in all shapes, sizes, genders, and educational and financial backgrounds. It was a great selling tool for her parents as well, especially Pops, who was still trying to warm up to the idea of women as police officers.

A couple of fast learning years on the force had matured Ann a great deal, gaining experience without becoming overzealous, she had handled her share of emergency calls.

Not voluptuous, Ann was a mannered and very pretty, young lady. Her hair, when not pinned up per regulation, was straight, chestnut and shoulder length. Her eyes were small almonds that played a perfect backdrop to smooth olive skin. Out of uniform, Ann would never be taken for a cop. Instead, she looked like that nice Italian girl all the boys wanted to take home to meet their mothers. Other cops would often kid her, crudely comparing her to the more formidable type of female cop newly ensconced within the precinct. "Where did you come from? Not from the same farm as some of these other animals around here."

Ann wasn't a crybaby like some women on the job; she wasn't quick to register complaints and she could take a joke with the best of them. Sure, some would hit on her, but subtly, not with the forthrightness and regularity reserved for the obvious takers. Of course, Ann was mindful that half the attention she received was exactly because she was not one of those 'takers.' She often stroked their male egos. "Great arrest John…You're such a nice guy Mark…You're the guys we rely on."

The male cops were going to have to be extra polite and attentive if they wanted to get in her pants, at least that's what they imagined. Still, the guys were mindful, some even resentful, of the special treatment females received just because of what they 'had between their legs.'

It was unusual for a female cop to receive a command discipline from any male superior. Those were minor infractions, usually a patrol guide tool reserved for male cops not wearing their cap, or an officer a few minutes late, or not on the foot post they were assigned. If a supervisor wanted to, they could find violations on any given day for any given cop. Even serious violations, such as a lost gun or insubordination (both fines that could cost a cop anywhere from thirty days lost in vacation time to possible suspension) were usually negotiable for the fairer sex.

* * * *

It was four hours before the New Year and pressure was on for party people everywhere. With all the new rookies assigned to the precinct and covering shifts, Ann and her friend from the precinct, Allison Ross, weren't pulled in for overtime. They decided on The Z Stop, one of Long Island's favorite nightclubs. They wore similar spandex mini outfits for the night to impress. Allison's a dark blue, Ann's a sexy black.

Allison was a little more open to the prospect of love for an evening even as she hoped to find Mr. Right. She was voluptuous, with seductive cleavage and light green eyes. Her hair, dirty blond, was cut short on the sides but waved big on top like many of the styles being worn during the ME GENERATION. Unfortunately, she had sealed an unwanted reputation by bedding two officers from the precinct who not only told each other, but most of their friends. Still, Allison was straightforward, a good cop, not a back stabber. She was a good friend and loyal.

New Year's Eve was a letdown. The club was too crowded, smoky and loud. The DJ played his usual thread of disco music, over and over. The girls drank a lot, met too many Romeos, and eventually wound up where many others sat their asses: at a late-night diner. Allison was a little sloppy, still wearing the complimentary red lei some guy threw over her head at midnight. She was pointing her index finger. "Next year were goin' somewhere different," she said. "We should stay local. We'd probably have more fun." Allison's hair, though stylishly sprayed, was disheveled and her mouth was visibly dry. Yet her faux gold earrings were intact and catching the light in a still festive spirit. "You get what I'm saying, Ann?"

"Yes, yes, we'll go somewhere else next year. Like maybe we'll just work the Times Square detail and maybe have a better time."

A bored waitress arrived with a pot of coffee and as soon as she poured the cups Allison attempted a sip, spilling some but thankfully not burning herself.

"You okay?" Ann laughed. Then she changed the subject. "My mother hinted I should be set up tonight with the son of a friend. I swear my parents think they can arrange a marriage like I was a virgin and it was somewhere in Italy." Suddenly she reached for her pearls and caressed them for a moment.

Ann laughed and Allison giggled. "Italians are obviously different than the Irish," Allison said.

"God, if my father got a look at all those Guido types he might think twice about a nice Italian boy. I know he didn't like Louis."

"They weren't all Guidos," Allison said. "Some of them looked like smurfs with mullets. And did you smell all that Obsession cologne? I thought I would puke."

"So, right, Al. Me, too." Ann laughed.

Ann thought of Louis DiMaggio, a blue-eyed charmer from Bay Ridge. He wore a lot of cologne also. A two-year investment that turned out to be untrustworthy. He was too macho to have any girlfriend of his become a cop.

"Who the fu---hell does he think he is?" her father had shouted. As always, she calmed her dad and life went on.

That had been awhile, she was getting lonely for the touch of a man. She imagined a lover like those she read about in romance novels. She also wondered about Louis. Two years now seemed like a waste of time. He had claimed marriage was important. Then his excuse for attentiveness with other women became her fault because she wanted to become a police officer.

Ann even thought of Anthony, her first love when she was just seventeen. Remembering him, his soft blue eyes. His solid build. Sweet in conversation, he had charmed the pants off her. Then devastated her when he backed off saying, "I'm confused. It's not you." Adult lines that even teenagers used. Still, Ann realized it was a hard lesson. Close to her mom, Ann remembered her elder's words, "Careful, my daughter, I know it sounds harsh, but it is true many boys want just one thing." Because her mom's sister learned truths the hard way, Ann's mom knew of the fast world of men. She didn't demand Ann's chastity stay intact, though she mentioned, "I was very careful. Sure, I was tempted, I'm not that old. But I only slept with one man, your father."

* * * *

Days after her conversation with Allison, Ann was still reflecting for the umpteenth time about why she couldn't meet someone. And she wondered about Louis. What was he doing now? Two years together, now two years over. Again, Anthony. A typical Italian kid who wanted to be a gangster like his uncle.

Her father had referred to Tony as an asshole. The whole family, *Pessenavontes!* Sicilian for a person who thinks he's a big shot. She told herself she had plenty of time to meet the right man. She worked the perfect shift for nightlife: four to midnight. She also thought of her neighborhood friends. They drifted. No one's fault. Sure, they really didn't understand the cop thing but there was also the natural gravitation for cops to buddy with their own.

CHAPTER 2

Frank Colleri was thinking how ironic it was that he was doing the very thing he tried desperately to avoid in the past. Only now it didn't matter. He was lying on his back with just a sheet covering the front of his naked body. When Nina went to the bathroom she shut the bedroom light off. Frank was glad she did; he was intimidated by the woman's casual forwardness, her obvious carnal intent. But that's what his friend Sean told him. 'This is not only an easy one pal, but a damned good one.' Sean Walsh was rarely wrong when it came to women.

She appeared from the dim-lit foyer looking like a street corner hooker, a pro inching towards her mark. Bright lipstick matched the red teddy she was draped in. Her dark hair was hanging long on the left side of her face. She moved her hands upward from her waist to her bra where the bottom of her breasts seemed tucked to her nipples. She climbed onto the bed like a large cat, teasingly, one limb at a time. Frank swelled to excitement and the night of drinking rushed to his head. He removed the sheet and displayed what he had been covering. She was on him, her fingers moving, and she whispered, "Poppy?"

He felt himself jerk at the sound of the Latin anthem, acknowledging he was her man, at least for the moment. He answered childishly, "Yeah?" He felt her breath when she went down on him.

In that moment, Nina was in complete control. Frank knew he had certainly chosen a winner for his first extramarital affair, unless he counted a hand job by a hooker at one of the precinct's wild bachelor parties. Nina was like hitting the bimbette lotto. Aggressive and quick, not much of a challenge… Drinks and a tumble. During his marriage, other women had tempted Frank. He certainly spent enough nights fantasizing. He was especially struck by one: Jenna, a dark-haired nurse from the local hospital. But he was non-committal in any pursuit of Jenna outside of a clumsy kiss.

As he lay next to Nina, he recalled the fun before marriage. Getting laid, no commitment. He lit a cigarette taking a long drag steaming the butt. If his wife had been this easy he probably wouldn't have married her and consequently would not be having problems. How easy if all relationships existed just too get laid. Find out right away and save the trouble of putting someone on top of a pedestal.

His buddies were still engaged in the practice of non-conformity. Probably better off. With Nina, all it required was an introduction from Sean Walsh and a little friendly conversation. Nina stirred to go another round. Feeling zero affection, he was free of the nervous trembling that accompanied pure lovemaking. He allowed Nina to take him to that place where he was quick in his ejaculation, even the second time around. He attributed this to the newness of a strange piece. *Awesome!*

Nina drifted off to sleep again and Frank's thoughts turned back to his wife, her timidity. The last thing he wanted to think about now. Yet, Kathleen, her phony Catholic innocence, only loosened when she liquored up. Teasingly she'd make him wait. That was fine because in those times he held the strings of happiness. The power to convince yourself you were making lasting love… And here next to him, a woman who would wake soon and want to make love again where there was no love at all.

The ice was broken. Frank officially joined the ranks of a cheating cop. Though, of course, a guilty conscious explained it was his wife who drove him to it. And like all indiscretions, this night began with a lie. It was Christmas season, Frank told Kathleen he was stuck at work with an unavoidable shoplifting arrest. Instead, he went to meet Nina at the bar where she worked. He planned on spending an hour or two drinking until she quit for the night.

The Tavern was really just a polite name. It was a real dive, a bucket of blood. The bar was dingy, too smoky, and the place reeked of stale beer as soon as the door was swung open. The bar reminded him of a small joint in Long Island where Sean met an intoxicated and forward girl with stringy hair, and five minutes later had her in the backseat of his car.

The Tavern hosted a small and apparently whacked crowd, lingering around an extremely loud band with overblown speakers. The clientele looked like they were perps in a central booking holding cell.

Frank found it hysterical that he would have to conjure up some story to his mistress, saying he had to work the holidays, only to spend a forced Christmas and New Year with his wife and her family. Nina didn't know Frank was married and he never offered such information. Nina hinted for sleepovers and breakfast. He felt it a desperate act. She'd only known him for a short time even though she introduced her life story. There were the bad relationships, the kid, the small apartment; all tiresome nonsense to Frank but he pretended to be interested. He was amused by her previous employment. Nina needed extra money so for a few months she worked with a friend at a sex phone company. What was even better was her nickname: Passion. *Really, original,* he thought. Still, he wondered what it would be like yelling over and over, "Passion, Passion." And she, uttering all the filthy phrases she burned up the phone lines with.

Nina explained she gave it up because the work was done at home and her daughter was now old enough to figure words out.

What a mother. How gracious.

So, Nina became a barmaid and food stamp recipient, certainly no worse than a phone whore. Maybe she thought she would hit it big sleeping with a civil servant.

Booze alleviated all guilt on that first night. When Nina's shift came to an end she asked Frank to stick around a little while so she could unwind on the other side of the bar with him. Her hair waved in his face when she hopped on the stool next to his and swiveled around to face him. She wasted little time positioning her hand between his legs as she fixed her dark eyes on his. Then she moved quickly to dart her tongue in his ear. "I want a favor, Frank with the beautiful eyes," she had whispered.

He loved the sound of his name falling from her lips. Though in a more romantic fantasy he would want the woman to call him by his proper name, Francis. "What would that be?" he asked. She pushed her palm deep into his crotch where he was beginning to harden.

The bartender brought more drinks and Frank lit a cigarette. He downed the shot and attacked the beer chaser. *Spanish women age early,* he thought. *Well the loose ones anyway.* Nina was only twenty-eight but already showing signs of weathering. Right now, he didn't want to know the numbers of men. Suddenly the thought of going down on her disgusted him. *Did Sean?* he wondered. A few cocktails and of course he had, the male slut that he was.

CHAPTER 3

This time it was the real thing. No peering through windows, no beatings for getting caught as a peeping Tom. His father wasn't here now. The old drunk was dead.

Levar liked what he saw; dark hair, dark eyes, and a slim body. He had seen her before. First, in a police car parked by a bank. Then as luck would have it, again in a grocery store. Some cop. She didn't even notice him spying as she shopped in the aisles. No one did. It was like watching her in slow motion, on a runway headed right towards him.

The courts would make excuses for him. Misunderstood or mistreated, neglected or rejected, cursed with a sickness that coursed his veins. A freak of nature given a raw deal. Paying for the sins of his bloodline. Well damn it to God, it was God's fault. Who else has the power to unleash such evil? The devil? His father? Who didn't make love to his mother but fucked her when he came home drunk. And Levar had heard the screams, could even now as he fueled the little glass pipe, inhaling a strong hit of the fresh rock of crack.

* * * *

Ann blew into her hands, checked the thermostat in the kitchen. Something wasn't right with the heat. She rushed to put on a pot of tea. She went to the mirror and pinned her hair up. She picked up the book she started reading last night. She laughed to herself, *This can't be real, can it?* On the cover was a glazed photo of a shirtless hunk with a blond-haired beauty at his feet. She placed the book on the kitchen counter deciding to read a few pages with her morning tea. The whistle of the pot was taking a little longer than expected so she quickly wiped down the countertop with a paper towel she then tossed into a full garbage pail. *Might as well get rid of this.* She pushed down on the bag then jerked it out while spinning it to tie. She decided against a coat since she was only going a few steps from the door. Besides, she was wearing a light sweatshirt and pants. She backed through the door into the walkway then driveway, where the garbage cans stood. A chill suddenly traveled down her back and she tightened her neck to temporarily keep the cold out.

A row of small trees separated the driveway from the house next door. They moved with the wind, eerie with no leaves on them yet. Ann lifted the lid from the can and quickly stuffed the bag in as deep as she could. She began to quiver and again arched her neck.

Her head jerked back! Something stronger than nature had taken hold. Suddenly, Ann was thrown up and turned against the side of the house. She froze facing him.

His dark face was slightly hidden beneath the huge hood of his coat. She felt hot air rush from his mouth like an angered dragon. His words were quiet but fierce. "I'm gonna fuck you woman."

Ann's eyes couldn't hide a mind gone in fear. She couldn't scream and her breathing became labored. *Im a cop. There must be something I can do, should do...my gun. If I could get to my gun.* Hidden under her bed, useless now. She prayed someone would save her. It didn't matter that she was a cop, she was a woman now and desperately needed to be rescued, saved by someone, anyone.

She was finally able to scream. "My God, My God!"

The animal was grunting. "I'm going to slip you my...I'll kill you if you open your mouth again!" Whatever strength Ann could muster beneath the panic was not enough to overpower the predator. His mouth was frosted. "They won't lock me up. I got me a freebie, a real cop."

How does he know I'm a cop?

He laughed at her lame attempt to kick him. And when her kicks fell short...

"Please," she whispered. Overcome with hysteria she felt nauseous and a sick feeling of doom. Under the hood of his coat the monster smiled, a twisted grin. He was a man thrilled to be a beast.

He then hit her with short stammering blows to the middle of her face crushing her nose instantly with the first one. Her ears rang and she blurred, falling into his arms. She was helplessly trapped in the grip of her worst hour. He eagerly carried her into the apartment. Through her haze and the wet feel and taste of blood she heard the pot whistle and knew what was to happen. He was an animal that was not going to be denied.

CHAPTER 4

F rank Colleri was assigned to the police precinct's new CPOP squad: Community Patrol Officers Program. The new unit was designed by the department to insure a more personal and active involvement with the community by extending a police officer on foot patrol to address problems in specific areas. The individual police officer was to become a fixture on this beat, recognized by residents and shopkeepers. The unit was modeled on the old foot cop concept, a cop on the street when you needed one.

Specific missions of this pilot program were:

- Exchange information with the community on a regular basis
- Address crimes and victims within the officer's beat area
- Be recognized as a general peacemaker in the neighborhood

Along with the assignment came community meetings and an abundance of paperwork to be completed and filed. Maps of each beat within the precinct were drawn up and officers were to mark various crimes and patterns on the board with colored pushpins. All designed to cover the mayor's egotistical ass and to give the public a feeling of security by reducing their fear.

For the unit cop, CPOP secured better working hours with weekends off. An incentive when compared to the regular patrol officer's schedule of rotating shifts.

Conditions on each beat came in waves. There were the basic problems of traffic, parking, loitering and street peddlers hawking their wares of reproduced designer products. There was also the more serious problem of violent crime. The recent staggering increase was number one on the unit's agenda. Officers were instructed to review all complaint reports pertaining to felonies, and then they were to call and visit the victims to explain about the new Crime Victims Board, and to instruct on the help the board was offering victims of certain crimes. The officers were to hand out pamphlets and assist victims with filling out the application. Most cops thought this was just another community jerk job.

Because of the size of each beat, some covering a couple of miles, other officers were assigned as alternates to assist each beat cop.

Officer John Bennett became Frank's alternate. Soon it was decided all the felonies having to do with burglaries or robberies with no injury would get limited visits and the rest would receive their victim booklets via US mail. Regarding the violent felonies, Frank and John split the chore by category due to the enormous amount of complaints.

Bennett, one year out of the academy, was just happy to be in CPOP. He agreed to handle felony burglaries and robberies where injury was inflicted. Frank would attempt the more delicate victims of sexual assault, especially the cases involving the elderly or a minor, because such sensitive cases were double checked in the Special Victim's category, and because the precinct, on word from higher up, recently made the sexual assault category a top priority.

Frank wished the whole thing could be done by mail or maybe phone. But he knew his supervisor, Sergeant Moore, was obliged to check on these felonies.

Moore specifically told his officers, "You guys know that normally I don't give a damn what you do. But this is a hot bed from the top. They're going to check on these crime victim things, and you know the sneaky captain has no problem helping the big guys out. Misdemeanors can take a temporary time out for now. He'll be checking logs and calling people to see if you're doing what you're supposed to. So, let's, for the time being, abide on this one 'cause I like it here in CPOP."

The officers knew shit rolled down hill from One Police Plaza's Ivory Tower to the borough chiefs, to the precinct captains, then lieutenants and sergeants, until finally mistakes were suffered by the patrolmen. The complaints (UF61s) over the past twenty-four months were stacked an inch thick. They were siphoned through patrol, the detectives, then police assistants, before making it to the beat cop.

Frank began the work skimming complaint reports and separating the sexual assaults from the others; the larger pile he would hand over to Bennett.

Sergeant Moore explained that though this was a priority, it was too time consuming to visit every single victim indefinitely. This would have the job screaming that there wasn't enough time for other police activities such as the issuance of parking tickets and high visibility to local shopkeepers. "For now, the workload will be heavy. The whole idea is we still have to be out there on the street visible for all to see us."

The powers that be were confidant the communities of New York would be pleased with the establishment of the Crime Board. Designed by the state, victims or their survivors could be eligible to collect benefits for losses that occurred in the commission of certain crimes. Benefits could include such reimbursements as transportation to court and funeral expenses. A claimant was to apply to the board explaining the circumstances of the crime and the ensuing hardship. Thus, the loss to the claimant would be evaluated on an individual basis where it may undergo both a medical and verbal hearing. The board would then decide what monetary awards were to be issued.

A noteworthy early catch made by an ambitious young and compassionate Queens CPOP officer led to the arrest of a three-time loser—a crack addict from an upper-class neighborhood who committed multiple burglaries and sexual offenses. The officer, who was black, and his inquisitive nature, managed to extract a specific profile from one of the victims. This gave wonderful front page accolades for the NYPD in regard to its new CPOP program, and great fodder for the PC, especially after recent complaints from minority groups citing the police were not very kind or concerned about them.

"See," the commissioner, jumping on a chance to publicly comment, boldly stated, "CPOP is working. This is the reason we implemented the program. My guys are out there paying close attention to their assigned beats and getting involved in the goings on with problem solving and concerns of the citizens who live and work in those areas, regardless of what the press or news media say."

Sergeant Moore reiterated to his new CPOP group that it wasn't brain surgery. Make a quick check of crime victims and ask them if there's anything the NYPD could do. Discuss the pamphlets and be done with it. And don't forget to write the time and date of the visit in the beat book.

Frank began the delivery of the pamphlets on a Monday. A fresh start. He figured to make two or three visits a week. It was early spring and street conditions would be the flavor of the month. There would be a few grungy homes to endure, some victims that would bend his ear endlessly; all meant little because they would be falling on deaf ears. He would just be there hiding out from the cold and complaints on the street.

Officer Colleri rode the elevator to the tenth floor. The young girl lived with her parents in apartment 10C at the far end of the hallway. Frank removed one of the pamphlets from his duty jacket. Before he rang the bell, he stuck his pinkie deep into his right ear to temporarily relieve the itching. This time of year was bad on his skin; the colder, the more inflamed his eczema.

A stout, strong looking woman of about forty answered the door. Pleasant to the presence of a police uniform, she invited Frank in and offered him coffee. He accepted gladly and immediately gave his reason for being there.

"Sit," she said. "Is it more questions officer? We already spoke to the detectives." This would not be the first person to need an explanation that his visit was not an interrogation of the crime. "Crime Victim?" she whispered. "My daughter is good officer, she really is."

"I'm sure ma'am. But what I'm trying to say is that there is help—" He thought this would be easier. He didn't want the coffee after all. "Please, ma'am, read it."

"Stay officer. I'll get you more coffee."

How do I get out of here? He had only taken a couple of sips from his cup yet the woman topped it off. She won. He was going to hear her version of the attack on her daughter.

"My daughter invited him, Carlos, her classmate, home after school on that day."

Frank started thinking these visits weren't a good idea. *Didn't the brain surgeons up in the Ivory Tower realize the victims and their families would be drudging up their misery all over again?* Surely they knew these poor souls regarded a police uniform like a priest. The trauma was obviously fresh in her mind; she began spilling. Suddenly, the cold pavement wasn't such a bad idea.

"Yes officer, like I told the detectives, I knew Carlos had a crush on my daughter. But I thought, only a couple of hours, then I would be home from work." She was looking away. "He must have construed this, as a way, to, advance the, *um*, relationship."

Frank noticed photographs of the daughter adorning the living room walls. The girl had to be one of the prettiest girls in school. She possessed a remarkably angelic face with eyes wide and blue. She embodied teenage innocence, the kind that was worth the respectful wait.

What the woman knew from her daughter was that Carlos seemed to be probing with his eyes. Certainly, more than he should have. "My daughter was happy just to be watching TV with him...He moved his hand to her knee, commenting on how nice her jeans were." The woman covered her mouth. "She was nervous at that point."

Oh God! She's going to tell me everything. "Ma'am, you don't have to," he said.

"He knew she was a virgin." The woman began to cry.

Oh shit.

"The boy said she'd like it. Just a kiss, he told her. He started licking her lips. He told detectives his parents would shove him in the closet. Have you ever? She shouted for him to stop and then my daughter blacked out."

Frank didn't want or need to hear anymore. Strangely, for a moment Frank thought of his wife. *Bitch. Maybe the sick bastard should have been on a couch with her instead.* He scratched his ear trying to excuse the thought.

"He took her panties…"

Frank stood and inched toward the door. "I'm sorry I have to go, partner's waiting for me. If you need anything call us." He made his escape, leaving the woman with questioning eyes.

The girl was a statistic. One of approximately seventy-five percent are attacked or raped by someone known to them.

Out on the sidewalk he thought of the woman and her daughter left with all that pain. He also thought about the panty sniffer. "Sicko," he said to himself. Could he sniff his wife's panties now that he was no longer fucking her? He laughed. Crudeness was a defense mechanism for cops. He hoped he wouldn't have to listen to too much emotion with every victim he would visit. Maybe he should have taken the burglary and robbery felonies.

He removed a report from his jacket. According to the time and place of occurrence, Leslie Lee, 35, was attacked on the same day as the school girl. Report time of a ten-minute difference. *Not today,* he thought. He put the report back in his pocket. He walked away digging his pinkie into his ear again.

CHAPTER 5

Ann Caputo had kept pace with a purse-snatcher for three blocks, wrestled the thief to the ground and handcuffed him, disregarding another of her father's pleas: 'You see those animals causing trouble, go the other way.' The irony was that her father did believe in helping the little guy. It was one reason Ann was drawn to helping others. She would forever remember her father, walking out the front door after witnessing a commotion from the window. Three neighborhood teens had surrounded another kid, who was calling on one of their sisters for a date. One of the teens smacked this kid in the mouth just as Mr. Caputo got close. He grabbed the teen. "Come on now Sal, what the hell is goin' on here?"

"Mr. Caputo, this fuckin' jerk off wants to go out with my sister, and I already told him no."

"Well, did he do something wrong or disrespectful?"

"No but look at him."

"OK, I see a kid bout the same age as you and he hasn't said a word, hasn't fought back trying to attack."

"He's a fucking---"

"Don't say it Sal. Just don't. I'll talk to your father but for now you leave this kid alone and let him walk away." Mr. Caputo glared at Sal and the other two boys. "Got it?"

"But it's a fair fight Mr. Caputo."

"It's not. Not when you're fighting for the wrong reason."

The teens knew better. Mr. Caputo was intimidating. The kid who was smacked rubbed his cheek and nodded in gratitude to the older man.

Mr. Caputo walked passed Ann. "Get inside sweetie." He looked at his wife and Ann. "Told you about that family, and the father ain't a bad guy."

Ann felt a little red in the face. Her father had no way of knowing that Sal's brother Anthony had deflowered her.

The whole fiasco was a lesson. Her dad stuck up for the underdog. In an Italian neighborhood where outsiders were frowned upon, her dad wouldn't allow kids he knew to pick on this innocent outsider, whose only fault was liking a girl from this block. This Puerto Rican boy who just showed up to say hello to his high school crush. So why did her father not believe in loyalty to a job he didn't understand? Maybe because she was a girl?

Yet, as fast as she could run or jump, she couldn't rescue herself from her own attack. Like many victims, she was haunted, perhaps forever, by a personal fear smothering her.

Weeks had passed since the brutal attack. The young cop took some sick leave, bruised and battered. The swelling in her face had dissipated and the darkness under her eyes could be covered up with makeup now.

She beat herself up with the *what ifs*. If she had stayed in her previous job she still would have lived at home, safe in the womb of family. She would have been safe in a workplace where she traveled with thousands of commuters. Safe in a tiny cubicle where she would noisily type until her eyes ached. Safe in a tough Brooklyn neighborhood where residents looked out for each other. She wouldn't have been able to afford her own place, nor would she have had the confidence. A lot of good her confidence had done her. Was her ex-boyfriend, right? She rationalized until her head ached.

Ann didn't have the heart to tell her parents about the attack. When she spoke to them on the phone she had to bite her lip to keep from crying. But she also knew sooner or later she would have to face them. Of course, she'd have to wait until the swelling in her face and black eyes totally disappeared. Thankfully, though badly bruised, and feeling tender to the touch, her nose was somehow not broken. How would they react? Would they think their only child a disgrace for being unable to defend herself? What would she say to them? "Oh Poppa, I'm sorry, it wasn't my fault...Mom it wasn't..." Ann felt like she was going mad. Of course her parents would understand. They would be sick with worry. Her father would irrationally try to take the law into his own hands and try to find the scum that left scars on his daughter.

The detectives who questioned her assured her that no one would know about the incident. Publicly anyway. She knew that her name could never be released to the media. As for coworkers, she knew it was nearly impossible to hide anything from the police department rumor mill. She would deal with it when the time came. There were those that would be sympathetic, but there would also be some behind the back snickering. There always was.

All the detectives got from her up to this point was a faint description. "A male, black...wearing a dark hooded parka coat...breathing heavy like a..."

Thinking he was out of earshot she heard one of the detectives, an up and coming self-proclaimed know it all, comment that it wasn't much from a trained police officer.

Like most police officers, Ann's closest friends were cops, yet many didn't want to intrude. After all, what could they say? Allison was the exception. It was Allison who Ann had called first. It was Allison who took Ann to the hospital and made all the proper notifications, and who sat with her through all the questions. It was Allison who hugged her as if she were her own child. Allison checked on her friend every single day.

The local precinct did its part with constant patrols by her home and radio car teams drinking their coffee parked out front. There were moments when she wondered if she should call a couple of her childhood friends just to feel separated from police and crime, but she saw them infrequently and that's simply just the way it was.

Ann had no choice but to confer with the department's counseling unit. She was free to see a doctor on her own but as a member of the department and victim of such a violent crime she had to go through department channels. Ann wasn't eager to trust a department shrink. Their motives were always suspect to the rank and file. As expected, the first concern was to remove the officer from her weapon.

Ann had been subject to hell, choking back tears as detectives had carefully, but none the less, relentlessly barraged her with a series of repetitious questions. "When did you notice him? Was he high? What did he say?"

Then there was the physical exam. If she could forget one thing other than the assault itself, it would be that exam. But she would never forget...

There had been a few times she was summoned to the hospital to assist a rape victim as a female police officer. Now she was the victim. She had lain there, legs up in the stirrups, the doctor prodding... all the horror engulfing her again. It took all her strength to fight back tears. Again, Allison held her. She had waited with victims for the evidence kits. Now someone waited for hers.

Ann knew the Vitullo kit was an integral part of the evidence chain supplied by hospitals. The Vitullo kit contained various slides, swabs, and envelopes to be collected and processed as evidence in each sex case. Other evidence, such as torn undergarments, were also placed in the kit then packaged and given to an assigned police officer who would bring the kit to the police lab. These kits were sealed, keeping a chain of evidence. It would be opened first by lab personal at the New York City Police Department. A lab that was staffed around the clock, accepting evidence at any time.

Ann wasn't deeply religious, but as any other who experienced human suffering, she would question the Almighty. Why hadn't the attacker just finished his work and killed her? The guilt questions: Did she deserve it because she wasn't a virgin? Did she deserve it because she engaged in enjoyable sex? Ann didn't really understand the work of God before, so she certainly doubted who or what he was now. However, religious guilt doesn't just subside. *Should I be grateful to God for giving me the strength to reach a phone that day?* That awful day, when she had finally regained consciousness, she was shaking all over and stinging with pain. She tasted the dry blood that filled her mouth. Her head was filled with dizziness and she felt like the bones in her nose were crushed. There were feelings of total disbelief and hope that what happened wasn't real. Then intense shame, realizing her bowels had softened from fear.

She cried uncontrollably then, and she cried all over again now. She was remembering the first shower afterwards. The necessity: to wash the filth from her body, as scalding water burned the wounds. Sitting in her easy chair she was not at ease at all. Once again, she felt ill, the tears still falling and all the while Ann wished she were dead.

* * * *

Frank scratched his itch by circling a paper clip in his ear. He didn't carry the cream ointment, that worked its best only when he remained indoors for prolonged periods of time. Frank was sitting in the CPOP office, shielded from the cold wind, totally bored. He decided to rummage through some of the reports hoping that not all the victims were going to be melodramatic. But of course, they would, it was their personal pain.

There appeared to be no set patterns to lone attackers. Frank was amazed at the geographical proximity and coincidentally, close times, of some of the attacks. He read on, also realizing that if it were not for the brutality of the crimes, much of the perpetrators' dialogue appeared to be straight from a low-budgeted comically-scripted porn film.

The Leslie Ling report went into the garbage. Ling was one of a multitude of Korean residents who inhabited northern Queens. Other than a few youth gangs who would terrorize their own people, the Koreans were basically a quiet lot who kept to themselves and rarely called on the police. Unfortunate because what they failed to realize was if nothing is said or done assailants would keep on assaulting. Often the Koreans were considered by police as people just passing through, especially in the shopping areas, carrying handled grocery bags and wearing diminutive smiles. The smiles were once explained to Frank by another cop, not as stupid grins, or insinuating insult, rather they were often worn as a mask to hide their embarrassment.

Many Koreans were not knowledgeable in matters of New York crime. They rarely, if at all, looked over their shoulders while carrying large sums of cash. Recently they were being victimized by age-old con games. Perpetrators were in the shopping areas following these citizens and watching them withdraw money or they would observe them leave establishments with valuables; in each case following the helpless victim to their automobiles where the thief would then go into gibberish monologue, pointing to the victim's car tires showing them the flat. And then the barely English speaking victim bent to look, still uncertain as to what was going on. So, when the victim's attention was focused on the tire, and they put their bags down or their grips loosened, the perp would grab the wares and take off. If the grips became a little tighter, then the victim might receive an unexpected blow to the head.

Many of these crimes went unreported. The community councils emphasized these serious and violent crimes were extremely important and to be reported to the police. Sexual assault, of course being one, though many people regarded such a crime too private to disclose. Frank wondered if the Koreans should have stayed where they came from. They were only here to make money, not friends, so why should anyone go out of their way to explain the laws of the land? The irony was, in Korea extreme justice was handed out quickly. Frank had heard stories of foreign countries reaping the rewards of vengeance. Ling's attacker would have had his balls cut off within a day. That wasn't happening here.

Would these folks be able to decipher a frog from a turtle in their descriptions? Frank wasn't the only cop to use callousness as a defense. Cops were taught early that if they were going to last twenty years there would be times when crass humor had to be interjected in misery. A rookie cop from the suburbs once cruelly commented after a sexual assault on a Korean woman, "They ripped that chink two assholes."

Frank never said anything to the cop, but at the time, he didn't laugh along, rather he thought it a remarkably heartless thing to say.

* * * *

Frank crossed the street tugging at his uniform turtleneck. Today was unseasonably mild, less windy then the last few days. As bad as other people's problems were, he wasn't thinking about how a crime victim could give a solid description, he was obsessing on his own circumstance playing out with his wife. He was feeling more miserable than usual. It had been at least two days since he'd spoken to Kathleen.

He walked past the busy intersection of Main Street up the cross in the road towards the public library when he was accosted by a young postal worker who told him there was a black kid sitting on a mailbox down the street who refused to get off. Frank walked up to the mailbox. He saw the kid wrapped in an oversized coat, sitting atop it and kicking his feet into the core of the box, his head turning left to right smoothly.

"Yo, didn't the mailman ask you nicely to get off the mailbox?"

"I ain't botherin' anyone. And no, he didn't ask nicely, he demanded."

Frank shook his head in frustration, he could sense where this was going. Still, he wanted the kid gone not arrested. "What's your name bro?"

"Bro? Is that racist?"

"Don't play fucking games with me. What's your name?"

"Levar. What's it to you?"

"Well Levar. You have only two choices. Get off and go. Or be forced off and arrested."

The kid jumped off and hiked up his pants. "Shit, all you motherfuckers want to do is harass us. Do you wanna search me for drugs?"

Frank sighed then responded, "No, I just want you out of here. I'm not gonna tell you again Levar..."

After the kid sauntered and swayed away, unfazed, Frank went back to his thought of a few days earlier when Kathleen was sitting next to him on the couch.

* * * *

Frank was flicking the television remote past every station as if he were a zombie. In a fit of anger Kathleen jumped up and turned the set off. "You're not happy, are you, Frank?"

Frank wasn't surprised by her question. But he was also not in the mood to comment knowing she would just counter with an argument. Kathleen was on her period and her right eye was squinting. Sure signs that she was ready for war, at the most deadly time of the month. What was the saying? Something strange about a person who could bleed for a week. She continued her line of questioning. "Well, where were you last night? And what time did you finally roll in?"

"Stop, will you please," he said. "I figured you were sleeping and since I didn't have to get up early---"

"Stop lying!" she shouted. "Answer the damn question!"

"It's not a lie, Kathleen. Besides what's your problem anyway?" Now it appeared he was headed exactly where he didn't want to venture. Kathleen wasn't going anywhere until she made her point. Her green eyes were like that of an unfriendly cat ready to pounce.

Snapping back to reality like a driver who doesn't know how he got where he wanted to go, Frank was oblivious to the walk he had just taken. He shook his head in an attempt to recycle his thoughts to the present; he also needed to be out of sight of John Q. Public. So on automatic pilot he quickly darted up one of the side streets. *What the hell is happening to my marriage?* Sleeping back to back. A year old, it was already disintegrating.

Finishing that round, back at the office he removed another report hoping someone else's misery would take his mind off his own. Really it was just going in circles, but along the way he was ingesting pieces of a world he'd known nothing about. Taking his boss's advice to read up on sex assaults, he was learning statistics were just numbers and figures with variances to the patterns of previous years. They were a census rather than a conclusive calculation to ascertain the why. Even the victims became students of facts. He learned about the cynics, other than cops. There were also many in the civilian world who didn't take rape seriously either. Through the victims, he would also understand why they chose to drop their complaints because of a horrendous justice system. The Catch-22. Not wanting to testify, yet not wanting the scum to walk. And on it went...

Frank gained insight into the victim's embarrassment, especially dealing with a heartless media. The victim's strong fear of being attacked again and the onslaught of continued nightmares. He would learn that rape didn't discriminate. And more statistics and ratios.

Another day, another patrol on the streets. Frank went deep into his ear before knocking on a big oak door. Sarah Kelly, a bright green-eyed college student in her freshmen year. She had been attacked by what she described as a very large Hispanic man who pretended he was the cable repairman. The girl also remembered his teeth. "They were disgustingly brown," she said. "He kept trying to rub them on my face. They were grinding and he was laughing." That's what Sarah remembered before recollection passed into a blur.

In circles Frank went...

Janet Korn, twenty-three, proper and Jewish, she lived only three blocks from where the Kelly girl was assaulted in this diverse, overpopulated ethnic neighborhood. The girls didn't know one another. People weren't as close as the stoop talkers that came from neighborhoods of old, where friends left their doors unlocked. Two men in dark clothing grabbed Janet as she was walking home from the train station. Now it was two, not just a lone wolf. They pulled her into the garage area of the building where she lived, said dirty things, and sexually assaulted her. Then they robbed her and instilled permanent fear by promising her they would keep her identification for insurance and would be back to kill her if the cops ever came after them. Janet never told her parents. She explained to Frank that the only thing that would have done is worry them to an early grave. "It's funny what you remember, the cold steel of a knife. The dark and the dampness. And one guy had to be oriental because he had the same atrocious breath as the corner grocer and his family."

I think I know that grocery store. Enough for one day.

* * * *

Initially Frank joined the CPOP unit promising his wife to work earlier hours to be home more at night. His good friends from the four to twelve shift, Joe and Teddy, tried convincing him to stay in the rotating patrol squad he had been comfortable in. "If you're going to make a change because you think it's what your wife needs then don't," Joe said. Joe was always the wise one but this time Frank disagreed, answering, "I don't know about that, Poppa Smurf."

In CPOP, he accommodated the hours to fit his social life; at night with friends and a cozy bar. Frank would lie to his wife claiming he had to work late, had an arrest or had to catch up on paperwork relating to conditions on his foot post. His friends predicted correctly. He was partying more than ever.

Kathleen would lament, "Yeah, whatever. Go get drunk. While you're at it, go smoke weed with your brother and get toasted."

What a bitch! At the same time his wife was falling asleep he would be bellying up to the bar with his buddies. This would prove to be disastrous.

Most of the people at Ferris Pub were regulars. By midnight the shift of drinkers were usually the cops, firemen and nurses just ending a day of work. A retired fireman owned the bar. However, judging from the décor, one would think he was a seaman. The bar ran the length of the pub and every ten feet or so hung large anchor-type ropes overhead to give a pirate effect. Sea and fish paraphernalia were displayed all over the bar in glass casings, and the small dining tables opposite the drinking area each had their own make believe windows in the shape of portholes for a low cabin effect.

The bar wasn't crowded when Frank arrived so he quickly ordered a shot and a beer. Until one of his friends walked in it was going to be small talk with Carl the bartender. That would be in between thoughts of Kathleen. He could barely believe he was wishing his old lifestyle back. In his heart, he wanted to be home. For sexual relief, he could have gone to Nina's. But…here he sat.

Ferris happened to be the place he met his wife. Unlike most of the cop's wives who never get to see where their beloved husbands play, Kathleen was a local resident who frequented Ferris often. Frank was planted on a stool close to the door and under the elevated television. The TV usually ran with the sound off allowing the jukebox to serenade the patrons. An old Motown song was playing when he slugged back a bourbon on the rocks.

"So, what else is doing Frank?" Carl asked.

"Not much, what about you?" Same old dialogue, but a necessary ritual nevertheless. Frank really didn't mind because Carl was a likable guy. Carl was well into his thirties but he looked like an average college kid. He was also curious about cop stuff. Frank downed the glass.

Carl was standing stick (the wood platform behind the bar) ready to pour again. He was smiling his toothy grin. "Do you want me to leave the bottle?"

"No." Frank laughed. Carl's mild manner loosened Frank up a bit. The two engaged in talk of sports. Carl was a Mets fan, Frank a Yankee nut. Frank wondered if Carl could tell he was in the dumps. Strangely, Frank felt at home here. He lit his last cigarette of the pack then asked Carl to change a five for the machine. "I need butts, buddy."

Handing Frank a fist full of quarters Carl asked, "How's Kathleen?"

There it is. The famous question bound to be asked. "She's good, you know probably sleeping by now. She has an early day tomorrow."

"Are you doing nights steady now? Thought you worked more daytime in CPOP."

"Just for a while I have things going on at work right now." Frank took a swig of the whiskey with a lit cigarette between his fingers, getting up for his getaway to the machine for another pack. He hoped a friend would walk in before he returned to his seat.

"Some of the other guys are coming, right?"

"I hope so. I left an hour early, I'm sure someone from patrol will be here any minute."

The length of the bar stretched north from the front door so anyone leaning right would be able to notice immediately who entered as soon as the sound of the door could be heard swinging open, especially tonight with a whistle from the wind. As Carl tended to customers, Frank began to think about his affair with Nina. It was so early in a marriage to happen.

The door whooshed and Frank turned to see Jenna Pendergast walk in. She was in green nurse scrubs. Suddenly, Frank's desire grew and he looked at her romantically, noticing dark hair dancing off her shoulders, wide brown eyes reflecting off light skin. *God, I must be lonely.* To think of a romance, before getting laid, that was the magic of booze and the music of The Righteous Brothers playing in the background.

For some time though, Frank had had the hots for Jenna. They were always friendly to each other, often kidding one another since their personalities seemed to mesh, even before Frank was married. But now he was taken. They had gone as far as sharing a kiss one night, then the issue of morality stepped in. *To hell with that now.* Jenna had such a great ass, and she was so easygoing and never cold to him. Maybe she didn't suffer the same swings of PMS. Who knows? After all, he didn't spend enough time with other women to experience their ups and downs so closely as husband did with wife.

A group of women walked in moments after Jenna. Frank's eyes widened when he noticed his wife in the formation. Almost in unison the girls were saying their hellos. Kathleen approached her husband and kissed him on the mouth leaving Frank slightly guilty about Jenna.

"Hi honey," she said.

"Hi," Frank replied confused. "What brings you here?"

"Well we wound up going to a movie. It wasn't that long and well...I figured you were working."

He blew that off and interjected, "I'm glad you're here." He kissed her on the soft of her cheek. *There's still affection,* he thought. *God, she can be adorable.* His romanticism entered again. He noticed his wife's skin: illuminating. Her strawberry hair seemed to bounce with every turn of her head. Her smile, perfect white teeth. Not to mention her ass and her brains. *God, is this what fighting is all about? You wind up lusting after your own wife?*

"Hey," Carl said. "Just talking about you."

Kathleen smiled. "Good things I hope. I'll have a Bud."

"I'll take a white wine spritzer," her friend Peggy said.

The harmony of the women snapped Frank back. He pointed to the money in front of his glass. "It's on me Carl." *Could I have a play with my own wife? Does she still love me even though things are frigid in our sex life?* He felt guilty now about wishing bad on his own wife during that assault victim visit.

Frank looked up to see Kathleen reaching for her beer. Peggy picked up her spritzer and was chatting it up with Carl. Jenna glanced at Frank a couple of times, he cautiously looked away. He wondered if down the road he should make a play for her. The reality was, he shouldn't. Their last kiss affected him. He would be in danger of falling for her and he didn't want to complicate his already troubled marriage. He knew Jenna wouldn't be like Nina. Nina could have screwed him until doomsday, finished his laundry till Sunday, and cooked him a feast every night and it still would mean nothing...

Kathleen snapped her finger in front of Frank's face. "Anyone home?" Frank blinked then smiled. "I didn't hear from you all day except to tell me you were working late, which I see was bull."

That's right. He sure lied. Again, he shrugged the work thing off. "How was your day sweetheart? How was the last-minute movie?" Both seemed to understand where their dishonest remarks could lead and backed off.

Kathleen took another swig and her cheeks appeared to turn rosy. "So, how is work?" she asked again, sarcastic, but not angry.

"A little boring," Frank said. "A few conditions on my post, you know?"

Kathleen pointed her little index finger. *"Umm.* Overtime?"

"I thought you would be asleep---"

Peggy interrupted as she squeezed between the couple. "Hey, it's pretty dead in here." Peggy was Kathleen's friend but also worked as a nurse on the same floor with Jenna. One of those small world things. Peggy and Kathleen grew up together, attending the same catholic schools. Peggy liked to party. Her looks were on the plain side, with a slightly blemished Irish face, a brunette with big hair, but everyone enjoyed her company. Frank, however, thought she was intrusive. She was always in earshot when he had something to say to his wife. He felt strongly that Peggy didn't like him and certainly hadn't wanted her friend to marry him.

"I'm gonna go after this beer Frank," Kathleen said. "I should definitely be home before you."

Maybe Frank was being a bit paranoid but he didn't detect an invitation from his wife. They had been arguing of late. He forced a phony tightlipped smile. He was not about to invite himself even if it was his wife. "You probably will," he said. Frank noticed that as the girls left neither Kathleen nor Peggy shot him a last glance. *Conspiracy.* He noticed Carl looking his way, the curious bartender was probably wondering why he would say his wife was home sleeping. But Frank had more important things to worry about, namely he and his wife both caught lying to each other.

Just as he was beginning to feel embarrassed, a rambunctious noise filled the doorway and in walked a crowd of off-duty cops. Fellow officers Frank knew when he worked the rotating shifts. Married CPOP cops like Gallo and Bennett were not usually part of the late crowd, though Eaton and Walsh might pop up at any time.

Carl began to assemble the cocktails and there were hellos all around.

It was the end of a long workday, but not quite the end of the night. The cops would tack on four hours of drinking to complete the notorious four by four shift.

CHAPTER 6

Peter Colleri was hell bent on leading the life of a hedonist. Just twenty-five years old, Peter's philosophy was: he wasn't hurting anyone, so he alone would decide when it was time to grow up. Unlike Frank, who possessed their mother's features of soft blue eyes, a pinched nose and light brown hair, Peter was more likened to their father having thick, dark, wavy hair (though Peter wore his in mullet style) and a slight roman nose that was not too noticeable because of the beauty in his grey eyes. Peter also had their father's barreled chest, and father and son were both short in stature, two inches shorter than Frank, who himself was no towering figure at 5'8" tall.

Since his brother's marriage, Peter lived alone in the family apartment in Briarwood, Queens. His ex-girlfriend, Liza, had long given up hope of a future with him. Peter exhausted himself with endless partying and strange women.

Frank loved his brother with deep affection. Their parents instilled tight bonds of family. When they were growing up the boys shared a room together along with enough toys and games for a dozen children. Like many siblings, one had to be a little more selfish, preferring to use up his brother's toys before his own. Frank was the selfish one. Their pops always insisted to the boys that no matter how fierce their arguments, they were never to raise a hand to one another or the winner would feel the wrath of dad.

Frank always felt guilty. When he was a teen, Peter was picked up for possession of marijuana and again when he was twenty for assault, after having punched out a guy who was trying to pick a fight with Frank in a bar. After these incidents, Mom and Frank banned together and lifted the father's strained view of his son. Frank was no angel he just never got caught.

"I'm sorry Pete," Frank once said. "You would have made a tougher cop than me."

"Hey Frank, I'm proud of you. At least one of us made it."

* * * *

The community patrol office was located in the basement of the precinct building. The claustrophobic room was tucked in a corner next to the patrolmen's dismal lounge. All this mattered little to the housed cops who had grown accustomed to tight quarters and stale air. Compared to the office type atmosphere in corporate America, most stationhouses in New York were filthy and cluttered, some were even unsanitary. It wasn't uncommon to share space with bugs and mice. Frank sat at one of four metal desks in the room; sleepy, insomnia had been a strong opponent of late. It was early in the morning and Frank was rubbing his eyes against an irritating burn. He felt as though the tour should be ending instead of just beginning. He was thinking about the warm bed he had been in only an hour ago. Warm with body heat, cold with love. For now, his wife was still there, still in their apartment, but he had stared at the ceiling a good part of the night wondering for how much longer. What was going to be the proverbial straw that would break the camel's back and send her packing forever?

Frank ran his fingers through his hair, and as if he did not have enough on his mind he now wondered if his hairline was receding. He was only in his late twenties. *Why think of this now? I need coffee.* He was mentally exhausted. Rejection was hell, an indefinable prison. Nature was capable of dishing out a force so profound it affected a person physically as well as mentally. And though Frank had come to dislike his wife because of their constant disagreeing, he still longed to curl up against her bottom at night. *God, I miss her touch.*

The phone rang twice before Frank was conscious enough to even contemplate answering it. "Yeah-*ah*-I mean CPOP. How can I help you?" *Idiot, who's calling so early?*

"Hello, is this the police precinct?"

"Yes, it is." *Brain surgeon.*

"I hate bothering you so early, but, I have to tell ya' that someone's gonna get killed if they don't leave my son the hell alone." *Here we go,* Frank thought. "I mean I'm gonna kill the kids keep picking on my son 'n tryin' ta take his money every day."

Frank said nothing, opting instead to ride it out then blow the woman off.

"Those scum, oh excuse my language officer. But they pick on my boy almost every day, and I'm tired of it. We don't bother no one and I work hard for my money, know what I mean? So, I'm just saying if nothing is done I'm gonna kill the fuckers."

"I totally understand ma'am so give me all your information and I'll be glad to send someone around."

"Will you officer?"

"I promise."

"You're so sweet, really. Cause I don't wanna have to hurt no one."

Frank left the woman neatly jerked off by the time they hung up. *Who the hell gave her this number?* A patrol cop, of course. The precinct guys were known to be upset and jealous of the CPOP unit and their nonchalant work routine. Many times, the patrol units would see a CPOP cop and immediately break their balls, 'Hey, that fuckin' job was on your post.' *Actually, I would do the same thing.* Upstairs, vicious cycle. He went back to lingering thoughts of rejection...his wife. The loneliness terrified him. An ache so heavy that nothing, even Nina's imagination, could fill the void.

Other CPOP cops began filing in, Harry, Grillo, and Johnny Pump Turris, who got his name from being stout but solid as a fire hydrant. First in though, was Officer Seabiscuit, who nodded at Frank with a country grin, no teeth showing. Seabiscuit was a native Long Islander, way out, a calm guy who got along with everyone, civilians as well as cops. He always wore his cap a little back on his forehead. "Just do what I have to do, that's it," was his motto.

The officers weren't as noisy as they might have been on a later shift but their presence was known. Some checked their message boxes, really for personal messages rather than job-related nonsense.

Officer Gallo entered smoking what was probably his third cigarette of the morning. Arthur Gallo was a striking and intimidating figure. He possessed a huge ego, a large hard chest and biceps that tightened his uniform. He could have doubled as a bouncer in a night club. Clouds of smoke steamed from him like a dragon.

Officer John Bennett was the first to announce something resembling a good morning. "Mornin' dudes." Bennett, unlike Gallo, wasn't a poster boy for a macho cop. He was short, wiry and quiet to a fault. He pretended that not much got under his skin even when some of the boys teased him about his thinning crown of hair.

Sergeant Moore trailed in just after the group. "Hey, Colleri, out of my chair. Bennett, I believe it's your turn for a coffee run."

"So, it's true," Gallo joked. "Old people are happy risers." They all laughed and Gallo choked out a cloud. "Do you fart when you piss?"

Moore just shook his head.

"Can't you blow that outside," Frank said to Arthur.

"How about if I blow it up your ass Frankie? It's not as if you don't smoke." Frank had just opened the door for Gallo banter. "No smoke today? You quitting? Frankie?" Gallo blew yet another cloud. "Or is it maybe you got no taint last night."

"All right knock it off. Blow that shit outside and stop making fun Arthur. You know you only smoke here cause your wife won't let you smoke at home and I allow it here," Moore said.

"It's not my wife. I don't smoke because of the kid."

"Yeah, right," Frank stated.

A couple of more cops were coming in. Gallo's voice was enough to draw tired laughs even though they missed the start of the bantering.

"So, who wants what?" Bennett said, hand out for money.

"C'mon sarge," Gallo quipped. "You're the big bucks guy." There was more tired laughter, then, as usual, reporting last were John Eaton and Sean Walsh. They were part of a trio of merry men that included Frank Colleri. The three finished the academy together and once they wound up in the same precinct became even more inseparable. When they were patrol cops, along with their buddy Teddy, they were taken under the wing and helpful hand of the veteran Joe, an old-fashioned Harlem cop with sarcastic wit, who aspired to the idea that the real job was patrol, out in the street answering calls every day. But against Joe's advice, within months of each other they decided they had enough of radio runs and roll calls and decided to join the CPOP unit. No more holdover collars, domestic disputes, car accidents or the rest of the other patrol shit.

Before Frank was married the three spent most of their nights staying out late, getting drunk and trying to score with as many women as they could, though Walsh and Eaton were much better at tackling a conquest. Ultimately, they all needed to curb the drinking and late nights of yesterday if they didn't want to age as badly as some of the old-timers who had spent their lives and careers in a tavern.

Sergeant Moore was barking an errant order. "Get your memo and beat books up to date. I'll scratch them now, I know I won't be able to find you guys later." Scratch was the term used when supervisors signed an officer's memo book for proof the cop was checked on.

Walsh was readying himself to tell a story. Of the three he was the least to slow his lifestyle by letting shift changes get in the way of a possible lay. Gallo recognizing the signs of bravado about to be spilled so he chimed right in. "Walsh! Not another fuck story? You know one day you'll get AIDS, *that* would be some story."

Walsh playfully slapped Art on the back. "Jealousy, will get you nowhere, big man. Besides, who wants to hear you complain again about how you're not going to be a sergeant. AIDS can only be caught getting it up Hershey Highway, something you would know about."

"Drop dead Sean. Up the ass? And I'm the wrong color that's all."

"Yeah, right," remarked Sergeant Moore. "Maybe you were the wrong brain size, and I do believe secretly jealous of anyone who passed the test. By the way, you guys are so ignorant about the AIDS virus. Try reading." Moore's easy way drew laughter from the men. The sergeant was unlike the typical grumpy old cop who stayed beyond twenty years on the job. Nor was he like the younger bosses who were getting promoted and relishing power the stripes gave over past friends. Moore was plain and simple; a good boss to his cops and the CPOP unit knew they had it good with him. Hence, signing their books when he saw them, instead of looking diligently for them out on the street.

There were infamous stories about Moore in his younger days; an imposing figure on the streets of Harlem. The time Moore as a young cop had no choice but to go head on with a psycho wielding a knife at a corner market. Escaping unscathed, he lifted the assailant into the air and hurled him through a laundromat window. The stuff of legend for a Harlem cop. Now nearing retirement with twenty-six years of service, Moore had mellowed. His cops guessed he could still throw someone a beating if need be. Moore had the largest pair of mitts any of them had ever seen. Fists surely capable, even now, of crushing an opponent's skull.

"Oh and again," Moore was saying, "I have to sign the beat books. Those wonderful guys from Borough Inspections are coming this week. Unannounced of course."

John Bennett was over by the message slots gathering papers from his box when Gallo surprised him, "So many damn Johns around here. Bennett, what if we call you loser?"

"Wise ass," Bennett replied.

"Don't fret," Frank said. "We're all losers around here. As a matter of fact, when we get the loser T-shirts you could buy one, fit right in."

When Frank retreated, Walsh moved to his buddy. "Hey Frank, everything good?"

"Yeah, why?"

"I don't know, you look a little rattled today, like you're in another world. How's it going with our little Spanish fly?"

"Awesome, everything you said," Frank answered. He rubbed his temples now hoping to push out some of the confusion.

"Then why the long face? Headache?"

"Yeah, huge. Female bitchy huge."

"Is your old lady on the rag again Frank? Well don't feel bad, my girl has been busting my balls forever. They all do, oh by the way, I was with you last night."

Frank managed a smile. *Not even married and he's making up excuses.* "Well, where were we?"

"Ah...shooting pool?"

"Okay, listen up," resounded Moore. "I'm going to breakfast since I no longer feel like waiting for Bennett to get the coffee and it's gettin' crowded in here, everyone out."

"So am I, damn it," Gallo said.

"Even if you were a boss I don't think anyone would want to eat with you," jested Moore.

"My skin is the wrong color to get promoted."

Moore threw up his hands. "Enough. And don't splash so much Giorgio on in the morning, it's nauseating."

"What do you wear, Canoe?"

They both laughed and threw the subject of race out the window. Of course, Moore couldn't agree with Gallo's assessment of promotions. In this climate of racial politics as the 1980s hit their stride, no one could. Most white cops were terrified to even joke about it. More than anyone, Moore had seen the huge curve in favoritism swing in favor of the minority and female population on the job. Still, he wasn't about to make an off the cuff remark with the chance of some loose lips overhearing and his pension being jeopardized. Moore grabbed his hat, reached for his paperwork, and headed for the reception desk, on his way out reminding Gallo about the prostitutes on his post. "Do a night shift this weekend Arthur, chase those ladies please. Furniture store on your post says they piss in his walkway. Help him out Biscuit." Seabiscuit nodded and smiled.

Gallo, always eager for the last word, replied, "I'll get you the day rate, boss. As a matter of fact, I'll get you John Wayne." This cracked all the guys up. John Wayne was the name of a young squatter on Gallo's post; when he wasn't finding shelter in abandon buildings, he was living out of, and turning tricks in, an old Dodge Coronet parked in the upper level of the municipal parking garage.

As the cops began filing out, Gallo philosophized about the city and its bowing to the ultra-liberal. "Another day of political correctness. Yes Mr. so and so. I'm doing my best Miss."

Man is he cynical. Worse than me, Frank was thinking. *Here's Gallo with just two years on the job and he thinks he knows it all. Another stupid hair bag. Look at him, gun strapped to his waist hanging below the hip like Wyatt Earp.*

"Oh Frank. Hello buddy, you in there," snapped Walsh.

"PMS...the headache. The ball busting." Frank always seemed to make Kathleen look like the bad guy.

As the cops climbed the stairs to the first floor, Bennett passed Frank and handed him a slip of paper. "Here you go dude. It was in my slot, and losers still give out their messages."

Frank laughed and said thanks as he looked down at the paper. Moore was behind the stationhouse desk and called to Frank to stick around. "What did I do now boss?" Frank joked.

Harry was walking out the door, "See you out there Frank."

Moore smiled and said, "Why can't all of you guys be as impeccable. Look at Harry's uniform, always ironed, neat as a friggin' pin."

"Mine's right out of the dryer," Frank quipped.

"Mine to," Moore laughed. Moore pulled a report from the top of his clipboard. "Listen Frank...I almost forgot...you know the female police officer that was assaulted, the one I mentioned? I didn't think they would want CPOP to visit, now they do. She lives on your beat and I want you to check on her."

"Ah, come on boss, don't they have sex crimes for that? Not to mention a female to visit her. What the hell could I say to her?"

"Listen Frank. Just check on her. You're not involved in the case. You don't have to get into anything uncomfortable. Just make her feel safe, you know, see if she needs anything...I have to check on her too."

"Like what could she need?"

"Frank, no jokes on this one please. Go easy."

"Should I go today?"

"Within a week...Now can I go to breakfast? And yes, before I forget, the deli near the bank on forty-first Ave. Graffiti problem."

"Anything else?" Frank mocked a military salute drawing a smile from his boss. Then Frank looked again at the paper Bennett handed him. It read: CALL NINA AND YOUR BROTHER! He tossed it in the trash basket. Frank's stomach growled for breakfast, maybe he'd call later.

Frank rubbed his temples. Hopefully his brother didn't get another ticket. The thought of another cop giving his brother a summons infuriated him. Weren't there enough idiots in the world to give a summons to? This scumbag, whoever he was, had to write up a cop's brother? The ticket and the phone call agitated Frank, but they were only temporary distractions. His thoughts selfishly wandered back to Kathleen. Last night he thought about slipping it to her while she slept. But that would be like forcing her and the last thing he wanted was for her to wake disgusted or worse. He felt like going home, like crying because he was warned from experience that trouble always loomed when the sex stopped.

Time. Do I have time to salvage my marriage? Negative thoughts penetrated deeply. His mother even recently commented that she hadn't heard from her daughter-in-law lately, even after leaving a couple of messages. All the signs were right there in front of him. The thought of his wife forever cold made him tremble with fear. The image of her fucking someone else, too much to bear. Yet hadn't she kissed him on the lips at the bar?

At breakfast Frank ate very little. His buddies were talking shop and chicks. Frank needed to vent, distract himself. "Cannot make this up," he said. "I'm thinking my brother got another ticket. This would be the second time in the last couple of years that some scumbag cop wrote up my brother. Probably Highway again."

"Frank," Walsh said, "you know those guys are a bunch of schmucks. They just don't get it."

"They think they're on another job. PBA cards mean nothing to them," Eaton said, chewing on an egg sandwich.

Gallo joined the trio for breakfast, his mouth full. "They think they're elite. Especially that tall black guy from the parkway station. I've known people been banged by him twice." Gallo raised two fingers. "Always two. One for being white."

Frank nodded. "As far as I'm concerned they could be lying flat on their backs with someone stomping on their head and it will take me a day and a half to respond to their call."

Gallo was still on the black officer. "Once when he was parked by the precinct I glob-spit all over his windshield." Egg fell from Gallo's mouth as he spoke.

"You mean like now?" They all laughed. "Gag me. I can't believe you're a father big guy. Are you teaching your kid to eat like that?" Walsh said.

"Get bent, Walsh," Gallo cracked.

Walsh snorted. "You know Frankie, you can't even call those guys to fix anything...ask our wonderful PBA delegate."

"I know, what would be the sense? It would only get me more aggravated," Frank said. "You know their greatest line is, 'Well your brother gave me a hard time,' or, 'he was nasty,' some crap like that. Cops are just full of it."

Gallo added, "They're full of crap. They would write their own mothers."

eter Colleri grew impatient waiting for the traffic light to turn green. He revved his engine numerous times. His passenger and good friend Richie remarked, "Be cool, it'll change." Richie passed a joint to Peter who took a quick hit then passed it back. Peter looked side to side and roared the engine, running the red light. A block further was a hospital and another steady red. Again, he looked side to side and ran that red too. Out of nowhere red, white and blue strobing police lights appeared in the rearview mirror causing him to squint. *Nooo, I can't get a ticket.*

Quickly Peter rolled all the windows down to clear the smoke. He pulled to the side of the road hoping his family connection could get him out of this one. "Toss it," he said to Richie as he tried helping the smoke out by waving a hand.

Two cops exited the patrol car and approached the powder blue Cadillac cautiously, one on each side of the car, both with their hands on the grips of their guns, ready to lift their weapons from the holster if necessary. Peter could see the taller cop coming up on his side and through the rearview noticed the other officer flanking his buddy's side looking intimidating, his hat lowered over his eyes, his hand on his pistol. Both cops were young. Probably rookies.

"License, registration, and insurance card," said the cop using a flat but cocky tone, his chest pushed out as if he were holding his breath.

"Officer---"

"Don't even try giving me a story pal," the cop interrupted. He was pointing his finger towards the hospital. "Good thing that hospital is there pal. 'Cause if you rammed a pole with this tank, or worse, that's where you'd be."

Peter flipped through his wallet. "Officer I know I was wrong and I'm really sorry." He retrieved his license and registration then leaned to the glove compartment for the insurance card. He noticed the other officer's attention was glued to the glove box while lifting his weapon slightly from the holster. Peter sat up and gave all his papers to the cocky officer who immediately snatched them from his hand.

"Wise ass," the cop said.

"I'm not really officer," Peter said. "Would it help that my brother is a cop?" He removed a PBA courtesy card from his wallet. Peter sensed a slight annoyance on the cop's behalf, yet he might actually consider letting him go with a warning. Yet maybe not, it would mean losing out on a number for his quota. No cop was legally bound to let a motorist go because he displayed a PBA card. Peter knew that chances were better if he stayed polite. He knew from his brother that the average patrol cop honored the card of family members, and more often than not, would do the right thing and cut the motorist loose. He also knew there were scumbags that would write their own mothers, like the last time he got a summons. Especially the Highway Unit cops. Even though this cop had an enormous ego, Peter was hopeful.

"Where does he work?" the cop asked.

"He works at the 117. His name's Frank Colleri. That's his shield number."

"Okay, okay, no more bull. Tell your brother this one was on me." He returned Peter's papers and walked away disgusted. The other cop had also backed away and Peter uttered a delayed, "Thank you." Though underneath he was thinking scumbag. But the bottom line was: no ticket.

The cops were back in their cruiser and sped away before Peter got his papers organized. Richie never moved. "Close one Pete. They had to smell the shit."

"Probably. Too lazy to make a collar. Just looking for a summons. I don't think they would've cared if we were smoking crack."

Once back in the neighborhood, parking was, as usual, a tough find. Peter found a tight spot for his large car, bumping both the car in front and behind him. He was still high, mumbling something about the rookies that stopped them. He said to his buddy that though he respected cops because of Frank, the majority of them were losers with a badge. Ego maniacs who think they can do anything they want.

The two said their good-byes agreeing to meet up later and go clubbing. Richie was a ladies' man. Incorporating a carefree attitude with looks, light green eyes and blond hair, he didn't have to work hard when he asked a lady to dance. He taught Peter about the night club world. Staying out all night drinking and putting the rap on until the last chick left the bar. "You could not shave, have bad breath and dirty fingernails, and still get laid," Peter once told Richie.

Peter entered the apartment he once shared with his family, with a sudden feeling of loneliness. *Should I settle down?*

It was times like this he missed his girlfriend. *Hell no, I'm too young to settle down and have plenty of party left.* He was going to be relentless in his pursuit of the wildlife.

He hit the bed for a nap wondering if the rookie cops had smelled the weed.

 week after Valentine's Day a coworker of Kathleen's was throwing a house party. Some of the girls in the office had found new boyfriends and wanted to show them off.

"What fun," Frank mocked.

"I shouldn't have even invited you if you're going to start."

He and Kathleen hadn't been getting along well for some time, a situation that was building intense stress. He would feel worse in a room full of people he didn't give a shit about. "I'm fine."

The few times Frank had met the girls from the office he found them annoying. Not that he wouldn't bed any one of them, if at least to shut down their ego, but he didn't like the way they pranced around like know it all smart asses. They were like many good Catholics: hypocrites. They assumed all women were whores except them. He thought his wife was different, though sometimes he wondered. Kathleen trusted in Frank when she confided some of her friend's secrets to him. He always felt like it gave him a devilish upper hand. Kathleen mentioned her friends often approached dating like the Virgin Mary. They would administer to their boyfriends the classic case of blue balls, until they held the belief they had entered into a committed relationship. Even then, they would profess that opening their wings might need an enforced higher degree of certainty. Still, this was always the part Frank loved... a perfectly good blow job was not out of the question. Frank always wondered about the rationale of the act. The girls would not spread their legs as easy as they would give head. Frank wondered if his wife was of the same mold. And though she confessed to sleeping with only two men before him, Frank often dwelled on how many guys she might have sucked off.

What is it about Irish Catholic girls? A challenge of the Graces? Apart from their guised purity they didn't hold much to an old-fashioned Italian girl, women who were raised on the art of caring for a man. Perhaps it was the chase. An attempt to break the coldness of Irish lore. Maybe melt away the ice and open up feelings hidden just for the right man. The coldness was generational he figured. Handed down from mothers and fathers. Frank remembered when he first met his wife's dad. He was greeted with lukewarm enthusiasm and a continuous string of Irish music on an old hi-fi player, as if he were doing it just to annoy

Frank. But Frank had gotten even at the wedding, having the band play a number of Sinatra songs.

Cindy's house was on a quiet block on the North Shore of Long Island. The kind of house city kids only heard about, with huge property, cozy sitting rooms and a country kitchen. Frank thought it was only rich Jewish folks who lived in these neighborhoods. There were no cops at this get together. As a matter of fact, there were no Italians either. The guys all looked the same. Khakis and loafers with button down shirts. They appeared to be corporate people, future stockbrokers, insurance salesman, and obvious nobodies as far as he was concerned. Frank knew the subject of police and summonses would sooner or later find its way into a conversation. It never failed that whenever Frank was with a group other than cops there would be the question of ticket writing raised by some idiot in the room. An obnoxious grunt, begging to be smacked in the face. Maybe a pretty boy showing off the newest fad: an earring in the right ear.

After the greetings, ten minutes was all it took for boredom to hit Frank like a ton of bricks. For a moment he wouldn't have even minded if Kathleen's friend Peggy was here. At least he could get into some sarcastic sparring with her. The Doors permeated the house, Frank hung by the living room bar. He downed three quick shots of tequila and grabbed a beer chaser. Tequila gave him a trippy feeling that other drinks like bourbon didn't. Kathleen was mingling. He held his beer to give the appearance of involvement as he said a few, 'How are yous?' *Fake.*

Then he noticed Heather, who he already had the annoying pleasure of meeting a few times. She was alone looking bored, her face more dour than usual. She possessed one distinct feature that protruded under her big hair and wavy bangs. A long nose hanging right out there past thin lips. No wonder her previous boyfriend dumped her. *What the hell, let's have some fun. She was one who sarcastically called me out at the last party. Almost demanding to know why cops were arrogant ticket writers.* He had kept his mouth shut that time because of Kat. Frank closed in on her. "Hi Heather?"

"Hello, Frank the cop," she replied with a thin smile.

"Are you alone?" He knew she was but wanted to dig it in.

"It's a long story."

I bet it is. He leaned in close sensing she was blushing with nervousness. "I have time, do tell," he said with a feigned interest.

"Well—"

He held up a forefinger then chugged the rest of the can. "Go ahead," he said.

"Like I was starting to say—"

"Wait," he interrupted again. "Why would you want to tell me? I hardly know you."

"You asked," she replied. She tilted her head, confused.

"First I want to tell you what I did last week."

"What's that?" she asked.

"I went skiing."

Heather remained confused. Frank waved his hand slightly above his head then slowly slid his finger down the bridge of Heather's nose and she jerked back. He let out a laugh and said, "Slope."

Her eyes widened, too embarrassed to speak. Frank walked back to the bar.

It was then that Kathleen noticed something was wrong. Looking at Frank she walked over to Heather who was standing in quiet desperation. She felt sick after her friend explained her husband's cruelty. "Just gag me," Heather said. "What do you expect from that scumbag husband of yours?"

Kathleen had no defense for Frank. If he thought she was cold in the marriage now, well then wait until they were home. *Why is he so cruel?* She told Cindy she wasn't feeling well and was sorry but she would call later. She said a few goodbyes as Frank waved to no one in particular through his drunkenness. She treated him to a big chill on the ride home ignoring him, all the while seething.

Once home Frank fell into the couch. Kathleen retreated to the bathroom. He was channel surfing when she returned. She stood over him and tore into him immediately. "I have had it with you, fucking inconsiderate loser! What could have possibly possessed you to be such a fucking asshole?"

"You couldn't tell me that in the car?"

"Dick."

"I'm a what?" Frank said. "C'mon, it was just a joke for Christ sake! Nobody even gave a shit. Heather is a fucking snob anyway!" He pulled his wife on to the couch with him but she jumped off just as quickly.

"Joke my ass! And don't touch me."

"What's your problem? PMS again?"

"You really are a sick dick," she yelled.

He got off the couch and moved towards her like some drunken husband in an old black and white movie. "C'mon sweetheart, let's forget about it and get back to being husband and wife."

She flipped him her middle finger. "Are you kidding? Go to hell, you fuck."

"What language," he mocked. "And from a good Catholic girl. That's not like you Kat. What's this really all about, those twerps from your job?"

"There you go...You just don't understand because you're the big shot cop who knows it all and done it all. You're lucky one of those twerps didn't kick your ass."

"What—"

"Let me finish." Her breathing was on the heavy side. "We've only been married for one year and already it's a disaster, ending with tonight!"

He put up his hands, in an act of giving up.

"You're out all the time. And when you're not, you sit around making wise ass remarks as if you're bored. I told you Frank, I'm not an old Italian woman who's going to wipe your ass—"

"I never—" And he stopped himself, sat down and let her continue.

"I heard that you flirt with a lot of women when I'm not around. Maybe you're screwing them, I don't know."

Who the hell told her that? Probably some jealous cop or a nosy friend of her ex-boyfriend, a New York City Fireman.

"When you drink too much you get nasty. You hate my family and you hate my friends. You think those asshole buddies of yours are the only friends you should have—"

"Could I get a word in now?" he said jumping off the couch. He poked his finger in his chest. "Yes. I know all those things, thank you. But what about *you?*" Frank went over to one of the end tables, opened the drawer and pulled out the last Valentine's Day card she gave him. He was getting steamed. "What the hell is this? What was Christmas? You gave me cards this year you would send to an acquaintance. And why don't we fuck anymore?"

Kathleen sat down on the arm of the sofa and ran her fingers through her hair. For a moment there was quiet... "Something happened to us. I don't feel close to you." She inhaled and exhaled. "This isn't easy Frank, feeling like I need my space."

It hit him. Saying the words made all the difference and suddenly he needed air, it was as if he were drowning. He needed to react and he did so swiftly and with typical male pride. "Well then go! I can always get what I need elsewhere. So, get lost."

"And you think I can't?" she said with a short laugh.

Those words sent his feeling of suffocation to complete rage. The thought of another man, of her sitting down and comparing notes with her friends at work...Until now he never thought it a possibility. At this moment, he wanted to punch her like he would punch a man but he mustered all his common sense to refrain. It was his turn to cut her with words. "You know what you are? You're white Irish trash. You'll be washed up in a few years!"

Kathleen lunged at him kicking up into his groin with all her power. Frank fell backwards over the coffee table, letting out a cry of pain. Then she resounded in a force of intensity she'd never used towards him before. A real indication of the demise of their marriage. "You are a real slimy piece of shit! I'm so sick of your childish games—of this apartment, of god-damned fighting with you!" She was heaving when she grabbed her jacket from the chair, headed for the door then turned for a last barrage. "I'm bored with you, you loser!"

Frank backed himself on to the sofa. Everything hurt. His head, his balls, and especially her words. "God," he uttered. "What's happening here?"

He made no move to chase her down.

efore crack-cocaine, Queens was known as the quiet borough. Cops who worked high crime areas in the Bronx, Brooklyn, or Harlem would often joke about their eastern counterparts, labeling them The Queens Marines. Other than a couple of south-based stationhouses, most precincts in Queens were considered B and C houses. Cops who worked the ghetto areas of New York were in mostly A houses: high crime locations, where they faced violence and deterioration on a daily basis. Queens was always New York's friendly neighbor to the suburbs. But that was a decade ago in the 1970s long before the crack epidemic reached prime time. That was a sobering reality when a young police officer was ruthlessly assassinated sitting in a radio car on a quiet night in Jamaica Queens while guarding a witness. The quiet borough was piling up an alarming number of criminal statistics, spreading like a cancer over and along the underbelly of greater New York.

The crime victim problem wasn't going to blow over in a few weeks. CPOP work was guaranteed for years to come. One reason for the immediate alert was because the Police Commissioner's daughter was pushed around in the filthy lobby of her apartment building. The young woman feared she would be sexually assaulted. She also noted disbelief at the number of crack vials in the stairwells. "A rainbow of different colors," she stated.

However callous and cynical Frank felt, he was definitely not looking forward to a visit with the raped cop. Thank God female officers had already gotten the dirty work out of the way. Still, Moore would remind him that it was his beat, he was just offering assistance, anything she needed, not personal conversation, not therapy. Hell, he didn't want to hear the whole sobbing routine. He had to be careful with a cop turned victim. She might sense an uncaring nature and get pissed off. Just this once Frank wished there was a female cop in the unit to switch assignments. No broads in CPOP yet, that must mean it wasn't much of a detail after all, he started to think maybe he should transfer back to shift work.

Anyway, there was no way around it. The female officer lived within the confines of Frank's beat, so he would have to eventually show his face, but he would put off the visit as long as he could. Frank's own problems still weighed heavy on his mind and the start of a new week didn't matter much. He was just showing up.

"Did you get to meet with Officer Caputo yet?" Sergeant Moore asked.

"I'm waiting for the right moment, boss."

"There is no right moment Frank. Just go and talk with her, she won't bite. See if she needs anything. I went to see her. Department already assigned people for the psychobabble. You're not there to discuss any women's issues. Just see if she needs anything. The PC wants a record of CPOP doing their job."

"Sure boss, I understand." *Should I go grocery shopping for her too?* He then moved to gather some reports from a file. He figured on three visits this week and squeezing in the business of what the job really wanted, summonses. No matter what crisis lurked in the city of New York, cops still had to write their summonses. Summonses, summonses, summonses. Preferably a book a month. That was twenty-five well-written summonses including two for red lights. All Frank had to do was stay in the ballpark range and he would keep his cushy detail and everyone was happy.

Arthur Gallo was spewing some rhetoric about the 'bitches' on the job. Frank wasn't paying much attention and decided to leave. He wasn't in the mood for humor or conversation. On the way up the stairs Frank bumped into his CPOP partner John Bennett.

"Hey, Frank, good morning."

"What's up, John?"

"Listen, Frank. I need a favor. Can you work a four to twelve for me on Friday? I have some place I have to go."

Frank slapped Bennett on the shoulder with his memo book. "Sure, that's what it's all about."

"Thanks, dude."

After a slow cup of coffee Frank went to see the Chen family. What he didn't expect was a frightening tale of babysitting molestation. Frank had heard parents joke about how loud a baby could cry. But here it was, the baby's shrilling screams that had miraculously kept the perpetrator from fully penetrating the child. The Chens were a humble Korean family who completely trusted the babysitter that night, the fifteen-year-old son of communal neighbors. Frank pretended he was leafing through the pamphlet so he wouldn't have to make eye contact. As the mild-mannered Mr. and Mrs. Chen quietly vented, Frank's tactic of in one ear and out of the other was getting stuck somewhere in his emotions.

Apparently, the sitter attempted to put his penis into their three-year-old daughter's vagina. And though the boy panicked and was unable to fully insert, the baby girl still sustained damaging bruises. Suddenly, Frank shuddered at the thought of the girl's screams. Horrific cries that scared the bastard off. Frank hadn't taken off his duty jacket. His plan was to not get comfortable or stay any extended time. Now he felt hot. The apartment's heat was on high and reeked a heavy odor of third world food condiments. All this combined with thoughts of the horror this little girl had gone through suddenly suffocated Frank. He quickened his routine and headed for the door.

Once outside, Frank took some deep breaths of cold air. He thought *he* had problems. Forgetting his torment, he imagined the agony the Chen family was going through. Frank and his buddies often joked about how they thought certain people should go back to their own country. Now he couldn't help wondering if they might not want to. He speculated again that in another country, it was probable that someone would take this cocksucker out back somewhere and cut his head off. The only justice that would be administered here in the good US of A would be a trip to a court appointed psychiatrist. Just more tax dollars. Taxes that cops did pay, contrary to popular belief. Presently the NYPD was working into an overdue contract in which the city they served was offering next to nothing.

"God, I hate this job and this whole stinking city," Frank said to himself. Then, as if he needed more aggravation, Frank went to a phone to call his wife. It was habit. He rang up her job and got no answer. She must be on a break. Yet, he was relieved. *She's still sore at me for how I treated her friend. She's so right. Why am I a jerk? Why do I go too far? What if I called and apologized to Heather?*

* * * *

The Captain was watching!

ANOTHER VISIT: A young high school girl, who left her bathing suit in the trunk of her car the previous summer, would live to regret it. The confessed rapist stated that after he broke into her car and stole the stereo he decided to check the trunk where he came upon the swimsuit. The pervert just had to smell the bottoms, which sent him into a frenzy.

He returned to the glove box and retrieve the girl's address from the insurance card. He then stalked the girl for a few weeks before finding the right moment to rape and beat her to a pulp...

When Frank entered the Lansing home and saw twenty-year old Diane, he couldn't take his eyes off her. She was a classic virginal beauty, with long silky blond hair and creamy fair skin. How could such a beautiful creature become damaged? Here was a girl who possessed the innocence of another time. A time when a young girl would have just moved on from Barbie dolls to 45 records.

Diane's horror began the moment she was surprised and accosted from behind. Even then, when she felt the brush of greasy hair on her face, she imagined it was her boyfriend surprising her. She remembered the attacker's hands were even as soft as Bobby's. But then a silver gun was stuck into her cheek and she was pulled into a nearby construction site where she was raped until morning.

"Maybe I could have done something, officer." Her face welled up. "Maybe it wasn't a gun."

No sweet girl. Please don't blame yourself for the actions of that prick. The whole story: just sad. Diane's boyfriend left her. He just couldn't handle the abuse this precious, intelligent girl endured. Twenty and scarred for life. It was certainly ironic. He knew men so obsessed they would crawl back on their hands and knees after finding out that their wives had been out screwing someone else.

Anyhow, the Lansing family was thinking of relocating to Dallas where the elder Lansing was originally from. Did they realize that there were three times as many sex attacks in Dallas as there were in New York? And as Frank had also discovered to his surprise, there were two times as many sex crimes in both Seattle and Boston as the sinking city of his own New York. He was reading and storing information he wanted no part of. *Why can't I memorize the Patrol Guide this well? Why can't I just say to these people, here is your crime pamphlet and all the information is self-explanatory. You really don't have to talk to me. Thank you and good day.*

When Frank reached the front of the precinct at the end of his shift he reached for a cigarette, the last one in his pack. He was going to have to buy another and the day wasn't over yet. *A second pack. Just great. Next it will be a third and then I'll drop dead.*

CHAPTER 10

The embattled borough was ushering in a new era. A diverse melting pot, taking on the sights, sounds, dress, and the worst cuisine smells of Korea, India, Pakistan. Busy intersections were bombarded with gypsy taxi cabs and the hacks picking up unsolicited fares was just another problem on Frank's beat, a situation only corrected so long as there was a cop in sight. Many of the drivers and supposed owners of these cabs could have been traced to a thousand relatives all with the same foreign names. It was the same with the Haitian street peddlers who all possessed identification showing they lived at the same residence, somewhere on the Grand Concourse in the Bronx.

Frank was determined to listen to Linda Beech's story dispassionately. He'd heard enough sexual depravity to last a lifetime. Citizens of Queens should only know the rottenness that lurked inside their quiet borough. Linda Beech had climbed the stairs from the subway on a drizzly, dismal day. A rainy day in the city made a commuter feel they were in an uncomfortable stampede. Linda wanted to get home and unwind, so she hailed the first cab available. Yellow taxi or gypsy, it didn't matter to her. Later, Linda would not be able to remember the name of the car service written on the side of the door. In fact, she wasn't even able to recall if it was a cab. With the weather as it was, not many would have paid much attention to a logo on the side of a car.

What she did remember was the driver. His dark eyes focusing on her through the rearview mirror. His brows so thick Linda thought they looked pasted on. His face a charcoal dust that made it look as though he had not washed the dirt off in days. Linda felt messy from her commute so she removed a small makeup kit from her bag as she announced her address to the driver. To avoid the driver's glances, she occupied herself longer than usual with the portable mirror and was therefore unaware of the route the driver took. Suddenly she was tossed back and forth and dropped the makeup when the car sped over a couple of speed bumps, like a rollercoaster out of control. The car stopped deep into a park. In an immediate panic, Linda tried focusing her eyes through the rain covered window. She remembered a lush of wet greenery, it was actually soaked brush.

"What the hell is going on?" she cried. Then that frighteningly sick feeling fell over her.

What made the rape more sickening was that she was three months pregnant. She repeatedly pleaded this fact to her attacker, it landed on deaf ears. The rapist told her, "Just sit back and enjoy my long-tailed goody." When it was over, Linda withered and broken, the rapist drove through a fast food restaurant asking Linda if she wanted anything to eat.

* * * *

Most cops knew the reality of their city. New York wasn't the gorgeous mosaic it was cracked up to be. Even before the drugs, it possessed a sick underbelly where havoc was always ready to be wreaked. The crime of rape wasn't one of prejudice. In fact, it reached all ethnic groups from the Chens of Korea to the heart of a lily-white family.

Frank's work was becoming too routine, only the names were changing. *I'm learning enough to be a detective,* he thought. But he wanted to be done with these visits in the weeks to come. *I definitely should've taken burglaries and robberies instead of these personal stories that are like third world invasions.*

Barbara Sanchez remembered arriving home that night to find the lock on her apartment door already open. Her first thought was maybe her husband arrived home early from work. She entered the apartment calling out to him. "Honey, where are you? You managed to come home early today!" Then the blur of a stranger standing in the frame of the bedroom doorway. Her first instinct told her that she was being robbed. "I told him to take everything. Take whatever you want and go, please just go."

Frank listened as her voice grew shaky and he imagined the fear she must have sensed at the actual moment of surprise. "He was thin, like a string bean," she said managing a slight smile. "Tall...skinny, and was wearing an ugly lime green jumpsuit." Barbara's hands had been moving upward and sideways to describe her attacker. "Then he told me all he wanted was my jewelry and some money and that he wouldn't hurt me..." She looked deeply at Frank as if a river of tears might flow any second. "And I felt safer officer. I actually believed him."

She looked away from Frank and started to cry but after a short moment contained herself and continued. "He threw me against the wall and ripped my necklace off..." She felt for the missing necklace.

Frank turned his eyes, his feeling of empathy was increasing. He in no way imagined that these victims would open up to him in such a way, to such a stranger, to a man. Why couldn't they just accept police courtesy, take the pamphlet and say thank you?

Then, as if he just asked for it, Barbara blurted out, "He said he was going to lick me." She began to breathe heavier. "Then he hit me in the face..." Barbara gasped, threw her hands to her mouth, coughed, then excused herself.

Frank rose from his chair. Distinctly he heard that fierce and heaving guttural sound. He grabbed his belongings, placed the pamphlet on the table and headed for the door.

He pounded the pavement thinking of Barbara. She was indeed beautiful with chestnut hair that was long and smooth and skin dark like her eyes. He hoped that being victimized by some lousy scumbag wouldn't cost her and her husband a lifetime of doubt.

Sexual assault was such a darkly hidden and undocumented crime he wondered if women took the fear of being attacked seriously enough. *God. Maybe paranoia should be in order for every chick in the city.*

Once again, a night out dominated his thoughts. He needed a drink and some serenity without his wife.

CHAPTER 11

After her mother pleaded, Ann agreed to visit with the parish priest, Father DeMartino, who held a PhD in psychology. Describing a tale of horror was not going to be easy. It was bad enough disclosing the story to a shrink, but to a priest? Reminding herself that she was a cop, Ann tried unmercifully to forget the ordeal, to no avail.

Initially, Father DeMartino offered to visit Ann at either her or her parent's home; wherever she might feel more comfortable. Ann thought it best to speak on God's turf. Father DeMartino was new to the parish. He took over for Father Dolan, the priest put out to pasture after some forty years of sermons. Nevertheless, the younger priest was an instant hit with the parishioners. He seemed to relate to all the faithful on their level. Still, Ann was reluctant. But she unselfishly promised to help ease her parents' pain as well, they were devastated by the confession of her attack. The senior Caputos shed a river of tears and their anxiety levels increased dramatically as if they were losing control. Understandable, but Ann and Allison worked feverishly to calm them.

Her father was becoming paranoid, demanding safety behaviors, proclaiming a chilling recollection of the first female police officer recently killed in the line of duty. Shot in the back of the head in a vacant lot after giving chase to a robbery suspect. "I don't want that for you!" he cried out. Her father's proclamation made her think of the time she, herself, separated from her partner to chase down a car thief.

Some jerk had stolen a new, sporty Camaro and crashed it into a light pole on Union Turnpike in Queens. As the police cars began arriving and the cops exited their cars to investigate the wreck, Ann walked away from her partner stating she was just going to look down a small alley that led to a children's park. There she noticed a stocky built white male in a tight black t-shirt limping towards the park, obviously injured from the crash. Rather than tell her partner, she picked up the pace and went to investigate. "Police don't move!" she shouted. But the guy took off even with the slowdown of his limp. Ann easily caught up to the perp but as she reached for him, he turned and swiped at her with his forearm, obviously drunk, missing her face by inches. Ann struck back with her police radio catching him in the chin where he lost his balance and fell to ground. She easily cuffed him then called for assistance on her radio. When the other cops arrived, her boss, now on the scene, chastised her for going it alone. "It's a no, no, Ann. You did good in the long run, but don't separate from your partner unless there's no choice, and even then, *radio first* where you are. What if this scumbag wasn't injured and got the best of you?"

Her boss was right. Being a little overzealous could have gotten her hurt. Many times she wondered, especially after the killing of the female officer, why she hadn't drawn her weapon and why she got so close to the disobliging perp without commanding him to drop.

Still, one thing had nothing to do with the other. But if her parents thought church was the answer, however reluctant, she would go. It couldn't be worse than any other grilling she endured. Perhaps she needed an answer from God. She certainly needed to calm her frantic parents before one of them got sick.

She stood at the rectory door and quickly checked herself in her makeup mirror. The powder had done wonders, the bruises no longer recognizable. She rang the bell three times in quick succession. She smoothed down her dress, covered with pretty flowers, and made sure the hem was below her knees. *Why is it that a visit to church requires one's Sunday best?* Probably respect, not to mention in her state of mind she needed to cover up.

The door was answered by an older woman who looked haggard and had probably been there as long as Father Dolan. She dispensed with the usual formality, guiding Ann to the east rooms of the rectory with an air of coldness. "Father will be with you in a moment," she said. Then, with a sort of bow, she left Ann alone.

Ann sat on a dark leather sofa her legs moving nervously inward and out, shaking, so she put her hands on her knees to check them. She removed her jacket and fidgeted with it before folding it over the armrest. She was looking around the room at the many books and familiar religious articles when she heard the door open.

Father DeMartino entered and closed the door before speaking. He was attired in traditional black slacks, button shirt and shoes, only the collar was missing. His hair was almost shoulder length sprinkled with salt and pepper. Ann imagined he was trying to appear Christ-like, though he sported no beard. "Hello, Ann," the priest said, offering his hand. "How are you? And how are your parents? Your mother is such a wonderful woman."

Ann lightly shook his hand without looking Father DeMartino in the eye.

The priest took a seat in the wing chair opposite Ann. Still she had not made steady eye contact. The priest leaned forward and spoke first. "Ann. Would you rather not? I understand if you don't want to."

Finally, Ann looked up, swallowing hard. "I'm sorry Father. This is very hard for me. And certainly, you know if my parents were not wonderful I wouldn't be here. You have to help them too, Father."

"Ann, you don't owe me any apologies. Like I said, I understand. Just take your time. And please try to remember that I'm here to listen, and to help, in any way I possibly can...No one will ever know what is spoken of here." He smiled warmly and Ann felt slightly better as he said, "You're doubly protected, not only by my vows as a priest but by my vows as a psychologist as well."

There was something in that smile that made her trust him. Father DeMartino possessed a young face and an infectious smile that maybe she could relate to. He was also very soft spoken. "Father," she said almost at a whisper, "I feel guilty...real guilty. Forgive me but I also feel God has done a terrible thing to me..." She waited to see if the priest was going to defend God. Instead Father DeMartino sat back, waiting with a comforting, encouraging smile.

"I can't get this out of my head," Ann continued. Her hands were moving nervously. "The attack I mean. Father I'm a cop. I, of all people, should have been able to protect myself...right?"

The priest leaned forward. "Wrong," he said matter of factly. "Listen Ann, I can't know how difficult this must be for you and I'm certainly not going to placate you by telling you all the ways you think we would tell you to exorcise your anger. You have every right to be mad, mad as, pardon the expression, hell. And you should be. Yes, I agree it's going to take a while to get out of your head."

Tears began to wet her cheeks. The priest was so understanding and comforting. He gave the air of being a poet or musician sitting at a cafe in a distant place, verbalizing the meaning of life. How nice that would be if she weren't raped and he weren't a priest. She couldn't believe she would even entertain such a thought.

"Father, I wish with all of my heart and soul that my---attacker---that black---" she sighed, "---were dead."

Still not preaching the rhetoric of forgiveness, Father DeMartino simply said, "It's understandable Ann, it really is."

"Father, what does the church think about such things? I mean...why?" She lowered her head.

"Of course, you could not think otherwise. There really is no explanation for such horrible wrong doing, Ann. Sure, the church has its theories, some saying that it is put there to ensure goodness...You know that God is good, God is powerful, terrible things happen, evil is the nature of mankind. I've been asked about guilt in the past. My wish is that you don't feel this way. Ann, believe me when I say to you that there is not one minuscule reason for guilt here."

She lowered her head but said nothing.

"You know we Catholics grow up with entirely too much guilt. My Jewish friends think they have that market cornered." A smiling sigh reflected his sincerity. "I promised myself not to be too preachy." He didn't move his eyes from her direction as if expressing his soul in a clear understanding for her pain. Suddenly Ann didn't mind if he talked for hours.

"Of course, there are a few things I'd like to advise though I'm sure you're aware of them."

"Sure Father," she said. "But I also know that many priests believe more in the power of prayer than the power of a psychiatrist."

"That's hogwash," he said. "Obviously, I believe that one should utilize whatever means necessary to help overcome tragedy in our lives."

Ann spoke freely now feeling at ease. "Father what does the church think about the bastard that, ra--assaulted me?" Her voice had turned up a notch and she realized that even the word bastard was a harsh thing to say within these walls. Still..."I feel nothing towards these scum, except bile contempt. I'm sorry Father."

He waved off her apology. "No, no. You're angry. Who in your place wouldn't feel contempt? However, you aren't going to get entirely all the answers you would most like to hear, such as burning these bastards at the stake. The church has moved out of the Middle Ages," he said with a little levity. "I know you want some justification from the church, but we're not going to nail anyone to the cross, no pun, though I see where you're coming from. The church, Ann, would know he deserves punishment but at the same time they would hope he could resolve his issues."

Ann uttered under her breath, "Right."

Father DeMartino gestured for moment's break by getting up and walking over to his desk where the old woman had left a cold pitcher of water and some Styrofoam cups. He poured the first cup and turned to offer it to his visitor. He poured a second cup and downed half of it before speaking.

"Ann, have you taken care of your physical needs? Have you gone for the pregnancy and HIV tests?"

"I'm not here for your medical opinion, Father. I'm not an idiot; I know what has to be done." Her eyes watered again and she sank further into the sofa.

The priest calmly walked to her and held out the water. "Please, drink some, please."

Ann looked up at him. He was genuinely empathetic even after the way she just snapped at him. She took the cup from him and Father DeMartino returned to his chair.

"You *are* going to recover. And I don't mean with just prayer and the help of God. I mean that you possess strength, real strength. You also possess a trust of this life, and of family, and even your work, or you wouldn't be here. Strength you haven't even tapped into yet." The priest got up again and fetched a box of tissues. He gave Ann the tissues and this time sat down next to her. Ann turned to him and noticed a small bead of water clinging to his chin. *He looks cute...If only...How could I?*

"Look, Ann. You're no doubt utterly exhausted. Now, for one moment I'm going to sound like a priest." He smiled at her and she reciprocated. "Ann try your best to put away guilt...Forget revenge. Forget what your boyfriend, your parents or anyone else for that matter, will think of you. I know it's easier said than done, but I believe you will be well."

Ann sensed her hands were no longer shaking. She looked into the priest's eyes, deeply, for the first time. And she felt a strange tranquility that she hadn't experienced since before her attack. His eyes were truthful. *I will make it,* she thought.

Father DeMartino continued, "I know you don't believe that now, but I do. I also know that you are good. Good to yourself, good to your family, and as good as anyone can be to others. I know you will move forward and get through this. And you will love and be loved wholly and completely." He smiled. "Even if I personally have to say a thousand Novenas for you."

Anna smiled at the priest and made him laugh when she said, "You've been talking to my parents, Father."

"Just your mother. Though I know your father is crazy with worry. I promise from here on I will be in constant contact with them. They will get through it Ann."

"My father brought up the female police officer who was murdered. He's worried it could be me. And he brings up my childhood, when I was a little girl, and my dolls, and our trips to the store for sweets, my soccer games. It's strange."

"I know. Be patient. He'll calm. He's trying to relive an innocent time in your life, when there were no hints at danger, when things were like a family postcard. And as for the poor officer, as you feel about your situation… who knows, maybe in those last moments before evil took over she wondered why she couldn't get the better of her assailant too."

Ann didn't respond to further the conversation of murder, instead she turned serious and asked Father DeMartino if he would make the sign of the cross with her.

"As many times as you wish," he said.

"Well, this was a help Father. Thank you. I had visions of Father Dolan and that stern look."

"Don't misjudge Father Dolan. He's a good man. In fact, maybe a saint." The two shook hands and smiled warmly with the satisfaction of some peace.

Once outside the rectory Ann lit a long-awaited cigarette. She was almost at a pack a day, a habit she had given up when she was in the police academy. The habit slowly found its way back and she relished the long-steamed drag on a Virginia Slim. She looked up at the church's bell tower, its image appearing as gothic as the old building itself.

Father DeMartino was still in his office sitting pensively in his chair. He recalled a recent sermon where he spoke of the commitment of the priest. He likened it to being the same as a father who would care for his children. But now he wondered if that were true. Surely, he couldn't comfort a child he couldn't keep an eye on. He wanted to hold her but considering the circumstance he knew he couldn't. He knew she would feel terribly uncomfortable. Maybe there was hope against the destruction of innocence. Her eyes were deeply soulful. Salvation and tranquility are no easy tasks, but like his own struggle and eventual guidance from his parish priest, perhaps one day, on her terms, he would be able to help.

'Listen to me when I say, you will be well.' The same words spoken to him, a lifetime ago when he returned home from war, stricken, not only with a physical wound, which caused undo ringing in his ears, but a deep and lasting spiritual void as well. He had lived, but why? What source of religious or cosmic enlightenment took part in his survival? Only to be rooted with an affliction that kept him on the brink of sanity. Did he deserve to be insane because of the very survival that gave him nightmares?

* * * *

Somewhere, on a strip of dirt road, in the Quang Tri Province, platoons were scattered in the hot moisture… facing him, distinguished by their uniforms. A North Vietnamese soldier, pointing the AK50. The round of deafening explosions… blood on his face, but for the grace of God, alive when he pushed off the ground and saw the young Vietnamese corpse lying in front of him, with the top of its head gone. To his right a grim-faced marine.

"It's alright soldier," the marine said. "Just looks like your ears been pierced with a rusted needle." His bottom lobe had been torn off. For the rest of his life he would wear his hair long.

He had hated after that. The likes of anyone who remotely resembled that Vietcong.

He thought he would never find forgiveness, either in his heart or his attitude.

Somehow, he made it through the regiment of books: theology and psychology. Then, the old Irish saint, Father Dolan… The religious retreat where he cleansed himself of guilt and pain, with tremors likened to withdrawal. Where the other priests, serving as brothers, instilled their life's teachings and echoed the words of the old priest: 'Listen to me when I say, you will be well.'

CHAPTER 12

Strange, the more Kathleen distanced herself from Frank, the less he felt compelled to use others for his pleasure. So instead of calling Nina, Frank picked up the phone and called his brother. Peter answered, his voice sleepy. His brother was having too many late nights and early joints, more waking and baking. *Who am I to criticize? My own life appears to be headed towards the crapper.*

"Can you meet me in the neighborhood, at The Hill Bar? Around eight?" Frank asked.

"Sure," Peter replied. "But are you allowed out? And why so early?"

"Very funny wise ass. I just want to catch up. Be on time please, I don't want to run into the late crowd, anyone from the old neighborhood and get an ear full of bullshit."

"Sure bro, but nothing you could tell me on the phone?"

"I could, but I want to see you schmo." Then Frank heard a strange cough and he laughed, knowing his brother had a woman keeping him warm.

After they greeted each other with a hug Frank ordered a bourbon for himself and a scotch on the rocks for his brother. "Who was the girl?" Frank asked.

Peter smiled. "Met her last night in Manhattan. Ah, the single life."

There was a pause and a smirk from Frank when Peter asked his brother how the cop business was doing.

"Shitty...I called you so why is it you look like you have something on your mind?"

"Frank...a friend of mine...saw Kathleen having lunch at that new burger and bun place." Another pause.

Frank felt ill. "Right to the point *uh* brother? What friend? One of those morons—"

"C'mon Frank, this guy knows you're my brother, he's not gonna mess around with something like that. He don't even want to get involved."

"Then maybe he shouldn't jump to conclusions."

"Frank...my buddy was sitting real close and it sounded to me like one of those yuppie dorks she works with. You know, button-down shirt and slip on shoes. So, I wondered—"

"What!?"

"I'm sorry, Frank. It could be bogus but I don't want my brother looking like a fool so I thought you should know."

Frank rubbed his temples as he felt his breathing accelerate again. "Funny...she told me she was going to go out after work with her friends… God, I was so mean to her friend."

"What?

"Nothing Pete, nothing."

"Frank, you're my brother. I know this isn't what you came to hear."

"Forget it. Anyway, Mom called."

"How is she and Dad? I have to call them."

Frank told Peter that their parents were worried because they don't hear from him as much as they thought they should. They were concerned he might be smoking those funny cigarettes again. Peter laughed. "I'll call them," he promised.

Once the brothers parted Frank was overcome with anxiety. *Please God, don't let her be having an affair. Time for a drink.* When Frank reached The Ferris it was filling with regulars. A comfortable crowd of policemen, firemen, nurses, and local customers. There were the casually dressed, in jeans and sneakers settling in for the night, and there were the sharply dressed group ready to move on to a club after a few drinks. Frank was in a black leather jacket, a light gray sweater and black slacks. Afraid to confront his wife, he was ready to go where the night took him.

Just then Jenna walked in with some friends. She immediately strolled over to Frank to say hello. It felt good to have a girl smile in his company. He felt hope. Hope and smiles. For a moment, Frank wished his life were different. He wished his troubles away, to wonder about a fresh start in a new relationship. Her smile, her warm manner, gave him a feeling of want, as if she sensed his new vulnerability and wished to help, but...

He remembered another time when desires could have been answered. One night, early in his marriage, Frank was out with friends and ran into Jenna. The downtown area bar was crowded and the pair were pushed together by the crush of people. With all the loud chatter and Frank feeling his drinks, he leaned into Jenna and jokingly remarked that they were close enough to kiss. Frank was aware that she knew he was recently married. He was surprised when she responded, "I think you should." So that night they shared a stolen moment. Frank remembered the light brush of her lips then the soft flicker of her tongue. It was nothing long and dramatic with bodies clenched in passion; rather, it was a moment in time that only the truly romantic could appreciate. Frank often imagined he was more romantic than his friends, even more so than some of the women he knew. Experience taught him that a woman could turn the tears on whenever they wanted during the relationship, but once it was over it would be the man left lingering in torment.

Anyway, back to reality and not some movie, Frank thought. The kiss with Jenna was not meant to make time stand still. After all, they were both drunk. She probably didn't even give the kiss much thought.

Jenna snapped her fingers in front of Frank's face and gently punched him in the ribs. "You were zoning out."

"Ouch, get me a nurse," he quipped.

"In your dreams," she responded. He was saved from decisions as his buddies closed in on them.

CHAPTER 13

The approaching Easter holiday brought a hint of real spring, especially on the busy corner of Main Street in the 117th precinct, where the influx of new rookies were assigned in a bunch to stand on the corner and robotically pull cars over for ignoring their left turn signs. If Frank watched from afar he could see the newbies, their uniforms a little baggy and the females with ponytails flying in the breeze as they trotted to catch a vehicle for a minor traffic infraction. They were not unlike himself when he was new, not realizing how dangerous it was for any cop to be standing out there in the street flagging down cars.

The job loved using the new kids because they were all on probation and couldn't play off union demands for a slowdown. Frank remembered when he was a rookie. The squad sergeants played sort of a game with the young cops. The Irish boss would tell the Irish cops they had to produce more summonses than those 'fucking Guineas.' And the Italian bosses would do the same, demanding they should make the 'Micks' look bad. In the meantime, both sergeants looked like superstars to their boss since the private competition scored the precinct hundreds of summonses.

For Frank, the only change in temperature was the coldness surrounding his now defunct marriage. He confronted Kathleen about the incident. She responded by calling him an asshole. The frost became palpable. Things went from bad to worse and Kathleen finally moved out of their apartment and back to her parents. *Looks like I'll never get that dream house like we planned on.*

Sure enough, that night Frank's dreams showed him a For Sale sign on the lawn of the house he always fantasized would be the place he brought up his own family. No more Leyland Cypress trees and big lawn for him.

Eaton and Walsh listened, advised, and cared as much as they were capable of understanding. There wasn't much they could contribute in the way of advice except, "We like Kathleen. She was always nice to us. She got along fine with our crew and our girlfriends of the moment at barbecues and such. But it's time to say fuck her Frank...be glad she did this now, before any kids...she'll regret it one day after a few guys fuck her around." His buddies were convinced that the only cure for their friend's woes was to get laid.

The trio had spent their careers partying and looking for girls until Frank dropped out to get married. Eaton and Walsh saw this as a reunion opportunity so tried their damnedest to revive Frank into the single world. Frank rationalized his pain was the result of someone else's heart he had broken coming back to haunt him. He wondered if the same ghosts would eventually haunt his friends. He hoped not, knowing that this kind of pain could only be wished on a mortal enemy.

The long weeks also brought Frank to some losing nights in a few Atlantic City Casinos, as well as a several precinct card games. On the home front, his lonely home was becoming a mess and there were a few nights when he had to hug the porcelain throne, often to the sounds of dry heaves.

The entire psycho-babble thing about, the 'I'm okay, you're okay crap,' was tossed right out of the window. If he wasn't careful he would be right on course to the same path of destruction he witnessed as a rookie, observing some of the old timers who were branded losers. Cops who had enjoyed the high life until they lost everything: their marriages, their children, some even their jobs. Now, the spring changing of the guard brought on an eerie familiarity and there were probably rookies laughing at him. Still, there were his friends from patrol who would never turn their backs on him and would act selflessly to help in any way. In the few years Frank was assigned to Squad Two, Joe and Teddy, who took an immediate liking to Frank, acted like mentors trying to sway him in the right direction in both personal and professional matters. With more time on the job than Frank, they were like his godfathers. Joe, though a prankster, was the nurturing Italian father who had experienced many life lessons, and Ted embodied a tough but likable bear of a man with a lumberjack mustache and infectious laugh.

Their shifts were now different, they saw little of Frank, yet he knew they were there for him. But he went out of his way to avoid them because a part of him didn't want to stop the lifestyle he was accustomed to. In a half-assed attempt at trying not to be shut out of the world, Frank tried to have sex with Nina. Both occasions ended with the same result. He couldn't bring himself to enter her without a feeling of nausea. He just couldn't stop thinking about Kathleen. There was no way he could tell anyone, even his friends, such a thing. Not being able to fuck was a death toll to a cop. As far as Nina was concerned, he just told her he'd been sick.

Sex was like trying to find a beautiful rainbow through a clouded window of dust. He tried to envision the beauty and the joy of lovemaking, but as his erections softened he dumped Nina for good. Now it was he who used the mantra, "Fuck her." The hope was that if he couldn't have sex because of Kathleen then maybe Kathleen couldn't either.

Whatever this was, it was becoming dangerous. There were growing casualties now. He realized he was hurting Nina, even if his pals thought she was just some dumb slut. Work was also becoming a hassle. Intellectually, the job didn't require much. He would nonchalantly breeze through any tasks at hand, his way. It was the dragging himself in to work and suiting up that was bothersome. Frank never realized how mentally distracted he was while on duty.

As Easter approached, two things happened with regards to his professional life. Circumstances on the job always happened to surface around a holiday to ensure a cop would be that much more miserable. The department seemed to derive pleasure from it. The first situation to arise was not too tumultuous. Sergeant Moore told Frank that the crime victim agenda was still priority and it appeared Frank's visits for the last few weeks were minimal. The captain wasn't going to stand for it and was willing to bounce any cop back to patrol if they weren't doing CPOP proud.

"There isn't a hell of a lot I could do Frank," Moore stated. "The police commissioner's daughter was accosted on Sanford Ave. Need I say more? It's not going away. Unfortunately, most of these assaults took place on your beat."

Frank responded with, "The commissioner should pin a special award on my chest with the shit I had to listen to."

"Yeah, well, the captain wants bad for a female and an Asian to join the CPOP ranks and he wants me to talk to a few of the patrol cops because it looks bad if he has to force them in. This precinct has a melting pot of third world residents and CPOP is made to address their issues. They would rather the cops be diverse even if the brass don't believe it themselves. Really who could expect you guys to immediately get used to all the diversity? However, you and your pals are expendable so get serious for a bit."

"I get it boss," Frank replied.

They laughed lightly ending the conversation, Frank immediately made a visit to scratch one off the board. The victim was a mentally retarded male who claimed he was accosted in the mini-mall bathroom by three other males who forced Robert to sodomize them. Frank spent about one minute interviewing the retard before dropping a pamphlet and blowing him off. But for the record, it counted as a visit. Frank quashed down a flashing feeling of guilt.

The second issue was a disciplinary complaint. Frank received a command discipline for failure to safeguard department property. Though it happened months ago it just surfaced now. Since the complaint wasn't in the category of a suspension, department sadists usually let the lesser charges string out until they were damn well ready to decide on a penalty. Of course, the more serious the complaint the more eager they were to cut a cop from his balls.

The radio incident happened the previous November, on a night shift. Frank and John were utilized as backfill for routine patrol. They were paired in a radio car patrolling the south end of the precinct; sector ADAM, a relatively quiet area. During their tour they received a complaint of excess noise. When they arrived at the location they were greeted by a crusty old woman in a house dress standing on the curb. The woman came to greet them. She began complaining immediately about noises and music the patrolmen couldn't hear. Frank placed his hand radio on the roof of the car to light a cigarette. Later he would obsess about the weather, warm for November. "If it were colder," he said, "I would have never gotten out of the car."

While they were listening to the lady rant, three quick beeps sounded through the cops' portables, signaling that the next radio run would be a heavy one. Up in the north section of the precinct, sector TOM received a call of an emotionally disturbed man possibly wielding a knife. This was the type of job situation that escalated a police officer's stress. If the job turned out to be a legitimate call then the cops had to be on their toes and careful not to intimidate the emotionally disturbed person. The last thing any cop needed was a psycho pissed off at authority figures. At the least, there could be a scuffle when the disturbed person realized it was mandatory to be handcuffed and carted off to the local hospital's psychiatric ward. That's what Frank was thinking when they jumped back into the car and responded to the EDP run.

As it turned out, there was no knife involved, but the EDP didn't want to be hospitalized, therefore, the predictable fight ensued. "Fuck you, officer, I ain't goin' nowhere." It never matters the size of the EDP because no matter how big, small, or whether male or female, an emotionally disturbed person who doesn't want to be taken is going to put up a fierce struggle. The experts say it's something chemical. It took four cops to restrain the psycho, cuffing his hands and strapping his legs with Velcro, before placing him in an ambulance.

When sector ADAM flew off into the night away from the crusty woman, so did the portable radio on the roof of the car. They searched their route to no avail. Frank had no choice but to tell the platoon commander, who in turn informed Frank that he had no alternative but to issue Frank an automatic command discipline. Frank was disgusted because what this all meant was that the loss of department property was officially on paper and had to be reported to and reviewed by the commanding officer, possibly the borough inspector, who could hand down a fifteen-day penalty. That would not be an easy thing for Frank or any cop who valued their time as much as money. Based on his mood, the captain could recommend a penalty after reviewing the cop's activity sheet, the cop's attitude, and of course the number of summonses that cop wrote.

Since the loss of the radio, Frank only met once with the commanding officer about the issue. Initially, the CO offered Frank a five-day penalty he thought he could satisfy the borough with. However, Frank along with his PBA delegate, Officer Callahan, turned the offer down. The PBA delegate assured Frank the penalty could possibly be knocked down to two days or perhaps just a warning if they were lucky to catch the CO on a good day. "Frank the circumstances in which the radio was lost, racing to aid a fellow police officer in trouble, helps us." The CO insisted, "Five days is a low ball number, and the bottom line is you were still negligent in leaving a radio on the hood unguarded."

The disagreement on the penalty caused the captain to shelve the paperwork. Now resurfacing at a bad time. For Frank, the climate couldn't have been worse. His personal woes affected job activity. Topping that, the PBA was causing the city problems and putting many COs in hot-tempered moods. The patrolmen's union was stalled in contract negotiations with a city that claimed it was broke and couldn't afford decent raises for any city worker. The Taylor Law was still in effect, police and firefighters were simply not allowed to strike because of the obvious hazards to the citizens. So, unofficially, the only way to react without breaking the law was conducting minor slowdowns. A job that demanded twenty-five summonses a month from a patrol cop, unofficially of course, was now getting half that. The terms: activity or production meant nothing to the cops who knew they were disguised words for quotas. The Taylor Law prohibited union leaders to sanction slowdowns, the city couldn't officially enforce quotas. So came unofficial threats and ball busting.

When the mayor was broadcasting warnings to any cop who ceased work activity, the union countered with denial of any job actions. And the mayor, who was a hothead to begin with, got extremely pissed off, then in turn pissed off the egomaniac police commissioner...rolling that down to the chiefs, inspectors, captains and so on until, as it usually did, shit rolled right over the patrol cops.

Commanding officers were ordered by their superiors to nip any out of control situations in the bud. Lieutenants and sergeants were delegated to ride in patrol cars and point out summonses for the cops to issue. Also, the same lieutenants and sergeants were ordered to hand out command disciplines to their cops no matter how minor the deficiency. Discretion's usually reserved for the minor violations log were now to be officially put on paper so the penalties could be upped from one hour to one day, depending on the CO's discretion, and of course, the cop's present activity. Such minor violations as shoes not shined, haircuts, shaves, smoking, or not wearing the uniform cap were now command disciplines. The climate of abusive authority was such that a cop who could joke about a minor infraction of years past, could now be subject to harsh penalties. Proof that timing was bad, Frank's issue coincidentally resurfaced from a pile of nothing, and the PBA delegate was told that the captain was now going to seek at least ten days. Cops were taking hits all over the city and it was becoming apparent their union was losing its balls.

Suddenly the sharp silver fox, the union president, was leaking to his membership, "Hold up a bit on any slowdowns." His battle cry was that he had forced new negotiations, that his members should hang in there. These were famous last words from a guy who took home a salary double that of a patrolman. He was also receiving this salary at a midnight tour rate. Then of course, there were other perks, including a free car and credit cards charged to the PBA.

The hint at a change of heart was both confusing and disheartening. What happened to the union's argument that cops now had to live in a two-salary family? Didn't this start with their leader? Yet without their leader's total and full support, there wasn't much cops could do. Precinct delegates did their part, reminding the president that in just one week the minor slowdown was costing the city $300,000 a day in lost revenue. A total shutdown could grab the mayor by his balls and drive him batty enough to reconsider. The public, for once, wouldn't complain. They were reaping the rewards of unlimited parking privileges. The arguments became heated. The union boss didn't want to be told how to run his union, so he shouted down delegates like a school yard bully. But he couldn't disagree. The PBA president endorsed the current mayor.

Meanwhile, Frank, unable to put the complaint off, decided to accept the findings but refuse the penalty. It would sit again until the CO decided whether to escalate the complaint past the borough to the trial room, where Frank would plead his case to the department's version of a kangaroo court.

Frank risked pissing off the captain. But he bargained for more time, hoping things would cool. Those five days didn't sound so bad now. Still, if the captain was going to be a real hard ass, Frank might find himself bounced from CPOP to a permanent and boring foot post. In addition, the CO could direct some no-good sergeant, someone other than Moore, to make sure Frank was highly visible on his post. He could also find himself suddenly getting stuck with assignments like guarding prisoners at the stationhouse, or at the hospital watching over EDPs at the psyche ward, until a slow as molasses doctor decided to treat the patient. Worse, Frank could be scheduled to sit with dead bodies until the funeral parlors or the morgue got around for pickup. He'd taken a chance and defied the 'take it and shut up' rule. His life could be made miserable at the behest of a vindictive boss.

To stall his climb down the shit list, Frank would have to bring his summons numbers up. Sergeant Moore was a fair boss but now there was only so much he could do for his officers. However, understanding the situation with the city, Moore assured Frank that if he took care of the conditions on his post, wrote just a few more summonses, he would back him to the captain.

Frank wouldn't be able to procrastinate visits to the crime victims, especially Police Officer Caputo. It had been weeks since he was asked to visit. Frank would also have to show a strong effort of ridding his post of street peddlers whose products were confined to a blanket on the sidewalk, ready to be covered and removed at the first sighting of a cop. There was still the annoyance of the gypsy cabs, flooding the legit taxi stands to steal a fare. The summonses would be the ones the captain was most concerned with.

Fortunately for Frank, the issue of his drinking had yet to reach catastrophic proportions. That only meant he wasn't drinking twenty-four hours a day. So, at the end of each four by twelve tour, Frank headed straight to the bar as if he were on automatic pilot. At The Ferris he concealed his pain from others. However, in the soap opera world of gossiping cops, most of the people who knew or knew of him, were now aware of his split from Kathleen. Frank had to act hard in the presence of people who knew both he and his wife. Part of his strategy was to animate the heckling that he and his friends would share with the opposite sex. Hopefully, people would interpret that as the boys were back. He especially needed to drive that point hard to Carl the bartender, who would eventually inquire into his personal life.

The other half of the battle would be Kathleen. Where had she been? She always enjoyed The Ferris for the local spot it was, and not just another cop bar. Although it was a saving grace not to run into her, Frank still wondered about what filled her days. If she finally did walk into Ferris would he fall apart in front of the world? It didn't help any that all the songs on the juke reminded him of her. This bar was where Frank first noticed Kathleen, from the back view. She was standing by the jukebox, swaying slightly to the sound of a psychedelic sixties song. A perfect ass in tight acid-wash jeans that accentuated her upside-down heart shape. Her strawberry hair, just beautiful. And then when he was introduced by a friend he was knocked out. She squinted one eye, bit her lower lip, and he was hooked.

Sometimes Frank would go to bars off the beaten path. But once away from Ferris, he would wonder if she was there. That fantasy was crushed when Carl told him he hadn't seen Kathleen. When the night would end clueless to her whereabouts, Frank would fall deeper into depression...

One night at The Ferris Frank was standing at the bar, glass empty, waiting to order another. He couldn't help but overhear a conversation about baseball going on to his left. One of the regulars, a loud-mouthed fireman, was carrying on to two guys about how great Gary Carter was and how overrated Thurman Munson had been. He was saying something about the world of baseball feeling sorry for Munson because of his death when Frank aloofly started towards them. Frank was a Yankee fan who held Munson high on the list of his all-time favorites, even before the catcher's death. Either luck, or the fact that the fireman's balls weren't big enough, something saved Frank from the large hulk of a drunken man. Carl, who could sooth his customers, was off this night.

Frank said to the fireman, "You big, fat bastard, you couldn't even squat to a catcher's position."

The fireman, who could have squashed Frank like a bug, responded, "Asshole." But that was it. He turned back to his friends. Maybe he thought Frank was just kidding or it just didn't matter since the Mets were finally headed to a World Series.

The next morning offered another unwelcomed surprise; Frank was the recipient of a civilian complaint alleging discourteousness. A cop receiving a civilian complaint was certainly not uncommon. Many who got tickets or were arrested make civilian complaints against a cop. Most civilian complaints were nothing more than retaliation against the cop just doing their job. Yet, no matter how frivolous the complaint, it stayed filed in the officer's folder for an extended time. This complaint read: "When I asked the Police Officer for directions to a certain street, the officer reacted rudely and his attitude was uncalled for. The officer said to me, 'How the hell should I know. Do I look like I have an information sign on my back?'"

Frank's acts of disregard were also extending to the family. His mother was leaving messages on his answering machine even while he was home. His brother stopped by the apartment and Frank didn't answer the door. He called his mother back when he thought she wasn't home. The old man, though concerned, wouldn't badger him with questions. His father just accepted all was well because Frank told him so. Frank finally told his family the extent of his separation. That he was close to a divorce. He couldn't tell them that he was dying inside.

Frank started working more four to twelve shifts to accommodate a nightlife escape. He was able to convince Moore that storekeepers were worried about vandalism and graffiti.

A few days before Holy Thursday, Frank was approached by Moore, who told him he needed to see him by the day's end. *Probably that damn complaint.* Moore and Colleri conferred in the CPOP office alone.

"Listen, Frank. I'm sure you know the captain wants to see you on that CD again. Maybe even answer it completely out by the end of the week, which is tomorrow."

"Sure, boss. But I already said I'm not accepting that outrageous penalty."

Moore was looking at his young cop, sensing some kind of turmoil. Frank was speaking in a low tone with a haggard look on his face. "Frank, you didn't visit that female PO yet. There is the civilian complaint. You're close to getting bounced out of here. I can't cover to the CO anymore kid."

"Ah...no, but I have two visits set up with other people this week and I figured I'd let it go till after Easter so not to upset her."

Moore looked at Frank through squinted eyes and a smirk. "Listen, Frank..." Moore took a moment to scratch his forehead..."Let's face it and cut the bullshit. I told you I would help you with the CO, and believe me you're hanging by a thread...if it weren't for that one cab arrest and that haul of peddlers my driver helped you with...Anyway. You're going to have to pay extra attention to this female cop once you meet with her. And I know it's something you might not want to do..." Moore leaned forward to make his point. "But the CO wants it done or you're gone from the unit. Get. It. Done."

"I don't understand why they can't send a female."

"I'm not gonna tell you again. Got it? She has all the female help she needs. This is a beat thing and you don't have to get personal. The next time I speak to you I'll expect that you went..." He wasn't into this giving direct orders nonsense..."I can't find any more excuses to back you if the CO finds out you didn't go."

"I understand, sarge. Shit aren't they concerned about the motherfucker's who commit these crimes?"

"Certainly, they are. You're flying off course here. There have been many arrests made on these complaints and more to come, you know that, this is serious stuff. That has nothing to do with you though, unless somehow you hear of a perp that hasn't been caught. The issue is *your* link is just to visit, not arrest or go to court. How's the summons activity?"

"To tell you the truth if I have a handful it's a lot."

"Speaking of which, you almost got another civilian complaint." Moore put up a hand. "Don't worry, I squashed it. The bus supervisor down on Main said he saw you giving tickets out only to minorities, especially Asians. I explained to the idiot he was misunderstanding the situation, the area was mostly Asian. Anyway, he decided not to pursue it. Just keep up the other crap: peddlers, cabs, security checks, you know, look busy until this PBA thing blows over. It all starts and ends with the goat-head mayor. But you're still going to have to write a few more. Have your delegate talk to me if there's a problem." Then Moore shook his head and tightened his lips with a rarely seen worried look. He gathered his things and headed for the door. He liked Frank and didn't want to see him get hurt. With his back turned to Frank he paused. "Have a good Easter, Frank. Tough it out with your other problems. Eat some good food, put some meat on those bones… And Frank, unlike your buddies, you seem like the type of guy who could muster up some compassion."

"Thanks, you too, boss." Frank sat back thinking, he was rubbing his eyes when Bennett walked in the office. "What's up John, working late?"

"Till ten thirty. I've been here an hour already; hey you're in early today."

"John, did you happen to see Brian Callahan upstairs?"

"Saw him when I came in. Everything okay dude?" Bennett asked, genuinely concerned.

Frank nodded, then called upstairs to the switchboard operator. "You missed him. he's gone home." He waited about ten minutes smoking a cigarette and flipping through a paper. He removed his PBA calendar book out of his jacket pocket and flipped to the names and home numbers until he found the seldom-used number of Brian Callahan.

Callahan picked up on the first ring.

"Brian?"

"Yeah, speaking, who's this?"

"It's Frank. Frank Colleri."

"Hey Frank. What are you doing? You know I was trying to get in touch with you," Callahan said.

Yeah, right. "What did you hear?"

Callahan's voice appeared to trail off. "They're talking a different penalty now, maybe eight, nine days…but don't worry it's just talk. That blockhead don't want to go to the trial room."

When were you going to tell me? Another PBA jerk line.

"Don't worry buddy," Callahan said. "Really. Listen, I'll meet you at the stationhouse tomorrow at two."

Feeling brushed off, all Frank said was, "Sure, Brian. See you then." Putting the receiver down Frank softly chuckled. "Douche bags," he said. "All of them."

Bennett was smiling now and changed the subject. "There's a lot of women out there...and between you, Walsh and Eaton there should be no problem—"

Frank's hand went up but he wasn't upset. "I appreciate your concern buddy, but really I'm fine. Thanks."

"Sure Frank...I gotta run." John reached the door and turned, "Don't let the bear eat you."

Why do we make fun of this guy? Frank wondered.

CHAPTER 14

Frank arrived at the stationhouse at two o'clock the next day. There was a commotion at the front desk. Three rookie cops had hauled in two Haitian peddlers along with a dozen bags of their wares. The peddlers spoke no English, gibbering in their native tongues. Waving their hands as they were searched, their pockets filled with money emptied onto the huge desk in front of the sergeant. Everything had to be accounted for before they received peddling summonses even though they all possessed bogus identification with various names all sounding the same. They were being ordered by the female desk sergeant to hush up or face being arrested. Still, anyone listening couldn't help but laugh; it was a comedy sketch.

Shit. Those are easy summonses on my post. The eager rookies should have held off. All about the summonses numbers, not the validity, Frank thought as he went to the cop sitting at the switchboard asking for Callahan.

The cop pointed to the muster room. Brian greeted Frank with a jovial smile and a handshake. He informed Frank that the captain was going to be off the rest of the week and this radio issue would wait until after Easter.

"Why does he play us like that? I just want to get this over with."

"Don't worry Frank. Maybe the wait is best."

"You think so? How many days is he going to want then?"

Callahan was acting the optimistic delegate. "It looks good, Frank. Him wanting to negotiate this thing again, can't hurt."

But waiting was something Frank didn't want to have on his mind. He had enough to think about, and this issue would never truly be resolved unless it was signed, sealed and gone. Frustrated he asked, "What do you think we're looking at Brian?"

"I'm hoping for the minimum, but like I told you yesterday—"

"We already turned down the minimum Brian. What happened to the good old, warned and admonished?"

"I hear you, Frank. But the way things have been if we get away with five—"

"FIVE?"

"Frank, he wanted to go to ten. Listen it's a schedule B command discipline. This guy could go to fifteen."

"I thought it couldn't go that high," grunted a disgusted Frank.

Brian's face was red with excuses. Frank couldn't help but wonder about the delegate ten years down the road. Would he grow into a craggy-faced Irish cop who had one drink too many? Fed up, Frank went downstairs after his disappointing conversation with Callahan. He found Walsh and Gallo taking advantage of Moore's absence. Both cops were seated in chairs behind desks. Walsh was on the phone and gave Frank a wink. Gallo now had something to do since Frank walked in: break balls.

"You look like hell, Frank. Rough night in the sack or are you still worried about all the vacation they're going take from you?"

"Do you ever have a bad day? Jerk off."

Gallo removed a tissue from the box on the desk and he wiped the corner of one eye pretending to cry. "Sean, Frank's having a bad day, *boo, hoo, hoo.*"

The phone on the desk where Gallo was sitting rang once. "CPOP, Gallo. How can I help? Hold on." He stretched the cord to Frank. "It's for you."

"Who is it? Is it my brother?"

"Not quite," Gallo said.

"Hello, Colleri here."

"Hello, Frank." And the soft voice on the other end nearly melted him. "How are you?"

Frank swallowed at the sound of the sweetest voice he had ever heard. It was the voice of forgiveness. The voice of making up and making love. Frank couldn't open his mouth, he hadn't heard from her in what seemed like forever. He should have been angry but all he wanted now was her assurance to forget the past weeks and bury them like some forgotten dream.

"Frank, are you there?"

"Hello." Frank inconspicuously turned his back to Gallo and semi-cuffed the receiver. The other thing that saved him from any further Gallo intrusion was that John Bennett happened to walk in and receive the instant ball breaking routine of Gallo, who said, "How's it going, dude? How's the Mrs. Number Two?" That was the last thing Frank heard before he faded the entire room out, back to the soft cloud of her voice he was drifting with.

"Frank," Kathleen said. "I'd like to know when it would be convenient for you, so that I could come over and pick up the last of my things."

She spoke these words so fetchingly that Frank couldn't believe what she had just said. "What?" he said, a bit stunned.

"I want to know—"

"No, no, I heard you," he said. A clamoring rush to his head now swept over the earlier relief. He was hesitant for a moment, for fear that he might choke up or sob right there in the CPOP office, in the presence of Arthur Gallo.

"I guess it's not a good time, Frank. Can you call me later?"

"Yeah, sure. I'll call you later." Frank was stunned when he put down the receiver.

Gallo was still breaking balls with Bennett, teasing him about a few days before when Bennett was called to an apparent suicide, confirmed when he entered the apartment of an Asian couple whose son was hanging in the bedroom by a sheet. "Was his tongue out?" Gallo mocked.

"You're an asshole," Bennett scornfully said.

Sean was off the phone and moved to Frank when he noticed the stone glare on his friend. Sean talked Frank out into the hallway without anyone else giving it a thought. He put Frank gently against the wall to steady him, then dug his hands into his shoulders. "Frank, tell me what just happened."

"Nothing happened." He made a feeble attempt to shrug Sean's long arms away.

"Who you kidding buddy? You look as though you've seen a ghost. This broad's turned you into scrambled eggs man, there are so many of them out there, why?"

"She wants her things, Sean." Frank's eyes were welling up. "She has a guy, I know it."

"Get a grip, Frank. This isn't the place. There's a bear in there in the form of Arthur Gallo that would gladly eat you if you let him."

"What the hell happened? We were good together. Did everything together in the beginning...lunches in the park..."

"Your fucking rambling Frank. Stop! Go relax in the lounge for a minute."

Frank put his forefinger to his eyes wiping. "What? So I could catch bed bugs from the retread couch someone pulled from the garbage?" Both friends laughed then Frank said, "I think I'm gonna be sick." He moved Sean aside and headed to the bathroom.

Then, with the urgency of a claustrophobic, Frank rushed to leave the precinct and hit the breezy air along his beat. The wind was kicking up a bit more than usual but it didn't matter to Frank who walked about eight blocks with a welcomed loneliness that seemed to be the only solution for now. Frank darted up a side street before some John Q Public accosted him on the street with another dumb civilian question or problem he was in no mood to hear. He was sick of people. Still, there was the matter of the work at hand and Moore's reminder that he couldn't back him up if he failed to make the visit. Well he would make *a* visit, not *the* visit.

First though, Frank stopped at a pay phone to call his brother. Maybe it would be a good idea to go out tonight to some old familiar places and see some people other than cops. "If anyone is interested I'll be bopping at The Z tonight." *Beeeeep.* Peter was in the habit of changing his messages often. Frank smiled but hung up not wanting to leave a committed message.

* * * *

Frank's guess was that some people approached a cop as if they were clergy, a psychiatrist or close friends. Some were willing to bear their souls in search for advice or just the need to let out their frustration, or just babble. Frank was sure these citizens didn't know that most cops really didn't give a shit. So rather than knock off a few summonses first, Frank hurried the three flights of stairs to apartment 3D where he was immediately greeted by a Mrs. Gennaro, something or another, he hadn't really taken a good look at the complaint report.

Frank was offered a seat on a plastic covered sofa where the complainant's mother sat across from him. She began almost immediately. A small black cat jump onto the couch beside him. A scraggly looking creature.

"First officer, I myself get robbed in the elevator," the mother began. "My God--but that's nothing compared to what those scum did to my daughter. My God, what kind of world do we live in? She's afraid to leave the house now for Christ's sake. She stays home constantly and says nothing. My God!" The pleasantly plump woman bounced in her chair after finishing each sentence and Frank thought she would fall to the floor. She also clutched her chest after each time she cried, "My God."

You better be careful you don't get a stroke.

"She's fifteen officer. Fifteen." She was whispering for fear her daughter would come into the room. "She cries at night. Her privates are swollen..."

My God! I can't believe she just said that.

"And they're so smug...Can, what they say, cop a plea, be true? Even after we picked them from the lineup? Even after we had to look at them?"

By now, Frank was becoming an old pro at quick departures. Yes, he was certainly sorry about what happened to the young girl. Time to go. "The detectives will inform you ma'am."

"My God," was the last thing he heard.

His head began to ache.

Good-bye lady. I know, you're 100% right. I know the lawyers and the broken-down courts, and everyone else involved all contradict themselves. I would love to smash those scumbags' skulls for you right now. These degenerates were probably the same kids who lived on anyone's block, the ones who would rip praying mantises in half after they caught them and leave them lingering in a jar. Moore was right, by God, these victims, they must face their attackers, lineups, courts, and the continuous questioning by police and lawyers, causing guilt and doubt. They needed compassion not cynicism.

He walked further away from the horror of that one family, but couldn't escape the only pain he would truly feel, his own. His wife's stinging words. His emotional wall collapsed, and he wished he had had the courage to say to his wife what he really wanted to. He wished he could have shown an honest self, vulnerable as anyone else.

He walked another mile before returning to the precinct. He asked the desk officer for the rest of the day off. Down in the CPOP office, John Bennett was sitting alone, staring into space. Frank mumbled a hello then signed off on the roll call. "You leaving?" Bennett asked.

"Yeah, I'm not feeling too great."

Bennett shot Frank his forefinger with a meaningful look.

"I know," Frank said. "Don't let the bear eat you." Adding, "Don't worry buddy, I was green my first few views of the dead."

Bennett smiled and nodded. Ironically, Bennett was being stalked by the bear as well, yet he still had energy to care about Frank.

In the locker room, Gallo was tearing off the Velcro sleeve of his bulletproof vest. He was also ripping some loud farts when he saw

Frank. "Hey, Frank. I'm gonna work out. Why don't you join me and get that sad shaped body of yours tightened up?"

"I'm gagging in here. Now you're gonna go down and stink up the gym for everyone else?"

"Hey, Frank, I think Bennett's second wife is about to fly."

"Where do you hear this stuff? Is that why you were breaking his balls?" Frank pictured Bennett downstairs sitting alone in silence.

"I was just kidding, Frankie boy. John knows that." He laughed.

That's Gallo. The big kidder. The Long Island guinea who knows it all. Who sounds like he was born and raised in Brooklyn.

"Don't you think Bennett's just a little weird? All that eat the bear crap and hey dude stuff?" Gallo asked.

Frank decided he wasn't going to get too deep with Gallo. He wanted to be rid of him, so he laughed along and replied, "It's an old cop term his dad told him about. You know? The job. Don't let it devour you. Give the guy a break Al, he's talking like all young guys."

The seriousness in Frank's eyes gave pause to Gallo who issued a rare, "I'm sorry Frank. Meant no harm."

Frank left the locker room hearing voices coming from the bunk area. The guys from patrol were sneaking in a quick card game. He decided to move on. Frank was suddenly exhausted, yet not tired. He decided against going to either Ferris or Zs. He stopped at a convenience store, buying a six pack of beer and a box of over the counter sleeping pills. Frank stood at the cash register while the foreign clerk slowly rang up the merchandise. He smiled to himself as he fantasized this store being held up with him in it. Since he didn't carry an off-duty weapon, he would probably be killed when he tried to interfere. The clerk looked at him funny and Frank left the store laughing.

Once he was home he popped open the first beer and downed five of the pills with a couple of swigs. He hit the button on the answering machine. "Between you and your brother I don't know...Call me. It's me, Mom..." His mother's usual flair for the melodramatic. At least he had a family that cared.

He bounced onto the couch and turned the television on. He finished off the beer as he was flipping through the channels. After a couple of more brews he realized he really wasn't watching anything. He was also starting to feel the effect of the pills and welcomed the drowsiness.

Frank needed to sleep. He needed to forget the day and the sharp words that resonated from her sweet voice, the finality of it all, 'When can I get my things?'

Ann promised her parents she would attend mass with them on Easter Sunday. A futile attempt to believe in something. During the mass Ann imagined herself standing at the pulpit shouting the words Jesus spoke before he died: 'God, why have you forsaken me!' Even after her talk with the good priest, no parable could seduce her into believing there was a purpose for everything. There was an older priest conducting this mass. Ann wondered where Father DeMartino was. He was one of the reasons she agreed to come. There was something soothing about that man. There had once been pain behind his eyes.

Ann was grateful when mass was over. She returned with her parents to their home. She helped her mother prepare dinner and felt safe in the womb of the family home. She needed the peace after a world turned upside down, a world in which she sank into sporadic states of depression. Yet even as she felt like a zombie, she didn't project any turbulence through her physical appearance.

Ann was presently in therapy and seeking further counsel; a female doctor she researched on her own yet hadn't set an appointment with. The other was the mandatory department shrink, standard procedure. The job relieved Ann of her firearms. The irony was that although it was supposed to be for the cop's safety, most just felt like less of a cop without their guns. A cop without a gun was like a knight without a sword, further sinking them into depression.

Still, the department was rigid about rules. The job had to cover its ass in case of a suicide, in which the department would be blamed or sued for their carelessness. Realistically, if the job removed every gun from a cop that had a crazy thought from time to time, there would be no cops on the street. Ann felt it was being too hard on her. What the powers that be didn't realize is work would have been a helpful relief. She loved her job and assisting people on patrol. She ached to be a real cop again instead of spending most of her time in thought.

After Easter dinner Ann's parents encouraged her to stay. Ann understood their concern, their unspoken fear of her returning to that apartment. After a day of them complimenting her about everything from her hair to her dress; she was ready to end the day.

She went to bed around one in the morning. As became habit, she turned on the television. She needed to hear the voices from the tube along with the light bathing the dark room. After her attack, total darkness had become impossible.

By two Ann was restless. She couldn't help but wonder if there was any man out there that would accept what had happened to her. If she were to find the right guy, which was hard enough, then she would eventually have to trust that he would understand. Ann's heart began to pump up the insomnia, so she got out of bed and went to the medicine cabinet. She swallowed two prescription tranquilizers instead of the allotted one. Finally, with her head rested back on the pillow her last thought before the forced sleep was the barrel of a gun pressed between her lips. *Hell, maybe the job's right.*

* * * *

Kathleen didn't call her husband for Easter. Frank spent the better part of the day willing the phone to ring. He spoke to his parents and his brother. "Peter called today," his mother said. "It took a holiday." Frank hated lying to them about the pending divorce. *God, this is only Easter. What will I do at Christmas?*

On a whim, late in the day he called Jenna. He got the answering machine and left no message. He was relieved.

To compound the gloom, it began to rain. Frank remained at home with the company of loneliness.

* * * *

Peter Colleri smoked a joint while driving his Cadillac. He carelessly blew a red light without slowing down. Bright lights and sirens again. The cop was naturally pissed off and asked Peter if he ever stopped to think that somebody could have been killed. Peter wanted to say that if he 'stopped to think,' he would have stopped. He knew the routine and was polite and apologetic to the officer. He produced his identification along with his brother's mini-shield and PBA card. But this was Suffolk County. He held his breath.

Once again Peter skated away. The cop told him, "Okay, but watch it." Peter knew the officer had to smell the pot. He was lucky. He got the right cop, and his brother had saved his ass again. "Thank you, brother,” he said, as he drove off turning the stereo up high.

* * * *

No one knew that John Bennett had fought off a near nervous breakdown after his first wife left him. Nancy disapproved of him becoming a police officer when she should have been proud. Not long after gun and shield day Nancy Bennett abandoned him.

Divorce left John bitter and untrusting. However, all appeared to look bright again when he met his second wife. Cynthia possessed a wholesome quality. She had fair skin, golden hair styled in feathery waves and quiet manners. John fell deeply in love with her.

The problem was that like many fairy tales, there was a skeleton in the closet. Cynthia was a girl with a past. John would learn that his wife still loved her ex -boyfriend. “I'm sorry,” she would tell John. The boyfriend had left the state to find himself, and now he was back and wanted to see Cynthia. He was leaving messages at her job and with old friends.

Her confession, even her apology, left John devastated.

CHAPTER 16

UNION BACKS DOWN AGAIN !

New York's finest once again found themselves highly confused during the current contract talk and on the front of every newspaper.

The week following Easter saw a return to normal job activity. Delegates from the seventy-five police precincts were now telling their cops to bring their activity up to par, including the summons numbers. A public announcement from the union was made by the union president: "We are currently in positive negotiations with the city and appear to be working things out...I don't understand what all the fuss is about pertaining to summonses and job actions. There's no union sanctioned job action now, nor has there ever been...If the city itself employs summons quotas instead of worrying about matters concerning law and order, well then we'll probably have a city become overwrought with bad elements...and I certainly don't think that to be the case."

Meanwhile Frank's command discipline wasn't finalized. PBA Callahan insisted it would be a 'good thing' to show increased activity performance before seeing the captain. Everything would be all right now that the union said so. Frank walked away from his delegate with mixed feelings.

Frank did manage to move forward with his 'visit a victim,' as he referred to them. He chose a young girl who lived in the housing projects. The girl was nineteen and Frank hoped to confront a hardened young lady with the possibility she was strong enough to overcome adversity. *Who am I kidding?* Sure, the girl was from the projects and sure, she might be a little tougher than the others, but the truth was, she was still a victim and would still carry scars like anyone else.

Frank entered the lobby of the building, one of four clustered behind Main Street's famous hub. He was instantly turned off, and immediately thought about turning around. Had it been a nicer day that's what he would have done, but the wind picked up and the grayness of the sky looked as though it was ready to spill some rain. The lobby was littered and filthy. A short elderly woman stepped off the elevator and spoke to the uniform. "Officer, believe it or not I can still walk down the stairs. But there so many a them crack vials in the stairway I'm just plain afraid." Then without missing a beat the woman moved along.

When Frank stepped inside the elevator it was worse than imagined. The graffiti covered elevator reeked of urine. Frank saw a few dead bugs at his feet. Arriving at the girl's apartment brought no solace. The wood floor was dirty, a clutter of clothing and paper everywhere. The furniture consisted of two low-boxed couches, the kind one would get at a flea market. Cheap dining room table and chairs were off to the side.

Frank needed a smoke and judging from the atmosphere there would be no problem if he didn't use an ashtray. The ashes would just blend into the floor. Nevertheless, he asked permission. The young girl smiled and said yes providing she could have one too. Frank lit her cigarette first, looking past her as she pulled back on a drag.

Then they sat and he explained the nature of his business. At first the girl seemed suspicious. After he assured her of the department's intentions she decided to tell her story; he wondered why she bothered. She spilled her tale with relative ease. She *was* tough.

The girl's smoke burned out, she asked Frank for another light. She was sitting in the chair opposite him, one she too had to clear off. She was bouncing one leg over the other as Frank watched her inhale a long drag. Her hair was pulled back tight, she checked the knot with the cigarette still in her mouth. Strangely, her street demeanor put Frank at ease, not having the know-how for showing the compassion he really did feel right now.

"I was asleep when the punk boy come in," she said. "My boyfriend was out. Copping some smoke probably." She flashed a wide grin displaying exceptionally white teeth with just a small gap in the front where she blew some smoke through. "His cuz, that little punk ass," she snarled. "When I woke up my panties were down..." She ran her hand down her leg leaving Frank to wonder about her dark thighs. "Then I felt somethin'," she said. "I saw that the little punk jerked off all over me." She pointed to Frank. "And yes, officer, I still want to press charges on that boy, 'cause he obviously has some serious problems. They gotta find him." Another hard puff, more smoke. "You know that boy's sixteen and he still pisses himself. His mama's excuse is he's unable to control his body evac or something, something the doctor told them. I suppose that's why he did what he did."

Frank smiled. The girl was actually amusing. She didn't seem all that bothered and she thought she had the answers to boot. *What a character. Good to look at and a real crackerjack.* He explained a portion of the pamphlet again and informed the girl that precinct detectives would again be in touch. Good thing they were the ones making the collars because Frank didn't want to rehash all the stories in court. The girl fell silent and Frank offered up another cigarette as he made his exit.

Back within the perimeters of his beat and the busy intersection, he leaned against the wall of a bank. Soon it would be rush hour and thousands of commuters would flow from the four-corner subway exits like a pack of wet rats. Rain appeared to be heading to Queens. It must have poured in Manhattan. For now, he could look at some women. He noticed his buddy Eaton on the other side of the street already in conversation with a long legged, dark-haired dream. He smiled for his friend, and sent a message through the air waves, using his friend's nickname. "Sharpy, I see taint on Main."

Eaton heard; he turned his head looking around then spotted Frank. "I'm trying buddy."

"Knock it off fellas," interrupted central dispatch.

Frank hoped one of the girls coming from below would catch his eye or vice versa. What better way to get a woman off your mind than to envision a possible replacement. It was Eaton who often reiterated, "It's all about the taint fellas." Unfortunately, the busy intersection was also a risk for problems if he stood there long enough. There was bound to be some annoying citizen with a problem or a dumb question about bus schedules or subway stops. That would be when Frank wished for a downpour. He walked a few doors down to a coffee shop.

A middle-aged woman with a pullover cap was headed his way. As she got closer she looked more haggard. Probably the years of long commuting. She then began to wave a finger, pointing it in the direction of the smoke shop above the subway entrance across from where he was standing. Frank was used to these annoyances, staying put as if he didn't notice her. Frank also glanced around for Eaton who was now out of sight. Probably buying that lovely girl a coffee.

* * * *

Sergeant Nolan had been assigned to the 117 only a few months. Transferred from a rough Brooklyn precinct, Nolan had certainly had his share of hard knocks. A connection he made was able to get him assigned to Queens, a welcome relief for the hard luck Nolan. He was mending his life and the change would be good. His late nights out, especially in Brooklyn, had nearly torn his family apart. Nolan developed friendships at his AA group. He met an alcoholic who was also a retired NYC police lieutenant and a member of Cops For Christ.

A changed life mattered little to the jokers in his new command who began a session of pranks. After Nolan reprimanded one police officer for being late, the pranks at the 117 started rolling. Those walking in and out of the stationhouse witnessed with hilarity changes made to three large bumper stickers affixed on Nolan's 1972 broken down Chevy Nova. Originally the stickers read: **Honk if you Are A Friend Of Bill W** (Mr. W was the founder of AA) the second **Today Is The First Day Of The Rest Of Your Life!** the third **Many Who Plan To Seek GOD At The Eleventh Hour, Die At 10:30.**

Honk was highlighted and word was passed around to anyone aware of the gag to honk like mad from their own cars when they saw Nolan driving to or from work. On the second sticker the word First was replaced with Last. The third sticker was changed with the letter L squeezed in, so now it read, GOLD. GOLD was the NYPD's line organization for homosexuals on the job.

Nolan was greatly pissed off when he noticed his stickers had been tampered with, yet there was nothing he could do, there was no proof that any of the cops had a hand in it. Adding fuel to the fire was when Nolan noticed a mock parable written with magic marker on a sheet of paper affixed to the passenger side of the car. **OBVIOUSLY GOD HAS NO MONEY OR I WOULDN'T BE DRIVING THIS HUNK OF SHIT!**

Nolan might have caught the religious bug but he still was quite aware of the cop mentality. He steamed when he had to scrub the vandalism from his car but refrained from taking official action hoping that the problem would just go away if ignored. It was true that if you let it be known your emotions were getting the best of you, things would get worse. Still, everyone has their breaking point and the last straw for Nolan came a few days after Easter when he returned to work only to find the latest gag posted on walls all over the precinct. The frustration of not being able to pin the prank on one person drove Nolan into a frenzy. "They crossed over the line, those sacrilegious freaks!" he was heard shouting.

Among the approving cops, suspects were already being crowned. Walsh and Eaton were known for their gags and cut-ups so most of the cops at the 117th laughingly figured it might be them. It was also Walsh and Eaton rumored to have had a hand in the vile Abruzzi affair. However, Abruzzi was not a boss:

Carmine Abruzzi was a veteran cop with twenty-three years in. He was a large fluff of a man who was quiet and kept to himself. His last few years on the job were spent as a paper shuffler for the administrative lieutenant. In his own estimation, he was content to finish out his useless career doing just that. His last time on the street was an eventful one—at Main in front of the citizenry which made it more stressful. Abruzzi was walking the crowded foot post when he was accosted by bank security stating there was a bum hanging around the front area. Abruzzi lumbered toward the bank hoping the guy would be gone when he got there. He wasn't. The so-called bum was sitting just a few feet from the entrance, a black man about 6 feet tall dressed in worn jeans and old sneakers. When he refused to leave, Abruzzi had no choice but to lift him onto his feet and shove him along. The man decided he would take a swipe at the cop but Abruzzi was ready and took the man by the arm, turned him around up against the wall and cuffed him with the mastery of a seasoned veteran. A patrol car arrived and placed the now perp in the back while Abruzzi asked some questions of the bank security guard, all in the presence of a now curious crowd of on-lookers.

When Abruzzi opened the rear of the patrol car he saw the perp had managed to wrangle his rear cuffed position into the old-fashioned front cuffed routine. This was an attempted escape, and Abruzzi acted by pulling the guy out of the car where the perp lost his balance and landed face first onto the sidewalk. There was a multitude of *oohs* and *ahhs* as the blood quickly poured from the perp's nose and forehead. The patrol cops called for an ambulance as they and Abruzzi whisked the prisoner to the stationhouse. The bum required a few stitches but it was the extreme amount of phone calls coming into the precinct switchboard enquiring about the 'poor guy' who the cops roughed up. Incidents like this left the police more afraid of management overreaction than the actual severity of the case.

Abruzzi, who survived the insinuations, now occupied a small room deep in the stationhouse, and out of sight, as he wished. Abruzzi was also something of a hypochondriac. He nursed himself like an overgrown baby, maintaining a mini drug store in his top desk drawer. Contents included: various cold tablets and syrups, aspirins, nasal sprays, a jar of honey, tea bags, antacids, and a large mug and spoon. The hulking cop also kept a pair of terry cloth slippers in the drawer since sometimes his feet would swell and he worked nights and out of sight so he would often slip them on during a shift.

Unfortunately for Abruzzi, he didn't keep abreast of precinct pranks. He was a trusting man who never kept his personal belongings under lock and key. As an old-timer he should have known better.

At the time of the Abruzzi incident Walsh, Eaton and Colleri weren't assigned to the CPOP unit; they were assigned to patrol cars working a rotating schedule. There were six musketeers then; Joe, Teddy, and Steve Renna rounded out the group. One had since been transferred to Manhattan to the elite Movie-TV Unit, Steve Renna. Eaton was assigned to the mapped area of sector MIKE, while Walsh and Colleri rode sector TOM, and Joe and Teddy sector HENRY.

One morning around three the six buddies were hanging around the station exchanging stories when they decided to have a few beers. The lieutenant on desk didn't mind so long as the boys bought him in his own 'square bag' (a six-pack in a brown paper bag). He also wanted them to stay out of sight and answer up if a job came over the radio. They retreated off to the back and out of sight to the unlocked room where Abruzzi worked.

Frank, single then, was telling a story about some slut he met at Ferris who he talked to for five minutes before she wanted to get laid. "I feel like you Sean," he was saying.

Joe and Teddy abruptly had to leave and answer a call for a 53-car accident. Suddenly Eaton began going through drawers with no purpose in mind. That was until he stumbled on Abruzzi's medic drawer. Eaton blurted out a laugh and the others turned to see him holding up a bottle of antacid. Walsh, who had a sixth sense about his buddy's sense of humor, laughed and put up his hands mockingly. "No, John, no, put it back."

Eaton unscrewed the cap, coughing up gross beer phlegm which he then spit into the bottle. "Oh, shit," Eaton said. They all roared with laughter. Renna tried to hush his friends as he peaked through the door to see if anyone was lurking around.

"Don't worry Steve," Colleri said. "The boss is happy, he's got his brew." Frank turned to Eaton. "What else you got there, buddy?"

"Well, let's see. We have some aspirin." He removed two aspirins from the bottle and stuck one in each nostril turning the pills around a few times causing his friends to once again roar. Renna attempted to quiet the party putting his finger to his big lips. *"Shhh."* But he was unable to control his own laughter spitting through closed lips.

Sharpy continued. "And here we have a cup, how nice." Eaton removed his gun belt then dropped his pants to his knees sticking his penis into Abruzzi's teacup and twirling it around a few times.

Finally, Renna and Walsh ran from the room bellowing. They were followed by a hysterical Colleri and Eaton.

The story surfaced after Carmine Abruzzi retired that winter as planned. And, as far as anyone knew, he never came down with a case of 'ballitis' or 'assotonis.' Later, Frank would feel remorse at having played a part in the disgusting Abruzzi affair. Even Joe and Teddy, who loved a good prank, said they wouldn't have allowed John Eaton to do that had they still been in the room. Abruzzi was a harmless guy. Eaton's reply to his friends about his warped sense of humor was that he heard Abruzzi was a rat and would spill the comings and goings of patrol cops to his own boss. And more than once. But that was never confirmed.

So, Nolan just became the latest target in a long line of off-color pranks. Now, Sergeant Nolan sighted the first picture above the water tank in the muster room.

"Son of a—" he mumbled. He noticed photocopies taped around the wall and on the chalkboard. On his way up the stairs to the sergeant's locker room he saw the same picture in the stairwell and then right there in front of him on his locker. Officers weren't supposed to be in the sergeant's locker room, yet there it was, staring him in the face. A pornographic picture with Nolan's face superimposed on the character. His first reaction was gut anger.

Nolan rushed down to the front desk in a state of rage. "Those sacrilegious…" He started checking the logs to affirm what cops should or shouldn't be lingering around the stationhouse. This was the only immediate recourse he could come up with. He took the desk copy of roll call, much to the disinterest of the desk officer who just nodded while taking a phone call.

Nolan entered the patrolman's lounge where five cops sat relaxed on couches.

"Officer Meade, I didn't see your name in the book to be on meal, and besides as far as this roll call goes, your meal is over. Where should you be?" The cops looked at each other confused. "I asked you a question Meade."

"I forgot to put myself in the book sarge, I'm on a personal, my partner's in the bathroom."

"Liar. I'm writing you up for being off post." Nolan looked down at the roll call. The others were properly on their meals. Nolan stormed out of the lounge setting off a fit of laughter among the cops.

Nolan was at the captain's door with one of the pictures. His face, blotchy red, he knocked a little harder than he should have.

"Who the hell?" the captain's voice resounded.

Nolan entered with no apology, immediately pushing the photo forward on the CO's desk. He carried on for five minutes, ranting about the pranks and insubordination, and that something 'has got to be done about it.'

Finally, after the captain felt Nolan had vented enough he responded. "The bottom line here Sergeant Nolan is, yes, it's a pretty bad joke, and yes I'll certainly put an end to them, but I also suggest you sit back a moment and calm yourself. I do think you have enough time on the job to curb your reaction."

Nolan was smart, he settled into a chair. He was worked up but not so stupid as to bump heads with the captain. Nolan apologized. In response to this prank the captain opted to attend each roll call over the next few days suggesting his troops layoff with the pranks, though the captain was not asking, he was telling. He even went as far as stating that using department property for pranks was a larceny.

The CO also decided to put Nolan on desk duty for a one month cooling period, a move that certainly surprised everyone. It was also during one of these roll calls that a bit of humor was injected into the seriousness of it all.

The CO was standing facing his men who were in formation. A new flyer was hanging to the right of the CO's shoulder between some tacked memos. A few of the officers began to smirk and a couple of chuckles were let out. After the CO reiterated the GLA (grand larceny auto) condition in sector ADAM he addressed the smirks. "I do not at all find anything funny," the captain said. Then before he left the muster room the CO glanced to see what all the giggling was about.

There it was.

The effect was little different now in a room full of cops. The CO took another quick glance before leaving. The superimposed picture of Nolan's face on the body of a preacher, one hand holding a bible, the other his dick, caused the captain to tighten his lips in an attempt to conceal a smile ready to burst out.

CHAPTER 17

rank Colleri witnessed the short fuse of Arthur Gallo the moment he stepped in the doorway of the smoke shop. Gallo had one hand on the back of a tall black kid's jacket as he slammed him into the magazine rack. The proprietor of the shop, one of the last old Jewish standoffs, was pointing and yelling, "Get him out! Get him out! Get that thief out of here!"

A crowd was swelling so Frank thought it wise to pull Art from the kid before any liberal folks got the chance to claim police brutality. Frank had Art's arm and was close to his ear. "C'mon, Art, just get the cuffs on the guy, deal with him later."

Gallo looked towards Colleri with unrecognized venom. He was breathing heavy and Frank knew he was a dangerous man. Frank felt Gallo's huge forearms tightening. "He spit at me, Frank."

"C'mon, buddy. You know it's not the time. Look at all the snoops out there. You want them lying about you?" *Where the hell is Eaton? This is his post.*

Gallo attempted to compose himself, clearing the way to Frank who now stepped in and began to cuff the perp. *Shit, this is the same kid from the mailbox.* Gallo attempted to close in again but Frank intervened. He patted Gallo on his shoulders. "We got him Art, relax." Then Frank radioed for a sector car to respond for transportation back to the precinct.

The perp was uttering, "Punk-asses." Frank squeezed him under the ribs to shut him up. Blood was glazed on the kid's swollen lips. His neck scratched by the fingers of a big hand.

Two sector cars rolled up and Frank quickly ushered the prisoner into the back of one away from Gallo. "Good thing for you two cars are here," he said to the kid. "Told you once before to get fucking lost. Didn't listen."

Once the beast in Gallo calmed, Frank persuaded him to ride in the second radio car, avoiding more troubled allegations. Frank then told the owner of the smoke shop to come down to the stationhouse and draw up the complaint.

"I can't leave my store," the old man said. "But please, don't forget to check his pockets."

Frank was furious but composed. *Unbelievable,* he thought. *It doesn't matter to the old man now that the kid is out of his store. Money first.* Nevertheless, Frank stayed behind to write the report. Under different circumstances he wouldn't have cared but a collar had to be made to cover Gallo's ass. Apparently, what transpired was the kid, who was sixteen, had already filled his pockets with candy when he was loitering by the magazine rack. He was about to fold a porn magazine and tuck it inside his jacket when the old man finally became suspicious and began to yell to the kid to hurry up and get out.

Officer Gallo was walking towards the busy corner moments before Frank exited the coffee shop. A concerned citizen approached the burly cop. When Gallo reached the doorway, the old man was in front of the much taller kid yelling up at him. The kid was flailing his arms and shouting back at the old man, "I didn't do nothin'-you crazy man---you bitch." Then the kid pushed the old man into the counter toppling a bunch of candies to the floor.

That's when Gallo rushed in first grabbing hold of the kid, non-aggressively. "Cool it, man," Gallo said. "No need for this, just tell me what's going on."

The kid pushed Gallo's arm away. "Chill! Get away from me you punk-ass pig. I didn't do nothin'."

"What did you say?" It didn't take long for Gallo to become enraged.

Then, without reason, other than stupidity, the kid spit outward to press his issue of rebellion. Part of the spit broke from its course and caught Gallo on the left ear, below his cap. With both hands Gallo grabbed him tightly and began tossing the kid from side to side like a rag doll. Finally, and noticeably scared, the kid attempted some remorse. "I'm sorry, officer—" But it was too late.

"You little shithead!" Gallo yelled grabbing the kid by his collar.

The kid was frightened by the enraged look in Gallo's eyes. "I didn't do nothin' man. I wasn't spittin' at you, it was a mistake—it's all cause 'a that old fool."

The old man was still pointing and shaking. "Check his coats, officer. Check his pockets." Now that the kid was in the big cop's clutches, he moved closer. "If I were a little younger I would beat the crap out of you, you little scumbag." The old man's whinny voice and attempted tough guy act broke the angry mood of Gallo's, but just for a moment. He even smiled as he told the old man to step away.

"It's because I'm just another black kid, ain't that right cop?" And before the kid could utter another word Gallo, who had waited to erupt, lashed out with a hard slap to the left side of his face, instantly stinging him to a daze. "That one's for spitting." Then Gallo grabbed on tight to the kid and smashed him into the magazine rack.

The old man was screaming, "You're destroying my store!"

But Gallo held on, smashing the kid's head and face again into the rack. The kid's lip was split open and blood was draining out as Gallo continued his verbal assault. "You low life black bastard!"

That was the scene when Frank walked in.

* * * *

With their feet up drinking coffee, John Bennett was telling Frank about his backfill in sector ADAM. "I worked with Tommy Whelan the other day. Of course he had to drive because he certainly wasn't doing any paperwork."

"The old guy's retiring soon, did you think he would?"

"Well there wasn't much conversation. Good thing we picked up a couple of newspapers...Any way we responded to a 53...west-bound on the Long Island Expressway and there were no highway units available to handle it."

"Are they ever?" Frank said.

Bennett took a sip of coffee and continued. "So, Whalen takes forever to get there and of course I ain't saying anything...traffic was already backed up and he didn't even throw on the sirens."

Frank breathed a smiled.

"A small car was hanging with its front a quarter over the divider. The other car was humpbacked on the back of it. All Whalen said was, 'Wow.' As amazingly slow as we were to get there, neither had any other emergency vehicles."

Frank joked, "Get to the point John, we have work to do."

"A young woman, blond, maybe in her twenties, forehead and hair all caked in blood. Finally, sirens blared, emergency vehicles coming. They rushed the car. Thankfully the girl was still breathing...the hump car driver, he wasn't even hurt. Whalen never even got out of the car."

"Are you shocked? Who gives a fuck?"

"Naturally I got stuck doing all the paperwork and notifications without a drop of help from that old prick."

"Naturally."

"Speaking of which, how are you doing on your visits?"

"Up to par." *Figures. Still wish I had given him the sex crime reports.*

CHAPTER 18

Frank brushed his teeth, dabbed on some Cool Water cologne and got dressed. He looked over at the phone. He collected his wallet and keys, counted his money. He headed out, locking the door right when the phone rang. It was as if he had willed it. Frank fumbled with the lock, rushing back inside, advancing on the phone; however, before picking it up he used a second to compose himself. "Hello?"

In the sweet voice that he missed so much she said, "Hello, Frank."

He was instantly nervous. "Hi, Kat, how are you?" He of course secretly hoped she was miserable.

"Fine, Frank. The question is, how are you?"

"What do you mean?"

"Well...a friend of mine said she saw you the other day and that you...you don't look so good, hung over and like you lost weight."

He was annoyed now. Her insinuations sounded as if she knew she was the responsible party. And of course, she was. "You're kidding, right?"

Kathleen tried changing the subject. "I saw your brother at the Z. He kinda' blew me off."

"He's just upset about our situation. Probably didn't want to talk about it."

"Well it wasn't right."

"First, it's I look like hell, and now my brother's rude. Did you call just to break my balls?"

"Yeah, right. That was my intention. What's wrong with you?"

Frank didn't want to lose this conversation so he fought for control. "No, no, you're right." He decided to go out on a limb. After all, she'd collected the rest of her belongings, so basically, she called for nothing. "Kat, why do things happen between men and women that are unexplainable?"

"Frank---"

"No please, let me finish. People... we forget...we forget what love really is. Especially when it's going well—"

"Don't," she interrupted. "Not now, Frank. I can't do this now."

He attempted humor. "C'mon, the laundry's piling up, the fridge is empty, and I'm one lousy shopper, you know that...And besides I miss you under the covers on a rainy night watching those shows you love so much."

"Frank, I really can't---"

"Then why the hell did you call?" he snapped. "Just to annoy me?"

"You're unreal, I called to see how you were."

"Are you banging someone?"

"See what I mean? You can't be nice."

"Or, are you doing what all the good Catholic girls in your office do—blow jobs first."

"You asshole! Is that what you think I'm like? What the hell have you been doing, since we met?"

"Since we *met?*" He fell silent and thought about hanging up. But he couldn't let her go. Her voice was his lifeline.

"Frank, I'm sorry I bothered you. Take care of yourself."

"Wait," he blurted. Feeling like he could choke any second, he confessed, "I still love you, Kathleen. Very much." There I said it.

"Frank---"

"No, listen to me. Listen to what I'm saying." His voice was quivering. "I really, really love you."

"Frank...I'm sorry."

"Listen," he said, stripping his soul to a nakedness only imagined in movies. "We aren't talking about problems that can't be worked out." He struggled to hold back tears. "I know my drinking got out of hand. I know I got nasty..." Again, she fell silent..."I've been spoiled by my own attitude but I never knew I could miss and love you so much."

"Nasty? When you start to pick things out on friends of mine like Heather that's more than nasty. It's cruel."

"Please." Then without being able to help himself he uttered the cliché plea, "I promise to change, to do anything you say. But please let me see you."

Her words sounded chocked. "Frank, I will always love you...but"...the word, but, hit him like a shot..."I don't love you in that way anymore."

"There is someone else. It's that guy you work with—that yuppie bastard—"

"Stop it!" she cried. "Stop it now! He's just a friend and this has nothing to do with him. Frank get on with your life." She made that statement as if she were a friend telling him to snap out of it, like she herself was never his lover. The fact was that no matter what a person does or doesn't do, there is that time when it is just over.

Frank gritted his teeth as he slammed down the receiver.

He was nauseous and ran to the toilet to throw up. He hadn't eaten much, so all he could do was wretch up gobs of colored spit followed by dry heaves. He hung over the toilet sobbing uncontrollably, a broken man.

When he awoke the next day, there was a pounding in his head and a sick feeling in the pit of his stomach. He called into work asking the desk officer for an emergency day off, feigning a family crisis. The sergeant on the desk approved the day. Frank wasn't going to worry about the NYPD on his day off. What for? Summonses; lost vacation days? Too bad. What else could matter if Kat wasn't in his life?

After a while Frank forced himself into the shower and turned the water on as hot as he could bear it, hoping the steam would clear him a bit. Exhausted, he sat in the tub with his knees up, the water pelting his head. Rather than think of the honeymoon, he remembered their last trip before they married, when they professed real and honest love for each other. It was at a small inn in Cape Cod. They had even gotten silly drunk and climbed into the tub with their cloths on laughing and getting soaked.

Frank began feeling drowsy from the hot water. Yet he continued to fantasize about Kathleen. He thought about the sweetness between her legs as he took hold of his limp dick. And though he had not had sex with his wife in what seemed like an eternity, he couldn't jerk off. Thoughts of her depressed him more than aroused him.

CHAPTER 19

Before Frank knocked on Officer Caputo's door he stopped in the driveway and lit a smoke. A couple of things had come to light that afternoon. In regards to the lost radio, there were harsh words in the captain's office; obviously because he was just fed up with the whole idea that Frank was dragging it out. Frank and Brian were there, said little, while the captain seated behind his desk scowled. He looked like a mean school dean about to expel a student for smoking in the hall. The captain immediately brought up summons activity. Frank tried using the excuse of visiting victims as time consuming. "I don't give a crap about your excuse Officer Colleri! Victim visits are ordered from the commissioner's office. My office needs productivity. The only victim I do care about is the one you didn't visit. Officer Caputo! Do you remember her? She should already know who you are so you better get your ass over there soon-real soon officer, understood? The only reason you're not bounced yet is because of your sergeant." In the end, it was a ten day penalty. If Frank disagreed he would have to fight it in the department trial room. He was warned his days in CPOP were numbered if he didn't get on board with activity. To further the perverse amusement, Callahan thanked the captain as they left the office. *What a suck ass. I could have done a better job defending myself.* Frank said nothing to his delegate, instead he just went on patrol.

Frank stomped his cigarette. Caputo answered the door dressed in a plain dark sweatshirt and blue jeans. Her hair was pinned back with a white clip exposing a lovely face and dark, but soft eyes. "Officer Caputo?" he said.

"Come in. I'm Ann....and you?"

"Frank."

Ann offered tea or coffee. "Tea," he said. He liked coffee but tea sounded more soothing. He looked around to get a feel of the person. The living room was small but cozy, with a long couch, a sitting chair, some decorative lamps, family photos and nice knickknacks. One photo struck him, it was Ann in a family portrait with her parents. She was wearing beautiful white pearls, the size of baby peas. *Aren't pearls the jewels of innocence?* It was hard to imagine a crime had been committed right here. What was even harder to believe was the girl's strength, to still live in the place she was brutally attacked in. Frank thought he was going to meet some strung out cop broad who would still be an unbelievable emotional wreck.

"Sit," she said. Ann put down a cup in front of Frank then sat at the other end of sofa. She was smiling and Frank eased into his purpose for being there. His rhetoric would be a bit different since he didn't have to go into the whole crime pamphlet thing. The police department was taking care of her financial and immediate personal needs. Instead, Frank talked of the small things he could possibly assist her with, maybe errands or something, to make her life a little easier. He also apologized for his presence and having to drudge up the incident. He told her he was sorry and that he felt uncomfortable.

Ann suggested he drop the police formality. She'd heard it all, knew why he was there, but she wanted him to know it wasn't necessary to behave like he had to be there officially.

"I know about the whole, 'can I get you something bit.'"

"It's not—"

"Yes, it is. You're thinking why not a female? And you're right, in theory. But I have all the female help necessary. I understand it's your beat, but I don't need a gofer. Leave if you want. I won't say a word except that you did your job politely."

Frank explained the CPOP scrutiny and the PC's personal involvement.

She smiled benevolently. "I know, and it makes sense. The PC figures the citizens of New York will be comforted by more police being geographically sighted according to where these things occur."

"Exactly."

"Not to mention his daughter was busting his balls."

Both laughed and Frank asked, "Would it be too much if I stayed for another cup of tea?"

"Not at all," she replied.

He watched her move into the kitchen and he couldn't help but wonder why bad things always happen to good people. Ann was surprisingly pleasant for a cop who had just been through hell.

She returned with two slivers of coffee cake. "Cake?"

"Sure."

"Are you married, Frank?"

Frank smiled. "Why ask that famous question?"

"Perhaps to start a conversation," she said coyly.

Frank's face retracted to a frown. "Well...yes I am."

Ann picked up on the sadness. "I'm sorry," she said.

"No, it's fine. I guess I don't really know what I am at the moment."

"Any children?"

"No." He looked away as if asking to change the subject.

"Do you like being a CPOP cop Frank?"

When she said his name, it brought back another memory. Jenna asked the same question once. There was an unexplainable feeling that you've known this person longer than you really have, and maybe you're about to embark on something really special. He wondered if his arrival here was leading to a friendship. Or perhaps it was his loneliness, his longing for a female friend. Of course, the guys would find this all amusing, and Sean, and most likely Sharpy, would try to take her out, but weren't female friends really the best kind...

"Well?" she prompted.

"Truthfully?" he finally said.

She nodded yes as she gingerly bit into a forkful of cake.

His face displayed seriousness in his hesitation. "It really sucks," he said. They looked at each other and laughed. There was a familiar connection.

"I'm glad I turned it down then," she said lifting her fork in a mock toast. "Heard it was probably going to be boring, community meetings with civilians, discussing things that might never pan out, you know, the more things change and all that jazz. Sounds good in theory but I like the radio car and 9-1-1 calls myself."

Without trying to get into too much detail Frank explained with brief cynicism the sour taste he had towards the job. Not just the CPOP unit but the entire NYPD, its patrolmen's union, and civilians at large.

"Small group," Ann joked. "But that's no surprise. Many cops start hating the job after a while. We come on with certain hopes of I'll do this or that but—"

"But all the losers make you hate it," he said. "Our own people."

Ann then surprised Frank by working the conversation into her personal life. She told him about her visits to the psychiatrist, of course explaining it with humor. "It's no secret that I visit, or should I say the job orders me to visit, a department shrink." Ann positioned herself to a Freudian mimic pretending to have paper and pencil in hand. "The guy is straight out of a movie. Round glasses, beard and all...'Tell me officer,' he says, 'Tell me how do you feel? Are you angry? Are you sleeping well? Are you eating well? Do you have all the support you need? Tell me of your family, your background,' and of course, the all important, 'Do you feel like committing suicide?'"

Frank was astonished to be allowed in the window of her life.

Still in Freudian mode, she said, "'Would you like to resolve issues of guilt officer?'" Ann sat back and spoke as herself. "What bull. And these are the people who will decide when I can carry a gun again."

"Some job, eh?"

"Sure is."

"How come a male doctor?"

"Oh, because it's the job, it's all generic. I don't mind. I actually found a nice woman therapist through my own but haven't made a definite appointment yet."

She reached for a smoke, offering Frank one. After lighting a cigarette Frank tried a desperate attempt at humor by imitating his wife. He squinted one eye and pitched his voice. "I'm sick of you Frank. I'm tired...I don't love you that way..." He stopped and sat back.

"Frank, I had a feeling. Obviously, your wife, right?" He nodded. "Don't worry, Frank. I get the feeling you're a nice guy. It will work out. Your wife should realize that all couples hit snags, saying and doing things they don't mean to."

They were sitting there, two people who didn't know each other, connecting through honest and humorous grief. Naturally, Frank was sorry about what happened to Ann, but he was glad to have met her and he genuinely enjoyed her company. It was true, he despised some female cops, like most male officers. Whether they were doing nothing at work and still getting all the breaks, or just because a few of them were vulgar whores who had screwed over cops stupid enough to fall in love. A different reason for each male cop.

With Ann, it was as if she weren't even a cop. And now he didn't want to ruin it with the extension of time, so he excused himself by lying that he had an appointment with the captain. He thanked her for the tea and cake and the talk they shared. He handed her a card with the CPOP office number on it and told her to call if there was anything he could do.

"Stop by again, Frank," she said.

"I probably will have to anyway," he said smiling.

Ann extended her hand. "Goodbye."

When she closed the door, Frank was sorry he decided to leave.

* * * *

Ann sat back on the couch, turned the television on and wondered for a moment about Officer Colleri. He possessed a melancholy, and strangely they clicked as human beings, not so much sexual as bonding in a sadness that seemed to hang in the air. Did he understand her great pain? That if she didn't feel that connection she would never have offered tea or extra time because she was tiring of all the forced attention?

Later Frank was walking down the stairs to the CPOP office when one of the female cops passed him. Officer Kane was short and squat, with a bowl like haircut, not at all feminine, but she was friendly. "Hello Frank."

"Hey Rita, how goes it?"

"Were 62 (in stationhouse), Beatrice has a robbery collar."

"Cool."

"Easy one. White trash kid, over eighteen, robs a kid's bike. Your buddy Gallo tells us exactly where he is." Kane started laughing. "Kid gives big B a hard time, she smacks him right off the bike. Anyways I'm not bad. Haven't seen you out."

"Been laying low, but I'll see you soon."

"See ya soon." Officer Kane continued on her way.

"Hey Frank. I heard you. You looking to go out with that hose monster?" Gallo joked. At the bottom of the stairs Gallo playfully dug his fingers into Frank's shoulder blades. "What's getting into you? Just because there's trouble in paradise don't mean you should go slumming for the first blow job you can get. Be choosy."

"Your right, Art." Frank was stringing him along. "I must be losing it. By the way I heard you gave them a robbery collar. You do have a heart."

"Easy one from a snitch, and I think Bea needed to get on the sheet."

The snitch has to be John Wayne, Frank thought.

"Hey Frank, I heard you had to take the heavy hit."

"Word, as usual, travels fast."

"Don't sweat it Frank. You'll make it up." Gallo covered his mouth feigning a cough. "Flu can be a bitch. Keep us out for at least ten days."

Frank faked the same cough. "Yeah, you're right Art, as a matter of fact I feel one coming on real soon." Gallo walked away laughing. Frank sighed.

CHAPTER 20

There was only a light mist falling when Peter got to his car. Still, roads were deceptively slick and could be a gliding battleground for tons of metal machinery. The entrance to the parkway was short and curved, almost circular. There was at least one light pole and a half-dozen trees lining the grassy area.

When the police found Peter Colleri he was lying face down towards the passenger side of his Cadillac. Blood soaked his hair. Since the officers were first at the scene, and an ambulance had not arrived yet, they nervously began to administer first aid. They felt a pulse, and thankfully, heard moans and groans. The ambulance arrived and the medics took over. They treated Peter's initial wounds, wrapped him in a blanket and rushed to the nearest hospital.

Peter's injuries appeared to be severe so the cops on scene had no alternative but to call in an accident investigation team to decipher a logical reason for the cause of the accident. Was it drugs? Was it alcohol? Was it a mental incapacity? Or did the driver just lose control?

Peter's Cadillac was crushed, the nose mangled from the impact with a tree that fell like a timber. Glass from the windshield and headlights was strewn everywhere, looking like pellets of ice glistening on the tarmac. The dashboard was cracked in the middle, opening through the gape in the front hood. The steering wheel had also been split open where the driver might have first hit his head. Since the driver couldn't carry on a conversation it was undetermined if he crawled across the seat or was thrown by the impact. "Man, I hope this is anything but a drunk incident," one of the cops said. One thing was certain. Had the driver owned any car smaller than the tank he was driving, he would have been killed instantly.

After the cops retrieved the driver's wallet, they found that his emergency contact was Frank Colleri, a New York City Police Officer.

Frank panicked at the sight of two uniformed cops at his front door. However, when they assured him his brother was conscious, Frank was then able to take a deep breath. He was told, "If a family member had seen the car first they would immediately think their loved one was dead." The officers handed Frank the wallet. "Obviously, it was the mini-shield and PBA card that made it easier to notify you," the female cop said.

"He's at Nassau General," the other cop said. "Come on we'll take you there."

"Thank you, officers. But I think I'll drive over."

When the cops left, Frank picked up the phone and dialed the precinct desk number.

"Sergeant Nolan, how can I help you?"

Oh no. Just what I need. He was sure Nolan suspected him and his buddies of the photo distribution and knew Nolan would give him a hard time about the day off, though he would go over Nolan's head if he had to. "Hi Sarge, it's Colleri from CPOP."

"Yes, Colleri." Nolan was firm.

"Sarge, my brother's been in a car accident. I don't know all the details, but I have to get to the hospital. I need the day."

Nolan told Frank without hesitation, "It's done. Praying everything is alright. Let us know if there's anything you need."

A very tall nurse with bright eyes stopped him at the emergency door. "It's my brother—the car accident!" Frank informed her as he flashed his shield for courtesy.

Her voice was pleasant. "Sir, I understand your worry, just give us a minute please."

"I'll be right here miss. I want to know soon. Real soon."

The nurse reappeared a few moments later. Frank moved to her quickly. "He's stable Mr. Colleri. Give us about fifteen minutes. I'll let you see him. In the meantime, you have a call. Use the phone on the wall hit seven."

"Thank you," Frank said.

"Frank, how's Peter?"

"Sean, hey. I don't know the extent of his injuries but judging from everybody's demeanor I think he's gonna be okay...Word travels fast."

"Nolan got in touch with Moore. Me and John are gonna meet you at the hospital."

"No. Sean I appreciate it but you'll just be sitting around. No problem, but I appreciate it."

"You sure, Frank?"

"I'm sure, buddy." After he hung up he thought about calling his mother and father. *Better wait. No sense in scaring the shit out of them.*

Amazing what one can think of in an hour. Frank reflected on the past and tears began to water his face. His brother. "We're close? Aren't we God?" He thought of the small problems when he and Peter lived together. He smiled as he thought of dirty dishes, an unwashed tub, and socks everywhere. When they were kids: little league, Peter would comfort him when he struck out one too many times. Sitting on their bedroom floor playing with toys all day...Oh how adult life snuck up on them.

Despite the sight of Peter wearing a helmet of bandages like a turban, along with taped gauze extending the length of his right cheek bone down his swollen jaw, his eyes appeared alert.

"You're so lucky you're not dead, or crippled brother!"

With clenched teeth and barely audible Peter was able to gasp, "All good bro."

"Don't talk." Frank stayed with his brother through the night.

* * * *

When he returned home there were phone messages from Arthur Gallo, Sergeant Nolan, John Bennett, Joe and Teddy...and Kathleen, her soft voice expressing sincere concern. Nolan and Bennett. Frank suddenly felt guilty about his two-faced participation in pranks against those two.

A few days later Peter, though banged up, was going to be just fine. Frank returned to work and the real world. Almost every cop in the stationhouse offered well wishes, especially his CPOP squad where the back slapping seemed more intimate, almost embarrassing.

"Everything good Frank?" Moore asked as he offered up a fond smile and a handshake as he got up from his desk. "See you later, Frank."

Another nice guy, Frank thought. *He didn't even bother me with any work, not to mention he backed me the whole way with the CO. Now, where do I begin? I have to catch up somewhere.*

Frank went through his message box hoping for another word from Kathleen, there wasn't any.

CHAPTER 21

Frank had never given the crime of rape or its victims much thought. The mention of rape around the job usually made for coy remarks inside a misogynist locker room. 'Was she good-looking?' 'Probably said yes, then last minute said no.' Now that the brass turned down the heat, concentrating once again on crack cocaine and biased incidents, there was no reason to continue these visits on a regular basis.

Leaning back at the desk he skimmed the newspaper hoping to read just through entertainment articles, the ones that didn't require much of an attention span. But it seemed that whenever Frank picked up a newspaper or magazine, articles about relationships, divorce or drinking loomed. Lately, he also noticed, rape and its tentacles of sexual assault or sexual harassment were all over. There had been a number of high profile rapes in New York City. Specifically, in Central Park and another on the Downtown Ferry. Even the advice columns contained questions and answers about the issue of rape. Frank found it interesting that most rapes go unreported, and the ones that are reported, are usually not false claims, regardless of opinion.

Many victims refused to prosecute. Embarrassment being at the top of their list. Many were terrified with doubts and being ripped apart on a witness stand by defense attorneys who would attempt to portray them as whores. 'WERE YOU DRINKING MS?' 'DID YOU AGREE TO THE DATE?' 'WHAT WERE YOU WEARING THAT NIGHT?' 'WEREN'T YOU THE ONE WHO APPROACHED THIS MAN TO GO OUT WITH YOU?' Compounding these issues was the fact that most perpetrators prosecuted for rape don't get convicted.

Most victims were attacked near their home and not by strangers. Another sad fact was that many husbands and boyfriends of the victims refused to discuss the incidents with their partners. Frank moved to the back of the paper, to the sports. His interest in baseball always peaked this time of year with a fresh new season and high hopes for a new ensemble of Yankees. As he fingered through the paper he noticed a small article: **Police Chief felt racially profiled!** Apparently, a black NYPD chief was pulled over in Bayside Queens by two young white officers, they choked and couldn't give a good reason for the car stop. It was under investigation. *Well, now I see why priorities are going to switch to racial bias.*

* * * *

Ann Caputo also thumbed through the news, though maybe she shouldn't have. Women were often writing in search for validation. Becoming a victim wasn't their fault. Even in the cases of date rape. This caused her great concern about her own future. As a rookie, she had responded to an alleged rape where the perpetrator was a police officer. She wondered why she and her male partner gave the cop the benefit of the doubt.

"Ann, this guy will lose his job. We have to be certain." Thankfully, the patrol sergeant responded and made the final decision to arrest.

Ann wondered if someone had intentionally stalked her because of the way she dressed or how she might have acted on one occasion. She read that many women escape potential danger by remaining near families; protected in numbers. Did seeking an apartment to be independent cause the assault? Yet she chose to return to her apartment. Her parents, aware of her determination, didn't push the issue too much. As compensation Ann allowed them to purchase new carpets, drapes, a couch. Her father even painted the walls a bright color. When Ann overheard her father say to her mother, "I'd have no problem cutting that scumbags balls off," she felt a sense of pride. Her father wanting to exact revenge, for the little guy. In this case, his little girl. She truly admired her parents.

Ann's thoughts were on the laws of castration. The notion that therapy could help these tortured souls was ludicrous. Ann read about man and his dark side, his primal urges and prowess. Irritation turned to disgust. Statements about male identity struggles, and sex as a tool for manhood, and aggressive eroticism. Men themselves were victim of horrible abuse, vulnerable and as frightened as children. She was appalled. How dare they. How dare they have any excuse for their testosterone filled self-gratification. A woman could be naked and still have the right to say no for Christ sake.

She would eventually have to stop reading newspapers and distract herself with a book. Not a harlequin romance, but some historical adventure from another time and place. She would also need to spend more time with her best friend Allison.

* * * *

"Crime sells Allison. Listen to this article on prevention..." Ann read aloud: Avoid walking and cycling paths, not wearing headphones, no tag keys for car or home, demanding ID for anyone calling or coming inside the home, only put initials on the mailbox, keeping doors and windows locked while sitting in traffic. Ann shook her head. "What if it was 100 degrees and the air-conditioner didn't work? Do we live in such a primitive world? Are you fucking kidding me? This is how I have to live?"

"Ann, that's how it is. Those really aren't off the wall suggestions. Stop reading all this. Come on Ann let's get out of here and get us something to eat."

"Have you ever heard any of the guys joke, 'Beautiful stuck up or snotty bitches should be put in their place?' Does that mean guys we know are capable—"

"Please, Ann, let's eat, I'm starving...you need to get out." At diner, Allison apologized. "Ann, I shouldn't change the subject on you. If you want to vent then go ahead. I'll listen to you every day if need be. But I still want you to keep the appointment with the female therapist, it'll help."

With sadness and downward eyes Ann replied, "Thanks Al, you've been such a constant in my life that it's taking away from yours. And yes, I'll get on that."

Allison put Ann's hand's in hers. "No way."

Her mind still off the charts, Ann wanted to tell Allison a story about a TV show she'd seen but unselfishly refrained. One evening, avoiding news channels she stopped on channel 13. The focus was on the history of the American Indian. The narrator was reporting about some of the wilder tribes who roamed the early nineteenth century. There were tribes who believed it honorable to descend upon innocents and savagely rape and murder them.

"What are you thinking about?"

Ann took an exaggerated breath. "Al. I confess, of course only to you...The idea of flirting with a priest, and the CPOP cop. Oh, my God...I do sometimes wish I were dead."

"Not unnatural. Give yourself a break. I can't say for sure but I probably would be worse. You know I responded to an EDP run once, before all this. A young girl's home. She had previously been sexually assaulted and now felt like killing herself. She was seventeen! She trusted her boyfriend. I was immediately sympathetic to her because I too thought it was a normal reaction...but because she said it, well you know, she had to go to the psych ward. Having to put handcuffs on the girl broke my heart."

Allison leaned forward. "Sometimes nothing we can do. Ann, look at me." Ann's smile was slight as she returned eye contact, her dark eyes soulful. Allison continued, "Sweetie, I promise you will be fine. And, yes, this won't prevent you from eventually finding that right someone, keeping in mind that boys will be boys."

The girls giggled a little and Ann said, "I'm not stupid. I know what most of them want, especially the guys at work."

"Well they ain't all bad. Sure, they have high testosterone but it comes with the territory. The job has never seen so many women hired. Now the boys club is surrounded by us beauties," Allison mockingly pursed her lips together, "and they don't know how to handle it. The old-timers taught them it wasn't natural for women to make decisions regarding serious police matters yet here we are and they want to sleep with us."

"Even the old-timers Al, don't kid yourself."

"Oh, I know but they won't admit it. Still, even as we complain you know most of the guys we work with will back us up in a second remembering we're cops first."

"I agree," Ann said. "I realize their plight. A male cop is supposed to be a tough guy and a horn dog." The girls laughed out loud.

"Sure, take my partner."

Ann squinted. "Yes, the macho, Tommy Labertino."

"Believe it or not he's a softy. Sure, he brags about notches in his bed post but the guy, when mellow, talks heavy shit."

"I know. I've seen him in action in the bars and I've worked with him. We talked about life and relationships. The loss of his parents. I knew he was hurting when his last steady girlfriend left him." Ann winced and whispered, "But I could still feel his body language. And he wanted me."

"Everyone wants sweet innocent Ann," Allison joked. "But yes, he was devastated. Especially since the girl left for another woman. How's that on the male police ego?"

"When I go back I'm afraid of the reception I'll get," Ann said losing her smile.

"Ann, of course it will be hard. But you're well liked. It won't be that bad, and I'll smack down anyone that gives you a wrong eyeball." Allison waved her hand and blew a short whistle and Ann's smile returned.

Allison shook her head slowly from side to side mocking, "Sure you are the princess who doesn't want a steady partner, and you prefer bouncing around, filling in sector cars and you like your foot posts, and no one could figure it out, but it's only because everyone wants to work with you. You're a good cop my friend."

"We should have been partners, girl."

"I know," Allison replied. "But if I dumped Tom for you it would really crush him. A second time a woman dumped him for a woman—geez, I'm sorry…"

Ann leaned in and grabbed her friend's hands tight with sincerity, "You made me smile today Al. Thanks my friend. You made it normal for me."

Once home and alone Ann sat at her kitchen counter and starred into a cup of tea. She picked up the spoon and clutched it tightly in her hand. She flipped it and pressed the thin edge into her skin, wondering what it would feel like to drive the metal through her wrist. She was shaking when she dropped the spoon and began to cry again.

Too much time on my hands. I need to work even if it's desk duty.

CHAPTER 22

Eventually, Sergeant Nolan decided against any supervisory retaliation against the cruel humor inflicted upon him. Since he'd been on desk duty there were no further pranks directed towards him. On a Friday night Nolan was back on patrol filling in for another sergeant who needed the day off. That same day John Eaton and Arthur Gallo were all doing an odd CPOP tour of 1400 x 2235 (2pm x 10:35pm). They didn't have to stand in formation roll call, all that was needed for them was notifying the desk officer they were present for duty, then signing the CPOP log.

After roll call Nolan dismissed the troops. The cops began hanging around the muster room as well as the area in front of the desk and the radio room, waiting to relieve the day tour. Gallo, trying not to appear suspicious, was hovering around the switchboard pretending to be taking a call. He was counting on Nolan going to the bathroom before going on patrol.

If any of the patrol cops tried walking into the bathroom Gallo planned to quickly intercede or warn not to use the middle urinal. And if the dumb cop did, then so be it, the boys would still roar with laughter and there was always tomorrow for Nolan. Gallo was delighted to be on a prank with Eaton. The big guy was forever breaking balls and this was right up his alley. It was Gallo who noticed that Nolan liked to pee in the middle.

As if on cue, Nolan walked to the bathroom. There would be no tomorrow.

"Yes," Gallo murmured to himself. He moved to the stairwell and let go a short whistle to signal Eaton. The outgoing platoon was bustling about, chit-chatting; nightsticks, keys, cuffs and utility equipment clinking and clanking from their waists, waiting for their assigned radios and RMPs.

Suddenly, a frantic Nolan came running from the bathroom and all heads turned. Nolan began screaming. "Those sonavabitches. Those sonavabitches!"

There wasn't a cop in the house who didn't burst with laughter.

Nolan surveyed the room for possible suspects, it was hopeless. He wiped his wet hair and shirt with his hands to no avail, then, turning away embarrassed, he walked straight to the stairwell and up to the sergeant's locker room. He was unaware that he passed the culprits responsible for him being soaking wet from the waist up. From the moment he flushed and was hit with an immediate burst of spraying water, he knew the pranks wouldn't stop.

Nolan opened his locker and grabbed an old towel. He began dabbing his head and shirt. His piousness was feeling thin as he slammed his fist into the locker. His teeth were clenched and he could not help mouthing a couple more 'scumbags.' After changing his shirt and running a comb through his hair he headed back down to try to resume patrol duties. He was casual as he went behind the desk to check roll call again. He mumbled something to the desk officer who was trying to hide his grin. Later, the desk sergeant told some of the cops that Nolan whispered to him that he had to get transferred out of this precinct. Nolan spent the rest of the tour quietly annoyed. He spoke to his driver and some cops only as it pertained to police business. This time he attempted no retaliation and no running to the captain. He remained a non-combative target.

Meanwhile the pranksters retreated merrily back to the CPOP office, their humorous task successful. "That was hysterical," Eaton said.

Bennett, sitting at Moore's desk said, "I caught the tail end. It looked like Nolan was going to go off the deep end."

"Well fuck him if he can't take a joke," Eaton said.

"My sentiments exactly Sharpy," Gallo agreed.

Bennett gathered his things and headed for the door.

"What, dude? Afraid you'll get in trouble if some boss winds up coming down here?"

Gallo snickered.

CHAPTER 23

Peter Colleri was adamant. He wanted to go to his apartment, to recuperate, though he appreciated Frank's offer to stay with him. "Don't worry brother. I'm good. Between you and friends it'll be fine. So what if I look like a mummy, I feel okay."

"Can't wait to fuck up again? Recuperate? Yeah right...you just want to go out again," Frank joked. "Just remember to call our parents and not let on about the accident." The brothers parted with an awkward side to shoulder hug.

As he walked to meet Walsh at the diner Frank wondered if he should call Nina. He hadn't had sex recently and his fantasies were making him yearn for a warm body. Still, it was a bad idea because after sex with Nina the warm feeling would end. Even though he was horny, he also needed to hold someone with genuine affection. He lit a smoke taking a deep drag.

Walsh surprised Frank with news that he was thinking about letting his girlfriend move in with him. Karen was a beautiful stewardess with bright green eyes, blond hair, and a killer body.

"How long do you know Karen? About a minute? I only met Karen a few times—"

"What's the matter, buddy?" Sean asked. "You don't think I'm the domestic kind?"

Frank burst out a short laugh. "Since you mention it...no I don't. Besides you're asking the wrong guy."

"What about nurse Jenna?" Sean asked.

"What about her?"

"C'mon, Frank. The girl is obviously hot for you. She lights up whenever we run into her, and always mentions you. Quite frankly I'm surprised it's not me she's really after...Are you gonna bang her?"

Frank smiled. "You're right. I myself am surprised that someone thought of me before you."

"Frank, a couple of dates and her pants will come flying off. But if not, there's always that Spanish chick. And you certainly don't need much on your mind to be with her."

"Well, to tell you the truth, it's bland, you know not being personal and all."

Sean peered at Frank. "Don't give me that. Since when? Hey, I told you about the poppy thing. No matter how Americanized, they still call you poppy. Besides you're a single man again."

"Not quite. And Nina's half Spanish."

"Whatever, get on with it. Soon you'll be back in business with the broads. Forget the Irish princess. The weather's getting nice, they'll be out in force."

"You really think Kathleen's getting laid Sean?"

"I'm sorry buddy. I know you think she's this good girl...there's no such thing as a truly good girl or a really bad girl." Sean paused, ran his fingers through his wavy hair, as if he wondered if he should continue. "Sure there're the girls that are easy; more so than other chicks. Sluts who do it for the sheer pleasure. But in the end, truth be told, even the good ones, given the right time, the right moment, they're like us. They need sex too. See that Greek waitress? I bet she would like it in the—"

"I get it Sean."

Sean was usually right on matters of the opposite sex. It probably was true. Kathleen feels horny too, and the recipient of her lust won't be me anymore. She has to be on someone's dick....

"You in there, buddy?" Walsh said.

"You're probably right Sean it's inevitable. She's getting laid."

"Well, believe it or not, that's a sign your getting better."

* * * *

Frank was enjoying the changed weather, wandering up a side street after passing the municipal lot where he saw John Wayne's old Dodge. Unbelievably the car was registered, according to Gallo, and since there were no civilians complaining about it Gallo let him park occasionally.

Frank's head wasn't in the game. He certainly didn't want to be caught in a situation with his head in a fog. He wished he could take the brain from his head and wash her out. But it was the same as if someone told him not to think about pink elephants. It would be planted in his head like a cartoon. Sean was right. He'd traveled far in his struggle. If he made it this far without total destruction, then he would hang in there a little while longer, and with time, peace would follow as well as meeting more women.

The day was getting dark and the wind was picking up. Frank leaned against a commercial building and lit a butt, unfazed by the dust kicking up on his uniform.

He had been smoking like a chimney of late. He damn well knew the reason. He didn't hate her; he loved her still. He looked at the cigarette and decided to toss it into the street where it landed next to a crack vial.

Drugs are here forever, he thought.

ohn Bennett slowly walked from the shadow of the ICO's office, slouched, looking like a beaten man. He would harbor his frustrations for days to come, no one would guess he was a cannon about to go off. In the world of buddy cops and the Thin Blue Line, if another officer had noticed Bennett's state of mind, the most the observer would do was tell a PBA delegate. Very rarely would a patrolman go to a boss and say this or that officer was a danger to themselves or others.

A few days after Bennett's meeting with the ICO, Frank noticed him sitting alone in front of his locker. No one else appeared to be in the locker room. Frank watched as Bennett wiped his eyes and choked out a grunt. Bennett's sneakers were untied and his T-shirt hung out over his jeans. He was obviously a man in no hurry to go anywhere. Frank purposely cleared his throat catching Bennett's attention.

"Hey Frank."

"Hey buddy, how's it going?"

"I'm fine dude."

"Sure?"

"Sure."

Frank squeezed John's shoulder but said no more; respecting Bennett's privacy, he moved along. It seemed to Frank, Bennett was desperately fighting the pain of another pending divorce. Frank understood such pain.

The precinct's Integrity Control Officer (ICO) was Lieutenant Patrick Reilly. He didn't have to pretend to be a scumbag, he fit the bill. He was a big man, over six feet tall, with a massive bald head and a large round nose that always seemed to shine a bit of blarney. He was a classic throwback from the old days when big tough Irish cops ruled the department. The difference was Lt. Reilly was a true rat. He spent ten years as a sergeant in the hated IAD unit until he was promoted to lieutenant. He was sent to the precinct to break the balls of every patrolman human enough to commit a minor infraction. He could spot a cop getting a free cup of coffee from a block away.

Reilly was determined to reward himself back into IAD. His motto, which was really his excuse, was, "If you take something for free you'll owe that someone. And a police officer should not be in such a position." His job as ICO was one of constant monitoring, checking the comings and goings of all the police officers, whether they were in the stationhouse or on patrol. He would continuously check the precinct logs to assess where a cop was at a certain time, and if that cop was supposed to be where procedure dictated. For instance, if the cop was in the stationhouse, that officer should be signed in a log and announce the reason, whether it was for meal, for paperwork, or for a twenty-minute allotted personal break. The same went for a cop out on patrol. Reilly should know their assigned sectors or foot posts, and check that they were within their assignment boundaries. Reilly's job was also to oversee a sergeant's evaluation of his cops, and if he disagreed, it would be duly noted, he would warn the sergeant that one of his cops hinged on negligence. But the key job as the title implied was **Integrity.** Here, Reilly enjoyed testing the officers. He would act as a trap, dressing in his own PD blues and wearing the silver shield of patrol rather than his gold Lieutenant's shield. He would then go into food establishments rumored to give their food to the cops on patrol. On the arm, is what the expression is, and that's what he hoped to find. And if the food was free, Reilly would gladly accept it as a perk then stake the place out spying for any other cop coming in to receive a free meal.

Still another duty was to monitor the precinct summonses, the issuance, and various paperwork insuring proper clarification. Reilly also would check the minor violations log, a book that kept a record of each police officer's small discretions such as shoes being not shined, need for a haircut, unshaved, tardiness and other unavoidable habits that come with any job. If a cop was put in this log three times or more, it was Reilly's job to draw up a command discipline against that officer.

If a cop signed off duty two minutes early Reilly would catch it. The CO gave Reilly free reign to do as he wished, thus he, the CO, wouldn't look like the bad guy. Reilly was commissioned to compile his own ICO paperwork trail. He even took the work home with him, dissecting the precinct's performance. His homework paid off. The precinct had racked up over fifty command disciplines for the year so far, most which would have been regarded as nonsense in the past.

Reilly had a knack for requesting penalties that were higher than what a violation called for. He would ask the CO for one-day penalties from any cop who was late three times.

Scumbag.

He requested four hours taken from a cop who failed to fill a car's gas tank at the end of a tour.

Scumbag.

He got four hours taken from a pair of cops who were out of their sector talking to some girls by the local college.

Scumbag.

He pushed to take a day from one cop who he caught off post just because he didn't like the lackadaisical way the cop fell in line during roll call at the beginning of the tour.

Scumbag.

The cops hated Reilly and were circulating ideas of retaliation towards him either through damage to his private car or maybe something in his office. But the PBA delegates rebuffed the idea. The delegate's position: Let's just wait. Reilly could get transferred any day. He could have people here transferred. Nobody wants to be set an example of and get kicked out of the precinct. Let's not make it worse for all of us right now. Even after Reilly would bag his biggest hit, the delegates still backed off; telling their troops to wait.

The veteran police officer had been at the 117th for ten years and enjoyed his steady foot post with weekends off. The officer, sort of a '60s reject, with an artist's mustache and hair growing over his ears, was well liked by just about everyone who owned a shop on his post. Reilly caught this patrolman having a free slice of pizza and decided that would be the most expensive slice the cop ever ate. 'Skinny' Polis lost fifteen vacation days and was transferred to another precinct, the furthest south in the borough. It was an extremely vicious move on the part of any supervisor. Also ironic, considering many of the 'rats' were hypocrites who enjoyed many a free meal in their past. It was a testament to Reilly's power.

Now Reilly eyed a new target: John Bennett. The accident report Bennett filled out in connection with the expressway accident would come back to haunt him.

The young girl who was badly injured in the accident later died of head injuries at the hospital. Bennett was the officer of record that day and should have notified the accident unit. Unfortunately, his mind was elsewhere. Adding to the problem, he worked with an old timer that day who just didn't care or help much, leaving all the paperwork up to the junior partner. When Bennett arrived on the scene the young girl, though badly hurt and bleeding, was obviously still alive, and when she was taken to the hospital by ambulance Bennett never thought to ask the seriousness of her condition. He also never checked with the hospital on an update of her condition. A careless oversight that wouldn't have been like Bennett had he been in his normal frame of mind. Usually cops would accompany the victim at a crash site to the hospital, stay until a notification was made to a family member, but Bennett agreed with the old timer to a short cut, to check the notification box and put the name of the person notified in the caption, the name that they found on the paperwork in the glove box, obviously a relative.

The trail of blundered paperwork led back to Bennett. Reilly advised the CO not to bring the matter up to the officer or his union reps just yet. He knew behind his back he was considered a scumbag. Reilly didn't care. He had no remorse when dealing with a cop's misfortune. He wrote up the command discipline himself, usually he would just order the squad sergeant to draw up the paperwork.

As much of a mean bastard as he was, no one could figure out why he wanted to take apart such a nice guy. Was he a union hater? Did the unauthorized slowdown of summons activity twist his balls?

Bennett arrived to work one day sluggish. Immediately after turning out of roll call he got called to Reilly's office, without a delegate present. Reilly, thirsty for his kill, wasted no time getting to the point. "We have a little problem, Officer Bennett," Reilly said, mocking concern by rubbing a hand over his bald head. "I really had no choice in the matter and I had to, by procedure, write you up for failure to take police action. Are you aware of the situation officer? Is there anything you can comment about it?"

Bennett responded, "Excuse me, Lieutenant. You know I need a delegate."

"You prepared a report officer..." Reilly picked up a copy of the accident report lying on his desk and he scanned the paper for the date, though he already had it memorized. He reminded Bennett of the exact time and date as if he were looking at it fresh. While Reilly spoke about the girl's death Bennett recollected the image of a small blue car hanging on a guardrail.

"Are you sure there's nothing you could offer, officer?" Reilly asked.

"Well..." Bennett had a slight headache growing bigger now. He tightened his eyes a second. "Well Lieutenant, where's my delegate if I've already been written up and going to be questioned?"

Reilly was a man who thought any answer from a cop was a smart aleck reply and didn't like it even if it came from a cop not reputed to be a smart ass. "Yes, certainly..." The lieutenant was agitated. "That's certainly your right, officer. However, I didn't have the time to track one down and I felt it necessary to inform you, rightly I might add, of the disciplinary actions. Which, by the way, officer, look as though you're facing substantial time, probably the maximum if we don't straighten this out."

Bennett uncharacteristically raised his voice. "What... what are you talking about? The maximum?"

"Officer, I would watch my tone if I were you." Reilly lowered his head, sat silent for a moment then suddenly waved Bennett off. "You know what, officer? You can go now. We'll discuss this another time."

"But Lieutenant, what the hell—"

Reilly cut him short and shot Bennett a cold stare. "I told you, about your tone. You're dismissed. Now go." He pointed to the door like some high school principal.

Bennett turned and left. He tried to decipher this surprise attack from Reilly. *The max,* he thought. *What the hell did he mean by that? Ten days? Fifteen? Twenty? That scumbag is out to get me. What next?* He assumed his delegate would be told and then he would officially be offered a penalty.

A couple of days passed and reality was sinking in; yet still there was silence from Reilly and from the PBA. What was Reilly's game?

Bennett felt a rush of panic. *He's going to drop the hammer right on my head.*

Bennett rifled his calendar book for Callahan's phone number.

CHAPTER 25

Frank never did get around to calling Jenna for a date. He did reach out to Ann Caputo. She seemed pleased to hear from him again as he apologized for not calling sooner.

"No," she said. "It's perfectly fine. As long as your brother is well."

How sweet, Frank thought. Her first thought was to ask after his brother. *How did she know?*

"Would you like to come by?"

"Yes, only this time I was thinking coffee, maybe we could go over to the new café on Francis Lewis Boulevard. Unless you'd prefer tea? Give you a chance, uh, maybe you want to get out?" He hesitated then said, "Tonight. I'll be off duty if that's okay? I don't want you to feel uncomfortable."

"Heard of it. Sure. And coffee will be fine. Off-duty is fine too."

Soon he would see Ann again. He couldn't understand why that made him nervous. It wasn't as if he were going on a date. He knew he couldn't even ask her for one. She certainly wasn't ready. And neither was he. It would be unfair of him to confuse Ann with any propositions.

That evening Frank drove to his brother's with a bag of food for Peter. Peter was almost back to his old self. The medical turban was to keep dirt and infection away from the opened cuts and stitches and keep the wound dry and the swelling down. Still, he decided to stay home from work and parties for a few weeks before a full recovery, or so he said. "This chicken's great Frank," Peter mumbled with a mouth full.

"Glad you like it."

Peter assured Frank everything was fine. He didn't have to call or visit all the time. Frank, not much of a believer, had prayed to God. His brother was his lifeline. Yes, he had close friends but he could confide in his brother like he couldn't with anyone else. "Frank how are—"

"Just like I worry too much, you don't have to keep asking me. I'm fine. And by the way someone else here appears to be fine." Frank pointed to Peter's dark t-shirt. "Are those pot ashes or did you take up smoking cigarettes?"

"Noooo." Peter changed the subject. "Frank if you want to leave your lonely apartment you know you have a home here."

"One day we'll talk about that."

* * * *

Before visiting his brother, Frank had showered, shaved, splashed on cologne, and even brushed his teeth twice, as if it was a real date. He was looking forward to seeing Ann. Since he was off duty he had to find something attractive to wear. He slipped into a pair of casual pants and comfortable shoes. In his closet he found a neat, blue, button down shirt not in apparent need of ironing. He grabbed his soft leather jacket, reached over one last time into the mirror, paying specific attention to the slight recession in his hair line. He tried convincing himself it was not that bad for a man pushing thirty.

His brother once advised him, "If you want to make a chick feel wanted and adored then you simply say her name softly, and directly into her eyes. That's key. You have to be looking in the eyes. She'll melt. They love the sound of their own names."

This wasn't any chick. Ann Caputo was the victim of a crime, fucked over by the recent past; like him. Driving, as his mind had done so many times, he explored the possibility of the darkness within maybe never lifting totally, and that frightened him. The lines between loving and hating. The demand to be loved. Strangely, he felt a sudden urge to demand dominance over the woman he once and possibly still loved, loved no matter how hard he tried to fight it. The feeling of loneliness Kat left him with gave him a total right not to be denied. He deserved to control her just one more time. To feel her closer, by force if necessary, the woman who had deadened his mind. Could he sneak up on his wife like a thief in the night and be with her once more? Hell, didn't most rapists use the excuse of being totally out of it anyway? *Banging my own wife like a wild animal could be interpreted as a drunken night that got out of hand. Just ravaging her. What am I thinking!? I promised myself I wouldn't lapse back to this?*

He dragged hard on a cigarette opening the window to let the air hit him.

Anxious now, Frank needed a drink. If he was going to spend a couple of hours with Ann he needed to regroup. A couple of drinks. Playing on the stereo was the white guy with red hair, who sounded black: Never gonna give you up. Ironic.

CHAPTER 26

After a quick stop at a deli, a couple of tall boy beers and some mints, Frank managed to seep through some of the fog when he arrived at Ann's place. He checked himself in the rearview mirror. He walked slowly up the driveway chewing a mint so it would be dissolved when he greeted Ann.

Somewhere between two roads traveled and nagging convoluted thoughts, Ann also tried to keep under control the obsession she was fighting. How easily she agreed to meet the CPOP cop. Earlier she was involved in a manic pursuit of article reading. She started a story about the mind of a rapist and why men rape. How it's impossible to decipher the sane person from the sick act. How the shock could sometimes linger for years. How hard it was for women to come forward. At least she had done that...and more statistics...and more brutal memories from victims...and exploitation from the scenes of brutality egged on by motion pictures and television, and concern, concern, concern...

What the hell is the difference between power rape and anger rape? And what about the profile. The guy from the ghetto, or the guy who works on Wall Street, or the married guy, or...she fought this for a while as she fought to compose herself. Then the knock at her door and Ann answering the call as politely as she had on their first meeting.

She smiled asking again about Frank's brother. Frank pleasantly suggested they move along to the coffee shop. Ann's slight hesitation gave a hint of discomfort and although she agreed it was fine to move on, Frank sensed that maybe she wasn't ready to venture out of her house for an evening on the boulevard. He surmised she probably was the type of girl that would normally have instantly responded to his suggestion with, "I'd love to" or "Sounds great, let me grab my jacket."

"Listen, Ann, I was wondering. Would you rather not go?" He appeared shy. "Would you rather stay in? I mean it's your place and I wouldn't mind..."

"Then let's stay," she said. "That is, of course, if you really don't mind. I know I thought it would be—"

"I absolutely do *not* mind," he said smiling. As he said the words he noticed it brought a look of relief to Ann. Frank awkwardly stood in the foyer waiting for his invitation to come in, soon received.

"Would you like something else Frank? I'm sorry but I don't have any coffee."

He was thinking about another beer but answered, "Tea is fine." He pointed to the lamp table. "Mind if I use your phone a sec?" He was already halfway there when she said yes.

Sean Walsh picked up on the first ring. "What's up Frankie?"

"I'm still at my brother's buddy. What do you got going for tonight?"

"How's your crazy brother?"

"He's great, thanks buddy. Are you gonna be up at The Ferris tonight?"

"As a matter of fact, I am. Why don't you meet me there around nine thirty."

"Ah, ten is actually better. Maybe ten thirty." Frank looked over to the small kitchen area where Ann was preparing the tea. She was wearing a loose fitting and stylish blue t-shirt and snug jeans. Frank suddenly hoped it would be no earlier than eleven.

"I'll see you later Frank. Oh by the way did you hear about Bennett?"

"No. Bennett? What happened to Bennett?"

"All that commotion with Reilly. Well it turns out he's breaking Bennett's balls, pretty good. Something about an accident report Bennett screwed up. He forgot to notify AIU and the person went DOA."

"No," Frank said, looking at the phone surprised, as if his friend were there in person.

"Yeah," Walsh continued. "Reilly's got him all bent. He's threatening to bang the balls off him. We have to plan something for that prick."

"What's John looking at?"

"Get this Frankie. Bennett supposedly got all flustered in Reilly's office and even lost it a bit."

"Bennett?" Frank knew that was out of character. John who was usually quiet to a fault, for a cop anyway.

"So, listen. Reilly's gunna take it to the trial room if he has to."

"That's not good Sean. They'll hang him in that kangaroo court."

Walsh sounded bored. "Hey, what are you gonna do? Anyway, I'll catch you later."

"Okay, buddy," Frank finished. He put down the receiver and turned to see that Ann had already placed the white teacups on the table. She was smiling holding her lips with one finger.

"You male cops are worse than the females," she quipped.

"What—oh, the phone call. Just cop stuff, you know."

"I know." She pointed to the sofa. "Please, Frank, sit, make yourself comfortable."

As he sat, he watched Ann sit cross-legged into the wing chair. She was barefoot and he thought that utterly attractive. When did she take off her shoes? For a moment, he wondered if they would have met under different circumstances might this be a legitimate date. "So," he said nervously, hoping to fish for a conversation to get the evening going and hopefully lasting. "How are you anyway, Officer Caputo?" A touch of humor in the tone, he hoped.

"Well Officer Colleri, I'm just fine. And how are things at work and with?" She pointed her chin and Frank knew what she meant.

"Well actually it never did work out between me and my...other." He looked down into his cup, a little embarrassed, and when Ann apologized he glanced up and smiled. "It wasn't meant to be I guess."

"What is meant to be Frank? What does it really mean, meant to be?" Ann appeared serious for a moment but then she swiveled her chin and smiled.

"I'm sorry—"

"For what?" she cut in. "Hey, I forgot to bring out some of that cake you enjoyed last time you were here. I bought another box." She got up to go to the kitchen and spoke with her back to him. "Your parents must be so happy that your brother is better I'm glad for them."

"How did you know about my brother anyway?"

"My friend Allison. She knows everyone, including the guys from your precinct."

Frank answered with a polite thank you for asking after his brother. He admired her from behind as he watched her walk. He felt somewhat guilty considering what happened to the poor girl but wished he could right now put his hands on her beautiful ass.

When Ann returned with two slivers of familiar cake she asked Frank if he would mind a question. "Shoot," he said, pointing his index finger. "No pun intended officer." It worked, Ann laughed. "Go ahead and ask away."

And as nonchalantly as if talking about the weather she said, "Frank. Did you ever think about eating your gun?"

It was not only the question that took Frank by surprise, but the way in which it was presented, with an air of irony that was neither serious nor humorous. Frank didn't realize his hesitant response until Ann stuck out her chin, pointed her fork and said, "Sorry. Just a curiosity question."

Frank breathed in and answered, "Tough question Ann. I had no idea our first date would be this serious."

In a sly nonchalant manner Ann simply said, "I didn't realize this was our first date." She succeeded in throwing Frank off.

A woman's mystery always worked. *Damn. What a fool. She's not sitting here in her own place for a date you idiot.* He felt like smashing himself in the forehead. Instead he responded matter-of-factly. "Yes. I've thought of eating my gun."

"Wow, I don't feel so bad now. I guess misery loves company."

Frank couldn't figure this girl out. Was she serious? Was he being too serious? He had discussed the gun issue with other cops before but the conversation was always with guys he knew, and then the discussions were either totally eerie or lighthearted. What was her point? He sipped his tea. "You're not the type."

"You know Frank; I sat with a priest one afternoon and was totally frightened to tell him what I just told you. But he was very cool. My mom says he helps out, connects with the young people. It's tough to believe in God."

"That's all right Ann. There's no need to say all things all the time to everyone, especially a priest." He wondered if her name rolled off his tongue the way Peter said it should. And did he stare, into those soft dark eyes!

Ann reached under her chair and came up with a handful of magazines. "I read such junk lately Frank." Then she quickly pushed the magazines back under.

Frank was thinking he loved the way *his* name sounded coming from *her* lips. "I don't think you should be reading too much of that Ann." This time he purposely uttered her name but it didn't sound as soft as before. "Whatever you're reading might be upsetting you."

Ann gave a short laugh, attempting to conceal embarrassment. "It's habit now. Almost an obsession. I've now read and heard it all."

Frank was busy romanticizing. He sensed a trust that he had felt when they first met. There was definitely a bond that was no fluke. He nervously decided to ask, "Would it bother you if you talked about it with me? I mean what you've been reading up on."

Ann was lighting another cigarette and it prompted Frank to join her. "It's weird but would you mind, should be the question."

He leaned forward and spoke softly, "Ann, I really don't mind. Believe me, it's weird but I'm truly not being nosy, just interested."

Ann came to the point. "You know not every woman, at least where I come from, contrary to belief, fantasizes about being raped..."

Frank sounded off an embarrassed short laugh. "I'm sorry."

"Do men really think that?" she continued. "Do you Frank?"

What a time to be asked this. Right now, his male one-track mind was saying to him, *how delicious does Ann look right now?* Yet, this conversation was almost manic, not normal. Then again, his friend Joe told him that nothing will shock a cop after some time on the job. "Of course not," he said, straightening his face.

She smiled and said, "You're the one who said you wouldn't mind the conversation."

"No, no, go ahead," he said, puffing on his smoke.

She puffed in response, a little nervous. "I've studied this from all points of view. The people that write this stuff are certainly getting their ideas and surveys from somewhere right? The male writers do believe they know women from their earlier dating experiences or something and their interviews imply that women definitely, and there might be a smidgen of truth to it, enjoy sex without attachment."

Where is she going with this? Why does she trust me so much to explore all this? Isn't she afraid I'll tell someone? The bond? "Well," he said. "Of course, that could work both ways. Women certainly enjoy thinking they can figure us men out." *Where am I going with this?*

"Yes, but women, I don't think, feel the absolute need to get laid just so they can belong to some kind of club."

Frank laughed. "Spoken like a true feminist. Listen I don't condone pushing the envelope right up to the point of a definite no. But some men do. They feel if a woman gets close, extremely close, then it's a yes. They're probably wrong."

"Probably?" she sneered.

"Anyway," Frank continued smoothly not wanting to make her angry, "I did read somewhere about married men forcing themselves on their wives and in some instances, it even made them feel closer to their spouses, you know, head of the household."

"Bull, would be definitely correct Frank. Masochistic."

Frank sat back and took a long drag then put the cigarette out. For a moment he fantasized about tearing at Kathleen's clothes, ripping them off and having his way with her. This is what flashed so suddenly in his thought process, Ann-Kathleen. Frank went forth, his tone taking on a serious edge. "Ann, as a guy, I really don't know why you knock yourself down over all of this." He uttered his next words so softly they were barely audible. "That's not—"

"I know," she interrupted, saving him. "But like I said I've been over these things a thousand and one times." She reached for a friend and found one. She gazed off and allowed a moment's pause between them. She took a long drag and filled the air with smoke. Then her eyes welled, but she continued to speak. "I didn't think this could happen to me Frank. I didn't think that I would wake up one day..." She looked away.

Frank wanted this to be a compassionate time but his own thoughts were selfish. *I came here for a pleasant evening. I should never have asked. This shit is for her doctor's ears. What did I get myself into? Next, she'll be telling me the internal stuff.* He pictured a dry vagina...*Sorry,* he thought. He apologized to himself for the strange mental wanderings. "I don't know what to say Ann."

"I read in this pile of junk I accumulate," she laughed a little, "I read that some son of a bitch said that after he molested his thirteen-year-old neighbor he wished he could burn his hands off. Well, you know what? I would like to burn." Ann leaned forward and offered more tea.

"Another piece of this cake," he said. A grin appeared and it formed wider when she reached for the cups. Her hand brushed Frank's gently and he conjured up some sympathy. *She just needs to vent,* he thought. She was tough. She knew when to break away with a sniff, rather than cry her eyes out right there on the couch. He watched the sway of her bottom, admiringly. *Sorry,* he reminded himself. When Ann returned with the fresh servings, Frank was unaware he had been watching her the whole time in a daze so strong he forgot to offer a helping hand. He reached up too late. "Sorry," he mustered.

Ann was coy. "Is it the way I'm dressed or something?"

"What?"

"You were starring, Officer Colleri."

"Oh, jeez, I'm sorry...I mean...I just zone out once in a while."

"Oh, then you weren't starring. Now I feel safe Frank." Gingerly she pressed her fork into her cake. "You know Frank, police officers aren't exempt from perversion."

Does she think I'm a perv just for looking? Yet Frank was enjoying her minor flirtation heeding the conversation at hand with a feeling it was something literary that prompted her to say such a thing. He responded accordingly. "Something you read, no doubt?"

"Of course," she said with a smile.

Frank wanted to change this whole subject, but since they appeared tied to it he remembered something he read a while ago. "As a matter of fact," he said, "I read somewhere that law enforcement people do get themselves in trouble from time to time."

"How so?" She asked in a way that suggested she already knew the answer but needed to hear it from a man.

"Well. Supposedly cops and such get off on the whole power trip...the need for dominance and control..." *God if I could control Kathleen one more time.* He squinted at Ann hoping it came across light humored.

Another smile followed by the holding grin put Frank at ease as she flowed into conversation. "I read the same thing," she said. "Isn't that funny? And judging from the cops and detectives I've known it's quite possibly true."

"What do you mean?"

"Some of the detectives I met after..." She was unable to say the word that had changed her life. Instead she choked a short intentional cough. Frank caught on and attempted to help by fumbling for a cigarette. She continued, "Well put it this way. Even if I weren't on the job I would be able to detect that macho sarcasm a mile away. Cop or no cop, I could tell, even though they were ordered to leave the case open, they just want to close their case load."

Frank said nothing. Ann lit a butt herself, tossing the match head into the fast filling ashtray and blowing another blocking cloud. "The first to show up were a couple of male detectives. They just went through the motions; you know the routine bull questions they would ask anyone, with only a slight hint of compassion. At the hospital, they were hitting on nurses for Christ sake. They walked around with their chests stuck out as if they were in a nightclub."

The two simultaneously dragged on their butts forming yet another large cloud of smoke, almost like a shield between them. Ann continued, "I mean some of those guys were manicured and groomed to get laid. I don't want to sound feminist, but Frank, I really couldn't wait for a female officer to get assigned to me. Thank God they assigned my friend Allison to be with me through it all. I would have had no problem with the guys if they just faked it a little more. I mean here were a couple of guys from the sex crimes unit no less. They were up there at the hospital and I hear one tell the other how he wanted to get a certain nurse up there in the stirrups. I mean come on."

"That's detectives for you," Frank said. "Maybe they were just uncomfortable with the whole, you being a cop thing. I'm sure they meant well." He was not being condescending, because for a moment, though he knew he didn't have the stuff to make detective, he wished he was one. Then he could open a case and catch the kind of prick that hurt Ann.

"Wrong Frank. That's a lot of cops." They put their cigarettes out at the same time, neither paying attention to the grinding of butts in the ashtray. "A friend of mine worked in the Central Park precinct when that teacher was raped then killed." It was easier for her to say the word when it didn't pertain to herself. Frank leaned back. Ann still had the floor and he wasn't going to interrupt. He was interested in listening to her and he had never been a good listener.

She finished the story about a bunch of cops from the Central Park precinct who got a hold of the crime scene photos from the detective squad's unlocked file cabinets. "These losers were gawking at the dead woman's naked body discussing parts of her anatomy. I mean come on, what the fuck is that?"

Frank was silent. He'd realized Ann didn't curse much and because of that habit, now she was simply more attractive than vulgar.

"I'm sorry Frank," she said. "I hardly know you and I'm laying all this weird stuff on you. You're right. I could be dramatizing a little. It happens these days I guess. If they treated me that badly Allison surely would have put them in their place. I'm really—"

"No, it's all right," he interrupted.

"You're being polite and I'm carrying on. I'm really sorry, so let's change the subject." Again, she displayed the grin.

"You got it," he said. But he was thinking how much he was starting to enjoy her talkfest. He was suddenly a little frightened at the thought of not having anything to say. He acted quickly on the assumption that their bond held true. "You know something Ann..." God her name did sound nice, like a saint... "This is going to sound like a line." She was still smiling making it easier for him to continue. "I really feel at ease and very comfortable with you."

Ann lowered her head for a moment then returned her eyes to him. "Frank, I feel the same way," she said, warmly. "I just wish we didn't have all this..." she used her hands for conversational enhancement, "...stuff in our lives."

A hint of rejection might have been in those words. However, at this moment he wanted to climb over and squeeze into the wing chair with Ann and kiss her mouth softly and then passionately. To hug her and assure her everything would be all right. This was significant to Frank because he hadn't felt romantic about kissing or holding another woman since he shared a stolen kiss with Jenna. Then, he resisted with excuses of alcohol and moral obligation.

If Frank knew for sure Ann would allow him, he would gladly pour his heart out to her, but the skepticism clouding his past made it painful for him to try. Something uncertain tugged him back, so in a way, really, he was once again being denied.

"Frank," she said. He replied with a nodding glance. "You're starring again." They shared a light romantic laugh that seemed to break the thicker air of attraction.

"Do you think I'm weird Frank?"

"Not any more than the rest of us," he replied.

"Good, because I would really like us to be friends."

He wondered if that was an awkward invitation or girl talk for back off. "Absolutely," he said. "So would I. And not to sound like the visiting cop or anything, but if I can do any—"

"I'll let you know. And I really think you mean that."

They finally did change subjects chatting about respective families and recent movies. They drank more tea and managed to finally fill the ashtray to capacity. When their time was over Frank related back to their movie interest and asked Ann if she would like to go to one at another time. She did, although he knew any flick with a happy ending would be just too corny given their circumstances.

Frank left, but that was fine because this night signified hope and Frank felt better than he had in a long time. As a matter of fact, he felt so good it was cause for celebration with a night of good partying ahead, certainly better than the usual drown your sorrows evening. As Frank was walking into The Ferris he nearly knocked Jenna over when he opened the door as she was coming out. Jenna, with one of her friends, both dressed in green nurse's scrub uniforms. "Wow," Frank shouted.

"Hey, Frank, I mean stranger. Long time no see, what have you been up to?" Jenna asked.

"Meeting some friends. What about you?" Feeling tall tonight, Frank reached for Jenna's hand, she didn't object.

"On my way home."

"Come on back in for a drink, Nurse Prendergast."

"I can't Frank. I mean I'd love to, but I have a six a.m. flight in the morning, I'm going to Florida."

"Ah, that's too bad. About the drink that is. Have a great time." He was still holding her hand but knew it was time to let it go for another night. Besides, Jenna's friend was wearing one of those hurry up jealous faces when she chimed, "Say it with roses."

Frank leaned and kissed her softly on the mouth. Jenna accepted his kiss completely and he felt the full wetness of her lips. "Bring back the heat babe."

This must be my lucky day. He felt like a teenager again, possessing the goofy charm of a high-schooler. He watched Jenna walk away imagining her lips if they had parted and Ann's if he had felt those as well. He blew Jenna a kiss and then he let the words and her name fall from his lips. "See you soon, babe. See you soon."

* * * *

Ann Caputo sat in her wing chair.

hat did I just do? A rape victim flirting with a cop with strange conversation. God I was just trying to be normal? I should have just gone to the coffee shop and made small talk? What will my doctor think? And Allison? Weird. Chill.

CHAPTER 27

There could not be a job on the planet, not any job, be it the police, or any office job for that matter, which could possess the infinite wisdom to detect the nature of a person's limits. No one could have known until it was too late that Bennett would erupt in such a manner as to send shockwaves through the corridors of NYC's law enforcement community.

Bennett, not yet a seasoned veteran, still possessed an untarnished record. In the academy he passed the required written and physical tests as well as the preliminary psychological screenings which consisted of a one-hundred word test where answers were sometimes repeated and recycled in different sentence structures in an attempt to catch discrepancies in a recruit's answer. Other testing for all rookies included a drawing exercise. Here the young cop was required to draw three sketches. The first of a person. The second of a house. And the third of a tree. This was supposed to determine to some department shrink where the recruit's head might be. Bennett, like most rookies, was no artist. So his drawings, like the thousands before his, were just a cut above stick figures, the point of which no one really understood.

Still, in the end it didn't come down to the department's psychological profile or drawing skills or the lack thereof. Bennett cracked under the pressure of one past divorce and one pending. Nothing was known about his first wife. He never mentioned her except to say he had been married to a witch. Later it was revealed his recent wife told him straight out that she never loved him. She split with no follow up communication at all. The idea of another woman abandoning him and the pressure of facing job write-ups were just the right chemicals to cause an explosion.

The 117th was preparing for its annual Atlantic City bus trip. Not all the officers who worked at the 117th attended the gambling drink fest but usually the bus was filled with takers. Sean Walsh was a regular, as was Arthur Gallo, John Eaton and other cops both male and female from the patrol squads. Frank was usually involved in the precinct outing, and though he already purchased a ticket, he fought himself to stay away this time, fearing it was just not a good time to lose a paycheck and bring his mood down again. In the end his decision came down to the theory he shared with his gambling, peer pressure buddies. The final assumption that he would win, not loose, and in the interim, make one big party out of the day.

Since Frank decided to go, he also made a last ditch effort to talk Bennett into joining the guys on the trip. He felt sorry for Bennett especially since the day he saw John sitting grim faced in front of his locker. Frank tried assuring John it would be a great time, he would enjoy himself, get his mind off other things. Frank joked that even for John a day of drinking was always a good cure. "Come on dude," Frank had said. "We'll all get drunk then come back and beat the shit out of Reilly."

Bennett smiled but again refused. "Maybe next time."

As the boys and gals boarded the morning bus, Frank was stopped by Callahan who looked as though he was late for the bus himself.

"Hey Callahan. You afraid we were gonna leave without you?" Frank joked.

"No, no, Frank, I'm not going. I would love to, of course, but I have things to do today." Callahan was huffing so relaxed a moment before he continued. "Frank, I don't want to worry you especially since your mind will be on money—"

"Then why worry me Brian?" Frank quipped.

"Listen. I heard some rumblings this morning about a civilian complaint—actually it's also a bias complaint and they're looking to drop it like a bomb on you guys."

"Who Reilly again? Who cares?"

"No, it's serious. Don't tell Gallo. I don't want to alarm him before I know all the details, but supposedly he's the subject and your name might also be on the damn thing. I also heard the CO is shitting himself with worry that the Reverend is gonna get wind of it. The good preacher is already on our backs that there aren't enough minorities working in the precinct."

Frank's expression drooped. "I'm not gonna worry about it." But suddenly connected with the word bias, he *was* worried. He knew that a cop should possess an extra layer of tough skin with an **I can take it** attitude. All that was going out the window as he recollected the incident in question. The thought of being on the tail end of a bias incident caused him to curse Gallo. He also knew if Reverend Wilson got involved, it would be a nightmare. Frank had been to a community meeting held by the demanding preacher, it was a bite your tongue evening with Reverend Wilson pontificating what the police must do, how they should act, and where they should be stationed during what times of the day in what he called *his* precinct. At one point he shouted to Moore, "Stop your cops from giving everyone out here dirty aggressive looks. You act as if you police aren't a group. You say we stick together, like a mob, or cult, well what is it you fellas' do?"

Callahan turned back to Frank calling to him before he got on the bus. "By the way Frank. Good luck down there." Frank jokingly flipped his delegate the finger.

The trip to Jersey lived up to expectations. There were three male cops to every female and all were on their way to drunken madness. Beers were being flipped open at record rates and there was frolicking up and down the aisle of the bus as music blasted from a portable boom box. The chorus of entertainment and loud chatter bellowed for the entire trip.

Some of the cops were playing cards as others, just as boisterously, hammed it up. The bus driver, a heavy man of sixty, left his blinders on to anything that might ensue, especially after receiving a one hundred dollar tip up front and expecting at least that, if all went well at the tables, on the much quieter trip back to Queens.

As usual, a few of the male cops were trying to suave the pants off their female coworkers. And of course, living up to police lore there was sure to be a couple of unusual pairings on this trip, as there had been on others. Stories were in the making for the gossip mill and ripe for future conversations about who was getting or giving blow jobs on the way there or back. The trip, which always seemed quicker going down, ended with the bus emptying into group clicks. Some took off to the Resorts and Trump towers. Colleri, Eaton, Walsh and their new tagalong Gallo, headed to the Showboat. It really didn't matter though, because by the end of the six-hour trip, all of the cops would have eventually rotated their way through the strip of casinos. The true gamblers let it be known that there would be no losers standing and looking over their shoulders, either at the tables or the slots, breathing bad luck down their necks.

Eventually Frank found himself sitting at a poker joker slot down to his last hundred dollars, wishing he never came. *Thank God the drinks are free.* Frank motioned for one, then slipped in a twenty-dollar bill for eighty credits appearing in the right corner of the screen. He hoped to kill time by doubling his credits and moving on to another machine.

Instead, the machine was cold and dissolved the twenty dollars in the time it took for the waitress to return with the drink.

Now he had just eighty bucks left, down from the six hundred and some odd change he brought. Frank stood to the side of some machines feeling anxious, so he lit a cigarette figuring seven minutes to smoke, providing he didn't take too many drags. As he inhaled and exhaled the sound of coins dropping and machines running vibrated a space in his head, and sometimes the succession of dropped coins would be accompanied by loud cheers. He learned that the cheers did not necessarily imply large sums of money, rather, just a good time for the hordes of retirees who traveled to the casinos for a cheap day and a lunch. He was nearing the end of a long and expensive day.

* * * *

That morning had been worse than a gaming loss for John Bennett. He awoke bleary-eyed with a feeling of being hung over after spending the better part of the night tossing and turning with a restlessness that couldn't be comforted. During a period when he had pressed the fluff of the pillow into his face, he imagined the pillow swallowing him up and smothering him like it would a child and then he would die peacefully in his bed while he slept.

Sleepless nights had mounted up for the young cop. The waking moments were like nightmares, containing uneasy thoughts of his wife and possible reasons why she abandoned him. He couldn't come up with one good one. He had always been good to her. He was not like the self-absorbed macho cops who needed various other so-called manly outlets. Bennett would dream up things to do to please his wife. He didn't miss a holiday to bring home a card. He would plan romantic drives to quiet lunch destinations for no other reason than to see a smile dance on her face. Now he sobbed at the foolishness of it all.

As the reality of work emerged with morning light, darker thoughts prevailed. Why would Lieutenant Reilly give this much of a damn as to what he did or didn't do on the day of some accident? Why was Reilly so vicious? Bennett knew the public could be jerked off in just about any situation and even if they couldn't then why not just give a minimal complaint and get it over? Why would this guy carry a vendetta for any reason other than he was just miserable?

With his thoughts vigorously flip flopping from wife to Reilly, Bennett pressed his face hard into the pillow once again. He thought over his dilemma at work. That scumbag Reilly. Bennett heard that Reilly was unofficially going hell bent on finding out who the cops were that messed with Sergeant Nolan. Sure, he had laughed along, but he was no instigator; he was a decent guy and decent cop, others should be getting the flak. As tired as he was he jumped from bed with a nervous energy speculating the phrase, Nice guys finish last.

Before leaving home, Bennett scanned the living room like it was the last time. The house had become messy, clothes everywhere, unwashed plates, it now possessed an air of loneliness. Suddenly he lowered himself to the floor and began to sob. "Let it out," he cried to himself. "Let it out. Isn't it best to cry it out?"

Bennett wished he had a close friend. Someone to talk to, to confide in. Someone that would encourage him. He went to the sink and ran the tap splashing cold water on his face. Then he dried himself and blew his nose into a rough paper towel. He was thinking that maybe he should have gone to Atlantic City.

When Bennett arrived at work the big bus was still parked in front of the precinct. He had secretly hoped it would have left so he wouldn't feel pressured once again into making excuses. But he was an hour and a half early since he didn't want to just sit around at home. If he was slightly tempted to join the guys it was out of loneliness rather than the desire to gamble. Sure enough, Frank Colleri approached him once more, but this time John was able to gracefully refuse. Other than an ironic joke of dealing with the lieutenant, later, Colleri respectfully didn't push. But Gallo was lurking ready to back him into an embarrassing corner so John quickly ducked into the stationhouse and began his day.

Bennett changed into his uniform hearing the roar of the bus pull from the curb. A sense of relief lifted his dark mood. Earlier he noticed Sergeant Moore descend the stairs to the CPOP office; it occurred to him that other than Moore, he might be the only cop working CPOP today, which meant he wouldn't be noticed all tour, could probably hang around the office once Moore left to his own hideout and would have plenty of the down time he needed. But he still had to inform the front desk that he was present for duty. The desk officer was a newly appointed sergeant and slightly embarrassed about giving orders. He informed Bennett that his assignment had been changed for the day. So...he didn't go unnoticed. The desk officer informed him that prisoners were coming from central booking to be lodged here in the precinct and Bennett was to be the cell attendant.

Bennett felt an immediate rush of anxiety about the prospect of eight long, boring hours guarding disgruntled prisoners. The tedious task of nothing to do in a confined area was sure to get him all worked up, especially with all that time to do nothing but think too much. Bennett tried not taking his assignment personally. He heard that the new sergeant wasn't a bad guy so he must have really needed to change Bennett's assignment.

Fate, in the form of a question, stepped in to change the course of John's life, as well as many that worked at the precinct. Bennett, not the type to question an assignment turned back to the desk officer. "No one else *eh* boss? I had some CPOP work today."

The young sergeant tightened his lip and produced a look of embarrassment again. The boss pointed in the direction of the back rooms. There was no need for further explanation. Reilly gave the desk officer the order to pull Bennett from CPOP. Then, as if in a veil of misty clouds, Bennett made his way to the stairway, never taking his eyes from the back corridor until he cleared the stairwell door. At his locker he dressed down for cell duty removing his heavy gun belt and street equipment feeling numb, then a strange thought occurred to him.

What if I were to bring my firearm into the cells with me and hand it to the worse felon of the bunch who has nothing to lose. I let the felon escape if the prisoner does one thing first. Walk into the back room, take out the good lieutenant.

The fantasy brought mild relief and by the time the prisoners arrived and Bennett was ready for cell duty, a weird smile enhanced his face.

CHAPTER 28

Brian Callahan, precinct delegate, was standing on the top landing to the precinct entrance, grim faced, smoking and furiously pacing. He watched as the bus pulled in carrying its weary, anxious and angry travelers who suffered a long drive knowing the tragedy which occurred at *their stationhouse*. This was by far the hardest thing he would ever have to do as a delegate. How in Heaven's name was he going to explain the carnage?

He didn't want a bus load of frantic people waiting nervous hours to hear conflicting stories. He would stop the troops before they entered the stationhouse and rustle them into the muster room, not here where the street was inhabited with news trucks, reporters and yellow crime scene tape.

* * * *

Earlier that morning, John Bennett stood at his post, assigned to cell watch unwillingly. At some point his fidgeting caused him to pace the front door of the cellblock rather nervously. Once in a while directing a glance in the vicinity of the ICO's office. Around the time of this pacing Reilly surfaced from his office causing Bennett to instinctively turn away. John was not good at direct eye contact; therefore, he didn't notice when Reilly leaned into the young desk officer to whisper a comment. But John would soon be made aware of what was said.

After Reilly disappeared back into his office the desk officer stepped from behind the desk and approached Bennett. The sergeant informed Bennett that it would be a good idea if he stepped inside the cellblock since that was where he was officially supposed to be posted. Outside the door would technically be off post. Then the sergeant shrugged pointing to the ICO's office, Bennett knew it was Reilly's order. He also remembered what that bumbling instigator, Gallo, said and it rang true. 'He'll let you know that you lose.'

Bennett complied immediately. But not out of fear, rather he didn't want the desk officer to notice the frustrating emotions that were causing him to choke up. Once within the cellblock he began pacing the sidewall where even the prisoners couldn't see him. His heart was racing, his throat felt hard. He wished he could just let it out, sob right there and release some of the bile that was eating him up. Fighting his emotions only made Bennett feel ill. It didn't help that the entire cellblock was at capacity, the prisoners grunting, spitting and moaning repetitively: Hey, when we goin' to court... when we eatin'...I need a cigarette! Not to mention the cells reeked of body odor and piss.

"John. Johnny Bennett," a voice called from the outer doorway.

John took a deep breath after he recognized the voice to be Sergeant Moore.

"There you are," Moore said. "I was wondering—"

"I'm sorry sarge," Bennett said. "I forgot to tell you they assigned me in here today." Bennett's appearance was flustered. He pointed his thumb in the direction of the offices in the rear. "It's him sarge."

"No, no, I know John." The boss sensed Bennett's uneasiness when he rested his large hand on the young cop's shoulder. "You know, even old man Whyte isn't here today, so they might have had to use you anyhow."

John was comforted momentarily by his sergeant. Moore might have possessed the physical stature of an ex-prizefighter with the accompanying gruff voice, and huge, even gross hands; but now he was comforting, like a father. "Listen kid," Moore said. "Don't take him personally." Moore lowered his voice speaking from the side of his mouth. "The guy can't help that he's a schmuck." Moore smiled and for a moment so did Bennett. "They come and they go, John. This guy won't be here forever. Hang in there, or as today's generation might say, just chill." Moore gave Bennett a couple of pats with those mitts of his then he winked and was on his way.

If only momentary relief could have been bottled, because this certainly would have been the time and place to corner the market. For John, it took only a couple of minutes for the slight relief to reverse back to an irate anger that filled him with the will and courage for confrontation. Bennett walked steadfastly out of the cellblock and B-lined it to the ICO's office. Reilly's door was surprisingly open, perhaps because of the quiet stationhouse. Bennett knocked once, hard enough to ensure a quick glance from Reilly shuffling papers cool and calm as a cucumber at his desk.

"What can I do for you officer?"

"Lieutenant...I just want to know..." *Don't back down now...* "Do you have a problem with me?" *There, said.* His chest seemed to pound harder and his hands were moist with nervousness.

"Officer. Who's on the cells now?" Reilly was sardonic.

"I am sir." Bennett's words hinted sarcasm but still he remained anxious within.

"Officer. I have no time right now to answer any of your questions; however, I do suggest that you return to your post."

Bennett stood there unaware that his face was taking on a contorted expression. 'Don't be a coward,' Gallo had said. 'Kick that fucker's ass.' John said nothing though as he turned and quickly left. He felt humiliated. Like a coward. He walked down the hall then detoured past the cells to the stairway to the locker room.

The precinct was quiet.

The desk officer had his nose in a newspaper unaware Bennett left his post. Then the desk phone rang sharply. The young sergeant's eyes widened as Reilly's voice immediately tore into him. "Sergeant. Get your face out of that paper now and tell me where your cell attendant is at this moment."

The sergeant looked over in the direction of the cellblock hoping to be assured by at least a moving shadow. "He must be inside the—"

"No, he is not sergeant. And if you weren't sitting there half unconscious you would've noticed me noticing you, and would've realized your cell attendant left his post—again. By the way, weren't you supposed to have an officer assigned to stationhouse security?"

"I'm sorry Lieutenant—"

"Never mind that now," Reilly interrupted. "If that officer isn't back on post in two minutes sergeant, you better well have the complaint written up already or you know who gets one next." The lieutenant hung up on the desk officer before the sergeant could get another word in.

The desk officer slapped his hands down hard on the huge desk shaking his head and huffing nervously. Now he knew why sergeant's got so pissed off at cops. He looked over at Lisa, the civilian telephone switchboard operator. "Lisa. Did you see Compton?" He was referring to the officer assigned to stationhouse security.

"No sarge," she replied. "Actually, I think he might be on a break." She said this to him without ever looking past her fingernails. "Oh, and the LT called me to see if Bennett was in the cell area."

A little late, the sergeant thought then looked over into the complaint room where another civilian was mundanely typing reports. It wasn't even worth the time questioning that one. Meanwhile, Reilly returned to his papers casually, as if the conversations of the last twenty minutes were so trivial to him as to not give them a second thought. Unlike those he conversed with.

Reilly closed the folder in front of him and put it on top of two other files on his desk. The folder he was looking over contained a civilian complaint review, and the two files were those of police officers in the command. It was a complaint of bias, constituting a serious incident involving racial slurs made by a member of the department against a civilian of the city of New York. The two officers mentioned in the body of the complaint were police officers Arthur Gallo and Frank Colleri. Earlier Reilly was giving their records and evaluations a go over with the hopes of finding past discretions. He had also spoken to their sergeant questioning the job performance of both officers. By confiding to Sergeant Moore, Reilly knew the cat would be let out of the bag thus triggering immediate worry for the cops, giving Reilly the leverage he needed to start something brewing.

Unknown to the cops, Reilly also instructed Moore to choose one of them to be assigned to the broom on their next tour. The stationhouse was in need of serious cleaning, especially the prisoner cells, inside and out. He smiled at the thought of one of those cops cleaning toilets. He scanned a clipboard, gathered his keys and portable radio, and glanced at his desk again before venturing out into the field to spy on the patrol cops' comings and goings.

It was routine for Reilly to give his office a last look, this way he would remember to the best of his ability where everything was so if someone did manage to get in and rummage through his desk he would have an early beat on it. Before he left he decided to take the complaint with the officer's folders off the desk and stuff them in a crowded drawer.

Bennett had returned from the locker room and was now in the cellblock doorway. He was wearing a twisted expression yet he appeared calm with a tranquil stare in his eyes.

The desk officer called to him, "Bennett." John didn't seem to hear. The sergeant tried again in a sort of loud whisper, "Bennett." When John looked over the desk officer motioned John forward with his finger.

Bennett approached the desk saying nothing. He looked to be staring past the boss but at this moment the desk officer's only concern was getting Bennett to stay put in the cells.

"Listen, Bennett. He's busting my balls to no end. He wants you in there or it's my ass. And that means yours. Just get in there Bennett. I know the guy pissed you off but he's the boss, so for both our sakes just stay in there. When Compton comes back from wherever he is I'll make sure he gives you enough break time." The desk officer didn't mention a possible complaint.

Bennett complied with a methodical nod. He turned and walked to the cells. This greatly relieved the desk officer who didn't want to be on Reilly's hit list. This time, instead of putting his nose in a paper, the sergeant turned slightly to view the back offices, and then picked up the phone for a quiet personal call.

It was a relatively quiet morning at the precinct. The civilian clerk was busy typing reports in the complaint room while the other civilian was still admiring her nails. There were many other mornings that had seen hordes of people standing around waiting to have a report taken, or people there just to talk to a cop about some problem they were having with their spouse, landlord or stranger. But such was the nature of a stationhouse. Some days busy, others not.

Reilly returned from the field several hours later. He eyed Bennett on his post then retreated to his office where he sat and opened the bottom desk drawer. Suddenly he felt the faint air of someone else present in the room. He looked up and for a second was startled to see Bennett standing there in front of his desk with his arms folded. Bennett's eyes were squinted and glazed, and though Reilly knew nothing of Bennett personally, there was a brief moment of sensing this was not the same person.

Reilly finished closing the drawer as he regrouped leaning forward on the desk with his head stretched towards Bennett. Relying on familiar tactics he became aggressive. "Did I not tell you officer, that your place is in—"

In that instant, almost robotically, Bennett unfolded his arms, reached into his uniform and came up with his snub nose .38 revolver. Reilly's last expression was one of a cartoon-like grimace rather than shock. The first shot ripped into the lieutenant's left shoulder, spinning him sideways. It was a bad shot at such a close range.

The desk officer and the two civilians reacted in almost the same manner, turning their heads in confusion, first in the direction of the pop, then at each other. The second shot rang out and the bullet tore into Reilly's head above his right ear discharging a spray of blood and flesh along Reilly's massive bald head, into the air, and on the desk. Then the lieutenant's body just slumped sideways out of the chair.

Bennett remained as tranquil as he was before the moment he reached for his gun. He just stood there. Then Bennett slowly backed himself into the door, and in one unrehearsed motion, raised the gun upward, and putting the barrel in his mouth, he pulled the trigger.

The two civilians began screaming and the desk officer finally ran to the sound of the gunfire with no instinct that someone else could be hurt. The young sergeant walked in upon the insidious sight unaware his mouth gaped, his face contorted. After he heard the second shot he called over the air waves: shots fired in the stationhouse—10-13. And though it would be a matter of seconds before he heard the sounds of sirens wailing and cops converging on the precinct, those few moments looking down at the dead cops would seem a lifetime.

When Moore reached the corridor to the ICO's office the first sight he saw was Bennett slumped sideways on the floor against the door. *My good God.* He approached cautiously still unsure of what lay to the right of Bennett. Moore, who was second to converge on the scene, had almost an identical reaction to the carnage. He looked down at Bennett then up at the young sergeant who was standing over the downed lieutenant. Now Moore knew what had happened. He knelt down to Bennett's crumpled body. There was no question that the young cop was dead. He reached out his big paw and squeezed the dead cop's shoulder as his eyes welled with tears.

Moore stood up when he heard the thunder of cops piling into the stationhouse. It seemed like every cop in the borough was racing through the doors as if everything were taking place in a fast action cop film. As Moore stood erect to position himself back, he caught sight of cartilage and a glob of crimson bloody hair stuck on the door, the spot where the bullet smashed through Bennett's brain. Moore suddenly thought of the cop's father, who he had known. *You let the bear eat you kid,* he thought. *You let it get to you.*

As senior man on scene Moore collected himself and turned to the sight of what looked like a hundred stunned cops, he knew what he would do. He had seen and he had heard it all, and now he had crossed the line into having enough. The job became a job about nothing, except maybe egos and too many bosses who made it a job about some things that were really nothing.

It was not the same job he once knew. Not the same job that Bennett senior knew.

Unnecessary trouble brewed faster now.

Right then as he walked from the death scene, Moore decided he would retire. He would draw up the necessary papers and submit them as soon as he could think straight.

CHAPTER 29

The murder/suicide of Lieutenant Reilly and Patrolman Bennett sent shock waves shivering through the spine of the New York City Police Department. It was also a tremendous blow to the confidence of the media-following citizens of the city who were absolutely horrified that the very men who were supposed to be protecting them could go around shooting each other.

It was impossible to believe that anything like this could ever happen in the city of New York, but indeed it did. In line with forgotten recollections, City Hall was certainly not about to leak a forlorn fact: that in 1963 a police officer in a Queens precinct walked into the stationhouse one afternoon with murder on his mind. Let the reporters dig that one up. The officer apparently had been dragging his ass for hours on a desolate foot post he was ordered to work by a scurrilous captain. When the officer entered the stationhouse the captain was conveniently behind the desk talking with the desk sergeant. The officer walked behind the desk and without malice shot the captain through the heart killing him. However shocked the officer who was answering the phones, he reacted instinctively and fired upon the disgruntled cop, fearing that others were in danger. Unfortunately, in that incident there were also two dead cops.

In 1963, there were no equals for the emboldened media of the 1980s. So when a city with no memory of that long ago incident heard of the present one, they were astounded. The story of the young cop killing his boss commanded front-page headlines.

At One Police Plaza, the police commissioner, on the mayor's orders, convened all his deputy commissioners and top chiefs. They were to devise a plan, first in the form of a speech for His Honor. The mayor was to go live in conference with his usual flair and rhetoric and attempt to quell any cause for panic and alarm. He would dismiss the incident, though tragic, as an isolated one. The mayor and his aides could only cross their fingers and hope this disaster would somehow dissipate into the city's thick air, along with 1963 and many other historical calamities. For now, though, the powers that be were not really expecting a miracle. Still, it could not drag on for more than a few months as the administration edged closer to re-election.

As expected, the days following the shooting were a virtual media blitz. The networks and the newspapers were gigantic in their coverage, all vying for the predominate story to satisfy curious readers. They would all be winners though, especially the newspapers, all outselling the previous week's circulation. The editorials of public opinion were mixed. Responses ranged from mortified, to favorable, to not caring one way or another. In every neighborhood where a person was seen walking, a reporter was there. Newsmen were waiting to interview anyone looking in the direction of the camera or anyone wanting to be quoted. Microphones were shoved in faces of weary midtown commuters and outer borough transients. The comments were such: I just can't believe it---It's such a shame, a horrible tragedy---Absolutely tragic---Those poor cops, my God---Astounding, just amazing it could happen---I haven't given it much thought---Their poor families, what a sin.

In the game of ratings both sides of the coin were a wise path to follow. Responses in the lower-class sections of New York were harsher---That sharp police commissioner, he has his work cut out---Those cops can't be helped---Who cares. Would they if it was us? Let them kill each other---Cop was probably on crack. Of course, there were those who hated cops just because of receiving a parking ticket.

What was more appalling to read were reactions from the cops themselves, who naturally insisted on anonymity. Understandably, most cops refused to talk about the incident at all, but many who did, had sharp responses: We lost one of our own to the hypocritical bureaucracy---This job's been declining for years---It's tragic---Right here in the city's backyard. They had to expect something like this sooner or later.

Then came more shocking comments certain to frighten the citizenry into an unprotected state of confusion. One officer was quoted, "I feel terrible for the cop and his family, but the son of a bitch that he blew away, never." Said another, facing a reporter without the camera on, spitting on the sidewalk, "That scumbag lieutenant deserved what he got. It's just too bad the cop did himself in." Another, "The rat lieutenant died like the dog that he was, at the hands of a proud cop in my book. It was only a matter of time before someone went postal."

It was also learned that many cops secretly hoped that the tragedy sent a terrifying message to their bosses. "Maybe they'll think twice before they needlessly screw with a man's life over nothing." Another young cop, a rookie, apparently learning cynicism fast after graduating the academy stated, "I think it's okay that the piece of trash got shot. It's just too bad he didn't suffer longer."

Needless to say, the brass fumed over these rank and file remarks. In a frantic shift to put an end to the disparaging remarks that would tarnish the city and damage the trust of the department, the brass threatened serious retribution to any cop caught giving comments to media. It was beginning to look as though the city was being protected by a bunch of deranged cops who possessed no regard for the life of a person who dared to cross their blue line.

The mayor's task: Resurrect the city before the election.

The man was already a controversial figure, cutting through his command with a Napoleon-like leadership: blunt, no nonsense, tough on crime, especially the drug scourge, and a disregard for criticism. But now he had the task of preserving the integrity of a police department he earlier divided himself due to contract negotiations. The cops didn't enjoy the tough battle he gave them. And the police unions had already sent word they wouldn't be backing the present mayor in his reelection bid.

Within the walls of the 117th precinct there were reactions of grief for their fallen comrade. There was also guilty relief for the loss of a scumbag. Management's threat of retribution kept any cop from an on the record remark, however it was unanimous; they agreed they weren't sorry Reilly was gunned down by one of his own.

Though many precinct cops hadn't known Bennett as intimately as others, their grief was a fear that came from just being blue, which meant being close to home. And of course, there were the tears of those who knew him.

The patrolmen's union called a meeting at the stationhouse. For those who wished to attend it was an attempt to restore some unity and sanity to the troops. For moral support, the PBA brought along retired members who were injured in the line of duty as well as members who had alcohol or mental health issues and survived the worst and reached way down and around to fight the obstacles.

The department had its own agenda, dispatching bosses from its early intervention unit to the 117th in an attempt to stroke the backs of possibly troubled officers who just might happen to use this tragedy as an excuse to fuel their alcohol consumption, as well as the possibility of becoming new boss fighters. The first few days were mayhem and confusion leaving many with profound feelings of doubt.

The mayor implored media to interview prominent psychiatrists who would explain that no matter what profession a person was in, it was nearly impossible to know if such a person could or would commit the act of homicide/suicide. Members of the CPOP unit were especially affected. They were the ones who talked with Bennett frequently. Though Bennett was not extremely close to any cop, he was still a link and this was made all the more clear by the heartfelt emotions of the unit's leader, Sergeant Moore.

To provide the proper sendoff the cops would have to be strong and band together as one. The CPOP unit acted as the ushers at the funeral from beginning to end. Patrol cops attended in force. It was still their command and a member was dead. Adding heat to the situation was the dead lieutenant's insistent family. They were demanding a full inspector's funeral insisting that Reilly was gunned down in the line of duty regardless of who shot him. When word of the Reilly funeral leaked to the members of the 117th, and that cops from this command would have to stand honor guard at his casket, they became furious. The conflict heightened when it appeared the department was planning a low profile funeral for Bennett.

If Bennett killed himself and was the only victim, then the PBA would have no problem with the funeral proceedings as ordered. However, the union was strongly opposed to standing by and watching as the lieutenant received full honors. They insisted Reilly receive a similar funeral as the young cop.

Eventually it filtered back to the patrol force that the higher ups were adhering to the demands of the PBA. There were political reasons. The union president hoped to be resurrected in his member's eyes and the mayor unwillingly caved in for his own selfish reasons. If the mayor had to attend a funeral for the lieutenant with no cop present under the rank of sergeant, unless they were officially ordered there, it would have been like banging the final nail into his political coffin. The commanding officer became so unnerved that he refused to allow the customary hanging of the purple and black bunting that was to be draped across the top of the precinct's doors, symbolizing in public that a member of the service had passed on.

"We'll just try to wash this whole mess away and get on with it," the captain said to the PBA delegate. "We can't recognize the police officer only. We must recognize in some way, to the community, praise for the fallen lieutenant. After all, we can't forget this man was killed."

"With all due respect, his family will benefit from line of duty money. As you already know, the PBA won't go along with any official praise for that scum—"

"We certainly can't encourage any memorial on behalf of a cop who shot down his boss in cold blood!"

"It's already been worked out captain—"

"Well, we will see about that one."

"Just so you know. A banner should be hung for Bennett."

When Callahan left the office the CO made as many calls to One Police Plaza as he thought he had in him. To no avail. He was ordered, not persuaded, to disregard any banners.

It was also ordered that both funerals would be arranged in the same manner: short, with no run over rhetoric during the eulogies. The city would, with difficulty, attempt to satisfy the Bennetts, the Reillys, and the job. The powers that be also were aware the press would swarm the churches, furthering their wish for quickness on the burials. Falsifying unity, the police officers attending both funerals were put on fair warning to shy away from the press. Any one person caught fraternizing with a member of the press would be severely reprimanded.

The dampness left over from the night's rain seemed to be ordered from the Grim Reaper himself. The funeral was not a city-wide ordered detail, nevertheless more than two hundred and fifty cops, including high-ranking police officials, stood chilled on what was supposed to be an early summer day, outside the small church that would bear the casket of John Bennett. As the coffin was lifted into the black hearse the sound of bagpipes filled the air. A funny thought crossed Frank's mind. He recollected the time on his wedding day during the reception when his father-in-law insisted on an hour of uninterrupted bagpipe playing. To Frank and his Italian side of the family, it seemed as though they played all night. Perhaps he should have taken the bagpipe incident as his first warning of a failed marriage. But then again, if everyone could foresee marriage certainty, Bennett wouldn't have suffered divorce twice. *Poor guy.* In this small moment Frank felt a slight admiration towards his own strength. He too had lost the woman he loved. He also had problems with the job. Yet he was still here unscathed, able, through mysterious strength, to resist the temptation of putting a bullet through his head.

When the pipes fell silent the quiet in the air became mesmerizing. Frank felt a surge of grief. Grief not only for Bennett, but also for himself and his friends, anyone one of them could be carried out of a church like Bennett for various reasons.

When the hearse drove off and the lines of blue broke away, one of the officers in Colleri's row broke wind causing a few laughs. Leave it to a cop to break the thick silence in a crude manner. Cops broke away in small circles. Some wore sunglasses to shield their tears; others had reddened faces from fighting back theirs. At the graveside where the crowd thinned out, Frank sensed that in a short time the only one who would truly remember Bennett was his mother. She would be the only one to care what had happened to John. His wife would move on with no problem and more money. And even after his death, the first Mrs. Bennett hadn't surfaced.

Finally, with the funeral at an end and the remaining cops in uniform gathered together, a precinct sergeant reminded them IAD forewarned the precinct that any cop in uniform on or off duty, under no circumstances was to be caught drinking. Since it was heavily advised not to drink in a bar or in the presence of an IAD rat, a few of the precinct personnel not scheduled to return to work found their own spaces within the precinct to slug back a few beers. Though there was a slight risk, the CPOP cops retreated to an outer maintenance room, off to the right of the CPOP office. Present were Colleri, Eaton, Walsh and Gallo.

At first, they were all quiet just sitting there sipping beer, Colleri puffing a butt. Eaton remembered to lock the door just as Gallo decided to break the silence. "Can you believe the balls on his wife to show up?"

"Just because she left him? Other than his mom that's all he had. I guess she had the right," Frank replied.

"Broads. Who the hell can figure them out," Eaton said.

"Broads," Walsh said. "At least his first wife wasn't there to star for the cameras."

"Hey Frank, are you a philosopher now? Right. That bitch will be on someone else's knob within the week if she's not already." Gallo was getting red.

Eaton changed the subject on his friend's behalf. "Anyone see how the boss was today? Where he was?"

"Yeah, Moore was around. Kind of looked like he was off in his own mood though," Gallo said.

For a moment, Frank felt ridiculous. He had seen Moore at the funeral, shook hands with him, and just assumed everyone else had also seen him. He felt as if Gallo took the words right out of his mouth and with that feeling came a weird sense of *déjà vu*. How many times did he want to say something first? Hence the *déjà vu*. Times he noticed from the car a violation or people fighting on the street and said nothing to his partner assuming they also saw and chose to neglect the situation. Or was he now being ridiculous? Did it turn out the cop he worked with on a given day wondered why he didn't notice things the way Gallo was wondering why he hadn't seen Moore. *What is with this obsessive thinking?* Frank panicked. *I gotta get out of here.*

"I gotta tell you," Gallo continued, "I didn't think the guy would have the balls—shit I didn't think he would take me seriously."

"What the hell are you talking about?" Eaton asked.

"I set the kid straight. I told him if that fucker keeps harassing you—shoot the bastard."

"Are you nuts Art?" Eaton gasped.

"It's not his fault. Who can control what a guy does?" Frank said remembering giving Bennett his own off the wall advice.

In a moment of sincerity Gallo added, "Maybe he should have just let his anger out, haul off and knock the prick down. He would have been in deep shit but he wouldn't be dead."

There was a knock at the door and the boys got quiet. Then a couple of more knocks and Eaton gave in. He responded in a rough attempt at a disguised voice. "Who is it?"

The young voice of a patrol cop filtered through the door. "If anyone is interested some of the guys will be up to the Ferris. Gonna make a day of it."

Eaton looked around at his buddies. "Guess no hiding place is sacred...C'mon guys, let's lighten up. Besides, you know how sympathetic broads can be, and there's bound to be nurses up there."

Sean Walsh popped out of his seat. "The kid is right guys. We might as well make an Irish wake of it and see if we can get laid in the process."

Gallo poured his remains in the corner on the cement floor as Eaton quickly gathered the cans, hiding them deep in a bag to dispose of.

Frank was relieved just to get out of there. Eaton unlocked the door then stopped in his tracks. "Oh man, no."

"What is it?" asked Walsh.

"I have to stay on duty till six."

Gallo, who was already getting sloppy, laughed and wobbled from his chair. "Your loss, loser."

Since the cops seemed to be frozen around the door Frank leaned back against a desk and lit a cigarette. A little more time to be miserable. He felt like retreating to the precinct lounge. Though it was filthy, with the lights off it would be tranquil and he could relax for a minute. He wondered if anyone cared about anything. Frank suddenly thought about Kathleen; why, he couldn't understand. Maybe because she had been the last woman that had held him during any kind of crisis, and the memory of her arms around him inspired a craving to have himself tucked in a pair of delicate arms at this very moment. His three-ring fantasy also brought thoughts of Ann. Would she respond to him? Maybe not right now. Jenna? Who was he kidding? His light-headedness was making more of a romance with the two women than was the reality.

Walsh asked as if they were waiting on Frank the whole time. "Well are you coming buddy? Or do you like it in here?"

"Of course, you schmuck," Frank quipped.

As the cops were leaving the stationhouse they got a last whiff of the department's *business as usual* attitude. Eaton was at the front desk trying to finagle the rest of the day off and the desk sergeant was heard saying, "Sorry, there's a sector out at the hospital with a psycho and they need relief from a footman to resume patrol."

"But they said we could all have off," Eaton pleaded. The decision was final, Eaton wasn't leaving. He was told to stand by for a ride; he was to watch over a twenty-year-old female nut case found at home acting like a throwback from the '60s dropping acid. She was found ranting and strumming air guitar to no music. A cop would have to babysit her until a shrink saw her. Later it would make for a short story when Eaton finally made it to the bar. He told his buddies how this chick kept uttering nonsense.

"She kept asking for pop," Eaton said.

"Who's pop?" Walsh asked.

"Where's pop? Eaton mimicked.

"Who's pop?" laughed Colleri.

"Where's pop?" Eaton said mocking a tear.

"Who's pop?" said the others.

"Pop," said Eaton softly..."Pop, is Jimmy Hendrix."

"Jimmy Hendrix?" Walsh sputtered.

"*The* Jimmy Hendrix?" chimed in Frank. "Couldn't be."

"Of course not schmuck," Eaton said. "This chick was lily white and Hendrix was long dead before she was born."

The following morning, with both officers in their graves, the mayor called a press conference in another attempt to put close to the hysteria. The administration was banking on a carefully prepared speech and two late night busts (one involving drugs in Brooklyn, the other stolen cars in Queens) to touch the citizens of New York and fill them with encouragement to carry on their business without fear.

The key to the message was New Yorkers were tough and resilient, able to move forward. The speech, designed to hit home to the citizens of his city, was not easy for the mayor. The forthcoming election, premature erratic polls and the all night preparation for this speech sent the mayor to the podium hunched and pale. Tiny beads of sweat perforated the crown of his large skull. The city room was full of bright lights and camera equipment and even the usually dark textured and high reaching stately mahogany walls appeared to have a different shine to them.

Woven in the spirited speech were constant and strong words of calm aimed to uplift the administration. No cause for alarm or worry that a great number of police officers were mentally troubled. The shootings were an isolated incident. The citizens could rest assure that something of this extreme nature was more than likely to never occur again, and that in the end, the NYPD stood together. Then with a chance to excuse himself and save face the mayor added, "We, the officials of this city, along with the hierarchy of the police department, religious organizations, and top psychological profile experts have been in discussions for two days now and we have formulated a plan in which I assure you that new and immediate measures are right now being implemented to deter future incidents at the hands of a troubled police officer."

The mayor also made these statements as a means to assure the cops and their families that he had been very busy huddled with the media and the masses, therefore as a strong reason why he couldn't attend the funerals of the dead cops. Of course, everyone knew better. The mayor then had his political machine recap to add credence to the conference. He introduced the police commissioner who was flanked in excess by a number of high-ranking uniforms. Hoping to accomplish the rest of the mayor's mission the commissioner spoke, his stone face masked by a thick mustache. Training would start as before but more intently at the beginning, when the recruits were in the police academy. It would be mandatory for every cadet who passed through to be evaluated on a one to one basis with a trained professional: at the start, in the middle, and extensively at the very end of the completion of the training program. Also, problem cops would be monitored throughout their careers and...

Lastly, the mayor commended the policemen who made two late night important and newsworthy arrests. In Brooklyn: a drug arrest garnishing crack vials in the hundreds of thousands. In Queens: where the stolen car rate was off the charts, undercover officers came upon a house garage in Middle Village acting as a chop shop.

The average cop saw through the political smokescreen, smelling the politics brewing in an attempt to create a safety net for the voters of New York. Many cops felt it was a truly condescending performance by a police commissioner who would just as soon fire you than look at you. In reality, the PC was overly paranoid with concerns about corruption; and less worried about the number of police suicides.

However, to seal the mayor's promise to the city, the PC himself devised a plan to send a personal message to all active members of the department. He had a short film made, starring himself, sent through the mail, and addressed to the families of police officers, urging the family members to get involved and to convince their loved ones to seek proper guidance through the department if necessary. The message on the tape further promised that there were no limits the department would not go to in order to help its officers including a promise of anonymity.

"We are a family," the PC insisted. "And we encourage the confidence of those who wish to help themselves."

Again, the cops weren't buying this feigned concern. Word around the police world was that the tape was just another weapon for a disgruntled family member to use against a cop. The job was enticing family members to 'give them up' for even the slightest act of angry emotion or for just having a few drinks.

The outspoken Reverend John Wilson of Queens Ebenezer Baptist Church, community activist, and staunch critic of the mayor, was also not buying this propaganda. "If they're going to kill each other, imagine what they'll do to us!"

CHAPTER 30

"**n**o way—Don't!" she shouted in her sleep. When she woke in a sweat, she knew it had been a nightmare. The dream was ambiguous; faces and locations, no hint about the time of day. Just people. Three to be exact. Two naked. And though there were no faces to go with the bodies, Ann knew the victim in her dream was Frank Colleri.

She wiped her face with part of the sheet, grateful to be consciously awake. Still, the context of the dream was maddening. She realized how much she suddenly cared for Frank and began to cry softly at the thought of anything harmful happening to him

The afternoon of the police shootings Ann turned on the television just as one of those ridiculous soaps was breaking to a commercial. Moments later the news broke in. Still lost in her own thoughts she was not quite sure what she heard the newsman say. Shooting? Police Station? Queens? She became anxious, almost disbelieving. She paced her kitchen wondering if the nightmare she had was some kind of omen. *Could it be Frank? God no.*

Details were sketchy at best and she flicked through the channels getting more soaps and more commercials. She turned on the radio which confirmed the shooting of two police officers at the 117th precinct in Queens. She paced again for what seemed an eternity then she heard the news come on the TV and ran to it, crouching, peering into the screen. "Oh no, please," she said aloud.

It was the same stoic anchorman and his beautiful blond partner both looking and acting as grim as a newsperson should. The man began the tragic story; yet no names were released leaving Ann as confused and worried as before. She went to the phone in a frantic attempt to contact the 117th. The precinct line was busy, as she assumed, but she was too anxious to wait. Ann dialed Allison asking her friend to find out as soon as possible the name of the officer who killed his boss then turned the gun on himself. "Please," she pleaded to her friend. "I don't need details, just the name." She made her friend promise to let her know that day.

Ann then tried the 117 CPOP office, which was, of course, busy. She paced some more stopping to light a cigarette. There were probably cops scurrying to call loved ones to say they were safe, and likewise loved ones would be calling the precinct. *Besides, would Frank really think to call me? Relax.* She put the cigarette out and rubbed her palms down her legs.

She couldn't help but recall the dream. Did it trigger some kind of fate? The cloud of bodies lying naked, Frank in the middle, obviously in pain. It was as if she had known him her whole life, and though she had never seen his naked body she knew it was his. The bodies were horizontal; Frank lying sandwiched against a large man with no face just a hood and a blond female whose face was also unrecognizable. Though the assailants were white, Frank paled in comparison. Perhaps an illuminated metaphorical meaning. Frank was writhing, face down on the woman. He began crying, his face contorted uttering pleas: 'no, no.' The man on top, grabbing Frank's face, pulling his head upward. The blond woman was crying, the hooded man on top was angrily asking the woman, 'Do you want me to fuck this bastard for you my love?' That's where she woke up.

The ringing of the phone suddenly startled Ann. Her emotions swirled as she rushed to answer the dreaded call. Though she was sad for the young cop who killed himself she was also overjoyed with relief when her friend informed her it was not Officer Colleri. He was on a precinct junket to Atlantic City. Ann expressed the heartfelt thanks of a wife who just received the great news that her husband was alive and well. Now, more than ever, she wanted to call Frank, if just to offer condolences, an ear, or a cup of tea. She wondered if he was a participant in the immediate cop reaction of joining buddies on an unannounced bender to medicate their pain.

Again, she dialed and again the CPOP room was busy. She was still wondering if she even carried the distinction of being considered a loved one trying to find out if all was well. Finally, she decided that there would be plenty of time to talk with Frank now that she knew he was safe. Still, she needed to calm herself, so she lit another smoke.

Later, thinking more clearly, she thought about attending the cop's funeral. She wouldn't appear to be crowding Frank; rather she would be just another police officer mourning the tragedy of a comrade. Of course, she would run into Frank, offer her condolences, and if invited, would accompany Frank to wherever he was going. She could handle that now. She would be all right in a social setting, as long as Frank was with her. But she wouldn't frighten him with a story of such a bizarre dream where he was victim. He would surely think her nuts. Finally, she decided not to go.

* * * *

The Ferris Wheel was, as expected, overflowing with cops not only from the 117th but other precincts too. Carl was working the bar at his respected pace and there was also a number of nurses present who knew many of the cops. They were all there to talk about what happened and then to move on to life's curiosities and party commencement. The cops seemed grouped off into precinct clicks but circulated around to shake hands and catch up with guys they hadn't seen in ages. As the men got drunker, the bar filled with more ladies. The conversation grooved from cop talk to chicks.

As crowded as the bar was, there was always a chance of running into someone you not only didn't want to see but someone you didn't even want to wave to. Frank now noticed some friends of Kathleen's. Naturally, he scanned the heads in the crowd to see if she was there. It was more comfortable not to see her, yet he found himself hoping she was there. Rather than getting depressed about his ex-wife's non-presence he turned his thoughts to Jenna. Maybe she was somewhere in the crowd. He had already spotted some of her friends as well. He scanned around but didn't see Jenna.

Frank was fighting to overcome a case of the solemns and was quickly snapped out of it by a strong pat on the back from Gallo urging him to another drink. Frank looked over at the bar and noticed Walsh in conversation with a couple of other nurses they knew. Frank agreed to another drink slithering away from Gallo. He suddenly felt a weird loneliness among the group of people he should naturally converge with. It was similar to the feeling of being high on pot and feeling paranoid, exiting a situation only to feel as though he was looking back in. Good thing he hadn't smoked in years.

At least the cops were together. Strangely, Frank thought if others were wondering the same thing he was: Who would be next?

He grasped for a third fantasy hoping to refocus his mind. Should he call Ann? Would she wonder what happened? Of course. But would she be worried? Again, it was Gallo snapping him out of it, this time with strong vocal cords. Gallo was in Frank's proximity as he addressed the court he was holding and loudly announced how he was going to piss all over Reilly's grave.

When the cops had had their fill and began to spill from the bar, there were good-byes and secret good riddances.

Frank left with no female companionship, but he comforted himself with the thought of needing some rest any way. His head was pounding and he would probably throw up on top of any girl he was screwing.

Even though he convinced himself he needed time alone, the last thoughts he was thinking before sacking out were the sex stories his friends would be bragging about tomorrow. Frank passed out as soon as he fell into bed, neglecting to even remove his shoes.

Well at least I made it home and didn't vomit.

CHAPTER 31

The somber mood around the 117th began to level off. Life went on, even more so now that the weather was getting warmer and cops could revert to short sleeves if they wanted. Frank's life remained on hold. He wasn't moving on as planned. Instead, he felt doomed in a nowhere land. First, he was going to fix up the apartment, buy a few things to change the mood of a failed marriage. Now, he thought, for what?

There was the matter of his love life. Frank promised himself to call the women he thought he had at least a minimal chance of getting involved with. Then he decided rejection might cut too deep. The excuse he gave himself was that it was all for the idea of the chase, and since his motivation diminished, it was sure to be less aesthetic at the seduction phase.

He passed the time doing what he seemed to do all his life at different intervals. Hanging out, watching TV, more hanging out, talking with the guys in the bar, and at the end of the night dwelling on recent events.

He had hoped that the tragedy at the 117th would have an upside, as tragedy had for others in the past. It could bring loved ones together. Reconciliation with Kathleen remained out of the question. She was concerned but not much of anything else. As far as the nurse situation, it appeared that too much time had passed. He hadn't seen Jenna since the night he held her hand in the doorway of Ferris. He should have gone for it right there and planted a kiss on her. Others were leading their own lives, as they do, as they should. No person should stagnate in their world with thoughts of others. The reality of Kathleen in a new relationship crushed him.

Ann Caputo. She had left one message that he knew of: *Hope all is well. Please call me if you get the chance.*

That was right around Bennett's funeral. Frank never called back, and he still didn't know why. Well, perhaps he understood a little. Strangely, he had never given her his phone number, leaving the relationship safe within the bounds of professionalism. For whatever he felt for Ann physically, he also cared for her as a person; she didn't need the imposition of his troubles cast into her life.

Frank didn't know Ann would have gladly welcomed him into her life, troubles and all. That she wanted to call him a dozen or more times before she finally left that one message. She wanted and needed to hear his voice to see for herself that he was okay under all the macho cop crap. Frank had no way of knowing that many times after Bennett's funeral Ann felt remorseful for not attending. That she was stricken with fear. That she rehearsed what she might have said to him. 'Frank I know it bothers you a great deal, it does me too. I'm so sorry. Just let me hold you.' And she would have wrapped her arms tightly around him and he would have let her console him. Perhaps he would have cried and they would have cried together.

She would always regret not tracking him down, other than the one attempt. She knew that after the funeral the cops were probably at their favorite bar. Maybe a few drinks would have loosened her up, taken the edge off the panic. But that was all past now and obsessing wasn't going to help. She certainly would have been terrified to be out there, in the crowded atmosphere of peers, with hang-ups made worse by the stares of eyes wondering over her. She knew there would be those asking themselves if she had asked for it. Especially if Frank said anything to anyone about her flirtatious behavior on the day he was at her place.

Then there was the blurred one attempt to see Frank in person. An attempt that was a secret unto herself... A few days after Bennett's funeral she gambled on a visit to the precinct. It was a perfect early summer day, the kind capable of lifting the dreariest spirits. Ann lived close to the 117th precinct, and since the day was gorgeous, she decided a decent walk would do her good. When she turned the corner about a block from the station she immediately thought of a dead cop she never met. She thought of Frank. Then... *Who am I kidding?* She unexpectedly stopped walking. *What's really his story? Did my dream imply he might not be the nice guy I imagined?* She began to tremble with panic. Yet, she forced herself to walk further with quick paces trying to compose herself.

Ann certainly didn't look like a cop, especially on this morning. Her hair was combed straight and tucked girlishly behind her ears. She wore light makeup and a loose-fitting sundress that matched the small clips in her hair. She carried a white sweater folded over one arm so she appeared like any innocent strolling along.

She didn't realize they were staring until she almost reached the front of the building. Three uniform cops were standing at the top of the precinct steps practically gawking at her. She now noticed their smirks and became uncomfortable. She knew these cops were not giving friendly smiles, rather they were 'I want to have sex with you' smirks.

One of the cops already moved himself from the front door, feigning a queen's entrance by bowing and waving his arms as if throwing out the red carpet. "Let this beautiful lady through, boys."

Maybe a slight case of overreacting, but that was it for her, she felt nauseated, even as she knew they were harmless, like kids, hanging out on a corner. Luckily, none of the cops would associate her with Frank, so she turned and ducked up a side street just short of the building edge. She heard laughter and was glad she had escaped. *What was I thinking?*

* * * *

Frank found himself thinking more often than not, that there must have been something he could have done. Some kind of last ditch effort to prevent Bennett from committing the ultimate act. After all, he worked with the young cop on a number of occasions. Should he have spotted something? Instead he made those stupid comments about shooting Reilly.

Then there was the time in the locker room. Obviously, Bennett had been depressed. Why didn't he force the issue with John? Consciously he knew that answer. If a cop didn't want to be bothered then you didn't bother him. Certainly, you would never give him up to the boss. Still, one moment of complete compassion might have helped.

Frank hated these feelings. He'd lived with them for too long in recent months. It was the same with his brother. *Have I failed Peter?* Thank God Peter was still alive. But Frank had known about his brother's habits. He knew Peter was forever climbing behind the wheel of that huge car stoned. Who was he to be self-righteous? Everyone he knew drove drunk, including himself.

So, as Frank's pendulum of doubt and guilt swung to its lowest, he fantasized about his own demise. His mind was creating more imaginative thoughts than just suicide. He had temporarily gotten over that trip and moved on to the idea of going out in a blaze of glory. A drug bust gone bad. Or perhaps ripping an old lady out of the street before a bus hit her, only to have it crush him into the pavement. He would be the quintessential hero for the city. Helicopters would fly over the church at his funeral. City officials and maybe even political dignitaries would attend the mass.

The reality of these fantasies however was the catch-22. Frank hadn't even reached his ten-year mark on the job and already he was a hardened cynic. It was all nonsense to him now. The city, the job, the pay, the citizens, even many of the cops themselves disgusted him with bullshit war stories about tough guy bullshit he knew were complete fabrications. He wasn't about to go crashing any drug dens or diving in front of any buses for anyone. This city was a lost cause and nothing was worth trying to save it. All that was left for him was to ride an even keel and go with the flow of things. Just do what was required. No more, no less. Well maybe a little less. Ironically, the last time he got involved with anything resembling serious police work, he was with Bennett...

A while back the two filled in a sector when suddenly a GLA call came over the radio. Bennett answered immediately to respond. As they turned up Main Street near Kisena Boulevard Bennett spotted the blue Toyota. They pursued for five minutes, with a heightened adrenaline rush. Lights and sirens, they pursued. "This is real cops and robbers shit," Bennett exclaimed. In and out of streets, up Franklin down Barclay. Colleri at the wheel trying to hold steady but swaying plenty. They gave each other a look as if to say, *Holy Shit! It's like on TV.* Then the screech and sounds when the perpetrator crashed into a city bus on Union. The perp was cracked out of his mind, didn't even know his arm was broke. Other than the thief no one was hurt. Bennett made the collar. Frank remembered Bennett's sensible comment, "We could have been killed. It's crazy this city thinks of GLAs and burglaries as just property crimes."

The fallen Bennett... time was passing, the dead cop was becoming a memory, though not the incident itself. That was one for the storybooks. There were a few who were touched by Bennett's life that would still suffer lingering thoughts or nightmares. Certainly, the young desk officer on that morning would be one. The new sergeant wouldn't be quick in forgetting the carnage that began with shots being fired. The bodies, the blood. He became a seasoned vet overnight.

Sergeant Moore was another casualty. There wasn't much the tough Moore hadn't seen in his day. Over the years, he witnessed many cops lead self-destructive lives. Many of those cops sunk their own ships by either hedonistic behavior or loose lips. But the downfall of Bennett was different; maybe it was his age, maybe it was because he knew the kid's father, and now was relieved the old man wasn't around to witness his son's demise, or maybe he could have helped. Bennett's death was tough on the old-time boss.

So, Moore would retire, and never again worry about a soft spot for kids like Bennett. In the end, it was simple. Moore put his papers in, cleaned out his locker, said a few good-byes, and left the precinct. After all the friends, all the arrests, the good times and bad, the fights, the lonely posts and the stress, Moore felt as many cops did, it was the end of a prison sentence. His parting words to the CPOP guys were simple and uncharacteristically cold. "I've seen the city go under. From heroin in the 70s to crack. Now you guys will have to do some work. And learn how to read; if anything, just for knowledge."

Ironically, the last cop Moore said goodbye to was another old-timer. Whyte was a burnt-out veteran who had spent too much time on the violent streets of Brooklyn before finally settling in as the arrest processing officer and basic security guard at the 117th. After 35 years with the department he utilized his final days gathering paperwork for police officers to proceed with their collars as well as taking photographs and fingerprints of incoming prisoners.

The two dinosaurs found they were on the subject of Gallo. "What makes these young guys act the way they do?" Whyte said. "I was in the arrest room that day. He was blowing his cork, banging on the cells, 'black this, nigger that.' I told him to calm down, it's over now. It's not like he worked in the ghetto and was actually involved in fights with these black guys. I don't know. Are we to blame with our old war stories of the street? Streets these kids never saw. And they don't even fake it with words like tar, they go right to the N word."

"Who knows," Moore replied. "All I know is half these guys from the Island had maybe one black guy in their school when they were growing up. It isn't even as if they are really prejudice. I think they fall into this historic cop culture of tough attitudes, everybody and everything sucks and they don't even know why. Maybe saw it on TV or learned it from their fathers. They just want to be part of a judgmental club. Anyway, it should've been explained to everyone, but it is what it is, and might always be the cop culture, which is sad." Moore shook his head knowing even Whyte wasn't getting it.

"I had a reason to be slightly prejudice, which I'm not. I had to beat off a few blacks in Harlem during a time when these kids were sucking on their mother's tit," Whyte stated.

Moore patted the older cop on the back, eager to leave. He really didn't want to hear anymore, it was finished for him. "Well you know what the CO called this new breed of cop? Uninvolved, selfish, hedonistic little bastards! True eighty's Me Generation. The kid went too far on the wrong day. He knows it. Anyway, take care Whyte, and don't wait so long to collect that pension."

"It just sucks," Eaton said watching Moore walk off. "Everything's changing around this place. We all figured a few years on patrol then a cushy gig like this. But watch. They'll send a real schmuck-head down here and this CPOP crap will peter out before you know it."

As the boys finished up and were on the brink of melancholy, Walsh walked in. "Hey, I just saw Moore getting in his car. Guy looks sad or something..." And then with the Walsh flair to turn a story, he moved in another direction. "I just spoke to Callahan. He found out that rat Reilly was after Bennett for something else besides the accident report."

This piece of info caught their attention. They stared directly at the messenger. Even death couldn't cure the need of the curious for a good story; gossip or otherwise.

"Well, what?" snapped Gallo since Walsh paused too long.

"It seems that Bennett had accidentally, and knowing John I'm sure it was, well he put a summons on a car that had previously been summonsed and reported stolen."

"So? Big deal," said Gallo. The others knew the extent of the offense, especially with a guy like Reilly who would think it was a planned indiscretion to accumulate bogus summonses.

Eager to finish Walsh continued, "It seems John did this twice in one week on the same car. The second time a civilian called to complain that cops were ticketing a car that was sitting there for weeks and didn't belong to anyone who lived on the block...Scumbag Reilly was investigating, and we know the rest."

Gallo snorted. "Big deal he made of it. You don't have to run plates every time you tag a car."

"I'm with you. But Callahan says supposedly Reilly found a door jam, full of summonses. Most were faded except the fresh ones—"

"Bennett's," Colleri guessed.

"Bingo."

Eaton said, "So he wanted to bang the kid for failure to take police action, again...Reilly deserved what he got."

"That's for sure," Gallo said. "But Bennett waited too long. He should've pegged him the moment he got assigned here and started stalking cops. He should've just given him any answer, stayed on his toes."

"You mean like you did before you beat down the nig--I mean black kid." Frank said this half joking, not wanting a confrontation with Gallo. Frank thought Gallo was crazy to ever let the corner store situation get out of hand. There was just no need for all the excitement when Gallo could have easily shit-canned the job and walked away without even making an arrest. Gallo could have smoothed things out with the storeowner and the black kid without uttering one racial slur and thus being forced into a collar.

"*Ha ha,* that's it," Gallo said. "You try getting spit at." He laughed gathering up his equipment. "I still can't get over the fact I got into it with some black guy over a Jewish guy's candy and magazines. Anyway. I'm hungry. Anyone down for pizza?"

"Count me in," Eaton said.

"Me too," Walsh added.

They all turned to Frank. "No, I'm full. Besides, I have some calls to make."

But Frank really just didn't want company right now.

CHAPTER 32

Frank was finding it difficult to shake the memory of John Bennett. He was sitting at one of the desks in the CPOP room with his legs swung over its end. He stretched for the Rolodex and scanned the stained cards until he found Officer Benson's home phone number. Benson was another mild mannered CPOP cop, much like Bennett, though Benson, more a street cop, liked to make arrests. The two got along like close friends until Benson was called by the Nassau County Police Department.

"Hi, John. It's Frank Colleri."

"What's going on Frank?"

John, Frank thought. *How many Johns have I known?* "I don't know buddy, I guess I was thinking of John," a short laugh, "and I wanted to talk with someone who was close to him."

"Jeez, Frank. What a shame. I mean I tried getting close. I knew he was hurting and offered to go out with him a couple of times, you know, try to cheer him up and keep in touch. I knew he was distraught over the wife situation."

"Women. To hell with 'em."

"How's everyone holding up Frank?"

"You know," another short laugh. "Miserable bastards. You made the best move taking the Nassau County exam. That's the job to have now. You know how much this job sucks now. You won't regret it."

"Believe me Frank, I don't. But I do miss the guys." There was a pause, the way two acquaintances circled silence when they hadn't yet reached a certain level of friendship. "It was a sad funeral," Benson said.

"A bitch. Sorry we didn't get to talk much." Then Frank attempted to lighten the conversation to stay afloat with his emotions. "Do you think the angels will give him some of that hair back he was losing?" Both cops shared a casual laugh.

"Sure, they will. But only white to match his wings. You know something Frank? Even though John was a little weird when it came to getting in with people, I really don't think he had a mean bone in his body…I'm gonna miss the dude," Benson finished. "I'm glad his dad wasn't around for all this."

Frank let out a sigh, "Well, he's with him now. Yes, he was a good guy."

"Never gonna figure out what makes guys like Reilly tick. Why they go out of their way to hurt someone."

"My guess is a really shitty home life. Whore or ugly wife, lousy kids."

Then the boys said their good-byes, leaving Frank feeling good he made this phone call. Maybe somewhere else people were also remembering Bennett. Benson was one of the good ones. *Good luck,* Frank thought looking over at the phone.

* * * *

Ann made it to her door. Once inside she felt an imaginary safety net. Her mouth was agape and she was breathing heavy, but not so much from the rushing than from fear. Finally, she dug deep for the courage to venture from home, only to encounter fear from outsiders. She started to cry.

She had been feeling better, more confident. Of course, there were the horrible flashbacks, but she was starting to feel grateful for life, a little sad there was no man in her life, but she also knew that would be the slower of things to come in her return back to a life she was fighting to protect.

Spending time with herself was the first priority. Conquering some fears and insecurities was a goal. So, she was killing two birds with one stone by venturing out, not only to a possibly crowded mall, but by driving there as well. Her black-cherry 1980 mustang was her baby and she hadn't driven the car any distances other than the local store since her ordeal.

She drove west on Queens towards the mall. The drive had moments of the usual traffic and double-parked cars, situations that could annoy the calmest of motorists. But Ann hadn't really minded like she might have in the past. It just felt good to be behind the wheel, a finger touch away from the stereo dial. Ann always kept her car in fantastic shape, polishing it as often as she could, however in recent months the car had gotten a bit dusty. Still, on occasion her dad would stop by to wipe it down. She reached for the stereo flicking through the channels where the beginnings or endings of songs once again sounded good to her ears. It was a gorgeous day, Ann had her window open allowing the breeze to blow through her hair.

She lit a cigarette thinking how it was good to be out without having to call a friend to come along. She smiled thinking of Allison. But she needed this time to herself. She had to face a world she tried to escape from for so long. Driving, thinking, smoking, the weather and the music caused Ann to reflect on the men who passed through her life. A good healthy sign.

The famous question: What did it all mean? There were good times, yet she spoke to none of those guys now. Rather than feel remorse though, she thought of the future and its possibilities. Perhaps the sad cop she made tea for would figure in somehow. Tea and talk; a refreshing change from meeting someone in a bar. If she did feel remorse now it was because she hadn't gone through with trying to see him after being frightened off in front of the precinct.

Does he think of me in any way other than pity? Was he just doing a job? He seemed sincere, though he never pursued anything further. He couldn't have been shy. Not many cops were. She certainly knew of their aggressive nature on the job.

Ann parked on the third level of the circular mall. The newly renovated Queens mall with its plethora of new shops psyched her up a bit. She felt like a high-schooler shopping for clothes to forget a guy, all the while hoping they would somehow meet and he would admire her new attire. She entered the mall through doors that swung open into a row of impressive new and glistening pay phones centered on the immaculate, brightly patterned walls. Ann was so busy looking around that she nearly tripped over a young man hunched around the curve and talking on the last phone in the row before entering the main part of the mall.

"Excuse me," she said politely. But then their eyes met and a flush of hysteria swept over her, blanketing her with dread. His eyes were black, and though he did not verbalize, he spoke through his hardened stare. She panicked at the sight of his massive head, wrinkled and shaved.

When it was too late to turn away from those hard eyes he furthered her troubles by pursing his lips and making a kissing sound. Then he winked, eyes big as coals. There was no hood covering his face yet his presence seemed strikingly similar. *Can it be?* She dreaded. She walked away slowly as if she needed help, then she heard his course voice.

"Hold on," he said, into the phone. Then he was louder. "What's you lookin' at? Hey you."

Don't panic, Ann tried telling herself. *Run!* Her mind then urged. Instead, she continued on slowly. She glanced over her shoulder. *Stupid,* she thought. *Why entice him?*

He was cupping the phone and smiling menacingly. "Keep walking you tight bitch."

There was no misunderstanding him. Ann picked up her pace ducking out of his sight around the next row of storefronts. Once she was out of eyeshot and she realized he hadn't followed, she lit a cigarette nervously. She walked again, looked over her shoulder and took a deep drag. Finally, she stopped in front of a woman's store, now a possible refuge from the wide mall. She fingered the butt in one of the barrels and entered the store.

"I'm not," she swore to herself, "going to let this destroy my day. I can't." Ann turned her attention to a rack of summer blouses as a young salesgirl moved quickly to assist her. The girl went through the rack with her, chatting about the best colors for this year. The girl recommended one of the yellow floral prints and Ann nodded holding it under her neck for mock fit view.

"We also have some great acid wash jackets and jeans to match," the girl said.

Then Ann's eye caught the windowpane of the storefront. There he was! The man from the phone was pressing huge lips against the glass, his eyes bulging.

He found me! Ann panicked. *It's him, the same guy.* She dropped the blouse and instinctively crouched behind the rack.

"Are you all right?" the girl asked. She was oblivious.

"Is he there? Is he still there?"

The girl knelt beside Ann. "Who miss? Is who there? Are you okay?"

Ann squeezed the girl's arm, more tightly than she meant to. "Check. Check if he's there."

The girl looked up. "I don't see anyone miss. Are you sure—"

"Never mind," Ann said standing. "I'm sorry. I'm sorry."

"Do you want me to call mall security?"

"No, no. But can I please use your phone?"

Ann sat in the front of the police car with a polite cop. His partner was following in Ann's Mustang, not something she anticipated. They walked Ann up to her door and asked again if there was anything else they could do, anyone they could call for her. Ann was apologetic and assured them that she was fine, now that she was home. She offered the cops something to eat but they begged off having to return to their precinct. When the cops left and she thanked them for what seemed like a million times, she closed the door suddenly feeling a complete loneliness.

There was a moment of heavy breathing and panic.

She went to the phone. "CPOP please," she said to the operator. After there was no answer the line switched back to the operator.

"One Seventeen, how can I help you?" The female's voice sounded immature with the sound of gum snapping.

"Is officer Colleri in today?"

"Hold on...Sorry I don't see him down on the roll call and I haven't seen him around. Take a message?"

"No, thanks."

Ann went into the kitchen and grabbed her phone book. Suddenly she realized she didn't have Frank's home phone number. He never offered it and she never bothered to ask. Now she wondered if he even wanted her to know it. Her intuition gave her reasons why a male cop would not want to release his number. Wives were at the top of that list.

Ann decided to call Allison for yet another favor. She would have to be quick and tactful though because if they had time to chat she would tell Al about the mall incident and her friend would want to rush right over. She was grateful for such a friend, but now she felt the need to be comforted by someone else. A man. Someone gentle like Frank Colleri. She yearned for caring yet masculine arms around her, assuring her that everything would be all right.

While she waited for her return call, Ann paced her apartment and attempted to suck up the negative. How would Frank react? Annoyed? Distant perhaps? She lit a cigarette, and just like anything that pops uninvited into the mind, she envisioned the man's lips pressed tight on the storefront window. Then by the phone with that hard sarcastic grin. "Hey, what you lookin' at bitch."----I AM GONNA FUCK YOU WOMAN---- "Keep walkin' bitch"----I GOT ME A FREEBIE ----A REAL COP.

She began spinning obsessively out of control. She was shaking the moment the phone rang but relieved for the outside intervention.

"Be careful," Allison told her. "Are you sure you know what you're doing? It's so soon. I know I'm the last to say, but maybe you're rushing things, obsessing over someone you hardly know?"

"I know, I know. You told me that, how many times? Look... I know you're concerned, but I'm fine Al. Really. Don't worry, I'm not obsessing, and thanks so much."

Ann sat back in her favorite chair to collect herself for a moment. *Am I doing the right thing here? Is Frank sincere telling me to call anytime?* She dialed quickly so as not to change her mind. The phone rang three times and now she felt a surge of relief that he might not be at home. She could put off her nervous proposal for another time. Just before she hung up a woman's voice answered. The woman sounded sweet and blissful. Still she didn't hang up hoping she now had the wrong number.

"Hi, is Frank Colleri at home?" she stated in a trained professional manner.

"No I'm sorry he's not. Can I take a message?"

It was not a wrong number and Ann suddenly felt foolish, but she hung in there. "Ah, yes. This is Officer Sullivan from his precinct roll call. Do you uh, know when he will be at home?"

"No I'm sorry. Actually, I thought he was at work."

He's lying to her too, Ann thought "No, he's not. Who am I talking with?"

"His wife. Are you sure he's not there?"

"I'm sure. Sorry to have bothered you Mrs. Colleri. I'll try again later." She's going to give him the message anyhow.

"No bother. I'll tell him to check into work when I hear from him. Bye now."

Ann lowered the receiver calmly, but she had a sense it might be the calm before the storm. She couldn't even dislike the wife who was so sweet. *How could I be so foolish?* Simple. She had fallen for Frank and the pain of sudden jealously confirmed how true it was. He must still be in love with and living with his wife.

Suddenly she was lightheaded. She hadn't eaten a thing. She had planned to grab lunch at the mall but as hungry as she was the lump in her throat wouldn't allow any food. Next would come the dry heaves. She went to her bed stretching face down into her pillow. She began to cry. First softly, then in sobs. When her eyes were soaked with tears and her head felt like a banging drum, she faded into a soft whimper.

* * * *

Kathleen turned back before leaving the apartment, which she knew was now Frank's alone. She sat in the kitchen and wrote a short note.

Dear Frank,

Thanks so much for letting me stop once more and get the shoes I was looking for. Silly me, I thought I got everything. As luck would have it a handbag was tucked away near the shoes. I'll mail my key back to you because I would rather not leave it in the hall, even though you are a cop. (Ha, Ha)

Anyway, thanks again. Say hello to Peter for me. I'm glad he is doing well. Oh, before I forget. An Officer Sullivan from your precinct roll call called earlier today. I thought you were working and let it slip. I hope I didn't give you up, as you would say.

Take care of yourself Frank. And I do hope you are doing well.

Love,
Kathleen

Two new bosses were transferred to the 117. One was a sergeant to replace the retired Moore. Since the new sergeant was also a rookie boss he was fit into a day tour squad while the existing day boss, the one who had his life experience changed on the morning gunshots rang out, was offered the CPOP slot. Sergeant Dempsey willingly accepted.

The other boss arrived the same day, a lieutenant. Rumor had it he was handpicked for the precinct by the chief. The circulating rumor also stressed that the new lieutenant, who was to be Reilly's replacement, was not going to just sit back and let things fall into place. It didn't help that he resembled the dead lieutenant in physical stature. He was not handpicked to be a sympathetic boss. Word was spreading that the new boss had a reputation as an A1 hardass, not caring one iota about what people thought of him. To further the rumors, the new boss was said to have leaked it out that things were not going to be easy just because some cop shot his supervisor.

The change in attitudes was noticeable immediately. The cops in CPOP knew no boss would be as easy going as Moore. However, there was no bad word on the younger Dempsey. As if he had a point to prove, Dempsey showed immediate signs of stringency which at first the guys attributed to his being a shaky newcomer in a cushy job. That's what Eaton analyzed. He said Dempsey was showing a nervous ass-kissing trait early on, there might still be hope after he settled in.

One morning during Dempsey's first week at the CPOP helm, a job came over for a patrol unit to respond to the old run down hotel on Franklin; a complex for emotional rejects who couldn't manage well on their own, subsidized by a generous city and state. The origin of the hotel was that it was a place which used to have class until someone threw themself out a fourth-floor window. This radio run was in regard to an emotionally disturbed individual needing hospitalization. Rather than have the sector concerned sit with the EDP in the psyche ward, Dempsey volunteered Eaton off his foot post to keep from putting a car out of service for possibly the rest of the tour. Dempsey thought he was doing right by not tying up a sector car, but his men felt they were being screwed. He could have done what Moore did many times in the past. Just say his men weren't available at this time.

Later, Eaton told his buddies how certain it was that Dempsey was just licking ass and would give up any of them to look good to the captain. "I was there," Eaton said. "He plucked me. I get stuck with all the nuts. I should be wearing a white coat instead of a blue one. I had to sit in the spaz-house with this old broad from that sleaze hotel and all the while, from the ambulance to the hospital, she's screaming and bitching and moaning, doubled over in pain like she's gonna puke any second. You almost feel sorry for the broad...anyway, you know what it was?" Eaton looked at his friends. "You know what all the fuss was about with this bitch?"

Colleri said, "Well? Are you going to keep us in suspense?"

"It was the little men," Eaton declared. Then he said nothing letting the punch line hang.

"What little men? Little man," Walsh joked.

"It was the little men this broad knew from her past. They were in her, inside her stomach, stabbing at her with little pitchforks." Eaton formed his fingers to simulate pitchforks. "The little demons wouldn't leave her alone."

The tale drew a rousing laugh and so much for another war story.

Eaton was the first to decide Dempsey was just a new loser on the block. Another morning had six CPOP cops feigning paperwork an hour into their tour, trying to kill time. Their beat books were open, poised for the active effect of showing concern for the goings on in their perimeters. *Yes boss, can't you see I'm doing my work?*

Eaton playfully tapped the nape of Gallo's neck. "Put your shoes on idiot, your feet stink."

Gallo reacted to the slap as if a small bug had crawled on his neck. "Watch it you moron. Good thing you didn't touch the hair."

Dempsey looked up from his desk but said nothing... yet.

"That's the only thing you have going for you, you glutton," Walsh interjected. "At least you have great hair."

"It's all the Chinese food he eats," Eaton joked.

Again, Dempsey looked up, but the boys paid him no mind. They were accustomed to banter and now there were the usual rounds of laughs.

Gallo's biased reply was not quiet. "That's right. How many bald Chinamen have you seen? And by the way fellas' any particular reason why my feet are being mentioned? No one happened to notice I've been itching today."

Walsh couldn't conceal his grin, which grew wider. "What are you talking about?"

"As if I don't know you guys," Gallo said. "I leave my shoes on top of my locker for one week in my whole career and one of you morons put some itching powder in them."

"Could have been worse," Eaton said.

"That's right," Frank added. "Could have been piss in your shoes."

"Then I would have pissed on your heads."

Dempsey looked up again but this time he spoke. "I see beat books," he announced somewhat seriously. "I see a bunch of cops. But I don't see anyone doing any work."

With their usual noisy antics, combined with the sound of a loud humming air conditioner, the boys weren't sure they heard Dempsey right.

"But my feet," Gallo said laughing, causing the others to stir.

"You guys might find all this funny. The bottom line is this unit appears to be jerking off. If you guys like it here I don't want to see it continuing." He said this matter of factly, without looking any one cop in the eye.

"Oh, and will someone tell that male hooker in the municipal lot his free parking days are over. He might have that AIDS thing and we don't need him spreading it around town. Tell him disappear or be hauled in. That's your post Gallo, isn't it?"

Frank made the first move with his body and everyone followed to exit.

"Jerk," Gallo whispered under his breath to Frank. "Moore never gave a shit."

"Screw it," Frank said, as he turned back and the room cleared, he stepped over to his mailbox. He began to nonchalantly retrieve complaints from the slot.

"I forgot to check these sarge. It'll only take a few." It was wise for Frank to announce his intentions since the chill from the air conditioning was not the only frost permeating in the air.

Dempsey returned to whatever was in front of him and Frank pondered why he really stayed behind because he was certainly not in the mood to decipher complaint reports. The day was too young to linger. He looked over at the moody boss and decided he really didn't care what the guy thought. Going through the complaints he noticed there was still an extreme amount of paperwork listed under the sex crimes category. *Damn,* he thought as he thumbed through the stack. *I thought this priority was done with. Dumb chick. Doesn't she know this is no longer the hot topic on beat 9?*

Frank was thinking of the female civilian administrator who did all the paperwork and filing in the office. He shared the opinion with most cops that she and many of the police aides were no brain surgeons. One of the cities easier civil service tests.

In an attempt to waste more time, Frank skimmed the reports actually stopping to read some of them.

SEXUAL ABUSE: The reporter states that the above person (perp) who is the grandmother's boyfriend did touch his penis...

RAPE: Victim states the above perp grabbed her in a chokehold by the neighborhood church. Victim further states that said person then dragged her into the dark alley of same church and forced her to take her pants down, where he then ordered her to turn around...

SODOMY: The person reporting states that the above perpetrator did approach her in front of the elevator in the building where she resides. Perp then put a knife to her belly and forced her to walk towards the laundry room, where the perp then forced the victim to her knees and ordered the victim to suck on his penis...

This is unbelievable, Frank thought. *You can't make it up. It never stops.* He glanced at a few more as if reading a newspaper that contained the same bad news.

RAPE/ROBBERY: The complainant states she took a ride from said person after her bus had not arrived and she was in a hurry. Perp, who was a stranger, then drove complainant to a secluded area by the boat docks. He forced her to have vaginal sex then he kicked her out of the auto after also stealing fifty dollars from her wallet...

Frank shook his head and in the interim caught Dempsey looking up at him then back down. It was a glance that if spoken would have said: I thought it was just going to take you a few minutes. Frank decided to read on. He just wasn't concerned today.

RAPE/SODOMY: Victim states that the above perp did force her into having oral sex, anal sex, and vaginal sex with him.

Period. That was the victim's statement. *Odd,* Frank thought. Such a bland description of a crime that carried such personal magnitude. Then again, he knew many of these victims kept their statements brief out of sheer fear.

RAPE/ASSAULT: Victim states while waiting for the elevator she was hit from behind with a blunt instrument that knocked her unconscious. Victim further states she did not see anyone until she awoke in the basement of her building. Though it was dark she was able to make out two male Hispanics who were laughing as they exited the room. Victim further states that she knew she had been raped. Her panties had been torn off and the pain was so great between her legs where in fact she also could not remove her tampon....

That's explicit. Definitely, cannot make this up. Frank looked over at Dempsey. *And this idiots' biggest worry in life is if his cops are on their posts.*

SEX ABUSE: Complainant states her mother's boyfriend who is male white, sixty years old, did try to touch her private parts on more than one occasion.

Now there's your classic dirty old man. The mother's probably a dried up, hard up, old bitty. The old broad knew and was desperate enough, or stupid enough, to stay in a relationship with the perv. The patterns of familiarity over the year in CPOP had Frank feeling as though he had already read these complaints. Something in the next complaint caught his attention as he spotted the words almost immediately:

I AM GONNA FUCK YOU WOMAN!

ATTEMPTED RAPE: The above female states that the said perpetrator did grab her breast while she was walking on the street. The perp then stated, "I am going to fuck you woman." The victim then kicked the perp in the groin and ran away to find some help.

"That's a good girl," Frank said softly to himself. Yet he thought of someone else who had heard those words. Someone who couldn't get away from her attacker in the moment of despair. A sadness for his friend fell over him with a chill. A strange feeling of guilt because he had looked up the separately filed report sequestered in the detective squad, where reading of Ann's report gave him a sickening feeling. He logged this report in the back of his mind wondering if this could be the same guy that raped Ann.

Tired of reading the heartache in other people's lives, Frank stuffed the stack back in his mail slot; all but one, he still held in his other hand and now felt compelled to read.

SEXUAL ABUSE: The mother of the victim left her father, the child's grandfather, to babysit her three-year-old for an hour so that she could run some errands. When she returned, she changed the baby's diaper, and found a small amount of what she perceived to be hair and sperm in the diaper.

My God, this is nuts. The report went on to state that the kit was prepared at the hospital where sex crime and special victims' detectives were on the scene. Frank shook his head and stuffed the final report in the slot wishing now he hadn't read it. He felt weathered after reading through the reports, only to top it off with another dirty old man story; Frank felt they should just cut the old pervert's balls off. He tried reminding himself what Sergeant Moore once said, "You're there to assist the victim, not discuss their problems."

This was all leading up to Ann. He turned to the phone with the idea of just dialing quickly so he wouldn't back down, but noticed Dempsey was looking up again. There were other phones in offices upstairs so Frank decided to use one of them. He left the CPOP office without as much as a slight acknowledgment to Dempsey.

Climbing the stairway didn't prevent him thinking of her. Was he really her friend? Would she remember him fondly, and the brief moments they shared? He certainly enjoyed her company. Cherished was too strong a feeling for now. He innocently remembered the smell of her perfume, the adolescent feeling of attraction he felt. The painfully shy way he refused to advance on her. The way she answered the door, with bare feet. In the macho circles he ran in, this would have to remain his own secretly exciting sensation.

Frank decided to use one of the phones lodged behind the wood plank of the telephone switchboard. He could call Ann using the excuse there was news her attacker might have surfaced. But then again, why get her upset, or her hopes up? As he reached toward the phone he couldn't help but notice the stack of paper in the police officer's courtesy message box. He thumbed through the messages and sure enough one of the folded white pieces of paper had his name on it. He thumbed it open and read the message: Call Your Wife! *Do I still have a wife?*

* * * *

Here's what Frank soaked up during his short time on the job: Social emotions in the police department are as flip and flap as stress and calm. There's the moment a cop could be sitting in a car in a secluded area enjoying the proverbial donuts and coffee, talking about the job, sports and broads, or just reading the newspaper while his partner catnaps. Then the static and squelch of the department radio, a sound their ears become accustomed to. The level of anxiety would then rise in accordance with the type of job about to come over the air. Maybe a robbery in progress, or a burglary. And of course, the all-important, adrenaline rush, of a 10-13 signaling a cop needs immediate assistance.

Cops young and old experienced high anxiety levels that went from sleep deprivation, to highly charged adrenaline pumping. Searching for a burglar in a pitch-dark house. Riding onto the scene of a high-octane street fight, perhaps weapons involved. Decision making had to be made spur of the moment and primarily for safety. Then other factors like how far one could push the system in the eyes of a politically motivated power structure.

There were other emotions just as dangerous to a cop, especially the younger guys. They were extremely volatile emotions that would statistically conquer the turbulent life of a cop destined for trouble: those who lost control, beating their wives or children, smacking perps around needlessly, or committing suicide.

And the emotions that followed the infamous social habits many cops wore as proudly as the shields on their chest. These social mongers like Walsh and his cohorts were not much different than the average construction worker or Wall Street executive. They were part of the male species who craved an after-work beer and the coming of the weekend. Still, the cop had differences. Most importantly, the confrontation of life and death.

Many of the boys in blue worked odd hours along with rotating weekends. The infrequency of a regulated life seemed to help them find more energy as the week moved forward. Any night of the week was an excuse to hit the gin mills. There was always a bar to frequent each night of the week. Another bonus for many, especially the young and charismatic cop, was the endless supply of young women, many enjoying their nineteenth birthday bash with finally legal cocktails. On a good night, girls could be found hanging out on the boulevards, in their cars or on their way to here or there, or in stores, wherever a uniformed cop could get a leg up to strike a conversation of feigned friendship while still on duty. The uniform was luxury in situations such as these. And though Walsh was naturally good with the ladies off duty, he picked up many women while riding the streets in a radio car. It proved a point he stressed to his friends many times. Being neatly groomed in uniform enhanced confidence. Possessing both, you were truly a blue magnet. He stated boldly, "Who else but us could stare women down, right in front of their boyfriends, and get away with it?"

Unfortunately, though, many young cops wanted their cakes and eating it too. Hence the ruination of many new marriages. It was also Walsh who warned Frank about some female cops he considered just good enough for a party. Some needed a little more working on than others, but in the end, they all could be had. They would get just as drunk and just as horny as the guys. Conflict arose when the ugly reality snuck up and bit many of them on their asses. Frank had never been with a female cop. His brain took over in his married life, and he was scared off by all the horror stories he heard from the guys.

One such story involved a young married cop, Paul Falcon, who worked in the 117th. This cop was screwing one of the rookies and when he wanted to break it off she decided to call EEO (Equal Employment Opportunities). She claimed it was sexual harassment. She also called his wife but when neither phone call dramatically went her way she called IAD and told them Falcon followed her into the female lounge of the precinct, pulling out his penis and whacking off. "He then begged me for sex and if I refused," she paused dramatically, "he would blow my head off." Of course, everyone who knew Paul knew this didn't happen, but they took his guns, sent him for psych evaluation, then transferred him. His wife finally divorced him. This was just one nightmare story of many.

Another factor was new marriages came with unconventional wives now, wives who wouldn't tolerate their men running amok and doing whatever they pleased. At the time, Frank had no intention of becoming a statistic.

He wondered if a girl like Ann could just loose it and decide to make a complaint. She could say Frank was coming on to her and sue the job. No, she isn't the type. She'd seen plenty and never hinted at going forward with any complaints. She could even have complained about the callousness of her investigating detectives.

And then there was the job. Lately it had become extremely boring, especially with all the changes in the precinct. Drinking as a single man was becoming routine. Simply, Frank was fatigued both mentally and physically and he wished he had someone of substance to return home to.

* * * *

Frank was totally surprised when Kat phoned to suggest they meet for coffee. His surprise also brought unrest. He was beginning to resign himself to the notion of not seeing her anymore. Now he was afraid of the yo-yo effect. They agreed on a weekday. Frank knew this would enable her to cut it short. There would be the bothersome idea all evening that she had work the next morning. Kathleen hadn't hinted what the talk was about. However, she sounded a little like the Kat of old rather than the confident and abrasive woman who insisted on a divorce. He tried to remember the tone of her voice, analyzing her mood. He had the car radio turned off so he could clear his head and think of her voice and the short of the conversation.

"If you're not busy Frank, I'd like to buy you a cup of coffee."

Strange. Not a drink. He thought of phoning Ann. But now most of the summer had gone by.

rank's night was, as expected, a restless one. As the wee hours approached he thought it best not to force sleep. His entire thought process recapped the entire marriage, highlighting what he thought to be important moments with his wife, conversations both good and bad.

Work was still hours away when daylight finally broke. Frank walked to the store for coffee and a newspaper. Once home, he sipped the hot coffee and scanned the paper. He didn't look for any police articles, in particular. Not interested. Nevertheless, any paper in New York had some article pertaining to cops. Frank stumbled on an article with a side photograph showing a blue and white car and next to it an artist's rendition of the same car painted entirely white. The column detailed a nationwide survey suggesting the color white be considered for police vehicles throughout the country.

Frank laughed, thinking about never-ending police propaganda, contrived to appease the growing number of liberals. Actually, Frank did remember hearing something about the push to have cars transformed to all white, at least in major cities. The writer of the article went on to explain; though Frank already surmised the reason: a positive survey explaining a white radio car was a more passive color. Therefore, the police would appear less intimidating.

A bunch of liberals thinking of the poor dirt bag in the street who might not feel the urge to commit a crime if he saw the 'light.' Frank's pun made him laugh to himself. This story was too unreasonable to read on. He turned the pages and spotted another article of interest. The next column dealt with driving under the influence. Was there a major difference between the driver stoned on pot as opposed to the driver highly intoxicated from alcohol? This columnist was offering the idea that a person who drove solely under the influence of marijuana might be less erratic or reckless in manner. Mellower, so to speak. The writer did go on to state that such a mellow effect would cause slow reflexes and diminished concentration, dangerous conditions on the roadways of America. *No kidding. Another brain surgeon writer. Tell that to my brother, Sherlock. He wrote the book on pot and driving, and his accident was certainly no fender bender.*

Frank suddenly devised a strange picture in his mind. In slow motion a white police car was ordering his brother to pull the big Caddy to the side of the road. Frank smiled. Then just like that, he closed the newspaper, bored with it.

* * * *

Many times, a patrolman would have to answer up for their troubles around the holiday's or coming up on vacation time. Such spiteful tactics would add pressure to a cop. Arthur Gallo planned a three-day getaway with his wife and small son. His vacation was less than a few weeks away. On that same humid morning that Frank was tiring of the paper, Gallo was reporting for an early tour at the 117th. At the front desk the sergeant handed him a notification slip. He read it as he walked away. "Damn," he whispered to himself.

The date was regarding the hearing for the smoke shop incident. The time to answer up had arrived. He was to report next Monday to the Queens Inspections Unit at 9 a.m. The notification also stated that GO15 was in effect. To most cops this was considered a trivial incident. If anything, it should have remained in house as a civilian complaint, maybe forwarded to the civilian complaint review board. If inspections services were involved, this meant management was taking it seriously. It was the GO15 that added to Gallo's worry. This meant he had to show up at inspections with a PBA attorney. Gallo folded the notification and tucked it into the sleeve of his memo book. He'd deal with it later. *Morons' in inspections. They love this stuff,* he thought.

At the front desk the sergeant signed the notification given and received sheet. He had one more to issue and it seemed of similar circumstance. However, the other officer was not due in until late shift. The sergeant stapled the notification to the four by twelve roll call. It was out of his hands now. Let the next boss deal with it. Still, like most cops who craved gossip, the sergeant wondered what kind of trouble PO Gallo and PO Colleri had gotten themselves into. No rumors of repercussions had circulated…as of yet.

* * * *

Ann was attempting an afternoon nap when the phone rang. Her body was tired, but it was mostly mental exhaustion which kept her down.

She practically had to drag herself to answer the phone. She was glad she did. Certainly, the last person Ann expected to hear from was Frank Colleri.

"Hello, Ann?"

"Yes. This is she. Who is this?" She hadn't forgotten his voice. She knew it was him after he said hello.

"It's Frank. Frank Colleri."

"Oh, Frank. Long time no hear from. How are you?"

"I'm sorry Ann. I really have been meaning to call you—"

"Its fine," she cut in. "I was kidding, I know you're busy." She wondered what Allison would have said to *meaning to call.* 'Yeah, right. They're all the same Ann.'

"Not too busy," he said. *Yeah right,* she thought, Allison style. Probably busy with Mrs. Colleri. "Has everything been okay with you?" he asked with genuine concern.

"Yeah, well, you know. I'm hanging in there pretty good. Hey, I'm told it won't be long before I get my guns back. A couple of weeks at the desk in the borough at most, I hope."

"That's great Ann. Are you going to go right back to patrol?"

"Nah. I'm going to get a nice cushy, do nothing post. Like all the other women." Her remark hinted sarcasm but with enough fluff not to sound too serious.

"Okay, okay, I'm sorry," he laughed.

"I think they're going to send me for range certification first, especially since the whole job's going that way anyhow. And...they did offer me inside—but before you jump, remember I've been out sick a long time, Frank. The job did take care of me."

"No, I know. I just..."

"Thinking of your friend John, aren't you?"

"Not just him Ann. I look at others, quiet like him, and I assume—"

"You can't run around thinking about that all the time. There was nothing you could have said or done to save him. Or anyone else. Just as if you were my guy," she said rather easily. "There would have been nothing you could have done for me."

"You're right. Now let's change the subject. Any chance of tasting some of that tea of yours?"

"Is my tea special or something? Besides I thought I was the only one who drank tea in warm weather."

"Yes, your tea is special, besides we could turn the air condition on to solve the other problem."

"How's tonight?" she said. He couldn't see her squint. *Stupid. First I allude to him as my guy now I am blatantly anxious.*

"Sounds great, Ann. But I have to clock in at two o'clock today."

"What time do you get off? Ten---ten thirty?" *Too desperate?*

"Won't that be late for you?"

"Oh yes. I'll melt."

"Sorry again," he said. "It's not too late for me if it's not for you."

"I concur."

"You know, let's play it safe in case I get stuck at work. How's this weekend?"

"Okay, call me," she said. And when they hung up she was grinning.

For Ann, it now seemed ages ago when Allison made a trip to her apartment to check on her, yet it had been only a few days ago. Al found her instincts to be right on when she saw Ann in a chair with tears in her eyes.

Funny what a phone call can do, Ann thought, the smile still there. Feeling ages beyond that night not long ago, with Allison and tears for hours. What a good friend Al was, through everything. Even after Ann attempted feverishly to convince her everything was fine, Allison still rushed to her friend sensing something was not quite right. She even joked with Ann telling her that her anguish was too detectable. Most people, even close friends, might have stayed away at Ann's request. An adamant **no** would have been enough of an excuse for some to not feel guilty. But Allison was special. Finding Ann in tears, listening about the phone call and the woman on the other end of the line.

"I told you to be careful," Allison said. Still, she listened, stayed a while, didn't preach, and then gave her friend a long hug when it was time to leave. She did leave Ann with one message: "Be careful of the cop you fall for. He probably belongs to another woman...you know they are just male whores...You're not here to stroke their ego; it's not your job to make them feel better, remember that." Allison spoke with the voice of experience and warned that Frank could bring more pain.

CHAPTER 35

The moment Frank felt the touch of Kathleen's mouth again was complete ecstasy. It was as if they were kissing for the first time. All that corny stuff about how a girl could take your breath away. It was true. What made it all the sweeter was that it was so unexpected. Frank never thought he'd be sharing an intimate moment with her again. Now it was certain, he would never forget the softness of her lips. The feelings of the whole moment almost brought him to juvenile tears. At least that's what his friends would think.

Kat's idea to share a coffee was supposed to be just what it implied. Not a snap decision detour to the local gin mill that also served food. They took a booth in the rear of the bar, though it really didn't matter since there were only a half a dozen or so people lingering about anyway. Still, sitting in a booth seemed more private. They were both nervous. Ironic that a couple that knew each other couldn't feel what occupied the other. Frank ordered a beer and fries while a hungry Kathleen decided on the cheeseburger deluxe with a bottle of beer.

They nervously engaged in small talk as if they were on their first date. Asking about this family member, or this friend or their jobs. Then the food came and Kathleen grabbed the butter knife and immediately concentrated on the huge burger. Frank grinned affectionately as he watched her slice into the bun. It was a part of the past that brought an instant recollection.

She smiled back at him. "Something funny?"

"Still can't just bite into it whole," he said.

"I still have my habits," she replied. "As I'm sure you still do." She pointed to the pack of cigarettes on the table to his left.

Frank worried that she was getting a little defensive. Perhaps they were both on guard with each other's thoughts and words. He hoped they would be able to just go with the flow and avoid any arguments.

"Oh, by the way Frank. I'm sorry about telling that cop, *uh*, Sullivan, that you were working. You probably were busy somewhere else."

"Oh, that. Seems like years ago." He laughed. "Funny thing Kat. You must have gotten the name wrong 'cause I don't know anyone in the precinct with that name."

"Then I guess you have a secret admirer." She winked at him.

"Yeah, you're probably right. I should be used to it by now," he said playing with her.

"Sure," she said. "No doubt with all those studs you hang out with. How could any woman resist you guys?"

Frank cleared his throat hoping to change the subject. He took a forkful of fries followed by a gulp. "So, anyway. Did you get everything you needed from the apartment?"

"So anyway, yes, as the note said...I see another one of your habits," she mimicked his mouth full, "hasn't changed. Close your mouth and finish your food."

Strangely he wondered if he'd put a finger in his ear yet. *No, she would have noticed.* "So Kat, I'm sure you didn't want to see me just to critic me. For what do I owe the pleasure?"

"You see," she said. "Sarcasm—"

"I'm not being—"

"It's okay. Can't we be friends? Can't we just talk, and hang out, once in a while?"

Frank reached for her hand. "Remember the house with those beautiful Cypress trees we were planning to buy?"

She pulled away. "Don't."

He exhaled in frustration. "We've been over this, my dear soon to be ex-wife. You know how hard that would be for me right now."

His confession obviously touched her and made it simpler to say what she wanted. First, she looked away, and then turned to him. "I'm not trying to screw with your mind Frank, but please try and understand...I know it's not right, but I do miss you Frank. I just wanted to see you. You know, sit and talk. If that bothers you, then I'm sorry."

He smiled at his soon to be ex. "Finish your burger. Listen, it's okay, it really is. I'm really glad to see you too. As a matter of fact, when I knew you were at the apartment, and I read your note...well it just felt as if..."

"As if we were still married?"

"I'm sorry Kat, but yes...It's hard for me to stop loving you." *There I said it.*

She bit into half the burger and moved the conversation. "How's Peter? Is he feeling better?" She whispered, "Did he quit...smoking pot?"

Frank hated how she easily changed the subject, but he promised himself no fighting. "Physically he's doing fine. But I don't think he'll ever quit."

"That's too bad. How about you?" She said this nonchalantly.

"Me?" he laughed. "You know I never touch the stuff."

"C'mon Frank. You know damn well what I mean. Are you slowing down?" She hoisted her thumb back mocking the definitive message of drinking a few. "And I'm not talking about just beer."

"What do you want me to say? That I don't get hammered now and again?"

She looked away again. "It's part of the problem."

"Did we come here to analyze my problems? What are the good ol' boys who wear them vested suits drinking these days? Grapefruit juice?"

"Here we go again Frank. All I'm saying is you're probably still going out too much. And those friends of yours—"

"Change the subject please," he interrupted. He was crushed that things were turning sour.

"Sure," she pouted.

"You're right and I'm sorry. Anyway, I would like to say that I think you look fantastic."

This drew the kind of smile he had hoped for all day. An eye slightly closed forcing genuine sweetness to form on her face. He must cherish this smile and this moment because he didn't know how or when he would see it again.

Kathleen talked a little about her job. Reports, paperwork, *blah, blah*...A subject Frank had never been interested in. He felt he was doing his best to sound enthused. Then she asked what was going on at his job.

"Same shit. One scumbag gets killed another just takes his place."

"Frank."

"It's true. The chain of rats keeps rolling through as if nothing ever happened. It was true of this job a hundred years ago and it will be a hundred years from now. That's what John would say."

"Still cynical. All of you."

"The guys Kat. All the guys are tired of these cunts."

"Frank!"

"What? You never heard that word? Oh I'm sorry, all women hate that word."

"Especially me."

"Okay. I'm sorry. But anyway, nobody wants to do anything. Nobody gives a damn. Work is down, or should I say quotas. Summonses as you know."

"Yes, I've heard that complaint."

"Not that me and the guys are big on work to begin with. But it's the whole place. Guys are pissed and rightly so. They're depressed and fed up."

"You and the guys don't know how good you really got it."

"Yeah, right. They screw with us all the time. That idiot captain gets a worse guy to replace the one Bennett killed, if you can believe that. Then again, he was happy they brought in the first rat…To top it off he's putting guys on crap assignments. Reverse psychology he thinks."

"Frank, you have to stop. Forget it. It's just a job. It's a thing that'll never really change if you look at history. Besides, you guys could be going through this and be working in a ghetto precinct. I'm sorry, I didn't think asking you about work was going to get your blood pumping this way."

"Yeah, well, they're all scumbags," he finished.

When the check came, Kathleen insisted on paying and Frank was touched, though he was still feeling anxious. When she got into her car she rolled down the window to say good-bye. Frank stood over her feeling rejected at her departing.

"Frank I don't know what today was really all about. But it was good to see you again. Even with the complaining." She smiled and there it was again.

"You too, Kat," he said. Now, instead of cherishing that smile, he felt hollow, like a lost soul staying friends with a woman he could never get to fall in love with him. "What the heck happened?" he said quietly. "Can't we go to a movie or something like we used to?"

"Frank, not now. I need to go…Take care."

He almost didn't hear because he was thinking about how long it had been since he shared a bed with her. He nodded feeling a lump growing in his throat. His pride hoped that she wouldn't sense his disappointment. *When did the honeymoon end?* He took a deep breath and straightened his back as if he needed to steady himself. He watched her pull out of the lot. The short time just shared with his wife knocked the party mood right out of him. He needed a real drink, even if it would be a quiet one. A toast to a relationship long over.

Frank stopped in at Ferris where the atmosphere was synonymous with his feelings. Now the place truly had the feel of an old boat. Other than a few regulars, the bar was empty. Frank sat on a stool under the television to the left of the bartender, in the corner. The bartender was the weekday man, a middle-aged stoic. Not much for words, he poured drinks in a friendly manner, was a Met hater, which Frank liked; it gave them something to talk about.

Frank downed three bourbons instead of the one planned on. After three he dropped a tip and headed home.

Frank locked the door behind him and stood in the foyer for a moment wondering if spending the little time with Kathleen did more harm than good...His heart jumped when he turned on the light to find Kathleen sitting there on the living room sofa smiling.

"You never do go straight home, now do you?" she said. She was tossing the key.

"*Phew*. You scared the hell out of me. You're lucky I'm not the kind of cop that reacts by shooting when scared witless."

He hadn't moved onto the living area yet. Kathleen got off the sofa and walked slowly towards him. Finally, he awkwardly moved a couple of steps. Once she came face to face with him she stroked his cheek with the back of her hand.

God. Does she still love me?

"Frank. You probably assumed I've been seeing someone...We're good friends, he and I." He arched back in disbelief. She grabbed his arm. Frank couldn't believe his ears. "I was supposed to see him tonight, but I needed to see you."

"Why?! Why are you doing this to me? Why are you here?"

Suddenly he felt sick but then Kathleen moved to his mouth touching his lips softly with her own, yet not opening her mouth for the total eclipse. It was a strange feeling of hope and despair.

Frank pressed his lips a little tight, trying to will himself not give in. He hoped, actually prayed, for this moment, every time picturing a different scenario in which he would have attacked her, like some wild animal. Now he was semi-frozen with fear. He closed his eyes, taking his chance, feeling destructive. He began to softly open his lips on hers. And then her mouth opened, colliding simultaneously, and the taste of her saliva came back from his memory in an instant. He moved her back in an awkward motion towards the sofa all the while his mouth not leaving hers. His tongue was reaching when they crashed on the sofa, then each letting out a tiny laugh, but their mouths never parting. He could feel her fingers probing his ear then her hand in his hair.

He was feeling as grateful as any man could who just received a second chance at a moment as profound as this one. He stopped kissing for a moment, only tilting back slightly so as to not break the passion.

He had to see for himself, to look her in the eye and know that what was transpiring was for real. Her eyes were half closed, twinkling it seemed. With his finger, he wiped away a wisp of hair from her face. He peaked down to see her nipples erect through her light pink T-shirt. He was grateful now, to himself for taking the chance of letting the animal emerge. He wanted to suck on her breasts immediately. He wanted to be gentle at first but then really suck them. He pressed his mouth to hers again, feeling as though he would burst in his pants.

Gingerly his mouth pressed harder, hands moving to her waist, then her sides. It all came back now. Her skin. Her ribcage. The spot where he instinctively knew where to turn in and cup her breasts. This was still love and he looked up at her as if to seek approval. Her eyes were closed and her mouth just slightly open. This always meant yes in their marriage: Do anything you want with me.

He licked small circles around her left nipple then moved to her right, hungry as he hardened to a greater height of near eruption. She was the one. He knew the difference in the feel of his hard on. This was the whole ball game right here.

He was nuts now, wanting more than anything to be inside her. He moved his hand to her buttocks then along her jeans while he went back to sucking the soft spot of her nipple, and he nearly came in his pants when he heard her whisper, "Francis."

His birth name was always reserved for the tenderest of moments with her. Frank never liked the name, preferring the more boyish Frank. The one time he didn't mind hearing it was when Kat spoke it in softness. Frank was—

Then, as if being kicked from a bed in the middle of an adolescent wet dream, she forced her shirt down over her breasts. *Oh God. No.* It was a plea that extended beyond sexual rejection. He looked up. She was crying. When their eyes met she sprang from the sofa. "What's the matter? Kat, what's the matter?"

"Frank."

"I know you have work tomorrow," he said confused.

"It's not that Frank. It's not you. It's really not you. It's not fair to you. I can't. For Christ sake, I can't be doing this one moment and planning to drop my married name the next."

He was stunned. "What? What are you doing?"

"If we're not going to be married anymore, I'm going back to Dawson. It's not like we have kids or anything to tie us."

He felt paralyzed and stuck to the couch. She was already at the door. It was the closing of the door that snapped him from the stupor. Frank jumped up and immediately felt the sting of blue balls. *What the hell just happened here? Should I go after her?* He raced over to the window where he saw her by the car fumbling for her keys. "Wait Kat. I'm coming down."

Kathleen never turned around instead she waved the back of her hand, got into her car and drove off.

Frank stood and stared by the windowsill feeling helpless. He knew a chase was futile. His hard on was still raging but that was neither here or there.

She stunned him to tears and it was a giant step backward into the hole he had nearly climbed to the top of.

CHAPTER 36

Frank was sluggish getting to work that morning. He worked the afternoon shift the day before, then talked on the phone in the CPOP office with Ann for a few minutes after his shift ended. He called to explain he was unable to meet her because he forgot he was going to work very early on the weekend and was extremely tired. Of course, he made no mention of his tryst with his ex. He did however feel slightly guilty, guilt for Ann or Kathleen he didn't know.

Most of the CPOP cops were in for early tours so when Frank entered the locker room the boys were already chatting it up. The place always smelled like musty old body and sock odors. Frank fell in with the banter to mask his agony. "*Mmm.* Fresh beautiful air," he said. "Sean, you back there?"

"I'm here buddy. With a throbbing hangover," Walsh said. "It's too early to scream."

"*Ahhh,*" snorted Gallo, stepping into Walsh's aisle to annoy him. "I see your head can't hurt that much if you're brushing it."

Walsh looked over, brush in hand, and feigned to throw it at Gallo. Also in the aisle was Eaton, quietly readying himself at his locker. Now Frank entered the aisle to complete the gathering.

"Schmuck," Walsh said to Frank. "Weren't we supposed to meet up last night?"

"Not that I remember," Frank said.

"Will you guys shut up? You're echoing in here," Eaton grumbled.

Frank playfully rubbed the back of Walsh's head. "You lush. This is a brain on drugs."

"Chill you schmuck. My hair, my headache," Walsh said, squinting. "What about your head?"

Eaton blew a thunderous fart. "Maybe that will shut you guys up."

Gallo instantly begun to laugh. Art loved that type of humor. "Great one," Gallo said, and now they all laughed.

"*Mmm,*" Frank sounded. "Like I said before, plenty of fresh air around here."

As the boys finally retreated to their own lockers a sense of being outside his body came over Frank. He'd had it before. He realized this job was no trip to the water cooler in a sharp pair of suspenders and a good morning to everyone. This was cop territory. Less than sterile stationhouses. Musty smelling locker rooms, messy radio cars, dirty dank bathrooms, roaches, mice, and in some precincts even rats. It was a life one had no choice but to get accustomed to because it would never change. The end of the tunnel was twenty years then retirement.

Another thought taking the edge off this morning was the feeling of possibilities. *What a difference when you have a girl, or two, on your mind, and you are probably on their minds as well. Time becomes different.* Kathleen had made some outrageous statements, but she kissed him. Now a new realization; perhaps he was depriving himself of a greater love. One waiting to replace the one he was losing.

Dressed in full clanging gear Gallo strolled into Frank's aisle. He stated loud enough for the others to hear, "Are we going for coffee?"

"Are you buying?" Eaton said.

"It's too hot," Walsh stated. "Then again, I guess if Gallo's buying—"

They all came to Walsh's locker. "Let's go to Tracy's on Rose Ave," Gallo said.

"I thought they hit you full boat last week?" Walsh said.

Gallo winked. "Don't you worry buddy. Their okay now."

"That's hard to believe," Eaton said. "How did YOU manage that?"

"What's so hard?" Gallo laughed. "I walked in the other day pretty thirsty. So, the old bitch, you know the one with the big calves? Well she bangs me for seventy-three cents, full boat for a small iced coffee. I drink it outside right in front of the store while at the same time I'm waving away every car that stops in front of her store, which just so happens to be a bus stop—"

"That worked with her?" Eaton asked.

"Let me finish idiot. After I shoo away about a dozen cars I see her at the window waving me in. I'm trying not to crack up. She says, 'Officer Gallo, why are you chasing my business?' I said, 'Fill this cup up Ms. Angie, when I'm done, then we'll talk.' So, I reach in my pocket as if to get money and bingo, she puts up her hand. 'No officer, it's on me.' So I look around making sure no one hears then I lean in and say, 'Ms. Angie, there will be plenty of cars in that spot today. Bye-bye."

"What makes you think she didn't do it just for that day?" Colleri asked.

"She didn't," Gallo stated. "And you know that coffee tasted better the second cup, on the arm."

"Just watch for the new ICO," Frank warned.

"I don't get it," said Gallo. "If the citizenry wants to give a cop a cup of coffee why should anyone give a fuck?"

With the mocked sternness of an ICO, Frank replied, "Because then you will owe them."

They began laughing, then quieted down when they heard the sound of a locker opening somewhere in another aisle. Gallo ventured over then returned to his pals. "It's just that crusty old fart Ralph," he said.

"He's not so bad," Frank said.

"Poor guy can hardly get his shoes on anymore," Eaton said.

"That's what I'm saying. Why doesn't he just retire then?" Gallo asked.

"Art," Frank said. "Don't let the guy hear you. It'll break his heart. He's a guy that would do anything for you if you asked."

"What could he do?" Gallo asked cynically. "Besides, did he get from this job what he put in? No. They screwed him royally."

"That's true." Walsh nodded. "That's why guys like him have to be a lesson to us all. This scumbag job is in no way on the level. Ralph legitimately breaks his ankle and by the time he returns to work they already stuck some rookie kiss-ass on his post. They offer him stationhouse grunt."

"And he accepts," Gallo said. "Again, would you retire?" Gallo put his left hand out. "Or would you clean shit houses?" His right hand went out as second choice.

"Poor guy has no home life," Eaton said. "His wife died a couple of years ago and he's just afraid that if he stays home he would—" Eaton quieted down lower then he was, hoping Ralph couldn't hear, "he's afraid of dropping dead or eating a gun."

"Why are we talking about this depressing nonsense?" Walsh snapped. "Let's talk about this chick I met who's going out tonight with a bus load of friends. Who's going out?"

Frank was wondering if he was still considered a married man. Gallo raised his hand even though he *was* a married man. Eaton nodded a yes as Ralph's locker banged closed signaling he was leaving the room, but not before the old timer let loose a loud fart, then jangled the lock a few times.

"Guy can't even hold it anymore, and he's obsessed he left his locker open, like he has a million dollars in there," Gallo said. The boys laughed.

"That guy could tell you a thing or two," Eaton said. "Ever talk to Ralph? There's a guy who has seen and knows some horror war stories."

Frank was secretly glad to be off the path of broad talk, still confused about last night with Kathleen. Even though it hadn't turned out well, there were still lingering thoughts about their mouths locked together. He cemented the Ralph conversation by inputting a story of his own. "I know there were a few guys who worked with Ralph over the years. Partners who got screwed real bad. One guy, nice guy, did his job. Made a lot of collars. Well this guy did so much work, too much work, even a couple of off duty arrests. Anyway, he did so much the CO thought he was nuts and sent him to psyche services. To top it off Ralph said the other guy jammed up over a broad—"

"Do we have to guys?" Walsh interrupted, bored.

Eaton, knowing Ralph better than his buddies, collaborated. "Another partner makes a huge drug bust, in uniform. Perps claim, falsely mind you, that there were plenty more drugs in the car, where did the rest of it go? This poor cop gets investigated pending an indictment. His life is miserable, turned upside down."

Frank looked at Gallo and said, "Keep that in mind when you want to play super cop jerk off."

Walsh was getting increasingly tired of cop talk. "All I know is that when old Ralphy boy worked the midnight shift he would go garbage picking for things people left at the curb. Now what about these chicks?"

Frank wondered about Walsh. *Will this guy ever be satisfied? Is the chase and conquest forever in his blood?* Hell, Walsh did so well with ladies. He had to consider love, once in a while. Real love. He claimed he wanted to marry his girl, but...Frank wished he could share the experience he just had with his wife. But he knew the guys would break his balls. Especially the part where he didn't get laid.

"I'm headed down to sign in before that rat moron Dempsey busts my balls," Gallo announced.

"What a hypocrite. Acting like he wanted to be one of the guys," Eaton said.

"He lost all his balls," Walsh said.

"If he had any to begin with. A real moron," Gallo snarled. "If he didn't have the stripes, I'd bitch slap him."

Frank lit a smoke. "His latest is, 'Get on board fellas.' As if we don't have enough paperwork. He wants collars and more summonses." Frank finally noticed Gallo's hand out.

"Do you ever buy?" Frank grumbled.

"You know I don't smoke much," Gallo said.

"I know you don't buy much either."

"Come on, Frank. We gotta' go."

"Stop being so shaky Art. We still have time," Eaton said.

"That's when he didn't let things bother him," Walsh said.

"I bet before he got screwed, Ralph not only was always doing the right thing by cops, I bet he also wanted to be like those cops on TV. The lone soldier, hero stuff." Frank blew a cloud of smoke.

"The big guy did have a sense of humor," Eaton said. "Even when he got a summons for being parked in the municipal lot by some rookie who was too scared to do the right thing. Not only did Ralph get his ticket evaporated, he tags the kid's car a week later."

"Great story," Walsh said. "But for once I agree with Gallo, let's go. I have to meet with the jewelry store guy later about scratches on his window, geez."

Eaton continued as if Sean hadn't said a thing. "And when I said to Ralph I was sorry about his leg, then getting dumped from his post, he just smiled that big ass grin of his and said, 'It just ain't worth it. When they don't need you, they'll dump you like shit from a high horse.'"

It was a great line and they all laughed, then Gallo added, "Then why is the old fart still here? He says things about how a young guy should think about getting out in fifteen and yet he's still here."

Frank blew a cloud in Gallo's direction. "Well he realized like everyone. When you get to fifteen you're trapped till twenty. Besides, I think Ralph knows that anyone leaves the job early gets no respect, and even less if you do more than twenty."

"Guys could blow their brains out from ridicule," Gallo said putting his foot in his mouth, causing the boys to think about Bennett. Eaton lightened things up. He leaned into Gallo and blew a machine gun fart. "You bitch Sharpy," yelled Gallo.

The smell caused the boys to finally scatter. Walking down the stairs Eaton was joking with Walsh giving Gallo the opening to grab Frank's attention. "Frank, I have to tell you something."

"What's up now?"

"I got the notification to appear at inspections. It's the smoke shop thing."

"It'll be okay," Frank said, as if there were nothing to worry about.

Dempsey was already at his desk. He sat with an anxious look quickly followed with a nervous command. "Some chief might be stopping by to check the beat books and monitor what we do. You guys should be heading out to post."

The cops knew the sergeant was, as usual, exaggerating, but they had to listen to the ranting. "And you guys just don't get it," Dempsey continued, "0930 means 0930, not," he paused to peak at his wristwatch, "not 0943."

Walsh tightened his lips and the others knew that could be catchy so they filed out. After everyone made it to the landing Colleri and Gallo laid back. "What a shaky guy," Frank said. "So what's up with inspections anyway?"

"Like I said before," Gallo answered, "I got notified to appear about the smoke shop thing. Incident date I recognize to be the day I slammed that," he looked around before whispering, "black moron."

"Now you whisper. Out on the street you lose your temper—"

"Yeah, yeah, yeah."

"So, what's the big deal? You just deny it, deny it, and deny it. It'll end up just a civilian complaint. It won't go anywhere."

"Says who? It's GO15. Chief of department's, in Manhattan."

"So? You still deny it. In front of a lawyer and a tape recorder." It was always easier to give advice when it wasn't your ass on the line.

"Why did it go there, Frank?"

"Who knows? Don't worry too much. It didn't go to IAB. And besides, it's your word against whoever. *I* certainly didn't hear anything to that affect."

"Thanks Frank. But you know how a GO15 can make a guy nervous."

"I know. There goes your great career, right?"

"Right." Gallo laughed. He offered to buy Frank breakfast. "Come on it looks as though the others forgot anyway. Foods good."

Before they made it to the door the desk officer called out. "Colleri. Dempsey just called up. See him before you head out. He forgot to tell you something."

"Go ahead Art. I'll catch up. Let me see what he wants. I have to make a call after that anyway."

Gallo appeared genuinely disappointed. Frank briefly felt sorry for the loudmouth who suddenly wanted a friend. For all of Gallo's banter he was a loyal friend in blue. There was not a cop in the precinct who wouldn't want Gallo there if they needed help. Eaton knew this all too well. One day Sharpy was entangled with three shoplifters on his foot post when out of nowhere the strong arm of Arthur Gallo reached in and tossed all three to the ground as if they were featherweights. Still, Frank knew GO15 was heavy. Especially on a bias incident. Gallo should stay on the straight and narrow for a while. Frank didn't know how long Gallo could keep it up.

He called to Gallo, "Hey Art. Don't worry." It wasn't much, but slight encouragement was better than none at all.

Dempsey was still at his desk. "Colleri, I forgot to give you this. Actually, I wanted to see you alone." He handed Frank the typed notification slip ordering him to appear at the Inspections Division, GO15 in effect. "I saw it at roll call, they thought you would be in later so I took it to give it to you now. Frank, between you and me, I hear this might be a heavy bias incident, in which case they'll be looking for Gallo's job."

Why are you telling me? Why aren't you telling Art?

"This bias thing is heavy you know, and the N word, with a witness— that's deep Frank. Deep enough where he might not climb out of it."

What a two face, Dempsey loves this. He'd love to see Gallo get sacked. Sure Gallo was an idiot, maybe even out of control at times, but Dempsey should know about Art's reputation of putting himself on the line for other cops on the street. Not to mention he also had the most collars in CPOP. Frank sensed it went deeper with Dempsey. Frank signed the top copy and handed it to Dempsey, then turned to leave.

"Colleri, wait," Dempsey said. "Listen. Gallo's a hothead. If you don't do the right thing you'll sink right along with him. Take my word. I've seen it happen before. Hell, I caught a mountain of trouble the day Bennett whacked himself." He lowered his head a little embarrassed. "And that was just because I had the desk. You were there with Gallo. Think about it...Hell, if Reilly were around he'd try hanging the both of you."

Frank decided to say nothing and just get the hell out of there. No sense to further the conversation. Still, he wondered why the boss was telling him this. He thought about a night Dempsey was out with the guys, before the shooting. He was getting drunk, trying to fit in. They were all friendly...and then Bennett. *The guy's acting like a real rat.* He was probably wired to be a shit all along.

Frank walked to his beat thinking and tried to reconstruct the events. On his way to post he past the municipal parking lot and saw the old Dodge. John Wayne was leaning on the hood. "You still around kid?"

The young guy looked tired and dirty, his eyes a spidery red. "I had a hard night," he said.

Colleri looked around the car. "They don't make em' like this anymore. My Dodge is a newer model, the compact size." There were a few empty crack vials, some beer cans and cigarette butts. "When are you gonna stop this shit?"

"You don't know what it's like officer."

"You're right. I don't know what it's like to smoke crack and give head."

The kid looked down as if he were going to cry. In another life, John Wayne could have had the world by the balls. Blond, good-looking, potential athlete even.

Colleri tightened his lips now feeling sorry. "Hey kid, I didn't mean that." He took a few dollars from his pocket and handed over.

"Word up, officer. Thanks. You're cool like the other cop, the big guy."

"You mean the cop with the crew cut?"

"Sure. Some fuckin' crack head, big kid, red hair, pimples all over, from the neighborhood, tried ripping me off, just as the big Italian cop walks by." John Wayne laughed out loud.

"What happened?" asked Colleri.

The kid pointed to his rear window of the Dodge. "Had to get a new window. Your compatriot slammed the ginger's head right into it."

Colleri couldn't help but laugh. "Hey kid?" Frank asked turning serious. "Any dirt on sexual assaults in the area?"

"Sorry officer, I've got nothin'. Drugs and burgs are one thing. Unless they crazy, no one gonna brag about rapes. Afraid if they get to prison they'd be fucked in the ass. Funny though. Some detectives were around askin' the same thing."

That was good news. Probably the guys who had Ann's case. John Wayne was right though. He wasn't a conventional informant but he gave guys like Gallo useful information for easy collars. "Take care kid," Colleri said. *If a guy like Gallo can feel sorry for this poor bastard, why can't I?* Frank read the stories, the AIDS epidemic taking hold. He hoped this kid didn't have it. He remembered Gallo's version of how this kid came to have the big name. His parents gave him the name because they loved John Wayne movies.

Frank turned back and gave the crack vials a second look. It hit him! There were red vials and purple ones, and a couple of orange ones. The colors meant certain IDs for dealers and junkies. He remembered the last snow fall when the publicity hound mayor was at the precinct shaking hands and smiling that goofy grin. Then the mayor stood behind one of the RMPs with a couple of cops pretending to be pushing the radio car out of the snow. What an asshole!

That day Frank wandered back in the precinct passing the arrest room and noticed Gallo typing away with two fingers, like many cops who were never secretaries did. "Collar big guy?"

"Yeah, felony drugs."

Frank looked on the desk and saw all the crack vials. Many of them the usual red and purple but there amongst the pile, a few orange.

"Just enough to get the felony," Gallo cracked.

There it was! Enough for a felony and the rest he gave to his informant.

Now on his route, Colleri saw a middle-aged Korean man changing a flat. "You know you haven't looked up the whole time I spotted you," Frank said.

"Wa?"

"Never mind," Frank said more to himself. "I'll stick around till you're finished."

Now that he had been GO15'd he and Gallo should come up with the same story. No question he was going to stick with whatever story Gallo and the PBA came up with. Yet he couldn't help but wonder about two things. Did they really want Gallo's job, and how far would they go to hang him? Secondly, if this thing went too far should he hire his own attorney? No cop could go in with their job on the line and some PBA attorney who would give an effort less than nothing. The PBA record of late was too negative to take a risk. Deep thinking time now.

Dempsey knew something.

Suddenly Frank thought about the little schmuck of an owner that Gallo ran to the aid of in the first place, yelling for help at the top of his lungs. *He* turned on Gallo. He had to. He didn't exactly love cops.

The rat squad had to have more than just a black kid's accusation. The storeowner was known to have remarked to a cop once about how his taxes paid a cop salary.

A selfish feeling of safety fell over Frank. If it was true about the owner, then his own ass was saved because with all the ups and downs, and screaming and yelling this old guy was doing, there would be absolutely no way he would remember the precise moment that Frank entered his store. Frank struggled remember, and he did.

He was in the doorway and the owner never turned to notice Frank before Gallo used derogatory words.

Frank's upbeat mood lasted until he opened the mail that night when he got home: It was official—divorce papers waiting for his signature.

CHAPTER 37

rank sat at Kathleen's old vanity table with a notepad in front of him. *How did it ever get to this?* he wondered. With that he took the pen to paper and began:

To the unfortunate bastard who gets to read this first, pass it along…

Frank completed his suicide note, dropping the pen. "Who said writing is supposed to be cathartic!" He was frightened at the thought of killing himself. And, he was feeling nervous sweat while writing.

If he had to, he could do it.

He wiped the table clean with one swipe of his arm. "Fuck her. I must be crazy," he growled. "I've lived through hell. I still don't have my head on straight. Kill myself over her? Fuck her. And why is her silly fucking table even here?"

* * * *

Kathleen was awake, her back towards her sleeping lover. She got pleasure from their sex earlier, yet now felt an unexpected guilt. It had only been a couple of weeks since Frank was caressing her and reviving old feelings. And though she stopped him from going any further, she couldn't deny it was pleasurable. It now felt like she was cheating on Frank. The husband she had had so many wonderful dates with. Quiet dinners and they both loved movies. She even managed to get the city boy to fall in love with Leyland Cypress, the way they romantically swayed with just a hint of a breeze. They planned to line their yard with the beautiful trees when they finally were able to buy their dream house. Now…

She turned. The Yuppie looking guy, her lover, younger than Frank, wavy hair and strong shoulders. She tucked the blanket under her chin and gazed at him while trying to convince herself it was definitely, undeniably, one hundred percent Frank's fault for the disintegration of the marriage. He couldn't commit on many levels. He was incapable of separating married life from his so-called social obligations. It was Frank who flirted with women at the bars.

Her lover restlessly turned in sleep. She looked around at the present surroundings. Signs of a man's room. Things were in disarray like Frank's apartment was before they were married, and again now after she was gone. It was clear when a woman didn't live with a man.

She turned towards the window and noticed the dull lifeless curtains, the beginning of daybreak attempting to push through. She felt his hands pull gently on her hips. He was obviously awake now. Guilt, as it was, took a backseat to desire as she nestled her body back into him, and in one motion he entered her. She closed her eyes lifting herself a little, biting her lower lip, consumed by pleasure. It was a pleasure that was certain; enough for her to realize that no matter what was left between her and Frank, she could never go back to him.

* * * *

The good news finally arrived for Ann. Clearance from the police department: two weeks at the borough then full duty. To help start her in the right frame of mind, the assignment of her choice was offered. She was going to think on that one. Either way her first couple of days back would have to be spent at the firearms and tactics range for retraining and re-qualification courses.

Ann was happy to be whole again on the job. A cop just couldn't feel right without the gun to accompany the badge. She was eager to begin re-training at the range at Rodman's neck in the Bronx. She was experiencing a sense of self, something she thought was reserved for the male cop. For a cop to possess a gun, then have it removed, was a horrible experience. Getting it back was exhilarating.

The first call was to her parents with the good news. Her second was to Allison. She wanted Allison to know she was a needed friend in moments of highs too. Allison was not only a shoulder to cry on, but also a friend to be happy with. Her last conversation with Allison was about dejected feelings when Frank canceled a date. Allison had served well with her input. Ann became more realistic about Frank's personal situation. Frank was probably lying when he excused himself. Allison even went as far as saying, "He probably still loves his wife," while still managing to make Ann laugh.

Now Ann was calling with some good news for a change. "Hey, Al, it's me."

"Hello girl. You sound good."

"You could tell, *eh?*"

"Were friends. Aren't we?"

"Its official friend. The job has deemed me well enough to give me my guns back."

"All right! Good for you. Do you think you can still shoot?" Allison joked.

"Yeah sure. The only thing is the man on the targets are all going to look like department shrinks."

The girls shared a laugh and Ann assured her friend that everything was looking up.

* * * *

Colleri, Walsh, and Eaton were spending the early hours of their tour yapping as usual. They just ordered the breakfast special and were complaining about the job. Familiar complaints.

"I'll tell you guys something," Frank said. "Lately I feel like I'm just wishing my life away. I really can't wait to retire from this loser job."

"Join the club," Eaton said. "But it's a long wait for us pal."

"You're getting too sentimental if you ask me," Walsh said to Frank playing with his spoon. "It's that whole divorce and regret nonsense. Start having some fun and you'll see the time fly without you having to count down or wish the next twelve or so years away."

"I wish it were seven," Eaton said. "But in a way, Sean's right Frank. You love, then it's over. You don't, it's still over. You have good days on the job and bad. In between you try to have fun...And forget trying to leave after fifteen. It's unrealistic."

"There you go Frank," Walsh said. "Take me. I was getting married and now I'm not."

"Gee, there's a surprise," Frank quipped. "Did you bother to ask her in the first place?"

Imitating Walsh, Eaton let loose with a straight man gag, "Not that I remember, except when I was fucking her."

"All right, I get the point," Frank said. "You're right. What else am I going to do with my life anyway? Dig ditches?"

"You're too lazy Frank," Eaton said. "Just stay a cop with us, and we'll all be in it together."

"You know though," Frank said, "so many imbeciles are coming on now."

"There've always been losers," Eaton responded. "They were here for a hundred years, and they'll be here a hundred years from now when we're dead and buried."

"Some you're gunna like, some you're not," Walsh said, as he grabbed a strip of toast when the waiter laid the food out. When the old waiter walked away Walsh pointed his toast. "Do we even like him?"

"Look at it this way," Eaton said. "None of us are cut out for manual labor."

Walsh jumped on the manual phrase. He pumped his fist up and down telling Eaton, "You're good manually. How many times a day you jerking off?"

Frank scooped some scrambled eggs on his fork. Walsh already had a mouthful before speaking again. "What I say is that, yeah, the job sucks. I hate it too. But if you didn't go to college, it's really not a bad stable job. You get what you need from it."

"That's providing you don't mess up," Frank added.

"Even then Frank," Walsh said swallowing. "Unless you do something illegal we can get away with screwing up a million times. Sure, they'll take vacation time, or we might get suspended for nonsense, but if you're not a criminal you won't lose your job."

"You got a point," Frank said.

"Besides," Eaton said. "When you do make it to the end of this twenty-year sentence there's a pretty decent pension waiting. And if you plan everything right, it's really one of the best jobs out there. Checks and benefits for the rest of our lives. For now, though, it pays the bills."

"John, remember, that's providing we live that long, " Walsh said.

"Not the way you eat." Eaton widen his eyes in a shocked look.

"Anyway," Walsh continued, "consider yourself lucky. I mean with the divorce and all."

The mere mention of divorce caused Frank an exaggerated heartbeat. If only his friends knew about his suicidal plot. *What would they think of that note I just wrote? Thank heavens I stopped.* Frank made a tiny and quick sign of the cross so no one would notice.

Walsh was going on, "You could have had kids. Then what? You really would have been screwed."

"That's right Frank." Eaton slurped coffee. "Just look around the stationhouse, Seventeen percent of our salary per kid. That doesn't amount to much."

Frank needed to change the subject. "Speaking of big mouths, where's Gallo?"

"Inspections," Walsh said.

"That's right." Frank remembered he had to appear soon enough too.

"He should have gone sick," Eaton said. "Go sick when you think they're going to get you. This way, they reschedule you. That bothers them."

"And they probably are out to get him. I mean I hope not, but that's the way it looks," Walsh said.

"You think they'll hurt him bad?" Frank asked.

"Frank," Walsh said. "I heard from Callahan, and others. They're probably going after his job. That's no shock. Calling someone the N word will always be a big deal on this job, now more than ever. The public wants to believe we're racist but crime stats prove otherwise."

"He helped the old prick at the smoke shop, now the old bastard's a witness against him. Some irony," Eaton grumbled.

Frank felt guilty not telling his friends about what the sarg suggested he do. Maybe it was too late now. The guys would only break his balls for holding out on them in the first place. This was another reason to despise a job that carried a million opinions. You're damned if you do and likewise if you don't. It was a constant walk on a path of eggshells. Always wondering if you're doing right by other cops. Forever second guessing decisions. Should I have done this or that? I did nothing. Am I a pussy? A coward? And if you said the wrong thing you were labeled a rat. Frank realized all of this, and more.

Sadly, whatever negative impression or perception, no matter how unwarranted, usually hung over a cop like a plague. Sometimes a perception followed that cop their entire career, no matter how many different precincts they were transferred to. Still, Frank now felt the urge to leak a hint. "I think Dempsey knew what was going down," Frank said. *There I covered my ass a little.*

Eaton picked at a tooth, then put his sunglasses on animatedly. "Don't you worry Frankie. We got plans for that rat loser."

Walsh was grinning now. "Yeah, big plans."

"As big as this check?" Frank quipped. Frank sat back then commented towards Eaton, "Who would think you were capable of anything wearing those faggy glasses?"

"You mean gay glasses?" Eaton said. "You have to see how many chicks compliment me on these." Eaton tapped his forefinger on the lavender Polaroids. "Hey Sean. Frank said the F word. Get the cuffs."

Walsh slapped Eaton playfully. "Come on girls. Let's get the hell out of here."

Frank again looked at the check as the three slid from the booth. "You know I'll never understand why a waiter automatically gives cops separate checks when we all had the same order."

"Shouldn't get any check," Eaton mumbled.

"That's easy," Walsh said. "They bank on three separate tips. Because we, as cops that is, have the distinct reputation for being cheap."

"Oh well," Eaton said. "No discount, no tip."

As the cashier rang up his check, Frank turned and said to his buddies in a low tone, "It's like playing breakfast chance. Some you pay for, some you don't."

CHAPTER 38

Frank, desiring a sense of home, went to visit his brother at the apartment they once shared. He looked around the place which Peter furnished with old family relics and photos, permeating warmth and charm from their parents, though minus the delicious aromas of Mom's cooking.

Peter Colleri was feeling ninety percent better since the accident and would soon be ready to resume his role as the party bachelor.

"I see you decided to light up before I even had a chance to bust your balls," Frank remarked.

"What are you talking about man?"

"Come on bro. Your eyes are beet red and the place reeks."

"*SShh*, okay, okay," Peter said. "So I had a few tokes. A small joint." He mimed the approximate size with his thumb and forefinger. "What are you up to anyway?" he said changing the subject.

"I'm a little lost these days."

"These days?"

"Don't be funny," Frank said. He was pointing the cigarette he removed from a pack.

"Those will kill you," Peter joked. "My form of smoke will be legal one day for medical purposes."

"Yeah, right," Frank said.

The brothers shared a laugh and Frank lit the cigarette before his demeanor turned heavy. "I've never felt like I couldn't talk to someone Peter. Everything before, it went smooth. It was all fun and games. Even the job was tolerable because of the fun..." Peter let Frank talk without breaking in with a joke, he sensed this was serious. "My place is a wreck. My mail piles up. I got nothing to share anything with...I mean I thought that must be okay. That it would be okay."

Frank took a succession of drags then Peter finally asked, "What happened Frank? Obviously, something happened."

Frank looked at his brother. He was reluctant to start spilling his soul. But if he couldn't trust his brother, then who?

"I saw Kathleen and—"

"Don't even tell me," his brother interrupted, holding up a hand.

"I'm serious Peter. I think it's still there. I think I still love her."

"Tell me why you think that. Did you fuck her?"

"We kissed. And well, quite frankly, I loved it bro."

Peter shook his head. "This ain't the movies Frankie. The hardest thing to do is to go back after you felt jerked around. I mean, I'm no expert, but think about it. You were a hurtin' dude. More than me and I was banged about the fucking head. And what about that other broad? It sounded like you liked her."

"Who? Oh, Ann. Yeah. But nothing ever came of that."

"Because of your wife?"

"I don't know, maybe."

"Well, remember something when you're out there making up your mind. Look, I loved Liza. But hey, I messed up. I dropped the ball so to speak. I still felt it. We all crash and burn, but I picked myself up, so can you."

"You have to use the crash analogy. And what are you now, a philosopher?"

Peter leaned closer to Frank as if he were about to spill a guarded secret. "I never told anyone Frank," he said in a serious whisper.

Frank looked at Peter quizzically then joked, "You're gay?"

Peter laughed and hit Frank in the shoulder, lisping, "How did you guess?"

"I knew," Frank said.

"Serious Frank. Maybe I'm philosophizing a bit. But let's face it. I do feel like I've had another shot. I mean I could be pushing daisies now."

"God forbid Pete. I got enough problems right now. Don't say that."

"Frankie, listen. When I said I dropped the ball...well in a way I think I did..." Frank now gave Peter his turn to speak. Peter looked away then back to Frank. "Frank, I think I dropped my joint that night."

"What night? What are you talking about?"

"The night I crashed and burned. Literally. I remember—I think I was taking a long hit on a joint before the accident. I dropped it between my—and then bam!" He hit his fists together.

Frank now hit his brother's shoulder. "Damn! You idiot. You're telling me you almost got killed because you dropped a lit joint in your crotch?"

"SShh—"

"Stop being paranoid. No one can hear us."

"That's not what I'm saying Frank. And now I would say no. Believe me. But we're also talking about you. About what you might do, that maybe you shouldn't. Think. Is she that important? Is an ex-wife—"

"She's not ex yet." *Not until I sign the papers.*

"Okay. Is a wife who probably, and I'm not saying definitely, rushed into another man's arms… Is she worth it down the line?"

Peter's statement stung Frank who was staring at the wall. "She is brother, and she's changing her name back to Dawson."

Peter didn't want to hurt his brother, but wanted to drive his point home because he was worried about what Frank might do. "I'm sorry Frank. But you know what? There you have it. You met her in a bar. Did you *really* have that much in common? I know, she was so nice to everyone, but fuck her!"

"That's what I said." Frank then leaned into his brother kissing his forehead. "I'm glad at least you're feeling better. Now do you have anything to eat in this place?"

Frank's thoughts were discombobulated as he drove away. He knew it really didn't matter much what anyone said in their attempts to help. Opinions were always listened to more than seriously calculated. The bottom line was, he would do whatever he had to, or his heart would agonize forever. Poets and musicians were right on about love. It was the strongest of forces.

Still, there was a slight sense of relief that Peter had hit the nail on the head about a possible romance with a different woman. Frank wondered if Ann was still an option. Suddenly he decided to drive to her place. It wasn't too late and just maybe she would be happy to see him; maybe that connection was still there and would keep him from writing another note to whoever might find his body; this last time had been minutes too close to the final act. He thought about calling first but was too nervous. *Just drive there. Pull the car over, get out, knock on the door and whatever happens will happen.*

Before long he found himself parked in front of her house. No excuses. No turning back. *Besides, I have to know how right it feels.* He got out of his car hurrying to the door and knocked. *No backing out now.* Part of him hoped she wasn't home.

But he did knock a second time establishing that it was not too late. *Last knock,* he thought. Then, the door opened and he could think of nothing to say except a fumbling, "I know it's late, and I'm sorry to bother you…"

Her eyes locked on his. Her hair blew with the slight breeze in the doorway. She didn't say anything. Frank felt uncomfortable. It was as if she did this on purpose to rattle him.

"I mean, I was at my brother's house. I passed and I, *ah,* saw your light. I'm sorry."

"Sorry for what? How are you?"

She finally spoke, but still had not invited him in. She stood rocking at the door, an old Beatles song reverberating behind her. *What did you expect idiot? Not all women will give you an instant invitation just because a man sensed she liked him once.* It was as though she were forcing him to take the initiative. His reaction was to search for a cigarette. "Do you have a smoke? Mine are in the car."

"Sure Frank. Come on in." The ice was broke. "Tea? Or is it too warm tonight?" she said, smiling.

He returned a smile. "Tea's fine." He felt the tension release.

She flipped him a brown package. "Did you receive yours yet?" She noticed he looked quizzically at the package. "I guess they assume we all live with our families."

"What is it?"

"A VCR tape. From the job. Addressed to the family of Ann Caputo."

"For what?"

"It's a suicide tape. Prevention, protection. Our families concern and well-being."

"Oh, right. Did you watch it?' he asked, lighting up thinking, *Suicide. Just the word I need to hear right now.*

"I did," she said. "Your typical job propaganda. It says that if we, the cops, can't handle our problems, then it's up to our families to step in and report the situation. Confidential of course." She was mocking. "Any feelings of depression, suicide, that kind of thing. Well the job is there to care for us, *blah, blah, blah...*"

"What bull." Frank was laughing. "The only thing they'll take care of is the removal of our guns, and vacation days if they can. Especially if our loving families report anything remotely close to domestic offenses. Unbelievable. They want to help? All they want is to make your life more miserable so you drink more, so they crucify you and call it help!"

"Didn't mean to upset you. You didn't hear about the tape yet?"

"Actually, I think I did."

Her voice was calming. He took a seat on the sofa. His spot opposite Ann's chair. He was unsure about bringing up the past, but he attempted an explanation anyway. "Ann. About the—"

"Forget it Frank," she interrupted. "You don't owe me an explanation if that was your intention. I don't need one."

"Okay," he said. "So how have you been?"

"Good, Frank, and you? And how's your brother?"

"He's great. Thanks. He's becoming a philosopher."

"Really. How so?"

"Nothing. Inside joke. Between brothers you know." He smiled with fondness.

Ann walked to her chair carrying the two cups easily. "I have some good news, for a change. I'm getting my guns back this week. Oh, I told you that."

"That's great. That's really great Ann."

"As a matter of fact, I'm going for the certification. The three-day course. Oh, that's right, I told you, too."

Fibbing a little Frank said, "I've been thinking about getting a re-cert. Can you let me know how it is? I've been too lazy to go for it... I'm happy for you..."

For a moment, their eyes locked as if each wanted to embrace. For Frank, the need was strong. He wanted confirmation once and for all. If their mouths were to touch, would it ignite something in him that had been missing?

As for Ann, she already knew the extent of her feelings. She couldn't imagine a kiss as anything but wonderful. But neither had yet committed to an approach. Instead both lit cigarettes, breaking the tension with a smoke screen.

"So," she said, a bit awkward. "It's good to see you Frank. Isn't it strange how we feel as if we've known each other for a long time?"

"You too, and yes," he replied. He meant it.

Just thinking about kissing her made him wonder if it was really time to move on now. Get past Kathleen.

"Frank, do you want to hear something funny?"

"Sure, go ahead—shoot."

"That's what I like about you," she said. "Your sense of humor. Real original—shoot." She pointed the same forefinger as he did and they both laughed.

"Don't get Buffy on me now," he joked.

"I hear you run with a pretty wild bunch," she said. "And, I have a friend that told me to watch out for you."

Frank grinned devilishly. He was proud of the idea that he and his friends possessed some sort of notoriety. "You hear wrong. Haven't I been pretty respectable? I haven't tried jumping your bones."

"No, you have been the perfect gentleman. But maybe that's because you don't find me attractive."

Idiot. Where have I been? There's the hint. Why am I being so stupid and amateurish about the whole thing? "Of course, I do."

"Then why haven't you tried to kiss me yet?"

The reasonable excuse he wanted to give, her attack, was inappropriate now. It would come off as insulting. He pointed at her. "I didn't think," he simply said.

Ann put her cup down, pushed herself off her chair and onto the sofa next to him. He appeared to be beaming and she smiled brightly. She reached behind and over him to lower the fluorescent light to a dim glow.

Frank reached for her hand bringing it to his mouth, kissing it gingerly, yet not enough for romantic corniness. Ann positioned herself so their lips had to meet and there would be no turning back. Frank was experiencing pulses not felt since meeting Kat. He knew this for sure recalling both Nina and Jenna, recent distractions.

Ann was gentle. Suddenly Frank felt hope even with all the despair that surrounded him. *Is possible to love again?* Above all he was genuinely and instantly aroused. It was more than he imagined. It was a moment to savor. They kissed for a time, and softly, once in a while, their mouths opened simultaneously widening to their impulses.

Ann pressed her body on top of his letting small groans escape. Embarrassing or not, he did the same. He felt like shouting out his groans.

His body moved back towards the armrest and Ann crawled closer pressing harder as their mouths stayed together at a moment where anything was now possible.

A moment to be savored in memory.

CHAPTER 39

The next workday, Frank's hours were again different then his buddies. Therefore, he had no way of knowing the precinct's morning news. Police officer Gallo had been suspended from duty. The other news was that it was done with no help from Dempsey, who hadn't put in a kind word for the embattled officer. Rumors went a long way, both factual and fictional accounts. The precinct delegate received an early call from someone who knew someone else through the inspections pipeline. A certain CPOP sergeant was called by one of the investigators in regard to Gallo. The detective wanted information and a synopsis of both Gallo's performance and his attitude in his position as a New York City Police Officer. The good Sergeant Dempsey was quick to deflate Gallo, calling him a cocky bastard capable of anything. But even before the backstabbing story, Callahan received a call from someone in the union concerning Gallo's status. Yes, it was true that Gallo was in serious trouble, but no, he hadn't been suspended from duty as reported. Instead, he was placed on modified assignment. No gun, no shield, and a temporarily changed identification card. Callahan attempted to explain. Of course it was bad, even humiliating if that's the way Gallo wanted to interpret it. But bottom line was the checks were still coming in. Modified at least meant Gallo would stay on salary.

Walsh and Eaton were anxious. They waited so Frank could be told in person. His buddies also didn't want him prematurely worrying about his own fate since he was also to report to inspections. However, though it was the same case, Frank was a witness not a subject.

In the meantime, Dempsey's treachery towards a fellow officer only fueled Eaton and Walsh's desire in their pursuit of revenge. They were definite on their plans now. The timing was right. There was no way they could confront the sergeant face to face and call him a rat. They would be perceived as boss fighters and surely face the consequences down the road. Instead, faint acting greeted the workday in the faces of Eaton and Walsh when they reported to Dempsey in the usual six a.m. exhausted manner.

The very same morning, seven a.m., Police Officer Caputo walked into a tin classroom on Rodman's Neck. It was a cool morning, heightened by the closeness of the island waters. She thought about having her long sleeve uniform shirts pressed neatly for patrol, to give a confidant appearance. Ann flipped the lid on her coffee cup and sipped slowly. There were four rows of folding desk chairs and she, not in the mood for idle chitchat, was glad to see she could be seated scattered amongst just a half dozen trainees for today's course. She felt a bit of agitation which began with the ride over the traffic jammed Throggs' Neck Bridge and its construction filling pavements. Drinking coffee instead of tea fueled her to remain awake. Still, this also enhanced a need for the few cigarettes she already smoked this morning.

* * * *

Gallo was quite upset when he explained to Callahan what transpired, and the sneak attack by a couple of Internal Affairs cops. "Scumbags," he shouted. To risk any further outbursts that Gallo might regret, Callahan wisely suggested he vent elsewhere. A few hours off to cool. Callahan offered his company but wasn't upset when Gallo refused. Callahan was just happy he was able to convince the cop to get out of sight for now.

"Don't worry," Gallo growled to Callahan. "I'll just go home and drive the old lady nuts."

* * * *

The range instructor was administering his usual tedious rhetoric about the firearm, its uses and abuses. Not that what he had to say was unimportant, but Ann, like most cops, had heard it all a million times, and it didn't help that the instructor added his own comic stint laced with machismo. This guy looked as though he had something tucked under his shirt to balloon out his chest. Guys like this that loved guns usually ended up wackos. Ann laughed as she remembered police academy days when she and a few other female recruits promised each other they wouldn't fall into the dumb broad group, easy prey for a male cop. They were going to insert themselves into the macho world of cops, where there would always be an audience for a female cop. Unfair as it was, they could tease, tantalize, then just back off.

The firearm instructor seemed to go on forever. He reiterated point after point on the subject of deadly physical force. After a few hours, it had been all talk and no shooting. The new officers in the class, last minute inductees to the NYPD, had yet to remove their clean new instruments from their box, not even for a look.

"This isn't the movies," the instructor was saying. Ann began to escape into her own world, while she listened inattentively..."Bullets go through many animals and many kinds of dogs..."

Ann was back on the couch... Frank's mouth was sweet and gentle. She had been easily and surprisingly aroused. Then she took on a state of confusion. There was the notion that she was moving too fast. Maybe she was leading him on. The thought of her even permitting herself to become aroused sent her head spinning.

Too soon. Guilt took over and she tried shaking it. She shook as her knees became weak and she was not even standing. She remembered needing a cigarette...*I'm just trying to get on with my life. All I ever wanted was to be somewhat happy and do the right thing by people.*

The instructor was still babbling. "You will see," he droned on, "these weapons are without a doubt, no fool's errand. Make no mistake. This weapon, this gun, will neutralize a person, an animal, or a thing, faster than you might wonder...Everything from the chamber..."

* * * *

Eaton and Walsh descended the emergency metal railing that was situated on the side of the precinct parking lot running to the building basement boiler room. It was also just through a couple of doors on the floor of the CPOP office and downstairs bathrooms. It was an effort for them to control their laughter as they snuck around crevasses like giggling school kids conspiring something dastardly against their teacher.

Once they made it to the men's room, they removed the rubber gloves they were wearing and flushed them down the toilet, then washed the remaining residue of grease off their hands.

"I hope it takes that loser a month to get that goo off," Eaton said.

"Probably longer Sharpy," Walsh agreed. "It will definitely give him something to think about the next time he decides to bang a cop. To think we thought he was all right."

"He's not in the office, is he?" Eaton asked, suddenly wondering if they could be heard through the wall.

"No, don't get shaky. I told you, he's out on some community meet. Probably kissing ass as we speak."

"Well," Eaton said, "he's got enough slime on his new car not only to kiss ass, but to stick a tree trunk of a boner in it."

They laughed loud enough to be heard even over the running water. And risk came with the usual cop paranoia. "Check the hall Sean."

"Clean up Sharpy. And stop it will you. No one knows. If someone heard us dying with laughter they'll think we were laughing at each other's dicks."

"Speak for yourself tortoise shell."

* * * *

Everything from the beginning felt right about Frank, except, of course, the reason they met. Maybe it was hexed for that very reason. How strange it would have been to meet and fall in love and live happily ever after with a man who was checking on your condition after you were assaulted.

Ann fished for excuses to retreat from a feeling she knew to be right. She had waited for a moment like this regardless if tragedy had anything to do with fate. Then there was the timing. Frank showed up on her doorstep when she thought he was gone forever. The long-awaited kiss. The conversations only soul mates would have.

It wasn't the course of tragedy or loneliness that had resurfaced her buried feelings. It was Frank, and his touch. His lips and his breath, together with hers. She had wanted the moment to arrive. And they were on each other, on the sofa, like anxious teenagers...So who could explain the frightening entrance of demons. The inability to make them disappear. It was as if someone told her not to think of green squirrels. There would come a hundred thoughts of them.

Frank's breath turned heavy and dragon like; he was suddenly wearing a big hood. He became dark and crude, his eyes black. 'I got me a cop. I am gonna fuck you...Hey bitch, whatcha' lookin' at?'

Ann shut her eyes hoping it would disappear. It was like she had been intimidated for life. She hid it well but the demons had done their job of humiliating and degrading her. When she turned away Frank stopped, but only for a moment before he went for her mouth again. Still Ann tried. She really tried, but again the green squirrels, the heavy breath, the cold air—the demons. "Please no," she had said. But Frank, who had no idea what was transpiring, went for her ear. *He won't stop! He won't until he's had---* "Get off me!" she screamed. She pushed him with force. Frank was obviously dumbfounded, even a little terrified. He immediately backed off the sofa.

"I'm sorry. I---I---"

"No, no, Frank, it's not you." She began crying. "Frank, no, please leave."

He nervously brushed his hair back with his fingers. "Are you sure Ann? Are you okay?"

"Yes, yes, I'm fine. Just go. Please go."

Frank left saying no more. Really, what could he have said? And so, for Ann, it was the beginning of a sleepless night with her demons. Later she would learn of Frank having a similar restless night. She turned to vodka instead of tea, an attempt to calm herself. But the booze only made her feel ill, so she tried these words: "Time is everything...Time. I've survived this far..."

* * * *

Dempsey could be heard yelling at the top of his lungs from the parking lot to the echoing walls within the precinct. "Scumbags!" As Dempsey rushed through the long corridor from the precinct's rear door, it rang with clarity when Dempsey stormed into the CO's office.

Dempsey hadn't noticed until he lifted the door handle on his car. He paused realizing the stickiness, not deciphering it until his eyes fixed on the greater mayhem. That's when the first 'scumbag' was heard. Dempsey looked from hand to car seeing his front windshield covered in a gel. Fuel was added to the fire when he noticed that every inch of glass on the car was also covered in the sticky thickness. At first, he just stood there. Then he poked his fingers into the wet thickness, as if to see if the shock were truly real. Ultimately it would cost Dempsey more money than he wanted to spend to remove the Vaseline.

"Scumbags!"

Walsh and Eaton were watching from a window by the front clerical office. As they exited the rear they were laughing so hard that Walsh thought he would piss himself. What he ultimately did, when the smoke cleared, was relieve himself on the door handle of the car parked in the spot marked, CO PARKING ONLY.

"That's balls," Eaton exclaimed.

CHAPTER 40

Reaching out for Jenna was a search for comfort to the increasingly lonely Frank Colleri. There was a time it would have been right to attempt a liaison with the pretty nurse, but it had been a while since Frank talked to her. He was reluctant, yet decided to drudge up some nerve and venture into Ferris. Frank was well prepared for the bar to be filled with familiar faces and reminders that he might not be up to socializing. But if he were to meet with Jenna, that would be the trade-off.

Earlier, Frank surprised himself when he called Jenna at the hospital. She seemed just as eager to meet, as if it were a planned date. However, as expected, she did have to stop at The Ferris Wheel to meet with friends and discuss plans for the group's winter party and skiing house at Hunter Mountain.

Every year, Frank thought. *Every year, it s Hunter in the winter and the Hampton's in the summer.* He recalled a time he went to surprise his wife in a bar in the Hampton's back when they were just dating. It was an annoying traffic-filled trip. He wound up at a bar besieged by drunken yuppies that got their kicks tossing cups in the air giving beer showers and pissing on the floor well before reaching the urinals. He wondered if he needed to go through nonsense like that again. He was in no mood for a long night of bar cliques. So, with some of his old charm, he persuaded Jenna into having a few drinks first at The Mexican Melon, a neat little place up the boulevard tucked around a corner. Intimacy to conquer the loneliness with help of a couple of shots of tequila for an instant buzz.

Since Frank was meeting her at the restaurant instead of picking her up, he got a head start. He was drinking a Tequila sunrise when Jenna walked in.

"Starting without me Frank?"

"Of course not, just a little thirsty. What are you drinking?"

"Ah, since we're going Mexican I think I'll have one of those big margaritas," she said removing a light jacket.

"Big it is," he said. "Bartender." He sipped his drink.

"So, Nurse Pendergast. How are you and how's the hospital business?"

"I'm fine. It's fine. How about you, and the cop biz?"

Frank lit a cigarette taking a drag before answering. "It sucks." The drinks came and Frank watched Jenna take hold of the large margarita, and then he lifted his.

"Wow," she said. "You think this will make me catch a buzz?"

"I certainly hope so," he said. Then he smiled and said, "So what's up?"

"Well, it looks like Hunter again this year."

Frank decided to keep his opinion to himself. He didn't want to be drinking alone. "Oh, great." He managed to make it sound neutral. He swigged a couple of gulps to get in the mood. Frank wasn't the overly aggressive type until he was well into a buzz, but his starvation for companionship and the beginnings of a buzz helped him to draw closer to Jenna, who for the time being appeared as though she would welcome him.

Although she did tease him. "How's the wife Frank?"

Coyly he responded. "Wife. What wife?"

"Come on Frank. It's not such a big world out there you know. Word has it that you're still pining after her."

Frank's remark was cocky. "Oh, it does? Well word has it wrong. And if I may ask, why are you so interested anyway?"

"No reason." She smiled.

"No reason. Well it is no reason that you look so pretty, especially when you're not telling the truth." He leaned in and kissed her on the cheek. When she didn't flinch, he leaned again only this time closer to her mouth. Her response was as if on cue. She turned her lips slightly as their mouths opened simultaneously. Frank felt a flush of something lost. But as if she were in cahoots with Ann and his wife, Jenna pulled away on alert.

"What's wrong, Jenna?"

"Frank, I'm seeing someone and I really don't think I should be--you know."

"I understand," he said. "But you should have told me. I'm sorry if I was out of line." He was thinking, *haven't I heard this before?*

Jenna smacked his arm. "You know Frank, you had your chance. Even when I knew you were a rebound and I was scared to get involved, you had a chance. Why now?"

"Just bad timing I guess," he said. It wasn't the timing. It was hard for Frank to understand why three women recently shot him down and now he was rethinking not following through on that suicide note. Still, he tried differentiating the circumstances. He ordered another round; soon realizing that was a mistake.

He fought not to be distracted or bored. The conversation shifted to Jenna and talk of her work, the girls, the Hampton's, Hunter…exactly where he didn't want to be. Everything entered in one ear quickly and rushed out of the other.

What he thought about was the why. Why the women in his life were starting him up, and then stopping him at the wrong time. *Is it ever the right time?* There shouldn't be room for regrets, at least in the developments involving Jenna or Ann. He would assure Jenna, like he had Ann, that they would remain friends even after she hinted he could better his chances.

Frank made a lame excuse to cut the evening short. Jenna was able to finally catch all of his attention by telling Frank that it was her hope it was the job that had made him callous, and not that it was his true self. She also wished for him that he would be able to see through it all one day.

Frank was certainly taken aback. He was also curious. *What the hell is she talking about?*

Jenna further informed him it was no secret and obvious to many that when Frank and his friends were together, their arrogance let it be known that anyone's personal misfortune was up for grabs as the brunt of a joke. She also told Frank that others thought his friends treated women like garbage.

"What people?" he retorted. "Haven't a few of your friends been with a few of mine?"

"Oh, come on Frank."

Finally, she acknowledged his bailing out of the evening as just one of 'their' kind of acts. Frank resoundingly assured her it was a complete exaggeration. Secretly though, he enjoyed the idea that he and his pals possessed an aura of notoriety. He thought of Ann. He certainly hadn't been mean to her, and she wasn't the brunt of any jokes where he was concerned. But, what about Kathleen's friend and the whole ski slope business? A new angle to think about.

* * * *

A day at the firearms range was usually a bonus since it was a short workday. When Ann made it home it felt like it had been an eternity spent out of her house. All she wanted was to spend a few moments in her favorite chair, an attempt to reshape her mood and try to mellow out. She poured herself a tall glass of white wine, adding some ice. Then she took two sedatives and a long painful swig to wash them back.

As her body began to relax she couldn't shake the paranoid thoughts. She wandered into the startling realization that the only relief might come from death. Other than its persuasive presence and handling ability, her issued weapon suddenly held a different attraction. The powerful handgun was more than capable of blowing her brains free of her demons.

Ann laughed to herself. All she wanted was the comfort of her favorite chair like some grandmother. Now, it was 'let's shoot myself.' She laughed again at the thought of complete mayhem. What a scene it would be if she took out that pompous range instructor right out there on Charlie Range before offing herself. Female suicides were rare in the police department. The ultimate act still seemed to belong to its macho men's club. Ann fantasized about changing all that.

She took a long sip of her drink then lit a cigarette and took a long drag. She went to the kitchen counter and fumbled around for a pen and writing tablet. Once she found her tools she began to write. She had no prior inklings of what she might write in a suicide note.

* * * *

Gallo showed up at the precinct the next morning looking pale and unkempt. Frank arrived early to talk with Gallo about their story, hoping to perfect their versions, not exactness, but to united believability, thus bettering Gallo's chances. It was Frank's turn to appear at the dreaded inspections services. Callahan was also present with the two ready to interrupt with his professional union opinion. It turned out that Callahan would be more informative to Frank since Gallo was not attentive, remorsefully the tough cop reiterated, "Whatever helps Frank, you know we're on the same page. Sorry again you were dragged into my fuck-up."

Funny. Here's Gallo who could crush a man's face with a short jab, weakened by the job which will pounce on him and attempt to completely destroy the life around him. His family. His mortgage. His career. Frank could see Art was a man in fear of losing his lifelines. And for what? For being a part of suburban upbringing? Gallo himself had said, "There weren't any black kids in my school growing up." He didn't get it. Sure, he used hyper-sensitive language but those who knew him really felt it was just talk, and at his core he wasn't at all prejudiced, he wasn't going to snap and hurt someone, why destroy his life over words?

And nobody was exempt from his razzing. "If the guy was Italian," Walsh explained, "Gallo might have called him a dumb wop." In his short career, Art had willingly assisted people of many races.

Frank remembered the time when an elderly black woman was hit by a bus on Main. Somehow the woman was knocked to the sidewalk but her foot was torn off, remaining under the bus. While cops and other emergency crews tended to the woman, Gallo instinctively put on his leather patrol gloves, crawled under the bus and retrieved the foot placing it in a plastic bag. It was unbelievable, like a horror movie. A tan soft shoe, inside it a bloody stump with sheared tendons, just gruesome. All to help the old woman.

Callahan reminded Frank that the lawyer waiting for him would be going over all the points of the case, to refresh his language before the scumbags turned on the tape recorder.

"It was this store owner who turned this into a big deal," Callahan said. "We have to do the right thing and make his remarks fall flat."

"Of course, Brian. I'll do my best."

"I know that Frank. But we have to get real precise. They slip you up and its worse for Art, and probably you too."

After Gallo separated from the two Frank asked Callahan, "Is he gonna be all right?"

Callahan looked around. "I don't know Frank. Art really put his foot in his big mouth. We were told this morning to report to the CO's office in an hour."

"For what?"

"I think they might transfer him while on modified assignment."

Frank shook his head. "Unbelievable."

Frank made it a point to be on time, so he arrived early for his appointment. He walked into the building located in lower Manhattan as if he were walking into another dimension. Immediately he felt the different, more authoritative presence of a department run in a totally different way than what he was accustomed to back in Queens. Recollections of academy days came to mind. Frank walked through the oval shaped corridor. The walls were dark brown, nothing written on them. Instead, every few yards were four foot standing signposts with directions to room numbers and which way to walk. A uniformed cop sat behind a huge desk situated before the oval. The cop sat, often just grunting, his main concern to check photo IDs.

Frank had the sense of an old espionage movie with Gestapo interrogations. Finally, one was lured, as if on purpose, to the marker directing officers to the last offices at the end, to the Inspections Unit. Frank entered and there was yet another small corridor and an approachable desk. *How big is this Nazi building?* At the normal desk sat an unusually small woman. Her hair was cropped short against a large head. As he got closer it became clear that her dwarf-like body was uncomfortable in the chair. She peered over round granny glasses and smiled, "Appointment?"

Frank smiled back, though more to hide a laugh. "If you want to call it that," he said.

"I know what you mean," she said. "Sign in the log over there please. And could I have your notification slip officer," she looked up at his name plate, "Colleri."

Frank handed her the slip, she told him to have a seat. He was fidgeting in his chair thinking about the security. He had to pass a guard cop in uniform, he himself in uniform, and still had to show photo ID. Now, he further had to prove his existence to a midget. *Unbelievable.*

Before long a thin man with horned rim glasses and a sixties crew cut was standing in front of him with his hand out. "Officer Colleri?"

"Yes, yes," Frank said, getting out of his chair and shaking hands with the pencil pusher although he really didn't want to.

"I'm Captain Connelly," the man said. "I'll be interviewing you today." He led Frank into yet another room.

Lousy worm, Frank thought. *Rat cops, midgets, and now I'm going to get my balls broken by this geek. The only thing this jerk off is missing is the plastic pencil holder in the shirt pocket.*

The captain didn't say much as they waited for the PBA attorney. The discomfort forced Frank to excuse himself to the bathroom. Upon the arrival of the lawyer, the worm quickly got down to business escorting them to a small investigation room.

The captain then left the two alone for a moment. The slick lawyer joked with Frank, tapping on the small tape recorder that was on the desk in front of them. "You never know," he said, "they've been known to leave them on."

After the two conferred on their story the captain returned, methodically turning on the recorder and beginning the proceedings. The captain asked a few questions and listened to Frank's brief and advised answers. He asked more questions, similar questions, then the exact same questions, harping on the N word factor, until finally it was over, the tape shut off. Frank tried not to act nervous, once in a while turning to his lawyer who looked thoroughly bored. Typical PBA man. He also glanced at the interrogator on occasion. The man definitely possessed a small-town worm-like appearance.

Nothing was going to be determined at this moment, so upon the conclusion of the thirty-minute session, Captain Connelly thanked Frank and told him 'they' would be in touch. On the way out, the dwarf smiled and said good-bye to Frank. This time Frank noticed that not only was she a dwarf, her legs were amputated from the knees down. Out on the street Frank welcomed the air, even if it was carbon-filled Manhattan. He was relieved to be out of what felt like a torture chamber. The PBA attorney assured him not to worry, that he had done a terrific job. The two said their good-byes as Frank thought about the union and its jerk jobs.

Frank returned to Queens. All the good times when he felt as though he and his friends ran the show came into a haunting perspective walking through those doors at inspections services. *Christ. If that was weird, what the hell is it like at IAD?*

Now he understood the dead expression on the face of Gallo. After all, Art was the subject of this whole mess, his interview had to have gone much harder. Frank stepped into Gallo's shoes for a moment. Walking through the big doors first. Facing the unconcerned fellow cop. More time to panic during the long trek to greet the cripple, until finally, the ball breaking geek. And a crafty geek to boot, attempting to trick at every turn.

These rat tacticians actually enjoyed what they did to other cops. They were the same guys who had been picked on all their lives, until gun and shield day. Now it was their turn. Gallo must have sweated his balls off.

Frank suddenly felt sure that they would go after Gallo's job.

CHAPTER 41

It was not uncommon practice for transfers within the police department to be sent down from personnel without warning. There were some situations when the cop would be told. But many times, the hammer would just fall. The one foreseeable transfer at the 117th was Arthur Gallo's. There was no surprise there, no matter how his case would swing. The department would predictably transfer him anyhow. But there were the other transfers. The ones that hadn't even got as far as the gossip mill.

Gallo's transfer to the building maintenance section was indefinite. It had to be since his weapons were removed and he was placed on modified assignment. Building maintenance was where broken equipment was fixed: from radio cars, to portable radios, precinct equipment etc… and Arthur Gallo.

Some thought the move turned out to be in Gallo's favor; for starters, his working hours were better. He wasn't required to wear the uniform, and he wouldn't be looked upon all day as the stationhouse janitor with a badge. Heck, at least the working pay was the same.

Next to go was Sergeant Dempsey. The captain was tired of the sergeant's constant ranting and ravings over the Vaseline incident. The CO felt the sergeant's one blow up should have been sufficient. Still, the sergeant was a victim, so the CO helped him along with some phone calls. When the wheels stopped spinning a satisfied Dempsey landed in the department's field inspections unit, borough of his choice. Now the young sergeant would be checking on police improprieties for a living.

And since everything was spinning, why not the captain himself? It turned out that the borough inspector was annoyed that the 117th precinct's commanding officer couldn't handle his men. Since the inspector had once had his car tampered with, he took the Dempsey incident personally. Rumors of the captain's possible demise circulated quickly with no sympathy. Still, the CO had his own agenda. He had his suspicions about certain police officers, though he couldn't prove anything, nor could he start dumping anyone from a command that housed over one hundred and fifty cops. This time he was on the receiving end of a style reminiscent of Reilly's and in the sneaky way the department relished operating.

Before the CO was finished, fate stepped in with the help of a bank manager who expressed his concern personally to the captain that he suspected one of the precinct cops was sleeping with his wife. This news, coupled with a poor performance rating from the departing Dempsey, was the perfect ammunition to bounce Police Officer John 'Sharpy' Eaton, not only from the CPOP unit, but also to another precinct.

Again, the wheel, the excuses. The captain, who at times was self-righteous about the job, was also to be swallowed up by disinterested management. For the captain of the 117th precinct, it was either accept a transfer to Staten Island or retire. The Staten Island transfer wouldn't be so bad if the captain lived in the city. But the commute from the east end of Long Island was a burden.

As for Gallo, he disappeared as quietly as possible, cleaning out his locker and facing as few people as possible on his departure. In the end, Gallo went from a somewhat enthusiastic police buff, (someone who overplayed their role as cop to the point of annoyance), a sergeant want to be, to a cynical shell of an officer.

Sergeant Dempsey left in the same manner, though not from shame. He never had a chance to befriend the precinct cops anyhow, especially since the Bennett incident.

Eaton however, went about the precinct shaking hands like a politician. There was a lot of the 'We still have to get together' talks. John made many friends during his stay at the 117th. As a matter of fact, he was planning a get together this very day. Everyone was heading to Ferris after work. Drinks were on him. Eaton even decided on a head start, taking four hours off during his last tour at the precinct.

Walsh and Colleri left early to join their friend, but first they helped their buddy clean out his locker. When Eaton's locker was nearly empty and the boys were hamming it up, he stopped and took a mood breaking stare into the open locker he had occupied these past years, as a ballplayer might after being traded.

"Everything okay Sharpy?" Frank asked.

"Oh yeah. you know, I'll miss it a little." They laughed. "The dinners at some great restaurants, you guys."

"Yeah, those sit-down meals are great," Walsh quipped.

"Rub it in you loser," Eaton said.

"I told you to be careful if you were gonna do that old broad," Walsh said.

Eaton playfully pushed Walsh. "You're the one who encouraged me to bang her. Besides they were breaking up anyway."

Frank shot both his friends a quick look. He suddenly felt left out. "You knew?" he said to Sean.

"Of course," Walsh said.

"Come on, Frank," Eaton said "You know I would---we would---have told you. But all that stuff with your wife and where your head was at. We figured the last thing you needed to hear—"

"Was that my buddy was doing somebody's wife."

"Exactly," Eaton said. "Actually, coulda been worse."

"Yeah?" Frank sighed.

"Banker could have locked me up if his wife confessed everything."

Now Frank was puzzled.

"One time," Eaton continued, "she wanted me to hold my gun to her head and make me insist on her sucking my dick."

"Are you fuckin kidding me?"

"He's not Frank," said Sean. "It was her reverse power trip not Sharpy's." Then they all laughed and Frank was no longer left out.

"You were supposed to be watching the bank. Not the banker's wife," Frank added.

"I'll probably see you guys more than I do now. I mean it wasn't much of a summer with our buddy here in a blue mood."

"Let's go," Walsh said. The three left the locker room at a fast pace leaving Eaton no time to reflect.

* * * *

Allison intended to go home after her shift. But like many times in the past, she was talked into another four by four. The extended shift to four a.m. at the bar with other cops. Later, the thought that she was too staggering drunk to notice the envelope lying on her carpet under the front door would haunt her for a long time.

If only she hadn't stumbled in at four-thirty...would she have seen the envelope? Would it have made the difference, those few hours? The bold large lettering that simply read: ALLISON MY FRIEND

Dear Al,

First let me say that I am sorry that I had to choose you. But it was after all you who had chosen to be such a good friend to me, though we really have known each other for only a few years. Anyway, I know Labor Day is approaching, summer was a blur anyway, and I hope you don't get assigned to that horrible parade in East New York. I know I won't be there. I have been feeling badly lately---and no it's not guy trouble, contrary to what you might think.

I cannot escape the torment Al.

Allison paused. That word, **torment.** So strong it made her tremble.

It is everywhere my friend. In my sleep. In my imagination. Even in those quiet moments of attempted peace.

Anyway, I will try not to bore you, but I would just like to state a couple of things.

First, I truly want to thank you for being such a good friend and being there when I needed you.

Allison felt an actual chill run up her spine. She read on slowly making sure there was no mistaking anything.

I know you really care and believe me I am grateful. Anyway. The thought process really intensified for me when I was up at the range today.

It's really hard to imagine myself taking my own life. But that is exactly how I felt holding my gun in my hand. I just wanted to pull the trigger, at myself.

Allison shook visibly. Still she believed in her heart her friend wouldn't do this to herself. She read on determined that this letter was going to end happily.

I even thought about shooting the instructor. You know the one who loves himself, only himself, and his gun. Of course, I'm joking and would never do such a thing. God Al. He reminded me of some of those guys from New Year's. You know the cool cops. I bet he still wears Capezios for dress and bargain sweats for leisure.

Allison knew the one. She laughed between the tears that had started to fall. Trying to convince herself this was just a joke. Just a joke.

I remembered my first visit to the range. The excitement about being on the job. My parents were so proud. And that's when it hit me. God, how can I do such a thing? Shoot myself in the face?

I knew it! Allison thought.

They have done nothing but love me. How could I disgrace and hurt them like that? They were so supportive when I finally revealed to them what happened. They still cry. You know what my father said? Other than shouting through tears, expletives of what he wished to do to my assailant. He said: 'When a child is as good as you have been your whole life, you can be nothing but virtuous in our eyes.'

Yet my pain is still intense Al. So I came up with a plan. I can only hope that you will do me one more favor.

"Anything," Allison said aloud.

Actually friend, almost my sister, I've been in a fog so much lately I don't even know how I'll get this letter to you. I already set a plan in motion. I called my mother and told her that I have had some trouble sleeping. That I have been restless for days. Blah, blah, blah. It was a funny thing. Mom asked me the very thing I was fishing for. She actually asked me if the doctors had given me any pills so that I could sleep.

Anyway, believe me Al, and I know you do. It has nothing to do with the money. I just don't want to be known as another suicide. For that matter, I also don't want to be known as a poster girl for rape. One whose case went nowhere. One who couldn't do a thing about what happened even though I carried a gun. How can that help anyone else for Christ sake?

Well Al, I have no survivor's sense of humor anymore.

Allison knew she was reading her friend's last moment of pain. God.

I would rather the whole thing be perceived as an accident. God knows the department doesn't want another suicide. They don't need the negative publicity. Anyway that's where you come in. Throw out the idea, in your opinion, that it could have been an accident. I want you to embellish on how I was happy about getting back on the job. That I called you and told you I was tired. That I had a couple of drinks and took some pills because I just couldn't sleep. And of course you advised me to be careful since I had those drinks. And you guess I was just not careful.

Allison began to sob.

One more thing Al. Please call my friend Frank Colleri. I think you know how I felt about him. I also think he should know about the (accident) of course. And maybe a little of how I felt. I am confident you will know exactly what to say to him. In the end, who was I kidding? God, it hadn't even been a year and I was forcing myself to get romantic. I even judged a priest on his looks. I guess I was just trying to be a girl again.

Oh. Of course destroy this letter. Please, please, please. Thanks again Al. I really am sorry to have to put this burden on your shoulders. I love you and have a great life. I really mean that.

P.S.

Remember Al. You must reiterate that I was certainly not the type to overdose purposely.

Love always,
Ann

After a night of boozing, Frank thought he would get home and finally be able to fall into bed and get an easy sleep. But then the phone rang, not a good thing at that ungodly hour. It was Ann's friend, though a stranger, still another police officer, and she told Frank about the death of their mutual friend.

She acted out her friend's request to the best of her ability. Cops can be good actors. After a brief conversation of what, why and how, Frank curled up with a profound and haunting feeling. He was stunned. He was guilty. He confessed to Allison he should have done more, especially in helping in the apprehension of her attacker. She in turn assured him that catching the perp wouldn't have made much difference, the damage to an innocent was done. She ending with words that rang in his head over and over: Her sad ending should tell us something. And I know she cared for you so be good to yourself Frank.

Frank got up to pace, smoke, and wait for a reasonable hour to call someone. But who could console him? No one knew of his relationship with Ann. It had been a secret of sorts. Even his family hadn't met the sweet girl. His brother only knew of her as Frank's mystery date and so called friend, with Peter stating he noticed Frank brighten at the mention of her name.

Now Frank wished he had invited her to dinner along with his brother. What a pleasant memory it would have been. And Ann, she would have certainly loved Peter and his playfulness. And though she never met his brother, she always asked Frank how he was getting along after the accident. She had said she would pray for him, for his health. Ann was genuinely concerned about Frank. Now it was horribly too late.

Frank also felt guilty. He wondered if some part of him might have been ashamed of her, of what happened to her. The way he was always secretly ashamed of his first name. He hid from his parents his name change once he joined the department. He never told them he was ashamed to be called Francis in the manly world of cops, so his nickname Frank became legally permanent.

He went to the stove and boiled water for tea. Since he was unable to sleep he might as well get some tea in him. Sort of in memory of Ann. As the steam rose from the pot, so to, did his memory as if in a cloud. Her small kitchen, her pot, her tea.

I need to talk with someone. I need to see my brother. Usually Peter wasn't the one to discuss serious issues. But his brother's accident had humbled his way of living. Frank knew Peter could reach to the depth and understand his brother's pain; they were brothers.

Frank heard the tiny pellet sound of rain on the window. *How typical. Death and rain. A funeral in the rain.*

There would be a police honor guard. The department flag draped over her coffin. The sad procession of mourners, Ann's fellow precinct officers, Ann's parents and family. He was guilty again. This time for not finding out about her death sooner, or her intentions. Guilty for not attending the wake. Yet, who would he have reflected with? Allison? No one else knew the extent of their relationship. Allison, the one who warned Ann about him, and was sorry for her judgment. In the final analysis, he didn't want to confront the death setting, the open casket.

Strangely he thought about asking Allison if Ann was buried with those beautiful pearls from the picture. He decided against the inquiry.

Daylight peeked through the rain clouds. The rest of the world would be rising for work. He lit a cigarette and began a string of calls, which strangely started with Kathleen. It rang three times before the answering machine came on. He hung up. A couple of drags and he picked the phone up again. Jenna's answering machine also picked up after three rings. Again, he hung up. A feeling of relief came over him and he wondered why he was calling two women he had no future with. *Is my life that empty? Yes.*

* * * *

Everyone at the 117th had received the circulated word that PO Gallo's status had gone from modified assignment to suspended from duty. No pay. Many of the cops were upset. The smart ones realized it could have been any one of them, for anything, at any given time. Callahan reiterated about the hypocrisy of One Police Plaza. The same assholes who beat minorities to a pulp a couple of decades ago, would now take a policeman's badge in a minute. The delegate was warning his guys passionately. Callahan also took a collection for the embattled Gallo, who now had the extra misfortune of trying to take care of a family with no paycheck.

The PBA, who ran around professing everything was we and us, would also assist in resources, to a certain extent. They wouldn't go out on a limb for Gallo's foolish actions. As for the department, their strategy was to wait, lingering to go in for the kill and crucify the young cop. In no way was the City of New York going to back Gallo legally or otherwise. The allegations were of too sensitive a nature. Frank's buddies were calling, leaving messages and wondering where the hell Frank was; they wanted to support Gallo and make sure each of them was prepared for further questioning.

* * * *

Peter got out of his chair to open a window. Frank smiled when he saw his brother take a small roach from the ashtray. "A little chilly today," Peter said.

"And wet in case you haven't noticed."

Peter wiped the windowsill dry from the droplets of rain falling in. "No kidding."

"There was a funeral today," Frank said.

Peter looked at Frank quizzically as if it were a joke. "A funeral? Who died?"

Frank was staring down at the windowsill where the drops were coming in. "Her," he said. "Ann Caputo."

"Ann Caputo? The girl? The policewoman? The new one?"

"Yes. The one I could have had something with."

"God Frank. What happened? On the job? A car accident?"

"Apparently, she had trouble sleeping." Understandable. "She took some pills—"

"Suicide?" Peter asked.

"No. According to her friend, Allison, it was an accident. And to the job's credit, they willingly accepted it as such. She had been out drinking or something, and just didn't realize how many..."

"Or didn't care," Peter commented as if to himself. "I'm sorry bro. I got the impression you were starting to like this girl. That's what I thought anyway."

To his own surprise, Frank's eyes welled and he turned to his brother. "I did. I really did. I should have done more brother. I told her friend, I should have asked around. All those sex crime victims, maybe I could have learned who the mutt—"

"Wait a minute Frank. You know damn well the possibility of finding someone's attacker is slim to none. Your job has big time detectives on it and they haven't found anything yet."

Frank put his fingers to the corners of his eyes. "I never got the chance to tell her how I felt. I thought it was all in my head, but the funny thing is, according to her friend, she felt the same way. Ain't that a kick?"

"I'm really sorry," Peter said again.

"I didn't go to the wake, but at the mass, I stood in the back of the church alone Peter, scarred in a way. It was weird. And the priest giving the speech, you know, the eulogy. He had long hair and this flowing robe. He looked Christ like... said he knew Ann. He praised her courage, her devotion, and you know anyone listening would be able to tell it was all true. She was someone who cared. Left after he spoke. Couldn't do the cemetery thing either. And suddenly I thought about the whole marriage thing and second chances. That there could have been that house and family, even if it wasn't going to be with Kat, like I dreamed. I don't understand Peter. Girl who's been through so much, only to die when things look on the upswing. You should have seen her parents Pete. Their anguish after what they had already been through. Inconsolable."

"Don't beat yourself up Frank. It's been one hell of a bad year for you. The shit you've been through with Kat and you've made it this far. You're a strong guy brother."

"Yeah, Superman."

Peter smiled warmly. "I don't know what else to say Frank. Maybe if you believe in God then you believe she's at peace."

Frank went to his brother and hugged him. "You're the only one I could share my feelings with. All I ask is that you stay healthy."

The tightness of Peter's return embrace caused Frank to cry for a moment. "Don't worry Frank. I'll stay strong as long as I've got these." He held up the small end of the joint.

Frank shook his head and the mood was lighter. "I guess I was too sentimental."

When Frank returned home he played back his messages. Walsh was the second message informing him fully about Gallo. Frank was not in the mood for work today so he called in for a day off. He made two more calls. First, he called Walsh, got his machine and left a thank you for the heads up. The Gallo news didn't shock him. Then he tried

Callahan and couldn't reach him either. He would have to wait. He wasn't too worried anyhow. After all, who could say that he heard Gallo call anyone the N word and prove it? Yet, they wasted no time in suspending Gallo.

Right now, still front in his mind, was the untimely death of Ann. The whole thing put his mindset in a different perspective. She was a victim. She suffered an unprovoked act of humiliation. She lived in perpetual fear about her future. And eventually, like many of her sister victims, would never taste the satisfaction of their perpetrator's punishment. Suddenly he remembered her words, 'They just want to close out their case load.'

Was it true what Peter said? If there was indeed a God, then did that God put him and Ann together for a reason?

He was smoking a cigarette when he noticed the tape lying on a shelf. It was the tape issued by the department for the families of police officers. He remembered when Ann explained to him about the tape. How good it would be if a cop could really and truly reach out to them. At the moment, he felt he could use a session with the trauma team. *Get real,* he said to himself.

The next morning there was still the miserable residue of drizzle outside. Frank hoped that going to work would help take his mind off things a little. At 0930 he reported for duty at the front desk.

"Hey, Colleri."

Frank turned to see Callahan. "Come on Frank. I'll walk up with you." Callahan said nothing more until they reached the quiet of the locker room.

"You heard about Gallo?"

"Not good."

"Listen Frank, but keep it to yourself 'cause there are a lot of jealous cops and it might bring attention to you."

"Could it get worse Brian?" Frank mumbled.

"What's that Frank?"

"Oh, nothing. You got my word."

Callahan gave Frank a congratulatory pat on the back. "You're off the hook Frank. We had a phone call put into inspections through one of the trustees. They have nothing. The old man, though he initially believed, really couldn't put you there during Gallo's alleged racist words. Stick to your testimony and it will all work out. Unfortunately, nothing could be done about Gallo. But they're not going to do anything where you're concerned, no matter how it turns out with Gallo. Although—"

"Definite? No perjury hoax?" Frank asked.

"It's definite Frank. It's definite. Knowing is half the battle."

"And Gallo? What did you mean although?" It was always a secret until the next guy knew.

"Listen Frank. I just got the call. Nobody knows yet."

For a moment Frank felt dread, that maybe Callahan was going to say that Gallo killed himself.

"He resigned."

"Resigned? Why? He's not the type to cave in."

"Well, that's why. His attitude was that at least there were no bias criminal charges and nothing hanging over him if he quit. So to hell with this job. He wasn't going to let this department climb all over his life for a year or more suspension before they decided to crucify him. 'Screw em' he said. He wasn't going to let these scumbags put him and his family through a nightmare. He wasn't going to let the beast devour him. And believe me they would have tried. It was a miracle Reverend Wilson didn't grab a hold of this one, especially since his congregation isn't far from here. Personally, I think that's why they were all over this. Nip it in the bud before he starts ranting and raving."

"Wow. I wish I had the balls," Frank said, thinking of the resignation.

"Well Frank, he stuck by his story, and yours. Hey, at least he had less than seven years on the job. If you're going to go that's the time to do it. Anyway, he's already lined up for good bucks in the construction business, his uncle or someone. I gotta' run."

"Thanks Brian, thanks," Frank mumbled.

CHAPTER 43

Other than the re-election of the mayor, fall passed with a whimper. Despite the intense protests of one Queens reverend, the mayor managed to convince the citizens of New York they were safer in his hands than in those of his democratic opponent. Reverend Wilson cut quite a figure in the last days of the campaign, puffing out his heavyweight boxer physique and accentuating his strong intimidating and lush voice. Up until the final vote count, and to no avail, Wilson was still spouting his famous anti-police line: "When you bring these white kids from the suburbs to join the police department, kids who have no knowledge of cultural diversity, and you mix that with a mayor who possesses brutal dictator tendencies, you are inviting a deadly combination!"

The reality was just another small-time borough activist with no pull city-wide making small waves; then life went on.

Frank felt as if the last twelve months were a convoluted blur. It was an increasingly brisk morning but Frank wanted a walk rather than to remain in the stationhouse or jump in a heated van. He walked down and through the precinct's heavy shopping area without worry of being bothered. It was the type of morning where shoppers and commuters would walk with their noses towards the pavement, hurrying to get out of the cold air and away from the swirling dirt the wind was kicking up. *If more of the garbage hidden in the city crevices was biodegradable,* Frank thought, *then this city wouldn't look like one big dust bowl on days like today.*

Noticing a bunch of kids ahead on Eaton's old post, Frank opted for peace and turned off from the main strip where he walked a few quiet blocks to the apartment where Ann had lived. Frank never cared for gloves except if he had to stand on a fixed post below freezing, or if he had to touch someone or something he had no desire to. All of a sudden he could feel the cold wringing through his hands. He blew into his palms then tucked them in his pockets.

Central dispatch was issuing another job over the portable airwaves. When Frank heard the location of the job he was glad that he had wandered off the main boulevard. Central was telling the sector concerned that there was a large group of disorderly persons, youths, congregating inside and in front of the smoke shop over the subway station.

The smoke shop was close enough to Frank's post, but he wasn't about to respond to that location unless a cop was in trouble, and right now it seemed to be just a bunch of kids cutting class or hanging out on their lunch hour. Frank guessed they were annoying the old shopkeeper. *Screw him. He gives up a cop and now he needs one.* Frank knew it didn't matter if the negative word spread about the old shopkeeper. There would always be a car carrying a couple of buffs just dying to fly, lights and sirens, through the streets of the city, aiming to be heroes. This image was funny. He laughed out loud.

Approaching the house Ann lived in he slowed down, making sure no one was around. He didn't want to engage in conversation about the dead policewoman. Frank reached the small path to her doorway. A feeling of loss engulfed him and he wished he could just go up to the door, knock, and step in from the cold to share some tea with Ann as if nothing ever happened. No rape. No pills. No death.

What a waste. If only...what's the sense? Still, he stood in the cold staring up the walkway. Then, as if he could walk beside her, he talked to her once more...

"I know how tortured you must have been sweet lady. You probably wondered what your life would have been like if...Wondered if you should have remained silent. My guess is you wouldn't have been able to because you wouldn't have wanted anyone else to. You probably know, being in heaven and all, that we thought we were onto that bastard that did that to you. Some poor girl, who did manage to get away, spoke up about her attacker. Still, I'm sorry to say it went nowhere. It just didn't pan out."

Frank looked around. He didn't want anyone in the neighborhood to see a cop in uniform just standing there in the cold with a blank stare. When he saw no one, he walked up closer to the door. Nothing much had happened recently. It was as if a storm had blown over.

"Who knows Ann? Who knows what might have happened between us? I'm not much for prayers but believe me, I have prayed that you be at peace. With all my heart, I have prayed for both of us to saints I don't even know exist."

Frank smiled remembering their first meeting. He reflected as if he were still speaking to her. It's great when you could use your official capacity as an excuse to bother someone, or at least get to know them better, without them knowing your intentions. *I'm glad I got to know her.* "At least I wasn't like my buddy, Sean Walsh. God Ann, this guy used to, and probably still does, use his authority to stalk his next lay. He might have talked you into the sack. Anyway, Peter is good and back at his apartment."

Frank smiled again but suddenly felt strange and the need for noise. He turned quickly and retreated back into the busy commercial section of his post. When he was once again back in the shopping area, he realized he was within eyeshot of the smoke shop. He could see there was no longer anyone lingering in front of the place. The radio car and its band of merry buffs did their job. He wished he could have done his. Somehow, he thought he was the one who should have helped get that bastard who attacked Ann.

He walked past the shop but on the other side of the street. He looked towards the entrance. A bus passed and belched some smoke as if in a scene on film. He remembered being in the doorway, watching Gallo, really doing his job, which was getting the bad guy out and instilling fear in him not to return. No one had heard from Gallo since he left the job. But, no news is good news. Perhaps the big guy was doing better than he would ever have done on this godforsaken job.

Frank also thought about Eaton. More fondly than Gallo. *Man, time flies.* Of course, the future never happens as planned. Walsh said it was because the new so-called movie cop might have been influenced by the job's tactics to change him. Frank still thought it was just time and distance.

Two endless nights of partying and vows of friendships since he was leaving. Since Eaton's transfer Frank hadn't heard from him. The only thing Frank knew was what Walsh told him. Eaton was feeling a little down because the CO at his new command put the transferred cop on the bottom of the totem pole with no regard for seniority. Eaton told Walsh that he had made a good grand larceny collar, only to have the CO's clerical knock it to petit larceny. John said it was happening all the time over there; felonies knocked to misdemeanors. He complained that the city was fudging its statistics for public relations purposes. Walsh told his friend to just forget it. It didn't matter anyway. They were all full of it.

Eaton was once again soured. In fact, he told Walsh, his last potential arrest was a shoplifter. After he cuffed the teenager and was about to cart him off, he got an idea. He asked the storeowner if he had a decision in this, what would it really be. The storeowner said he would like to kick these young punks in the ass. Eaton removed the cuffs, had the teenager bend over, and allowed the storeowner to blast his foot into the kid's ass. The storeowner was satisfied. No collar.

CPOP returned to its basics: crime visits, summonses; no dire situations to invite unwanted scrutiny. For now, it was quiet. Just do the job, be visible out there. For now the makeup of CPOP was still young white cops from Long Island, all except Harry, the good- natured cop from Trinidad. Every one of them nice guys, reliable cops, who got along well, did the minimum, and went home. But the precinct was going to eventually entice diverse patrolmen to the unit. The local population was growing with Hindus, Asians and Koreans. And of course, they would have to lure in a couple of women as well.

The boys from the 117th discussed a changed stationhouse.

The reverend was still screaming about minorities and the mayor who was always accentuating his fake smile and promising changes. *Maybe Gallo and Eaton are better off,* Frank thought. *Especially now that the new CO is breaking as many balls as his predecessor.* He wanted a tight ship, an attempt to bring the precinct back into the graces of the patrol borough. Break the patrolmen's balls, but suck the chief's, that was his motto.

Indeed, it became the same old story: summonses, summonses, summonses. And who better to harass the working community than the police department? The CO authorized roadblocks three times a week. This was nothing new, just a camouflaged public relations jerk job for the people, announcing to good citizens that the road blocks were protection for their holiday season, and if in the interim someone just happens to have defective brake lights, or misplaced paperwork, or worse, wasn't wearing their seatbelt, well then, the summons would be for their own good.

The roadblocks did nothing but create traffic jams and entice old ladies, mothers with a car full of kids, and exhausted commuters, to change their already muddled attitude towards the police.

What a bunch of imbeciles, Frank thought. How many times had he heard, 'They wouldn't have the balls to pull this crap in the ghetto.' The higher ups aren't the ones who have to deal with the embarrassment. Most cops knew that once the public became aware that these so-called safety roadblocks were practically unconstitutional, and the true meaning behind them, the public would hate the police even more. And of course, when some of the citizenry turn up to speak their minds at community council and precinct meetings, who will be there to address them but none other than the captain of the 117th, where he will play-act as sympathizer. Once again, the result would be the cop's reputation deflated and the public refusing to pick up the pieces, especially when some of them just received a useless and time consuming summons from a roadblock. *The more things change...*

All this seemed to revert back to a kind of logic that old timer Ralph mentioned. Ralph had stated, "The whole country couldn't give a rat's ass if our politicians were thieves and whores, so long as the cop out there in uniform isn't accepting a free cup of coffee, especially the cop that might have been the one to issue them a summons."

There was a lot of time left before he could retire, but Frank couldn't hold down the fantasy of life without the NYPD, that would be after retirement. For now, he had to see it just as any other job. The job had become as disappointing as a love affair, when one's hopes and desires are pumped on high, only to be unexpectedly let down, affirming a permanent chip in the armor.

The radio inside his pocket was crackling once again. "One-One-Seven, post nine, K." They were calling him. What could they want?

"Patrol post nine, on the air, K," he said this unenthusiastically.

"Ascertain your location post nine, and stand by for the patrol sergeant."

Wow. The boss trying to reach me?

The day tour sergeant, a bear of a man, was there quickly and told Frank to jump in the RMP. "Sorry, Frank, " the sergeant said. "You're the only one available to relieve sector DAVID on a DOA. It's not that bad though. Old guy. Family is present and the funeral parlor is on the way. Just wait there. The sector did all the paperwork already."

After officially relieving the assigned sector, Frank sat in the kitchen with members of the decedent's family. There was the man's wife, who sat quietly, and his two sisters. One of the sisters offered Frank a cup of tea, which he accepted once he noticed the kitchen was clean. The other sister looked stern in appearance, her gray hair pinned taut in a bun, her lips tight. It would have to be her that made inquiries that Frank really didn't want to hear.

"Officer," she said. "Can you come with me for a moment please?" It wasn't a question, she was already up and waiting.

Frank followed the woman down the foyer to the master bedroom where the brother rested in a permanent sleep. Frank saw the deceased as soon as he entered the room. The man was lying on the bed, on his back, propped on two pillows. A drab green sheet covered him to the chest. His face was of death, gaunt and ashen. There were large age spots on his bald palate and only a few wisps of hair on top of his head. But what were unusual were his eyes. They were still open revealing a glassy stare.

"He was only seventy-nine," the sister said.

That's all, eh? Frank thought, sardonically.

"Officer would you be so kind as to close my brother's eyes?" the sister asked.

Close his eyes? Now that's a question. Where the hell is EMS? They were the ones that pronounced anyone dead. They close eyes. "Ma'am, I don't—"

The sister cut him off. "Please, I don't want his wife to come back in here..."

Frank put up a hand. "I really don't want to offend you, but—"

"If you really wish not to offend me than please. Besides, young man, is it not your job?"

There it is. You, old bitch. As soon as you stop catering to these people they turn on you.

"By the way officer, now that I've had the chance to consider... I think my brother should have an autopsy. He might have taken too strong a prescription, or something, because he was really just too healthy..."

Suddenly Frank found himself thinking of Ann. It was she who might have taken the stronger prescription. Not this old man who had seen life, tasted five more decades than Ann. Sure, he had withered to this. But that was the downside of old age...

"Officer?" The woman sounded impatient. "Can an autopsy be performed?"

Frank attempted a bluff. "Ma'am, if that's what you wish, I could call the medical examiner and they'll take your brother to the morgue instead of the funeral parlor."

"If that's what it takes, then so be it."

Stubborn old shit, he thought. He was getting annoyed. This spinster was going to make everyone's day longer than need be.

"Officer? Can't they perform the autopsy at the funeral home?"

That's it! Time for a harsher bluff. "Listen ma'am. They can't do an autopsy at a funeral home. I'm going to call the M.E. and then we'll go into the kitchen and explain to your sister-in-law that it's going to take hours before they arrive. The M.E. is very busy. Right now, he's attending two homeless people who were found dead a couple of hours ago. After they pick those bodies up they will come straight here for your brother, who, in all honesty, could start to decompose. And the smell...well you know."

"I don't need to hear this from you," she snapped, lips getting tighter.

"I'm sorry ma'am. I just want you to be aware of what will be happening. I also think your sister-in-law has the right to know. Your brother will be put in a room at the morgue, with God knows how many other bodies, before finally, sometime in a few days, they will open him up, only to find the obvious, that he died naturally."

The woman suddenly became meek. Without saying another word, she left the room. Frank's lecture had done the job. He turned to the dead man, whose eyes seemed to be listening.

"Sorry pal," he said. "But that sister of yours is a real pain in the ass. But I guess you already know that." Frank left the room having conquered the old bitty. The dead man still lay with his eyes staring into nowhere.

After the body was removed, Frank decided to walk back to the precinct instead of calling for a ride. He tucked the second half of the toe tag, the precinct record of death was signed by the funeral director, into his duty jacket and he hit the sidewalk welcoming the fresh air. No matter how clean a deceased's house was, there still permeated the mist of the dead.

Once on Main he saw civilian workers from Flushing putting up a string of Christmas lights across the road from one building to the next. *Already?* He walked passed one of the furniture stores on his post then looked behind the display into the mirror. *I look beat. Circles under my eyes.* Out of habit he took off his cap and pulled back his hair. Still the same. He was grateful it hadn't risen further into his scalp. *This year has aged me.*

He walked another block, spotting the top of a familiar apartment building up the side street. He looked up and wondered if Nina still lived there. He walked up to the building. What he would do when he reached the front was still up in the air. Besides, Nina lived on the 16th floor, so there was still time for a rational decision. He was digging in his ear again. It was that time of year when the scratching could only be tamed with medicated cream.

He entered the lobby and the sudden change from cold to heat forced a sneeze. It was also that time of year for colds. That was okay with him. He would just go out sick. He had wanted to go on sick leave for months. He shifted back to the business at hand. Here he was standing in the lobby of a woman who would probably welcome the lay. Not exactly the woman he wanted, but something warm for the winter. It was not as if Nina disgusted him. They did share a good thing once. If anything, it would be for old times. There was nothing wrong with that. People did it all the time. He was trying to convince himself.

Besides, women weren't exactly beating down his door lately. Once he rang the buzzer he'd have to wait. He couldn't leave the lobby in uniform, feeling like a fool. His cynicism now made him think of the amount of time that had passed. Nina wasn't the type of girl to pine over the men in her life. What if she wasn't alone up there? This would be where the uniform could be a plus. If things got awkward, he would just explain he was on a call in the building and decided to ring her up on the spur of the moment. He thought about leaving. Maybe it was better to just slip into the bar on a night she was working. It would be less intimidating if he were a little stoned and with some of his buddies, instead of standing here in the hall like a jerk.

He drifted again. Friends, bars, drinks, loneliness, the sincere apology he never made to Kathleen regarding her friend. Eaton proving that no matter what precinct you worked in, it just sucked. Walsh, the same old Sean, still out there. Sean, the stereotypical straight-A captain of the football team, gets all the chicks. Not to mention the previous year both Walsh and Eaton were named cops of the month for running into an apartment on fire and dragging out an elderly man who fell asleep with a cigarette in his mouth. Even with the feel-good hero complex, cops often became cynical. Most of the cynicism permeated from within the department, like a large loving family that can't work out their issues no matter how trivial, no matter how much they love each other, and resentment festers until they forget their love and the resentment is more powerful than the argument and sometimes it's unrepairable.

Sean's engagement didn't work, not to any one's surprise. The guys didn't even know her that well. *Maybe I should take his advice and not be concerned with this entire settle down thing.*

New Year's Eve wasn't far off. It was the first year he could recall not having definite plans. He still didn't know if he was even in the mood for paper hats and horns. He might have been if Ann was around. Looking in those small soft eyes at midnight.

At the very least, Nina could be a backup. He could find out if her bar was open New Year's Eve, and if not, where she and her friends would be going. He could also tell her that he already had plans, that way he didn't have to commit the night to her. He could say he was assigned to the New Year's Eve detail in Times Square.

He would have to take his chances. After all, what were chances anyway? He screwed up enough of them. She wouldn't refuse. She couldn't.

So, leaving caution behind and with a touch of desperation, ready to lean on the bell, *Wait!* "What the fuck am I doing?" Frank Colleri decided he wasn't going to use Nina. He was, for once, going to do the right thing and let her be.

Love Books?

Support Authors – buy directly from their publishers. This puts more royalty dollars into the pockets of your favorite author – and gives them time to write their next book.

Visit us for links to many vibrant publishing companies to find the book for you: www.vanvelzerpress.com

These ARE The Books You've Been Looking For.

ABOUT THE AUTHOR

Vincent Casale was born in East Harlem, New York City, and was raised in Flushing, Queens. He attended Hillcrest High School in Jamaica Queens, where his favorite classes were those pertaining to the arts, especially the theatre, novel reading, and television history classes.

In 1984 after years of indecisiveness and no positive direction, he took and passed the entry test to become a proud member of the New York City Police Officer, the first to do so in his family. Most of his career was spent patrolling the streets of Queens, New York.

Vincent Casale retired in 2004 as a patrolman and now resides South Florida exploring his writing career. CPOP-1986, is Vincent's début novel.

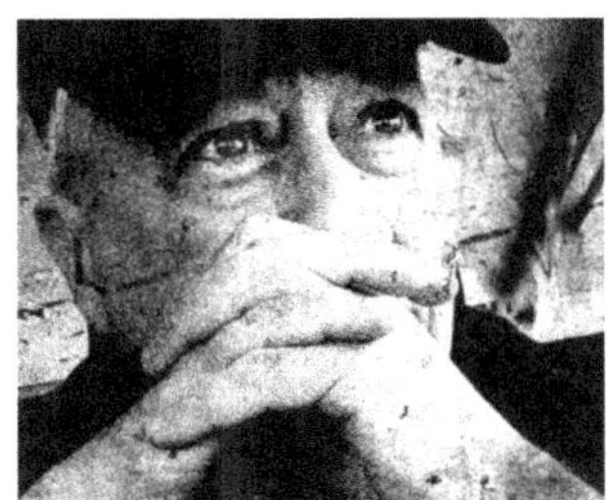